HEART of LEAD

Namesake Chronicles: BOOK 2

By Rachel Marie Lang

Special Thanks to my *Kickstarter* Supporters

Natalie B
Karen W
Sara Davison
Noel R
Stephanie Bertucci
Sara & John
Andrew Lang
Emily F
Sarah K
Anita K

ISBN-13:978-09920773-2-7

Dedication

To Jasmine and Sarah
Two of my biggest fans

To my editors, including Dave Radford – and my parents

To my brother Andrew for his hands

To all my family

Thank You

Signed Rachel Lang
May 2, 2016
Orillia, Ontario

Contents

Heart of Lead

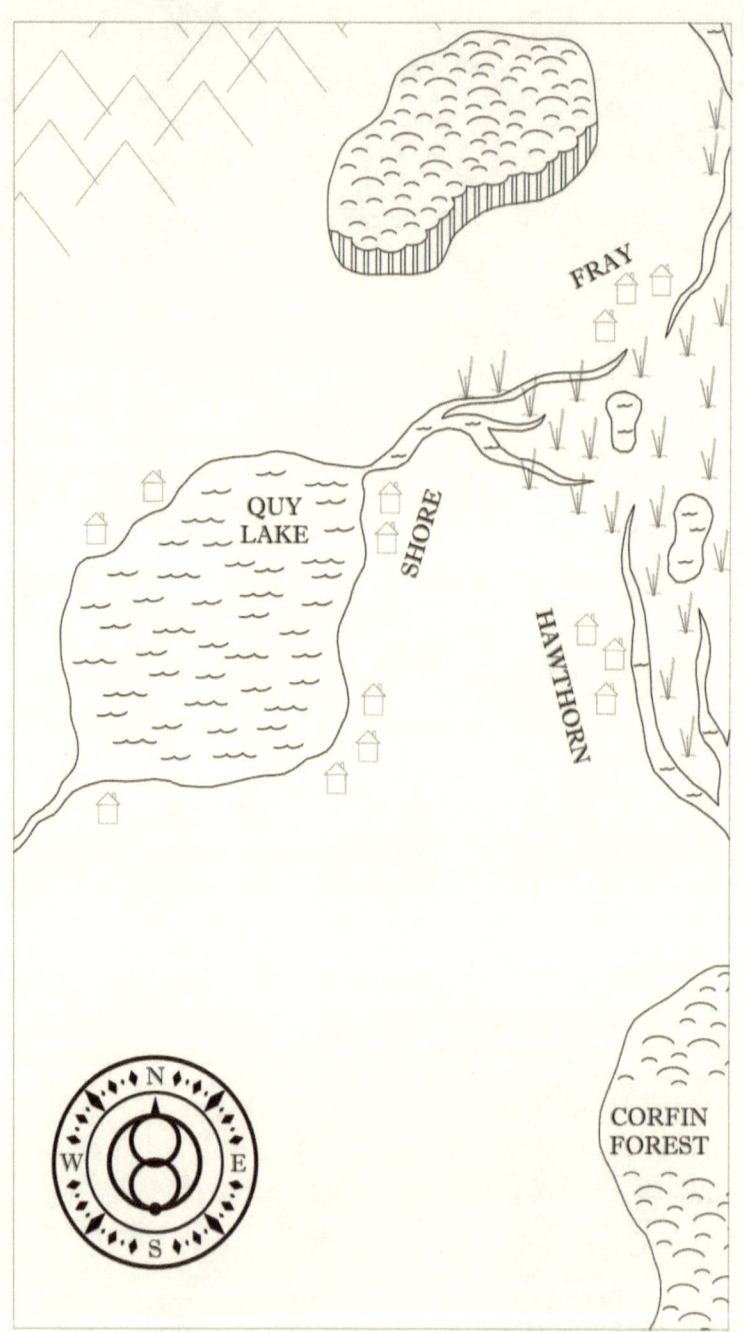

"Everyone knows what really happened." Anger was plainly seen on the Tarven's dark face, as he scowled down at the Garatin man. Sinister, also called Ister, sat in a high backed wooden chair behind a large oak table covered in papers and books. The table and chair sat on a raised dais so that Ister looked down on the Garatin man as if from a throne.

"I assure you, my lord," the Garatin man dared to look directly at Sinister. "The Garatin High Council had nothing to do with the unfortunate accident that happened yesterday afternoon." He was cut short and took a step back as Ister jumped to his feet and roared out.

"DO NOT DARE TO LIE TO ME! Do you think me a fool that I cannot see what is right before me!?"

There was silence in the otherwise empty chamber, the Garatin man lowered his abnormally pale blue eyes and shifted his feet. His discomfort seemed to mollify Sinister, and he sat back down heavily, and after a moment spoke.

"When I heard that a member of the Garatin High Council wished an audience, I assumed it was to confess!" Sinister snarled.

The pale-eyed Garatin seemed to gather his strength. "The delegate from northern Garatin was outspoken in the Council- he readily claimed to support the known rebel and now dead Eternity. Given time he would have stirred up the people and provoked dangerous riots in the city." He looked back up at Ister, with veiled contempt.

"His 'accidental'-", he stressed the word, "- death has saved you much trouble, indeed it would save you and the Garatin High Council a great deal of trouble if all of the 'Nity followers' were to meet similar ends."

Sinister's frown deepened. "You are driving at a point- say it plainly before you lose what little good will you have left with me- Garatin."

"Ever since that cursed man Eternity began street teaching five years ago, first he and now his followers have been a great insult to the ancient Garatin laws and traditions. Left unchecked any longer and they could seek to throw out the Garatin high council- by our law they are to be put to death for such insurrection!"

Ister sighed with great irritation. "So instead of a confession you come asking favours? I will answer the same as I have for years; I have neither the interest nor the energy to spend hunting down such insignificant rebels simply because the High Council finds them offensive!" he waved his hand in dismissal.

The pale-eyed Garatin stood firm and dared to speak further. "The Nity followers are a danger to you as well, my lord! They are numerous enough to challenge Tarva's hold on Garatin- do not fool yourself into believing they won't try. When you executed their leader two years ago you made them stronger than ever! They think of him as a martyr and believe his ghost lives on."

"I do not concern myself with superstitions!"

"My lord, if you will not deal with these rebels, then give me the authority to do it myself!" It was a bold statement.

Ister paused as though taken aback, sighing deeply he leaned back and thought it over. At last he spoke quietly to himself. "I have never dared touch the Eternity rebels- but if you, a Garatin were to arrest them…What have I to lose?" he paused to think more.

"Arrest and execute." The pale-eyed Garatin dared to ask for more. Ister smiled wickedly.

"You know as well as I that no Garatin has the right to execute- here in Garason that honor is mine."

He paused only one moment more before coming to a decision. "Yes; you will go throughout the city and arrest all found guilty of supporting the Eternity rebels." The pale-eyed Garatin straightened himself in victory.

"However- you will bring every last one to me to decide their fate… or else it will be your fate I decide upon." For a long moment Ister watched the man and let his threat sink in.

"I will draw up official papers for you along with my seal, as well as supply you with soldiers to carry out the arrests. I trust you can suppress your bloodlust." He looked up from his desk and waited for a response, but the Garatin only stood there. Ister raised one dark brow in question. The pale-eyed man seemed to force his next words from his lips.

"The Eternity rebels will be purged from this city and every one of them made to stand before you for justice, every last man, woman and child; I give my word on this!"

Chapter 1   Mag

The sun rose slowly over the hilly grasslands, its light red and its warmth somehow far off. The empty fields around the village seemed to stretch out to the very horizon, waiting to be plowed. The light of the rising sun slowly chased away all the shadows between the cottages, and the village of Hawthorn awoke. Men went out to their barns with lanterns in hand, while smoke began trailing out of chimneys, shrouding the village in mist. Looking down on the village, the manor of Hawthorn began to come alive as well; doors and shutters were opened, and lone voices could be heard on the chill morning air.

A Garatin boy of seventeen rode at a snail's pace into Hawthorn on a mule; following close behind, with his saddle empty, was a sad looking draft horse. The boy's namesake was Imagine. His shoulders were bent almost double and his head was hung low. He held on to the draft horse's lead with a limp hand and took no notice of his mule's loose shoe as it dragged and clacked on the cobbles. Turning a corner Imagine lifted his blue eyes and caught his breath as a sob escaped from his lips; before him, with thatched roof and closed shutters was his family's cottage. After four weeks he was finally home!

Suddenly he was overwhelmed by a shadowy flashback; *"Father!" Imagine called out, but the words were muffled and slow. Something bounced off of his boot, someone was running- suddenly he became aware that his hand had gone numb!*

The flashback gave way as Imagine choked on another sob, his eyes burned, but there were no more tears to cry. Driven by instinct, the boy's mule had walked into the yard and stopped before the little cottage. Imagine sat there a moment longer trying to gather his strength, this was the part he had dreaded; facing his mother and four younger sisters and brothers, and telling them... but he couldn't! He knew the words would never come. He slipped off the mule's back, his knees almost giving way beneath him. Leaving the mule and the draft horse in the yard he walked towards the cottage door with stiff legs and rigid back. Opening the door and stepping inside he looked up to meet his family's startled gaze.

Four weeks ago he had left a mere boy of seventeen with a heart filled with excitement and hope... he had returned with a heart filled with nothing- and yet it was as heavy as lead.

*   *   *

Perilous braced herself against the wood pile stacked beside her cottage, her legs felt weak and she feared that if she fell, she would never stand again. The light morning breeze ruffled her blond hair and chilled her face. She closed her eyes and forced herself to repeat the words her eldest son had said yesterday morning.

"He's dead..." saying it didn't make it any more real though. Effortlessly she brought to memory her husband's face- he was smiling at her. How could he be dead? Her mind rebelled against the truth, Imagine hadn't even been able to tell her how he died. Perilous and Obedience had been married for almost eighteen years, and they had loved each other very much- how could he be dead?

Even now she could hear his voice, "Peri-" Obedience had never called her by her full namesake, but always 'Peri'. "Peri I think the trip will be good for Imagine, to see the city of Garason- and the Vase! And besides, we'll be back in four weeks' time..." but he had been wrong, he would never come home- not even to be buried! What was she to do!?

'I'm a widow now!' the thought kept coming back to her mind, but each time it failed to take hold. Swallowing hard Peri took a split log in each hand from the pile, but she couldn't make herself go back inside the cottage.

"Mother?" a soft voice spoke behind Peri, she turned to see her eldest daughter Remember. Ember was thirteen, and third oldest of Peri's children next to Imagine. Ember was just a slip of a girl, with a long face and mournful eyes, her blond Garatin hair was tangled from a sleepless night. Out of all Peri's children Remember was the most gentle of heart. Ember walked up to her mother and said.

"Mother you don't need to bring in any wood, the fire is fine." Her soft voice cracked, and she sucked in her breath afraid that she would begin to cry. Perilous put the wood back and pulled her daughter close.

"Oh Ember..." Peri whispered at last. "We'll make it through this- we will!" Peri's own voice trembled but she had to be strong now. Ember pulled away so she could look at her mother's face. "How do you know that?" she asked choking back a sob.

Peri's face took on a fierce determination. "I don't know it... but we have to believe it." She pulled her close again.

"Mama!" they both looked up as Peri's youngest called from the back door, the girl's eyes were large as she said, "There's a man in the yard!"

She pointed to the front of the house. Quickly Perilous went into the cottage and opened the front door, her daughters followed her as she stepped out. Standing in the dusty yard, holding his hands behind his back was a Garatin man; it was the chief tax collector! He looked up and smiled at her politely. Peri frowned; why was he here?

"Good morrow Perilous." He didn't move from the middle of the yard as if afraid of getting too close to a common villager. The chief tax collector lived in the manor and did the lord's bidding, the villagers hardly considered him to be 'one of them'. Peri nodded and waited for him to explain his visit. He shifted uncomfortably.

"There is a rumor that your husband, Obedience, has uh… passed on," he said carefully. Peri bowed her head and swallowed hard. No answer was needed though. The tax collector nodded.

"That is most unfortunate, all of Hawthorn will grieve him," he said quietly. Off to the side Imagine and his two younger brothers came from the barn and stood listening. An awkward moment passed.

"It will soon be time to begin planting," the tax collector said with more discomfort. "Will your fields be… properly taken care of?" There was silence.

Obedience had been a serf, he worked his fields and paid a harvest tax to the lord of Hawthorn in return for a place to live… if their fields were not ploughed and planted, then the lord of Hawthorn could throw Peri and her family out of Hawthorn… the reality of their situation hit Perilous like a slap; what were they to do!? How would they survive?

"My father's land will be worked this season like everyone else's." All eyes turned to Imagine; Mag had stepped forward and was trying hard to look grown up.

The tax collector measured him up then nodded as if satisfied.

"Very well then-" he nodded to Peri, "Again I am very sorry." He then turned and left.

Imagine took a deep breath, Peri stepped towards him and placed her hand on his shoulder. They looked at each other for a moment then Peri nodded.

"Yes," she said sounding less than certain. "You and Vanished will work the field's fine," she said nodding to her second eldest, who looked less than sure. "We'll do alright," she nodded her head.

That same morning Imagine's younger brother, Vanished, lead

Thicket their draft horse, out to their fields while Mag struggled to carry their plough over his shoulder. Their field was surrounded by a little fence, the soil was lined with last year's ploughing, and weeds grew everywhere. Vanished who was fifteen, nearly whimpered at how much work there was to be done; but Mag was undaunted. Together they struggled to harness the cumbersome plough to Thicket, but they couldn't remember how exactly it went on. Slyly they looked around at the other farmers' ploughs to get an idea. When they finally got it right they were both very embarrassed, and hoped that no one had noticed; but their embarrassment had only begun.

Although both of them had worked alongside their father in the fields, neither of them had ever done it alone. The wooden plough with its rusty blade called a share, was heavy and they had a hard time controlling it, while Thicket was little better. The old draft horse seemed to know that they were only boys and would stubbornly refuse to move.

By the end of the day both Mag and Van's tempers were short, and their backs were sore and their hands were covered in blisters. And to both their dismays, the field wasn't even half ploughed!

They sat silently at dinner and ate quickly, after which Vanished climbed into the loft where everyone except Peri slept, and Van fell asleep even before he could take his boots off. Imagine sat at the table picking at the blisters on his hands and refused to meet his mother or his sister's gaze.

Perilous watched him, she had feared that the work would be too much for her sons- but what choice did they have? Leaving Remember to clean up, Peri went out behind the cottage to retrieve the day's wash from the line. Instead, she found herself standing at the fence looking out over the village and beyond.

That day had been horrid for Peri, to watch her children do their chores in a daze, all trying hard not to make eye contact with her- and she could do nothing to comfort them. As she stood there in the thickening dusk, a wave of fear and doubt rose within her. It started deep in her stomach, then settled in her heart like a heavy damp fog, her breathing became shallow. Her mind began to scream; how could she ever do this on her own? A young widow with five children might as well be a beggar! How could she expect Mag and Van to work the fields and bring in a good harvest- they were just boys! How could Eloi do this to her!? How could Dien leave her like this?

Her eyes became blurry with tears, shaking her head she covered her mouth with her hands. Somehow she knew, this was the moment when her future would forever be changed. It was now that it would be decided in her own heart whether or not she would survive and carry on... or give up. She began to whisper through her fingers into the evening air, her voice thick with emotion.

"Eloi, we lived as faithful Garatin's to you all of our lives... You never gave us any promises- I know Dien knew that. I know I have no right to be angry with you." For a moment she stood there, and it seemed as though a gentle breeze could blow her away. But then her face changed.

"But I am," she said harshly. "I am angry with you!" she shouted out for the whole quiet village to hear. A broken sob escaped her lips. Peri's anger faded into a dull ache as shame and helplessness flooded over her. "But I can't do this alone." Her chin quivered as she beheld this truth and a single tear ran down her pale face.

*　　　　*　　　　*

The village of Hawthorn was much the same as any village in Garatin, the lord of Hawthorn manor was a Garatin earl by the namesake of Favour. About a hundred serf's worked his land and were protected by him. There were another hundred nobles who lived in the manor and had their own serfs to work their land. Imagine and his family were just five of the serf's that made up the village of Hawthorn. In Hawthorn there was mainly two different jobs for serfs; animal farming, and land farming. A serf's life was not a bad one, as long as they could pay their taxes, they lived in the safety of a village. In times of war the lord would call upon them to fight- but that had not been necessary in Hawthorn for a long time.

Hawthorn was in the north of Garatin far from any excitement. The Quy marsh lay behind it to the north, and the Corfin forest flanked it to the East. In the east corner of the village stood the manor of Hawthorn- it was small and lopsided, with half of the stonework sinking into the ground. The manor had a two hinge gate instead of a drawbridge, and only one tower with the earl's crest fluttering in the wind. Leading out from the manor gate was the main cobbled street that then opened up into the market square. The other streets were crooked and the cottages had almost no order and were bunched together in clusters. Around the edge of the village was a shoulder high stone wall, broken often where the streets and foot paths lead out into the fields and then beyond to the hilly grass lands of northern Garatin.

Chapter 2   A Serf's Son

The Garatin with the pale eyes stepped into the tavern and cast his gaze about the tables and chairs. At one end of the room sat four men talking together, they fit the description that the tinsmith down the street had given. Behind the pale-eyed man five Tarven soldiers stepped into the room, stood about silently, and looked displeased to be taking orders from a Garatin.

The pale-eyed man walked up to the four Garatin men, they stopped talking and looked up at him.

"Who is Journey, apprentice to the tinsmith?" the pale-eyed man asked the group. They all looked confused, and glanced at the Tarven soldiers.

"I am he..." one of them said timidly.

"What are you doing here?" the pale-eyed man demanded. The man frowned.

"We meet here every week to debate and share the teachings of Eternity..." he said uncertainly. The pale-eyed man waved to the soldiers.

"By their own words they have admitted their crime- arrest them!" he ordered. The soldiers obeyed at once and took hold of the four men by their arms, the men protested loudly and struggled. Others in the tavern slipped out the door, while the tavern keeper came running up.

"What is the meaning of this!?" he demanded above the others asking the same thing. The pale-eyed man pulled out a rolled up paper from his tunic, a heavy seal on one corner made the paper unroll. A surprised and even frightened look crossed the tavern keeper's face. He sputtered.

"But- but these men have done nothing!" he said with a pleading tone.

"'Nothing' is what you have done to stop these criminals!" The pale-eyed man replied his voice becoming heated, then waved his hand for the soldiers to take the four men away, they began to pull them out into the street.

"We have done no crime!" one of the men's voices was louder than the others. "We are not rebels- we simply follow Nity's teachings- is that now against Garatin law!?!" the pale-eyed man replied loud enough for those gathered in the street to hear.

"Yes it is!"

*   *   *

Imagine pushed back his tunic sleeve to above his elbow and surveyed the disaster area. An old tree sat at one end of their field, and the night before a large branch had come down in the wind, it lay lengthwise crushing five rows of hip high barley stocks.

"I told you this would happen!" his brother Vanished said sourly. Mag felt his temper flare at his brother, but mostly at himself. Van was right, that tree was old and rotting and they should have cut it down before they even planted the field. But nothing could be done about that now.

"We'll have to move it," he said at last. Being careful not to trample any more of the barley they moved to either end of the old branch, slipping their hands under it Mag counted to three, and together they heaved. But the branch was heavier than it looked, they only managed to lift it to knee height when it twisted in their hands. Van lost his grip and jumped away.

"Watch it!" he shouted as the branch rolled toward him then hit the ground again with a thud. Mag stifled a groan and closed his eyes in pain; the branch had rolled out of his hands and bounced off his knees.

"You boys need a hand?" It was one of the neighbouring farmers who spoke. Van looked up at him in relief. But Mag spoke through his pain before the man came any closer.

"No!" The man stopped short in surprise. "We can manage just fine!" The man looked doubtful but he nodded and turned away. When he was out of earshot Van stalked over to his brother, only the branch kept them apart.

"What did you say that for!?"

"We don't need anyone's help Van!", he said with force as he looked at his younger brother. "I told the chief tax collector that we could do this- and we will!"

Van pinched his eyebrows together, his blond Garatin hair hung over his blue eyes that were clouded with anger. As Mag met his gaze, he didn't see his brother- but rather his father, whom Vanished looked so much like. It had been four weeks since Mag had come home, yet still it didn't seem possible that their father was really gone.

"Now let's try and move it again- and get a better grip this time!"

*   *   *

"Imagine, Trust stopped by on his way home to talk to you," Perilous said as Mag closed the cottage door behind him. For the first time in what seemed forever the ghost of a smile passed Mag's face.

"Trus!" Mag didn't even bother calling Trust by his full namesake. Trust had grown up with his father and was like an uncle to Mag, an awkward and shy one, but an uncle none the less. And Mag had come to appreciate Trust all the more since he had come home four weeks ago. Trust was a small man and soft spoken, he blinked a lot and was always nervous, and stuttered from time to time. Trus stood up and shifted his floppy felt hat in his hands.

"Hello Imag- magine." Mag knew at once that Trus was nervous from his painful stutter.

"How is your family?" Mag asked awkwardly when Trus said nothing more. Trust was married to a quiet woman, they had five daughters and one son- who was the youngest.

"Oh they are quite well." Trust said with a nod. "I-I came to talk to you about t-the meetings…" Mag blinked in surprise, from across the room Peri listened carefully. Mag hadn't even given the meetings any thought!

His father had started the meetings two years ago when he and Mag had returned from Garason where they had met Eternity face to face. His father had not needed long to decide that Nity was indeed the long awaited Eloi-man. And both father and son had been filled with the excitement that Nity brought with him, but when Nity had been arrested and then executed for high treason their hope had been shattered. However, a day later they heard the news- the wondrous news that Nity lived again.

Mag's father had been unstoppable after that, they returned home and Obedience told everyone in Hawthorn that the wait was over; that Eloi had sent the man to set them free. Mag's father tried to change the way things were done in Hawthorn, he tried to make people see that Nity had changed things- and that forgiveness from past mistakes was free for the asking. He even joined the Garatin Council so that he could have a voice in the decisions being made in Hawthorn. It had been on Council business that Obedience had made his last journey to Garason- the journey he never came home from.

Most of Hawthorn had brushed him off as a fool for believing that Nity could have survived his execution. But there were some who believed his wondrous stories, and they had begun the meetings. A place where they could retell the stories of Nity. But there were those in Hawthorn who strongly disagreed with what Dien believed, and they had given him no peace.

It was these meetings that Trust now spoke of.

"Now t-that your father is gone," Trus said looking at the floor, "You are the only one in Hawthorn who saw Nity… we hoped that you would take your father's place." He looked up at Mag shyly as he finished.

Mag was taken aback, he had been to the meetings before, but only as a listener. Could he really take his father's place? He wanted to say no, but what if he was the only one who could keep alive what his father had lived for? Trust believed he could do it.

"Yes, alright," Mag said at last. "I'll do it- at least I'll try my best." He stood up a little taller.

Trus flashed a quick smile. "Good! T-the next meeting will be at the end of the week, at-at the Inn. I'll see you then. Good morrow Mag- and thank you. Good morrow Peri," he said with a nod, then left.

Perilous stood there looking at her son, Mag returned her gaze.

"Mag, you don't have to do this." she said softly.

Mag nodded, "I know, but I won't let father's dream die with him."

Peri smiled and wondered how many other seventeen-year-old boys would do as her son was doing now. "I'm proud of you. And I know your father would be too."

Mag looked down and swallowed hard. Yet still, there were no tears.

* * *

Imagine made his way through the village at dusk, his stomach felt twisted and knotted inside him, the full gravity of what he was doing was only now hitting him. This meeting would be the first time he would be publicly acting as the man of his house. Mag rubbed his sweaty palms against his worn leather vest. Looking up he saw Trust waiting for him at the corner of the market square, he looked nervous but that was normal for him. Together they crossed the empty market square to where the Inn sat. The Inn was the only two story building in the village (aside from the manor) and it also doubled as an alehouse. The meetings had been held here from the very beginning.

Now as Mag and Trus walked up to the Inn, he took in the stone walls and sloping thatched roof. Off to the right of the Inn were the stables where the few travellers who came to Hawthorn kept their animals. On a swinging sign over the main door in white paint read the word 'INN', the white paint was cracked and faded and the sign squeaked on its hinges. On both sides of the door were closed shutters, hanging over one of these was a lantern. The glass sides were smeared and greasy but it still gave out a glowing light. Mag paused a moment before stepping up to the door and pulling it open by a brass ring. Inside the two of them were met by a dimly lit room with a low ceiling. At one end was a small fireplace and along the far wall was a counter with stools. Scattered throughout the room were mismatching chairs and tables of all kinds.

Spread around the room, some with mugs in their hands, were six of the men who came to the meetings; good men one and all. Command, the inn keeper, stood behind the counter wiping it down with a ragged looking cloth, he nodded at Trus but said nothing. The men throughout the room looked up as the two entered and everyone paused; they were looking at Mag.

"Oh!" said one of the men to Trust, "You brought Dien's son."

"It's a little late for boys," another man said under his breath but Mag still heard him and he felt his face flush. A man with the namesake of Victory spoke louder, "Well, I think that's everyone we need wait for, now we can begin."

Everyone made their way over to the table by the fireplace, a few of them finishing off their ales before sitting down. Before following them, Mag leaned closer to Trus and hissed under his breath with a touch of anger, "I thought you spoke for everyone when you asked me to come!"

Trust looked terrible embarrassed, "Y-You need to be here M-mag, you're the only one who- who has seen Nity in person."

Mag swallowed back his anger and wounded pride and took a seat at the table.

"W-we are beginning now? What about the others?" Trust asked aloud as he took a seat beside Mag.

"There is hardly any need to bother everyone else tonight," Victor said with a smile. Mag frowned, he and Trust seemed to be the only ones who didn't understand what Victor meant.

"Why?" Mag asked bluntly. Everyone looked at him, some even looked faintly outraged. Mag felt his embarrassment turn to anger; they expected him to be silent!

"Well…" Victor hesitated, and Mag felt his anger grow- he was being handled! "There are some important decisions that we must make as leaders of the meetings," Victor said carefully. Beside him Trust shifted and blinked rapidly, Mag took a deep breath.

"Well no one need fear what will become of these meetings; I am prepared to take my father's place." No one said a word but everyone seemed to shift in their seats, one man rubbed his forehead while another coughed, and none looked him in the eye.

"We all mourn the loss of Obedience," Victory spoke at last. All the others turned their attention to him and forgot Mag. "Your father was a good man, all of Hawthorn will miss him."

At this the other men all nodded in agreement.

"But, without him I don't see how these meetings can go on."

Mag frowned as he sat there awkwardly with a rigid back.

"Dien called these meeting so he could share what he had seen Nity do and say- but if we're honest, Dien didn't have all that much to say," he added.

Mag wanted to punch him! His father had known a great deal about Eternity. But instead, Mag took in a breath to try and calm himself before saying, "You forget Victor, my father wasn't the only one who met Nity. I was there with him- I too heard the teachings from Nity's own mouth. I know everything my father knew." Mag felt sure that that would settle the matter.

Victor sighed softly. "None of us doubt that you were there too, Imagine. But you are not yet a man, and you were only a child then, you can't be expected to have understood all that was said much less remember it."

Mag had never felt so belittled before in his life! He gripped the edge of his chair and held his lips so tightly closed they went white.

"And there's the other side of this," no one had noticed that Command had come to stand a few tables away and had been listening, but they all looked to him now. He stepped closer as he spoke, "I knew and respected Obedience, his loss is a tragedy. I agreed to let him and the rest of you use my place on the understanding that there was no risk involved; well his death proves that things have changed. I'm sorry, but this is the last time I can let you meet here."

All were silent for a moment.

"My father's death was an accident," Mag's voice sounded small, and he had to force the words out. Now he wished that he had been able to tell his mother the whole story, he didn't realize that the whole village would misunderstand!

"He was killed…" his voice caught. "By thieves, his death had nothing to do with following Nity." Just the thought of that made Mag's insides twist with pain.

An uncomfortable silence followed, Mag was forced to look up at everyone's faces; he felt small and childish.

"Your father had strong beliefs," one of the other men said with a low voice. "He upset many people, we saw it happen every month when the Council met."

The others nodded in agreement.

Victor spoke next, his tone suggested more then he said, "The Council made a mistake in sending your father to Garason in the first place. He shouldn't have been sent as a voice for Hawthorn in the Garatin High Council. You've misunderstood Mag, Obedience was killed because he couldn't keep his opinions to himself."

Mag felt like he was surrounded- with no way out! They were wrong- that's not how it happened! Was it? As he looked around the table he no longer saw friends. Even Trust sat quietly with eyes down as he blinked rapidly.

"Both the Garatin High Council and the Tarven's alike didn't want to hear what your father was saying about Eternity," Victor continued. "As far as they are concerned Nity died when he was executed and that was the end of him." Adding softly, "and maybe it was." He scanned his audience, "Dien's death could be the beginning of a war between Nity followers and everyone else. And I for one do not intend to be on the losing side. More will die before this is settled friends, I do not believe that Eloi would want that." He paused for a moment before saying with a note of finality, "I vote that we end these meetings and swear they never even happened- for the good of us all."

Victory then stood to his feet. Almost at once he was followed by the other four men, Mand also came to stand beside them. Mag sat there and crossed his arms as he tried to level his breathing; he would not let his father's belief die, there was no need to do so, there was no danger! He wouldn't give up- even if he was the only one in Garatin!

However, he wasn't the only one still sitting. Trust sat with eyes down and nervously rung his hands. At last he spoke. "It may be true-" he began with a shaky voice, "that Dien died because of what he believed. And if so then-then I too would rather die for what I believe then go back to the way things were." As he finished his blue eyes shyly looked up at the other men.

Mag felt a burst of hope; he wasn't alone. He met Trust's gaze and together they stood and looked for a moment at the other men.

"Good bye," Mag said quietly. Then the two of them walked to the door.

"Trust, Imagine!" Victor called out, "I am asking you as a friend; give this up! This is not worth dying for!" Mag paused on the door step at his words; could this lead to death? His face hardened, no! There was no danger. He and Trust left and made their way across the now dark square.

"They're wrong, Trus!" Trust looked over at him and even in the dark he could see the vulnerability in the young man. "They're the ones who have misunderstood. My father's death was an accident, a senseless accident. It had nothing to do with what he believed. He wouldn't do that!" he took a deep breath. "He wouldn't put his life at risk like that." He whispered, but the denial and fear could be heard none the less. Trus wanted to ask what really happened to Obedience… but he couldn't make himself ask. When they came to Trust's street they stopped.

"There is no danger for us- when the others see that, they'll come back around." Mag said, but his voice sounded less than certain.

Trus knew better than to comment, so he forced a smile then turned aside and walked away. Mag watched him for a minute then continued on his way home. 'This is not worth dying for!' Victory's words repeated themselves in Mag's mind, and he hugged himself. Just then he heard foot steps behind him, he turned and out of the dark came Command, the Inn keeper!

"Imagine- wait!" he said, his breathing was labored from running for he was a big man. Mag frowned as he looked up at him and waited for the innkeeper to catch his breath.

"Imagine, I wanted to tell you that you should take Victor's advice, don't restart the meetings." Mag felt the sting of disappointment; he thought that Mand was going to ask to join Mag and Trust.

"My mind is made up." he said turning away, Mand reached out suddenly and grabbed the front of his vest and tunic in his big fist. Mag stumbled and tried to pull away, but Mand held tight, panic struck Mag and with a flash he remembered that day in Garason; *"father!" Imagine called out, something slipped from his hands and bounced off of his boot. "Mag! Run!" his father shouted. Someone grabbed Mag's arm and he couldn't get away!*

"Listen here boy!" Command hissed. "Your father was a fool and should have kept his mouth shut in Garason- don't make the same mistake here!" he let go of Mag and pushed him away, for a moment Mag looked up into the face of one who he had thought of as a friend, then he turned and ran home.

*   *   *

Imagine didn't tell anyone what Command had said that night, but it haunted his dreams for many a night. However, it didn't deter him from leading new meetings, he and Trust went right on ahead, and after several months there was nearly twenty people who came to their meetings. They called themselves Nity followers. The other villagers tolerated them for the most part, as long as they didn't meet in the streets. Mag and the rest of Hawthorn had no idea of what was happening to the Nity followers in the city of Garason, and how could they? News doesn't travel fast in northern Garatin.

Indeed, life went on in Hawthorn the same as it always had, Mag and his family managed to plant and harvest their field every season without fail, and three years passed in this manner. The untold story of Obedience's death was never forgotten; however, it was pushed aside in the village's memory. The nightmare was for Imagine alone.

Chapter 3   Eamer

Appeared dumped his armful of letters in the trunk, then slammed the lid shut, picking up a candle he looked about the cottage one last time, if he had missed even one letter it could cost someone's life!

"Appeared! He's coming- we must leave now!" Quest whispered through the open window. The clouds had moved over the moon casting strange shadows on Quest's face. Just then they heard shouted orders from further up the hill.

"The rebels are attempting to flee- round them up!" Appeared felt his heart sink; the soldiers were too close, Quest and the villagers would never escape… He thought of the seventeen villagers who would be arrested only because they had helped him and Quest.

"Appeared- the others are waiting for us, we must go," Quest said when his friend hesitated.

"They'll never make it Est," Appeared said, they both knew he was right. "Go with them old friend- see that they make it out alive. I'll do what I can to keep the soldiers from spotting you." For a moment Quest tried to think of another way- but he couldn't.

"We were there with Nity in the very beginning you and I, I didn't think it would end like this." Appeared stepped to the window and gripped his shoulder in a less then steady hand and said, "May Eloi guide you and Nity keep you, old friend. I hope you make it."

"I wish the same for you," then Quest turned and ran into the night.

Moments later Appeared was alone, he wasted no time. Quickly he piled the letters in his fireplace then set them ablaze. True they were only letters, but they did contain namesakes of other Nity followers; those Namesakes could not fall into the hands of the soldiers!

Looking up, he watched as two soldiers came bursting through his cottage door. Dropping one last letter into the fire, Appeared threw a chair at the soldiers then turned and ran out his back door. He ran towards the center of the village- away from the fleeing villagers. He knew that in a few moments they would catch him, but perhaps the others would get away.

*   *   *

The tall golden grass moved in waves as a north wind blew over the vast wilderness, while white clouds floated peacefully across the blue sky. A pair of four horned deer settled down in the grass together to sleep off the noon day sun. Jack rabbits ventured out of their holes keeping a close eye out for hawks as they nibbled on clover, and birds fluttered here and there, low over the grass. The land went on this way right out to the horizon, only broken by soft gentle hills and little groves of willow and birch trees. If one stood on the top of one of those hills, they would be able to see where little streams cut through the grass land, stemming out from the Byla Marsh itself.

Running through the grass was a small girl, no more than two. Her little bare feet kept on stumbling in thick patches of grass, but every time she fell she merely picked herself up and kept going. Being shorter than the grass, she would sometimes disappear from sight completely. She wore a pale, simple yellow dress. Despite being only two she had unusually long hair- still wispy, but unusually long. None the less one could still see that it had a strange colour- it was copper coloured. With pale skin and tiny freckles around her nose, and blue eyes, it could not be missed that she was indeed Garatin.

Following the little girl was a young woman of eighteen, tall with olive toned skin and a long face. Black/ brown wavy and curly hair fell past her shoulder blades. Her dark Tarven skin made her cinnamon eyes stand out with their dark thick lashes. She wore a simple dress without embroidery or lace- but it could not disguise her dark and stunning beauty. The young woman was Promise.

The small girl in front of her fell down again and disappeared under the grass, as Mise approached her, she saw that the girl was examining a tiny ivory coloured, star shaped flower. Mise knew at once what kind of flower it was; it was a Cres`aren, a symbol of freedom, and the national flower of Garatin. Ten years ago the Cres`aren could not be found so far east from the country of Garatin itself, but five years ago Mise had planted a single seed, and since then the vine like flower had spread out, dotting the Byla wilderness with ivory stars. At her neck, Mise wore a curious little glass vial with a tiny cork, inside the vial she kept the petals from the very same flower she had brought with her from Garatin. The same flower that had died when Nity had, and had sprouted new growth when Treasure had brought news that Nity lived again. Mise wore the vial always, as a sweet reminder of what had happened so long ago.

It wasn't the first time the little girl had seen one but now she studied it as if it was all that mattered. After a moment Mise bent and scooped her up in her arms and said, "Come along Fate, time to go back for your nap." To her relief, Fa didn't seem to mind being put on her hip. Fa reached out one of her arms and wrapped it around Mise's neck and stroked her dark hair, while the thumb of her other hand went neatly into her little mouth.

Holding Fate snugly against her, Mise turned and walked towards the cluster of cottages that had become her home for the past five years. As the wind picked up and blew in their faces, Fa turned her head away from it and rested her head against Promise. Mise looked down at the little girl and smiled, she could hardly believe that she was already two years old. Destination and Treasure, Fate's mother and father, had also had a little boy a few months ago, they had given him the namesake Brave.

Just then Fa's mouth made a popping sound as she pulled her thumb out. "Mama!" Fa was not talking much yet but had indeed mastered that word. Mise glanced up to see Destination looking over their large vegetable garden. Hearing her daughter, Desti turned and smiled at them. Even after bearing two children Desti was somehow still slender. Ever since Mise had turned fifteen she had envied how petite Desti was. Destination was roughly the same height as Mise- but other than that they were very different in appearance. Desti was Garatin and as such had lightly coloured skin, and the same copper colour hair as her daughter. She had expressive grey- green eye's that seemed to tell just what she was thinking. Promise's mother, Loyal had once said that Desti couldn't hide anything with those eyes. The vulnerable and frightened rabbit look had disappeared over the past five years, but the pure innocence that was so very much Desti's, would stay with her all her life. She was a kind and gentle soul, whom Mise felt she could trust with any secret.

Promise was pulled from her thoughts as Fa struggled in her arms, quickly she set the child down and watched as Fate ran to her mother. When she reached her, Desti lifted her up and placed her on her own hip. "What have you been up to my little fairy?" Desti teased softly. In return Fa pointed her little finger back out to the grass and said, "Flowers! Mama!"

Desti laughed and said, "Yes there are lots of flowers!"

Just then Mise reached them and Desti looked to her and asked, "Did she give you any trouble? You were out for a long time."

Mise smiled, "Fa? Give trouble? No. But she is getting sleepy."

They stood there for a moment as Fa leaned her head against Desti. A wistful look came to Promise's face and she spoke softly, "I'll miss this little one."

Desti looked up quickly to see the younger woman's face, "I'm sure she'll miss you as well- we all will."

"It seems hard to believe I'll be leaving this place..." Mise looked about her. Desti smiled wistfully. "I know how you feel," Desti seemed about to say something more, but instead she only smiled.

Mise nodded her head, "I'll see you tonight." Then she turned away, feeling strangely heavy hearted.

*   *   *

Destination knelt down and sang softly to Fa, who listened silently as she drifted off to sleep. The little cradle Fa slept in, was hand woven straw- Desti had made it herself, lining the insides were several rabbit skins, soft and warm. Fa would soon be much too big for the little cradle, and her little brother would then sleep in it. Desti rubbed her daughter's tummy gently and sang quietly about a sparrow in a tree, but before the song was quite finished- Fa was fast asleep. Standing up, Desti rubbed her back and thought of how Fa was getting too big to carry around everywhere. Walking across the upstairs room, she was careful to walk in the centre of the room, away from the sloped, thatched roof, she smiled as she thought about how a day never seemed to go by without Treasure hitting his head off the roof. Being a half foot shorter than her husband she had to try a little harder to bump her head. Before returning down the narrow steep stair way, Desti checked on her three-month old son. Brave was peacefully sleeping, bundled up on her bed. Once downstairs, she went outside and circled around the back of the cottage, and there carving something out of some willow wood, was her husband.

Treasure was a few years older than Desti, about twenty-five this year. Having never known his parents and having raised himself for much of his life, he really was not at all that sure of his exact age. He like Desti, was Garatin, his hair was brown and just long enough to be tied back. He had a square jawbone, and blue eyes that could be startling at times. He had never lost the muscle mass he had built up five and a half years ago when he had been a slave in a silver mine. (But those days seemed very far away indeed and he didn't like to talk about that time in his life.) He was a kind and understanding man, even more so since the day he learned and believed the truth of what Nity had done for him.

The past five years he, Desti's father, Wilder and Promise's father, Courage had worked very hard to create a place for them all to live. Although Wilder and Desti had a lovely little cottage to begin with; six people could not all live in it together. Now five years later, there were three neat little cottages, a stable and several out buildings. A few years back they had started calling the place Eamer, after Wilder's wife Dream, who had died almost twenty years ago. Although Treas had never lived in any kind of wilderness before, let alone one as vast as the Byla, he had adapted quite well. He had used the time of quiet to learn and understand more about Eloi. He had even learned a lot about himself! Wilder had taught him much of living off the land, and what with having a wife that he was very much in love with- Treas was happy indeed.

Destination sat down on the work bench and watched as Treasure worked. Treas was perched on the edge of a smaller work bench near by. He had rolled up his sleeves and had to keep brushing his hair out of his eyes, but he worked steadily. After a time Desti frowned. "What are you making?" she asked. Treas looked up at her briefly.

"A chair for Fa," he said as he went back to working. Desti blinked in surprise.

"A chair!?" she repeated as if she might have heard wrong. Treas straightened up and laughed at her. "You don't think she can sit in our laps all her life, do you?" he teased.

Desti frowned again, "No... I suppose not. I just hadn't given much thought to her getting older."

Treas smiled at her, with a wistful expression, "Seems hard to believe that she'll be three in a few months."

"Don't rush it," she said with a smile. After a moment, Treas went back to carving. He was carving out the back of the little chair, as he bent close and blew away the wood dust, some of it stuck to his face, but he didn't notice. Desti watched as delicate wood curls formed and then gathered on the ground, absentmindedly she thought of how Fa would like to play with them.

"I'm worried about Promise," at last she spoke of what was troubling her.

Treas looked up in surprise, "I thought she was happy to be going back," he waited for her response.

Desti was quiet for a moment, "I don't think Mise has been 'happy' for a long time." Treas looked at her, and then set his tool down, stood up and went to sit down beside his wife. Desti looked at him. "She just wasn't meant for this kind of life."

"She has been acting strange since they decided to return to the west lands," he commented quietly.

Desti took his calloused hand in her own, "I think she's afraid that Garatin won't be what she remembers it was."

They were both silent for a moment. Treas grew grim as he looked out over the grasslands that had become home to him. "I think all three of them will find that out." Desti looked questioningly at him. "Five years is enough time for a lot of things to change."

Desti frowned as she thought it over. Courage and his wife, Loyal, and their Daughter, Mise had fled the west lands with the rest of them five years ago- but it had been harder for them to adapt to life in the wilderness than for Treasure. Courage and his family were Tarvens- and had been important, rich ones too, before Rage had decided that Nity and what he stood for had been more important than following orders. They had left behind a life of ease and comfort, and for a time they had been happy with their decision. But over the past year, Rage had grown unsettled, as if he had grown tired of such a simple life.

"Do you think they'll be alright?" Desti asked. "Is it dangerous for them to go back after what happened?" she felt anxiety build up within her.

"They'll be fine- if only Rage will lay low, and stay out of Tarva's reach," he said softly.

Desti's frown deepened, "Why wouldn't he?"

Treas didn't answer.

"Do you think Rage might.... do something?"

Treas sighed this time, "He was a General in the Tarvan army- that's what he was trained for his whole life- not to be a tradesman..." Treas ran out of words. But Desti understood.

"You and father don't think he'll be content until he has a position of power again..." Treas nodded sadly, but Desti shook her head. If Rage did strive for power in the Tarven world again (for Tarva was the only one who could give power in Garatin) then someone would be bound to remember who he was and what offence he had done five years ago. Surely this fact could not escape Rage! Five years ago he was sentenced to death for what he had done... what would happen to him- and Loy and Mise, if they were found to be in Garatin again? Desti could not accept the idea that Rage would knowingly put his wife and daughter at risk- just for the sake of power.

"You don't know that about Rage!" she said, not wanting to believe what he had said. "Courage wouldn't put them all at risk like that," she looked hard at Treas.

For a moment Treas only returned her gaze with concern- but then realizing that he couldn't argue with her he said softly, "I hope not."

To his relief, Desti relaxed and rested her head on his shoulder. They sat there together for some time.

*   *   *

Wilderness ran his hand over the wood panelled wagon wall, and inspected the carving work on the shutters. The construction of the gypsy wagon had kept Courage busy for the last year, and like most things he took great pride in it. The wagon wheels came up to Wilder's hips and were bright yellow, the paneled walls were a festive red while the window shutters and slightly curved roof were fir tree green making it all quite striking. On the back of the wagon was a yellow door, and on either side of it were several brass rings for tethering horses. Two big horses had been traded for to pull the wagon, but the two brown draft horses hadn't been given namesakes because Rage had thought it was foolish to name draft animals. The wagon had not yet been put into use and as such was spotless of travel dust. Wilder turned and leaned up against the wagon, crossing his arms across his chest. The past five years had done little to age him- but one could see several grey hairs. Other than that his Garatin blond-brown hair was still wispy and straight, and he wore it just above his broad shoulders. His face, with long chin and straight nose, showed no sign of ageing, but at this particular time his eyes looked sadder than normal and his heavy brows were pinched together as he watched his old friend.

Beside the wagon, on one knee Courage scraped dirt out of his horse's back hoof with a sturdy hook. The beautiful black stallion, that had been Rage's pride while he had been a Tarven soldier, had been left behind five years ago when they had all fled Garason. The horse that Rage had had ever since was a much humbler one at that, it was a pathetic looking bay gelding. The horse's namesake was Stream, they called him Stre. He was a fine enough horse for a common man, but Rage hardly thought of himself as a 'common man'. One of Stre's many faults was that at unexpected times he would lay down and roll on his bony back- regardless if he had a rider or not.

Courage by stark contrast was just the opposite from this horse. Tall, and dark skinned he had black hair that he had let grow long, it was slightly streaked with grey, his short dark beard was clipped to a point. He had high cheek bones that defined his face sharply, thick brows sat over brown eyes that could be very hard at times. He was a stubborn, proud and at times an arrogant Tarven. However, the past five years had done much to humble him. But running from danger was not in his nature. Five years ago he had been a high ranking captain, a rich and powerful man, and he had been respected by other Tarvans- and feared by the Garatins. And now? He was just a simple man living out in the wilderness. For him it was more than humbling; it was humiliating.

Wilder knew that Rage longed to be a man of power once more, and as he had discussed with his son-in law, there was great danger in that. But what could he do? Rage had made up his mind that they were leaving and only once before had Wilder ever been able to change Courage's made up mind.

Rage had determined to re-enter the west lands as a tradesman. In truth he had been preparing for this for the past year and a half by gathering and drying a spice called the Byla Star Anise. The plant only seemed to grow in the Byla, and it could be used to season any kind of food and had a unique flavour. Rage was convinced that he could sell it, and had accumulated quite a stock. It was a good enough plan, it would be a little strange that a Tarven tradesman would be coming from the east, but they would get by.... if only Rage could truly swallow his pride and give up all dreams of being anything more; but could he? Wilder would try once more.

"Is it really necessary that you return to Garatin?" he asked quietly, Rage looked over his shoulder at him.

"I understand that you must leave- but go elsewhere Rage. Go further west to the Mayfren forest, or north into the country of Mayvin, where Tarva has no power." He remained perfectly calm, but his voice was persuasive. "Don't tempt fate."

Rage, finished with Stream, rose to his feet and picking up two empty woven baskets went to the back of the wagon. "It is no use old friend," he said firmly as he opened the wagon door and stepped in. Wilder followed him inside- the interior was cramped but livable. Rage hung the baskets overhead and said with force, "I cannot stay here the rest of my life like a frightened child! It is different for you; this is your home." He leaned out and pulled the green shutters closed, a golden line of sunlight ran down his face and over one eye.

He turned to Wilder and said firmly, "but my home is back in the east. And it is not fair to Loyal and Promise, what future does Mise have here?" He moved to leave the wagon but Wilder blocked his way.

"And what future will she have if you are discovered- or if her death bed encounter with Nity is brought to light?" Wilder knew that it was unlikely that they would meet anyone who knew of that encounter, but his point remained.

"After Nity brought her back from death, there was talk of witchcraft. It was only because she was the daughter of a Tarven official that saved her then. Not so now; they would call her a witch, and you know how witches are dealt with."

"Her death and encounter with Nity will remain a secret, she will be safe." Rage paused, then went on with vigor. "Besides, haven't you longed to know what has become of Garatin? Or what has become of Nity and his followers. The Garatin rebels could have thrown out Tarva for all we know!" he paused and took a breath. "Wilder I must return."

Wilder nodded sadly. "Then I will not try to dissuade you again."

*   *   *

"I'm afraid this dress is too small as well," Loyal said dismally as she held up a dress. Loy had been the wife of Courage for over twenty-five years, but Promise was the only child they had. Loy was five years her husband's junior, and was in her early forties. Despite that, she was as beautiful as any young maiden. She had a long face with glowing cinnamon eyes rimmed with dark lashes. Her Tarven olive toned skin had tanned even darker in the Byla sun, and her black\brown wavy hair had only a few grey hairs. She was a woman of poise and grace, and she wore her dignity about her like a favourite shawl.

She considered proper etiquette and manners to be more important than looking one's best- but then for her and her daughter, looking good came naturally. Seven years ago, or even five, Loy would never have thought she would be living in the wilderness like a peasant, it was just so far from her world. But never once had she complained, never once had anyone heard her grumble about her present lifestyle- she was just too polite for that.

Promise, who was sitting on the floor in her little upstairs room of their cottage, glanced over as her mother held up one of the dresses Mise had once worn as a younger girl. The dress was of a deep red velvet, the sleeves dropped at the elbow and hung past the waist, and the hem was hardly worn at all. The neck line had rich gold embroidery circling it, and a gold belt hung down the front. Mise had once worn the dress quite often- but only once since coming to the Byla. Now as she gazed at it she sighed, although the dress didn't look that small, Mise knew she would hardly be able to squeeze into it, let alone do up the laces in the back. There was no use in trying- the result would be the same as the other two dresses she had tried on that morning.

Loy looked at her with a sorry expression, "That's all the dresses you brought with you from Garason."

Mise looked over at the trunk that she had been keeping the fancy dresses in for the past five years. When she had hastily packed them on that night so long ago, she had considered them her simple dresses. "Well I suppose it was foolish to think I could ever wear them again after so long."

"Still I wish you had something nice to wear when we go back," Loy said stubbornly.

Mise looked down at the dress she held in her hands; it was a simple brown dress- shamefully simple, but functional. It had once belonged to Desti, but Mise had been using it for quite some time, all the other dresses Mise owned were more of the same.

"It doesn't really matter anyhow, mother." Mise said. "There will be no reason for finery," she smiled grimly, "Not for a tradesman's daughter anyhow." It pricked her pride to think of how common place she would look.

Loy nodded and looked back down at the dress, "No I suppose not." Nor for a tradesman's wife for that matter, she thought to herself.

Loyal and Promise had been busy all that day packing. They would not leave for another week, but they were surprised at how much there was to pack. And for the past hour they had been deciding what clothes to bring, that's when they realized that neither of them had much of anything to be proud of. Loy tucked the small dress back in the trunk.

"Mother-" Mise spoke, "Where will father take us to trade his goods?" She had been wondering that for some time.

Loy didn't look up at her as she answered, "Northern Garatin, I believe, or eastern."

To Mise it sounded as though her mother did not know, but Mise asked no more questions. Just the thought of it all made her feel sick to her stomach. When Courage had first started talking about it Mise had been filled with excitement; she was going home! But the more it was talked about and the more she thought about it, the less excited she was. It wouldn't be the same. They weren't even going back to Garason- they couldn't. Instead they would wander about like common traders, and that was far from what she should be...

But Mise didn't even know what the life of a trader was really like! She would try and imagine the three of them traveling and living in the wagon her father had labored over. But every time she did, all she could think of was how cramped and confining it would be! She didn't know what to expect at all. Her mind kept turning round and round and she couldn't get it to stop. What would it be like? What would their lives be like? Would she ever see the city of Garason again? Or the summer manor by the Quy Lake? Would they meet anyone they had once known? Would her father be arrested if found? Would they learn of what had become of Nity? All these questions buzzed about like a million bees in spring time- only there were no flowers for them to find and likewise; no answers. Fear knotted in her stomach as she beheld her unknown future. She slept hardly at all in the week leading up to their departure.

The days passed in a flurry of packing and planning. Everyone helped and before Mise knew it, it was the eve before they were to leave. After one last mad packing spree, Courage, Wilder and Treas pulled out maps to take one last look. Meanwhile, Loyal, Desti and Mise organized the wagon. When there wasn't anything more to be done they all bid each other one last good night.

Mise lay in her bed not the least bit sleepy. Her cinnamon eyes wandered about her little room. On a window sill lay a small bouquet of wild flowers that Fate had given her earlier; they were already wilting. The stars had begun to fade when at last Mise fell asleep.

The next morning the two nameless horses were hooked up to the wagon. Barrels of Star Anise spice and trunks of clothes and blankets had been loaded into the wagon while the three riding-horses were tethered to the back.

Loyal knelt and hugged little Fate while Desti stood nearby holding Brave. Loy stood and took Rave's little pudgy hand. "Remember to rub his mouth with honey when he starts teething," she offered one last bit of motherly advice. Desti smiled and said, "I couldn't have gotten this far without your wisdom; thank you." Then Desti handed Rave into Loy's arms and turned to Mise.

Promise was afraid to speak for fear of a sob escaping her mouth instead; Desti had become so very dear to her. Desti seemed to understand and instead of speaking pulled her close. Unbidden tears came to her eyes as she wrapped her arms about Desti. When Desti pulled away tears shone in her eyes as well, but she smiled bravely. "I think I'm afraid, Desti," Mise whispered and shrugged her slim shoulders.

Desti tilted her head to one side. "Fear is what makes people brave, Mise. Only fools are fearless. It is the fearful ones who are truly brave," she said softly. Mise swallowed hard and nodded her head, the words sunk in and made her feel braver- if only a little. She hardly remembered saying good bye to Wilder and Treas and before she knew it, the cottages of Eamer were fading away.

Chapter 4   Leaving Shore

One day's travel away from the manor and keep of Hawthorn, to the west, and on the banks of the Quy River was a Village known simply as Shore. It was a small village without the protection of a nearby keep, or a lord to look after the villagers. The villagers themselves were an even mix of fair skinned Garatins and curly haired folk from the Quy Marsh. One day's ride south there was a small Tarven outpost, who sent a soldier to Shore and the other nearby villages every once in a while to check up on things. These 'checkups' were for the most part ignored by those in Shore- they were but simple fishermen who all together, hardly made two dozen people. The reason for the village's existence was merely one more place to buy a meal along the road that followed the Quy River.

A dozen little thatched roofed cottages were scattered about the narrow dirt road that wound northward. In the middle of it all was a crossroads with four signs nailed to a post; the top one read in black crooked letters 'Shore', the sign below it pointed north-east and read 'Hawthorn'. The one below that pointed to the west and read 'Quy Lake', the last one pointed south and read 'Garason'. In fenced in pens and yards, pigs and chickens mulled about happily, while sleepy dogs snoozed under trees and bushes. Inside the crooked and leaning cottages the womenfolk cleaned the house and kept the young children out of mischief. Just beyond the cottages away from the river the older children kept an eye on the village's cows and mules as they grazed in the common. Meanwhile, most of the menfolk were fishing in the river as they did every day.

It was early morning on a fine sleepy day as twenty-year-old Mag ran his hand through his hair. He hadn't gotten much sleep in the past few days, and last night had been no different. Two days ago Imagine had received a message from Witness; a good friend Mag had grown up with. Two months ago Wit had married Spell, a lovely yet shy Garatin girl. Wit and his new wife wouldn't have paid someone to take a message to Hawthorn unless it was very important. The message had only said 'come.' Of course Mag had left as soon as he could, he had made the one day's walk to the village the day before and arrived late that night. Wit had refused to talk until the next morning.

Mag might not have been so worried, if only things weren't so 'unsure' for those who followed the teachings of Nity. In the three years since his father had died things had changed indeed, ever since the last meeting at the Inn in Hawthorn, things had been tense. It seemed a day did not go by when those who attended the meetings in Hawthorn were not harassed and begged to give it all up. But no one had been hurt, and they hadn't been ordered to stop- so they kept on. Wit was one of these men who didn't stop believing, and he even held his own meetings in Shore.

Now Mag waited impatiently as Wit sat down at the table across from him. Beside Wit, Spell held a wooden cup of steaming tea and she glanced at her husband nervously.

"You'll be glad to hear that the meetings have been going well," Wit began abruptly.

Mag rocked back in his chair in exasperation. "If that's true- then why your message Wit? What's going on?"

Wit's blue, youthful eyes darkened as he sighed, beside him Pell squeezed his hand to encourage him. He took a deep breath, "I wouldn't have sent that message to you- only I didn't know what else to do!" Mag nodded, suddenly uncertain; Wit looked scared…

"A few days ago we received word that Tarva has passed a new law- one stating that any who teach or follow Nity's teachings can be arrested." Wit spoke softly as if afraid that the very cottage walls had ears. "I guess you haven't heard of this yet…"

Mag's eyebrows pinched together as comprehension of what Wit said washed over him. The people in Hawthorn were afraid of mistreatment for following the teachings of Nity- but being arrested!? Since when could Tarva dictate what Garatins could believe!? They had gone too far this time.

Mag shook his head slowly, "They can't enforce that law- even if it's true!" Wit and Pell looked doubtful. "Trust me! Tarva doesn't have the right to pass such a law, the Garatin high Council won't stand for them making laws about what people can and can't believe! We've nothing to worry about," he reassured them softly.

Wit frowned and opened his mouth to say something else- then they all jumped when a knock sounded at the door. Pell started to rise to answer it, when Wit insisted she sit back down. "I'll see to it Pell," he said as he walked to the door. Nether Pell or Mag could see who had knocked since the open door blocked their view. All they could see was the confused and surprised expression on Wit's face.

From the other side of the door a voice demanded, "Are you the man known as Witness?"

Instantly Mag tensed until his body was rigid, across from him Pell's face began to turn white. But it seemed that neither of them could do anything but sit there and listen.

Wit frowned, "Yes, I am he," he replied hesitantly. There was a pause.

"You are under arrest!" the voice exclaimed.

Pell gasped and jumped to her feet, her chair fell backwards and Mag did the same, but the table was between him and the door.

"For what?" Wit demanded to know as he took a step back and grabbed the door as if to slam it shut.

"Rebel activity!" the voice replied, louder than before.

Mag realized the speaker had stepped closer as Wit tried to shut the door but someone from the other side held it in place. Mag felt time slow down as he watched a brief struggle - there was a sickening sound. Wit's blue eyes filled with shock as he gasped and choked then doubled over. Holding his arm across his midsection where a gaping wound bled out, he wheeled away from the door. For a moment he gazed upon his young wife, then collapsed to the dirt floor, never to rise again. Pell's scream snapped Mag into action. Not waiting to see who was behind the door he grabbed Pell and pushed her to the nearest window. Mag practically threw Pell through the open window, and immediately jumped out after her. His foot caught on the ledge and he face dived into the dirt. Scrambling to his feet and spitting the dirt out of his mouth, Mag grabbed Pell's hand and began running. Staying close to the ground they ran through the fenced in backyard, then hopped over the rickety fence into their neighbour's yard. The yard exploded with the startled squawking of chickens as they scrambled out of their way.

Running past the frightened fowl they reached a large chicken coop. Mag let go of Pell's hand, as she collapsed behind the coop and heaved great breaths. Mag feared she would vomit- but there was nothing to be done. Crawling through the grass until he had a view of the road, Mag flattened himself as he watched. The angle of the cottages allowed Mag a clear view of Wit and Pell's front cottage door. Six men and their horses stood in front of the cottage, five of them were Tarven soldiers, their leather breastplates were stiff and their weapons gleamed. The last man among them remained sitting upon his horse, still and unmoving with his back to Mag. Even still, Mag could tell he was Garatin. Two of the soldiers dragged Wits limp body through the dirt and flung him atop one of the horses. Two more soldiers went inside the cottage and from the sound they were searching the place roughly. They came out soon enough and then one of them closed the door and nailed a notice onto it. All six of them mounted up and rode out onto the street; there they paused and the Garatin man (still with his back to Mag) looked about the village. Several people had cracked open their doors to watch- but they all shrank back when the man looked at them. Raising his voice, the man spoke, and to Mag it seemed as though the voice came from a beast rather than a man.

"Let it be known that any Garatin man, woman, or child found guilty of following the teachings of the rebel Eternity, will be arrested and brought to Garason to stand trial for treason before the Garatin High Council. None will evade justice! Those harboring these outlaws are as guilty as the rebels themselves, and will be arrested as such. A reward will be given to any who turn in these outlaws."

Beside him Pell gasped softly and Mag's head reeled. Then the six riders turned towards Mag's hiding place and came slowly closer. Mag sunk lower into the grass as they passed by on the road, just a few steps away.

The horse's hooves sent clouds of dust into the air and Mag looked up at the face of the Garatin as he passed by. Mag went cold... it was him! The man who had stopped Mag from going to his father's aid when the men were beating him to death! The man's cold pale blue eyes held no mercy just the way they had when Mag had last looked into them. The flash back of his father's death played again in his mind.

"Father!" Imagine called out as his father curled up on the street, the sound of coins dropping on the cobbles echoed in his ear. Mag began running towards his father but a strong hand grabbed hold of Mag's arm, he swung about and looked into the face of the man who held him. The man's eyes were icy blue without even a shadow of mercy.

Mag gripped his hunting knife, anger boiled within, and for a moment he saw red- die though he would by the hands of the soldiers it would be worth it just to kill this man. Just then Pell whimpered softly behind him reminding Mag of his duty to her; if he didn't- who would protect her? He clenched his teeth in an effort to gain control as the hunger for revenge contorted his face.

The company of men continued down the road south, but as Mag watched, the scene blurred as if there were tears in his eyes- but his eyes were dry! He wasn't dizzy, he wasn't sick, his vision was just blurry, he blinked hard but it didn't clear. He shut his eyes tight, and as he heard the riders getting further away, his anger faded. The moment passed; Mag became master of himself again. Mag opened his eyes as he released his hold on his hunting knife. His vision was back to normal; he dismissed the strange moment at once. Glancing up and down the road, he couldn't see anyone but he knew someone must be watching. There was nothing for it. He took hold of Pell's hand and led her out onto the road and back to her cottage as she followed dumbly. Around them the village seemed deathly quiet. He pulled Pell behind him through her deserted front yard, reaching the closed door he paused to read the notice nailed there. He had done his best to learn to read, even still he struggled to understand the large words.

The occupants of this cottage have been arrested
For rebel activity and will be held for trial. By
Order of the Garatin High Council, approved by
Ambassador Sinister of Tarva in Garason.

Realization hit him and with it came righteous anger; they had only come to arrest Wit- not kill him! Wit hadn't even had a hunting knife on him, and yet they had run him through without hesitation! Mag turned to Pell, thankful that she could not read. She stood breathing hard staring at the ground with glazed eyes and a white face.

"Listen Pell, you have to be strong! Now- you can't stay here in Shore-"

Pell looked up at him and frowned. "Why?" she asked in a faint voice. Mag was grateful that she could at least understand what he was saying.

"Because, the Garatin High Council ordered this- not Tarva-" even as he said it, it didn't make sense to him. "The villagers could turn on you- you're not safe here! Now- now think; you're not from here, your family's not from Shore- where are they?" for a moment her face remained blank, Mag feared she would be no good to him, but at last she spoke.

"South- in a village south of the Quy Lake, two days from here." Mag nodded.

"All right, I'll take you there, they'll look after you- no one there will know of Wit's arrest." He couldn't bring himself to say 'his death'. Mag leaned away to open the door, but was stopped from going in when Pell grabbed hold of his arm.

"What does it all mean?" suddenly she had changed from a frightened child who was too simple to understand what was happening to an adult who knew full well what had happened- but just didn't know what it meant. Mag wished he could comfort her somehow, but he couldn't.

"I don't know..." he answered. But in truth he did have an idea; it had started with his father, and now Wit too was dead. Before he had been too afraid to believe the others when they said there was danger, but now Mag could not deny the truth. Whatever was happening was something terrible and much bigger than he first perceived, and it would not be stopped easily.

They slipped inside where Pell went quickly about packing what few things she could not do without. Mag leaned against the wall as he waited for her, his blue eyes were clouded with deep thought. What was happening? Rebel activity? Was believing what Nity said really against the law now? Who was that Garatin man who had turned against his own people? Being against Nity was one thing- but letting his own countrymen die!?

Something caught Mag's eye from outside the window; across the road one of the village women was watching from a half-shut shutter. It was time to move. Pell came down the narrow stairs and stood with a vacant expression as she gazed upon the floor where only a few moments ago her husband had fallen dead. Blood streaked the floor in front of the door where the soldiers had dragged Wit's body out.

"Come, Pell," he said softly. She looked up at him. "We must leave now."

*   *   *

Imagine lay awake gazing at the stars from in between a clouded black sky, clouded over like his heart felt; confused and unsure. The tall grass around him would bend in the soft wind making a dome over him. His feet were sore and his legs tired, yet he could not sleep. It had been four days since Witness's death. In that time Mag and Pell had journeyed from Shore to her parent's cottage near the Quy Lake- they had reached them only that afternoon. Mag had not lingered and had left almost at once (he had been away from Hawthorn too long already.) He had given Pell strict instructions not to tell anyone the truth about her husband's death. If following the teachings of Nity really were against the law, it would not be

41

safe to be known as the wife of a man who had been killed for doing just that. It would be another two days before he would be back in Hawthorn, to be gone a week was too long, not only would his family be worried for him - but it was strange for a peasant to travel without good reason.

His thoughts ran fast across his mind; if he, his family, Trust and the others following the teachings of Nity in Hawthorn were in danger of arrest, then there were only two options as to what was to be done. The first one was to abandon it all together like Victory and the other men had done over three years ago… or, to stand by what they believed and hide it. Two weeks ago Mag would have thought all this nonsense - but now he knew better. No longer was it a time when men and women could believe what they wanted to believe in the open; the days of freedom were over.

Mag wondered how many more would abandon him in fear, just like Victor had. Would any stand by him? Would his mother beg him to give it all up to protect them all? Is that what he should do? It would be the safest thing - what would his father have done? Mag closed his eyes to try and stop the tears, but as he did a vivid memory came to him.

His father sat before him and hung his head, Mag, sixteen years of age stood before him with a hurt frown. Dien had listened to his son's outburst of anger quietly, but he had not been surprised. With all the embarrassment and shame directed at him and his family, it was a wonder why Mag hadn't confronted him sooner.

"Why?" Mag asked again. "Why do bad things happen to us if we're doing what Eloi wants?" Dien sighed, a sound to break hearts.

"Mag-" he said gently. "I don't know why. I don't know why Eloi doesn't save us from shame and disgrace. You're not the only one who has had friends turn away from you for what you or I believe. But son, Nity too faced shame and disgrace for what he said and believed - can we expect any less?" Mag hung his head and bit his lip. Dien's next words seemed to come from a much wiser man.

"Mag, at some point you have to decide what kind of person you want to be. A lot of people will try to decide for you, but only you can make that decision. Everyone must decide for themselves what it is they want to fight for, no matter what others think. For a long time, I didn't think there was anything in this world worth fighting for. But now I have decided in my own heart that Nity is, at last, something worth fighting for."

His father's words faded as Mag opened his eyes and found the stars looking back at him through the clouds, they twinkled and blurred as tears filled his eyes. It had been three years, yet the tears still had not dried up. He shut his eyes tight as if to shut out the truth that was begging to be seen. Even if everyone in Hawthorn believed it - Mag couldn't believe it.

He wouldn't let himself believe that his father had chosen to not only fight but to die for what he believed in. Mag couldn't let himself believe that, because if that was true, then his father had chosen to leave him...

Chapter 5   The Tradesman

It was one of those days where the weather was so perfect that one hardly noticed it. The sky was simply there. No one took notice of the way the clouds drifted by, or of the way the birds could be heard singing - if only one were to stop and listen. It was market day in the village of Hawthorn and everyone had either set up what goods they had to sell or was wandering about looking at the different goods. The square was cramped and noisy as the villagers bartered and haggled over prices and goods. But compared to the market day in a great city such as Garason, this market was quiet and peaceful. However, this day everyone kept a careful eye out to please, for on this market day, Lord Favour had come in person to see what goods there were to be had in his village.

The Lord Favour, the earl of Hawthorn, was a Garatin man of noble blood, though it could not be said that he in fact was a 'noble' man. For generations his family had been the lords of Hawthorn, his father before him had died only a few years ago, and although rumored, it could not be proven that Fav had hastened his father's death. He was in his late forty's, but was widowed, his wife having died some time past leaving him with a young son. Few in the village had ever seen the boy, and some even believed the boy had died with his mother, but that was in fact untrue.

Fav had a stocky build, thinning hair, and was clean shaven like most Garatins. His clear blue eyes sat under a wide forehead, they were shrewd and shifty. He liked to think of himself as a great man - but in truth he was a coward who was always on the lookout for people he could use to his advantage. He despised how Tarva controlled him - but he would kiss their boots if only they promised him gain. His only true love was power, and he would serve any who could give it to him. He liked to see himself as a great king ruling over his empire - but really he was just a small, petty, Garatin lord of a village too small to be of interest to Tarva. He was in a sour mood as he wandered the market with a body guard trailing behind him. Everywhere he looked he only saw sad little trinkets sold by sad little peasants. Nothing to catch an eye, or anything that was of interest or high value - nothing that could give him gain.

Fav looked up in surprise as a brightly colored gypsy wagon rumbled into the square. Sitting on the driver's bench was a man, his broad shoulders were stiff and straight, a dark mud-specked cloak hung from them off to one side. Dark eyes looked out of a dark face, his black hair fell just before his shoulders and his beard was closely clipped to a point, both were streaked with gray. Despite wearing poor cloth, he had an air of pride and nobility hanging about him.

Sitting beside him was a woman who could have been mistaken for a fairy queen she was so lovely! Thick lashes rimmed dark soft eyes, black\ brown wavy hair was braided away from her face then tumbled down her back. She too had an air of richness that her simple dress denied.

The man pulled the wagon to a halt in an empty spot of the market. Almost at once the back door to the wagon swung open and a young woman stepped out. Her cinnamon eyes flashed and unlike the older woman her own hair was free and wild about her. She made her way through three horses that were tied to the back of the wagon, giving them pats as she went by before circling to the front of the wagon.

Favour was taken aback for a moment as he beheld them, their olive toned skin gave them away at once; they were Tarvens! Fav froze and to him - so did the rest of the world, his mind worked double time; who was this Tarven? He appeared to be just a trader, but might he not be a soldier in disguise, or a spy from Garason, seeking to find corruption in the way Fav ran his village? If so, corruption he would find.

The Tarven man and woman climbed down from the wagon seat. Fav didn't waste another second as he walked swiftly up to this tall Tarven and pasted a smile on his dishonest face. Fav offered a little bow, and having the man's full attention, he spoke loudly enough to be heard by the people close by.

"I am Lord Favour of Hawthorn, and I welcome you to my village, humble though it may be, I place my manor at your convenience, my lord." He waved his hand towards the manor behind him, and was pleased to see that his body guard had taken up a stand behind him, making him look all that more important.

The Tarven looked at him with unreadable eyes for a moment, and then turning to his wagon, he said over his shoulder. "I am Courage the tradesman," it was blunt and to the point.

* * *

Rage had forgotten who the lord of Hawthorn was, the decision to come here had been made only two nights ago, now he wished they had gone someplace else. It was Favour! Rage hadn't given the man any thought for over seven years. Did Fav remember him? Suddenly Rage felt as though they should have stayed in the Byla. Loy and Mise stood tensely on the other side of the wagon, they could tell something was wrong.

"A tradesman?" Lord Favour blinked in surprise, but he recovered quickly. "You are from the south?" it was more a statement then a question, still Rage felt he had to correct him.

"We travel from the east, my lord." Rage turned back to him and held his breath as he waited for a response.

Fav frowned slightly, the question written plainly on his face; what Tarven came from the east?! "The east you say? Does not the world end after the Byla River!" he laughed at his own joke. Rage forced a smile.

"A friend made it known to me that there are treasures to be had in the Byla," Rage said in explanation. It was true enough.

"Hark! I didn't know there was anything of worth east of here!" again he laughed. "Of what treasures do you speak, I would know what they are."

Rage hesitated a moment. "Trinkets and woven goods made by Quy marsh folk, and goods from further east still, as well as 'Star Anise spice'. You will not find better spice anywhere north of Garason my lord." Rage could not keep pride out of his voice as he saw Fav's eyebrows rise at the word 'spice'.

Far from the five isles spice trade, Hawthorn along with all the other villages in the north hardly ever saw spice of any kind. Fav's reaction was what Rage had hoped for.

"Spice you say? Very good then! You may trade in my humble village for as long as you like, a good morrow to you."

Rage watched as the lord turned and left, his body guard following. Looking about he noticed that almost everyone else in the square was watching and had heard the exchange. Loy and Mise walked around the team of draft horses towards him, they both leaned closer.

"Rage do you know him- did he remember you?" Loy asked worriedly.

"I had one or two dealings with him in the past, but I don't believe he recalls me."

"Should we leave?" Loy asked.

Rage paused; leaving would be a wise thing, but it would be like running. "No, he didn't remember me, and he has given us permission to stay and trade." Then he saw how worried his wife was. "Don't worry we'll be fine. You and Mise take a look about the market, while I see about where we'll stay- everything will be fine."

With that Loy was put at ease for the moment; Rage knew best. She and Mise began to wander about the small village square, soaking in the feeling of being about people, even if they were strangers.

The little market was a bit of a disappointment for Mise, she didn't think the first place they stopped at would be so… small. Mise looked about and noticed people watching her, some with curiosity - others with distrust. She met the eyes of a Garatin girl some years younger than herself. The girl looked away quickly, but some of the others weren't so shy. They stared her down like she was an outlaw! It made her feel nervous - what was so strange about her? Then she realized it - she and her family were THE only Tarvens! Suddenly Mise felt like she was indeed an imposter, unwelcome and not wanted here. 'I hope we don't stay here long' she thought to herself. Rubbing her forearms with her hands, Mise felt terribly self-conscious in her worn out and fraying dress, but she tried to hold her head high.

The past three weeks had been like a breath of fresh air, and at the same time it had been torture for Mise! Each night she was either kept up by her excited thoughts or exhausted by dreams of uncertainty. Traveling through the Corfin forest, Mise had her first glimpse of what other tradesman were like; they had met a Quy marsh folk trader on the road and Rage had bought a few things from him to add to his own stock. When at last they left the Corfin behind them, they had come across a road sign that read 'Hawthorn'. And now here they were, and like all her fears come true they hadn't under gone some kind of magical transformation once entering Garatin; she was still only the daughter of a tradesman.

Loy had stopped to look at one of the stands, while Mise walked on by herself. She felt alone and lost, all she wanted to do was go running back to the Byla. She felt she was about to cry - and she wouldn't be able to explain why; for she didn't know herself. Fear gripped her, and her throat went dry. Suddenly like a soft breeze on a hot day, Desti's parting words came to her. "Only fools are fearless…" Mise took a deep breath. Fear or not, she was going to make it through this.

*   *   *

Beside a large fireplace with soot blackened sides, in a room with high ceilings and big, sagging tapestries hanging on the stone walls, and tables and benches spread about for banqueting, stood Fav. With brows pinched and arms folded as he stared at the dancing flames, one finger tapped his chin as he lost himself in thought. At long last he looked up and called out.

"You, page boy!" a page no more than fourteen who had been waiting in the shadows jumped closer.

"Yes, my lord?"

"There is a new tradesman in the market selling spice from the Byla; go there and watch to see how well he sells. But do not make yourself known."

"How will I know this man, my lord?" the boy asked. Fav looked at him for a moment.

"He is Tarven. Watch him all day and report back to me at sun down." The page ran to do his lord's bidding.

*   *   *

"Mother! He's back - Mag is back!" Peri's youngest called out as she tore out into the backyard, and then spun back around and ran around the cottage to the front yard again. The twelve-year-old girl was gone before Peri and sixteen-year-old Ember could say a word.

"Oh for my grandfather's namesake - where has he been!?" Peri exclaimed, as both she and Ember dropped the quilt they had been folding and ran around the cottage to the front. It had been a week since Imagine had left for Shore, saying he would be back the next day! Peri had hardly slept the whole week long in worry for her son. What had happened? As she and Remember came out into the front yard, they saw a very tired and worn out looking Mag. His face was smeared with travel dust and so too were his clothes. Putting his arm around his twelve-year-old sister's shoulder he looked up wearily as Peri drew closer. Perilous felt a dread come upon her as she looked at her son's face - something had gone terribly wrong.

"Mag!" but her words stuck in her throat. Sensing that what he had to say was serious, she said briskly to her youngest. "Go bring in the rest of the laundry from the line, there's a good girl. I'm sure your brother must be starved, Ember go and prepare him something to eat… please."

Ember, sensing the seriousness of the matter, nodded and pulled at her younger sister, who was protesting loudly. When the two girls had disappeared, and only Mag and Peri were left, they looked at each other as only two people who have shared hardship together can. Mag readjusted the shoulder strap from his bag, and walked up to his mother.

"I'm alright mother, really," he said as she looked him up and down for wounds or cuts. She breathed a sigh of relief.

"Then what's happened - why have you been gone so long?"

He sighed heavily, "Witness is dead."

Peri let what he had said sink in, "How?" she whispered.

"He was killed." He quickly told her of what had happened as she listened quietly. When he was done she nodded, then with nothing else to say, led him inside.

When Mag had finished the light meal Ember had made him, he and Peri sat in silence while Ember stood by the fire preparing food to bring to her other brothers who were out in the fields. At last Mag spoke.

"I don't know what it all means, but I think it would be wise to call a meeting and discuss with the others what should be done." Peri nodded her agreement, while Ember listened closely.

"Are Vanished and Survive out in the fields?" Mag asked of his two younger brothers.

"Yes," Peri hesitated. "Ember will be going soon to bring them some food... there's no need to tell them now, there'll be time enough for that later." Mag nodded.

Peri watched him for a moment more then got up to look over the meal Ember had made for Vanished and her youngest son, Survive; a hunk of cheese, some dried meat, and a small loaf of bread.

"What I would give for a bit of spice for the meat," Peri murmured to herself.

Hearing her and wanting to change the subject, Ember spoke lightly.

"There was a new tradesman in the market this morning, with a wagon and everything, he was selling spice."

"Was there now?" Peri asked offhandedly as she wrapped up the food in a cloth.

"Yes, I was surprised because he was Tarven."

Both Peri and Mag looked at her sharply.

"Tarven?" Peri asked tensely. Ember looked at her nervously.

"Yes-" she answered slowly. "There was a man and two women; all Tarven."

"Are you sure they were Tarven?" Mag asked.

More nervous by the second, Ember nodded, "Yes - the girl looked right at me - what's wrong?"

Peri looked at her son. "You said Wit's arrest was by order of the Garatin High Council, you said that Tarva isn't involved- didn't you?" she asked in a low voice.

He nodded.

"Besides," Ember said with a touch of uncertainty, "They wouldn't send a Tarven spy into a Garatin village... that doesn't make sense."

"It probably doesn't mean anything," Peri assured them after a moment, but Mag didn't feel reassured at all.

He spent the rest of the day going about the village and the fields telling those involved that there would be a meeting that night. Most hardly took him seriously and asked if Trust or Journey (he was a good man who had joined a year ago) would be there- but they all said that they would come.

When he found Trust he told him briefly that it was important and serious, and Trus spread the word further. By mid-afternoon over fifteen villagers had been told about the meeting. For the past three years the meetings had been held at both Trust's and Mag's cottages, but that night they would met at Mag's. So at sundown all fifteen villagers quietly made their way to Peri's doorstep.

Peri's youngest daughter and son had been sent upstairs while Ember was allowed to listen in on the meeting. Van stood close by eager to be involved, while Peri sat on a stool listening closely. Trus along with Journey, and three other men, and Memory, the woman who ran the bakehouse, all sat at the table. The other nine men and women stood or sat around the room quietly, as Mag stood and told them all of what had happened to Witness. His throat felt swollen, and his voice cracked once as he told the story a second time. But they all listened, and Mag felt for a moment like they respected him.

When he was done, one of the men turned to Peri and asked, "Where is Wit's wife, Spell?"

Peri looked to Mag, he hesitated before saying, "I moved her away from Shore to... I'd rather not say where..." he said glancing to his mother for support.

There was silence for a moment before another man said in a low voice. "You don't trust us to keep her safe?"

Silence filled the room broken only by the crackling fire. Mag swallowed hard, that's just what he needed now; a misunderstanding!

"I think the less people who know, the better," Mag replied carefully.

The tense moment was broken when Journey spoke with a calm and reassuring voice, "I think Imagine is right." All eyes turned to him, Journ was a good man and everyone respected him.

"At any rate; Pell is safe. We should really be thinking about our own safety - if Wit could have been arrested by Garatin order... Then none of us are safe."

No one said anything more and they only looked at each other as if to ask 'are you willing to risk it?' Even Van was quiet.

"I-I think..." Trust spoke up, "I think that if anyone here finds the-the risk too great for them, then I th-think that they should leave now." He looked around the room timidly.

"Trus is right," Journ said. "None of you are held by oath to stay. Surely, what happened to Wit could happen to anyone of us. If the Garatin High Council has deemed following the teachings of Nity rebel activity; we are now all outlaws," his voice betrayed his own disbelief at what he said.

"I disagree," Van said suddenly. Child though he was, he had everyone's attention at once. "The Garatin High Council are not our enemy - it is the Tarven's who we must fight against!"

"Here here!" one of the other men said and several more cheered at Van's rash words.

Mag glared at his younger brother; why was it the others listened to his idiot, childish brother and not to him? Peri pressed her lips together as though withholding the urge to scold her son in front of everyone. But Journ spoke before things could go further.

"We are not part of the Garatin rebellion - we do not start wars!" Again they all listened. "The only decision that must be made is are you willing to risk it? Your reputation, your livelihood, and the safety of your family for the sake of Nity? Because if you are not, now is the time to leave and break all bonds with us, for surely a dark time is coming for those who follow both Nity- and Eloi." His speech was sensible and there was not one in the room who didn't take it to heart.

No one could look each other in the eye, as they all questioned themselves. At last one of the women stood and whispered, "I'm sorry." She then quickly left. She was followed by another man and his wife who hesitated at the door for a moment, then they too left. They all waited, but no one else moved.

Mag looked to his mother, and he felt like a vise gripped his heart, he didn't want to believe that they were all in danger! But Wit's death made that impossible to believe, they were all in grave danger. 'It's not worth it!' fear whispered in him. Make no mistake Journ's words had a huge impact on him; but he couldn't put his family at risk! But as he looked at Peri she returned his gaze, and there was no fear in her eyes. Mag knew she was in this to the end. He wanted to argue with her - but the words wouldn't come. Closing his eyes, he determined in his heavy heart that no harm would come to his family.

At long last Journ spoke, "Well… If we are all committed to this- then we must be very careful in days to come!"

One of the other men spoke next, "I think we should have more than two places to meet, perhaps your cottage Journ?"

Journey nodded.

"We could hold them in my barn," one of the others offered.

"Do you think our neighbors can be trusted not to turn us in?" someone asked with fear. There was a somber silence.

"They wouldn't do that - we're all like family…" Peri said softly.

"We can't worry about that, we will have to trust them," Journ said.

"It's settled then!" Memory said with a curt nod. She was one of the oldest people in the village and had been in Hawthorn longer than most of the others in the room had been alive. She was an intense sort of woman with strong opinions and a sharp tongue - but had hardly ever spoke at the meetings. So everyone was surprised indeed when she spoke up with authority in her crackled voice.

"We'll all meet at Journey's cottage in one week after sundown- then we can get back to where we left off." No one dared say otherwise for fear of the telling off Mory would give them.

Journey nodded, "Yes alright, um… yes that settles it. Good night everyone- and don't tell anyone else about this."

Everyone got up, and although they had discussed dark times and how they might all be killed for what they were now doing - their spirits were high as they wished each other a goodnight and left.

Van grinned ear to ear like it had all been great fun. Rolling her eyes, Ember pushed him towards the stairs to the loft. While they climbed up, Peri watched the last villager close the fence gate behind them and wave her goodnight. She then closed the door and sighed. Mag sat at the table watching her.

"Are you sure we've done a wise thing?" he asked her quietly.

She looked up at him, she looked tired and worn out. "A wise thing? No," she said sadly. "I'm not even sure we've done the right thing."

Chapter 6   Moving Up

The wind snapped the colourful yellow banners back and forth, and filled the big sail till it billowed, making the green and yellow dragon of Tarva look like it was lunging out. The salty sea air was brisk and chill as it swept inland creating thick fog in the Moranna Mountains on the horizon. The seafaring village of Larsanne was a bustle of life as the Tarven ship came into anchor. Tarven seamen were busy unloading trunks, sacks and barrels into boats to be rowed to the docks and then taken into the village. It had been nearly eighty days since the ship had left the grand harbour of Tarva, making a stop in the Nyniver Isles, and another along the southern coast in sight of the Moranna Mountains. Finally, after a brief stop among the Five Isles it made its way to Larsanne. It was the season of good sailing, so they met with very few storms along the way. Yet even so it was good to know that the voyage had come to an end at last.

Walking slowly, giving his legs a chance to remember what land felt like, a Tarven man made his way into the village from one of the long docks. He was tall and slender, with short black hair and an over grown beard that he had neglected to trim over the last days of the voyage. His eyes were dark and intriguing, holding mischief within their depths. Thin lips that were almost always grinning in a lazy way, were now drawn tight in thought of the months ahead of him. For all his good looks, one would hardly guess that he was past fifty- but he was.

As he neared the end of the dock he looked up to see a Tarven soldier standing stiffly, two horses stood waiting behind him. Drawing himself up to his full height, the Tarven stood before the soldier. The soldier was a younger man, and he seemed to quake before this sea- faring Tarven.

"My Lord Thrive," he said and offered a little bow. "I bid you welcome on behalf of his Lordship Contrast of Larsanne." Sweat beaded down his face.

Thri smiled lazily, "Is his lordship too busy to welcome me himself?" he asked it offhandedly, but the soldier knew he was deadly serious. Thri never lost his smile as he went on. "Would his Lordship Contrast, rather welcome the King himself - rather than the King's right hand man?" The soldier only stood there, with open mouth. Thri felt cruel, so he put an end to it.

"We shall go ask his lordship himself." He then swung up onto one of the horses and let the poor soldier lead the way up to the Manor of Larsanne.

Larsanne was a fishing village on the southern shore of the Nennor Sea. As every year passed, more and more Tarvens arrived and the village grew, until now it was spreading out into the foothills of the Moranna Mountains. As Thrive and the soldier made their way up to the manor, Thri took the chance to look over the village. What he saw he was not impressed with. The streets were hard packed dirt; he made a note in his mind to discuss that with Contrast. As a growing Tarven village, the main streets would have to be cobbled. The market square was small and dingy; that would have to change as well. As a sea port it needed a large market square. As they rode past a narrow alleyway, Thri caught sight of several Tarven soldiers lounging about as if the King had declared a holiday! Thri frowned-things were severely lacking in this town indeed.

As they rode into the manor courtyard under a crumbling arch, the soldier dismounted and called for a stable boy to take the horses. Thri looked about the yard with displeasure, the stable was falling apart and the yard was littered with equipment that no longer had value. The Lord Contrast was Earl of Larsanne, and as such, looked over the surrounding area as well. Unless the fishing was bad (which it was not) Lord Rast would collect more than enough taxes to repair his own keep! Since he was so obviously not doing that- what was he spending the money on? Thri pondered this as the soldier escorted him into the manor and through the halls.

Thrive's answer came quicker than he had anticipated. As the soldier led him into the grand banqueting hall, Thri took in the sight; the hall's stone ceiling was not nearly high enough and was stained black from the many candles in the floor candelabras that lighted the large room. Rich tapestries hung on the walls, depicting glorious battle scenes from Tarven history. Spread about the room were a number of wooden tables and benches, and one at the far end of the room was set up with a great feast! Sitting alone, gorging himself, was Lord Rast.

The soldier nervously led Thri through the maze of tables, till they came to stand across from where Lord Rast was sitting.

"My Lord I present to you, his Lordship Thrive," he then bowed and stepped away with a relieved air.

Contrast was a man in his forty's with thinning hair and an ever growing middle. He had an air about him that said he thought he was better than most. Thri's disliking of the man grew at once.

"Welcome Thrive, please sit and join me!" he gestured to a seat across from him. "I trust your travels were pleasant," he idly popped a small fruit in his mouth.

Thri smirked, "It was- until I arrived," he ignored the invitation and began to slowly move around the table.

Rast sat up straighter, "Was my soldier not there to meet you!?" From a few tables away the poor guard opened his mouth with a stunned look.

"On the contrary, he was. You see, I expected to be greeted by you yourself. I see now you were - elsewise engaged," he said dryly. Rast frowned as if he didn't understand. Thri continued around the table. "I must tell you my lord, I am most displeased with the condition of the village, and surprised at the contrast -" he let the word sink in, "your life presents, compared to the rest of Larsanne." He looked pointedly at Rast's richly embroidered clothes and gleaming jewels.

Rast's face darkened as he comprehended the insult. He stood to his feet abruptly, his high backed chair falling behind him. Thri stood his ground toe to toe with him, and looked Rast in the eye, still smiling.

"Does his lordship wish to speak to me? Or perhaps, you would rather write what you wish to say in a letter and I could give it to the King upon my return - it can be arranged," he said it smoothly.

Rast growled in his throat as he realized he had met his match.

"Page! His lordship's chair!" Thri called out sharply, making both the page boy and soldier jump. The page almost leapt to the chair and righted it. Before he could escape however, Thri said, "His lordship's cup," the page picked it up from the table and held it out to Rast. "His lordship has a sore throat," Thri said with a grin.

Rast took the cup angrily and sat down again. The page was back against the wall in no time. Thrive walked over to a platter of wild boar and brushed away a fly.

"Shall we get back to all the things I found faulty in Larsanne? For of course you realize my lord, that the King of Tarva, may his reign go on, has given me full power," he paused and looked at Rast. Contrast sat and glared straight ahead.

Thri went on, "The King has sent me out into the eastern reaches of his great empire, to inspect his soldiers, his captains, and his governors." Thri paused again and this time pulled from his cloak a leather cylinder with a gold tassel hanging from one end. Removing the top, he pulled out a rolled up paper. Rast watched as Thri unrolled it slowly, revealing the heavy, red seal of the King of Tarva. Rast's mouth opened in astonishment.

"The King sent me with this letter - I could read it for you -" Thri said innocently. "But I think you'll take my word for it when I say, the letter holds a main theme," Thri laughed softly. "I really think he said it better when I last spoke with the King," he laughed again. "He said 'I've made it clear that you are to have whatever it is you ask for - even wings if you so demand!'" Thri let his laughter die slowly before saying. "I really rather think he was serious."

Rast swallowed hard. Thrive was pleased to see that Contrast was at last beginning to understand his position.

"You see -" he said, returning the letter to his cloak, "The King has granted me the power to do what I see fit. I can even give knighthood! I have the power to give land to those I see fit, and to take away land from those I see unfit. I have the power to uphold men whom I see fit, and to bring down those whom I see as... unfit." The pleasantness had faded as Thri drove home his point. Rast seemed to shrink back.

"I have the power to appoint men as barons, as counts, as earls, and as dukes. I also have the power to make barons, counts, dukes and -" he paused for a moment, "Earls into mere peasants. And if I see fit, to order banishments and executions." There was a long moment of strained silence. Thri watched as fear sunk into Rast's face. Then Thrive brightened.

"You will be pleased to learn I will be staying in Larsanne for two weeks before journeying over the mouth of the Arrow Sea and into Garatin. You will have until then to make the changes I will suggest."

The same soldier who had led him in, hurried to escort him to his chambers. Thri smiled to himself- back in Tarva he had inherited the title of Duke from his father before him, an important position on its own. But now, in a years' time, if he returned with a good report for the King about the eastern lands - the King had promised to make him Grand Duke. Then, he would be one of the most important men in the whole of Tarva. Thri's smile deepened, he was indeed, moving up in the world.

*   *   *

It had been two weeks since Rage had driven his wagon into Hawthorn, and in those two weeks he had not sold a single thing. After their first day they had set up camp on the outskirts of Hawthorn, making sure not to be too close to any of the fields. Every market day Rage drove the wagon into the village, setting it up in the square. Although people were obviously curious, no one had bought from the Tarven tradesman. He had even talked to Memory, the old women who ran the bakehouse in the village, about buying some spice to make special pastries with. She had been quite rude and had declared that she would never buy from a Tarven! She had nearly pushed him out the door after telling him, not to come back. Everyone in the street had heard the commotion. Courage had never been so humiliated in his whole life!

That had been a few days ago. A more experienced tradesman would have packed up and moved on to someplace else; but to Courage that would feel like defeat- and he would not accept that. Added to all this and the danger of Favour remembering him, there was also the problem of money. Unless Rage sold something soon there wouldn't be enough coins to buy more food. It was a great blow to his pride to think that his family would go hungry for lack of money.

So it was, that early on market day on the third week since arriving, Rage set up to sell in the square again. After hanging blankets on the wagon's open door, Rage set up crates and little barrels around the wagon to display his different wares. Among them all, the most important and profitable was the Star Anise spice- if only he could sell it. After setting up, Rage sat on the wagon wheel and rested his arms across his knees with fingers interlaced. And waited. The villagers went about the market, greeting one another, laughing, talking and buying and ignoring him to the best of their abilities.

As the morning went on Rage sunk lower and lower into a dark and bitter mood. In an effort to keep his mind away from it all he began to think about his life. First he thought on his childhood; he had grown up in a big cold manor in the centre of Garason. His father was an army general, and often away fighting in one war or another, so much so that when Rage was twelve and sent away to become a soldier- he hardly knew his father at all. Two years later his father died leaving him with all his wealth. When he was a year away from being a full soldier at twenty-one, he was called away to fight in the Five Island uprising. He performed so well that when the uprising had been put down, his captain had spoken of him to the Tarven ambassador. He had been so impressed he had knighted Rage on the spot! From there, Rage climbed in the ranks until he was asked to join a special unit who were being trained as assassins.

It was there that Rage had first met Wilderness. Rage had thought of him only as a half-blooded peasant, unworthy of such high training. He had had an immediate disliking to Wilder, and so had Wilder to him. Over the next six months of training they were in constant competition against one another to prove worth. Rage would excel in one skill and flaunt it to make sure Wilder noticed. Then the next day, Wilder would have topped whatever it was that Rage had worked so hard at. And Wilder would then, like everything else he did, quietly and humbly rub it in Courage's face. It had taken them six months to come to an understanding and appreciate the others skills. After they had accepted each other they found they really rather liked one another. After they completed their training, they were both married, and both seemingly, unable to have children. At the end of their training, Wilder was one of the best assassins in the whole Tarven army, and he had proven it time and again. Whereas Rage, had climbed in the ranks until he was the Assassin General.

It was then that Wilder had changed his way of thinking and had disappeared into the east with his wife. Eighteen years later, Rage went looking for him, asking him to do one last assassination. When Wilder accepted, they both found themselves entangled in something that changed their lives forever - Nity. Rage sighed, how would his life have been different if only he had not been ordered to take Nity down?

Courage's original plan to distract himself from thinking of how much he hated his current life had failed miserably. Bitterness took him as he sat there in the market. There was a time when he had been on top of the world - and now? His thoughts were interrupted when he realized a man was standing in front of him. And not just any man - but a Tarven!

"At last, a good honest Tarven tradesman!" the man said happily. Rage blinked and stood to his feet as he took him in; he was an older man, with fine clothing and a round face and just generally, round all over. His brown eyes sparkled in a way that not many Tarven eyes do. "What are you selling good man?" he said in a jolly fashion.

"Goods from all over Garatin my lord, and spice, the finest in the eastern lands," Rage said proudly.

The man blinked, "Ha!" he exclaimed. Then he turned and called out. "Here, Lord Fav! I didn't know you had a spice trader in your village! Very good I say!" Rage felt uneasy as Lord Favour walked up, wearing what were undoubtedly, his best robes. Fav looked confused.

The man went on, "I say, will you be using this spice for the banquet tonight?" Fav gave him a blank look. Suddenly Rage understood; Favour in his need to impress, had invited this Tarven to a banquet that night, and had been showing him about his village with pride. Rage jumped at the opportunity.

"I would be more than willing to supply the needed spice for the banquet tonight - if his lordship has a desire for such a thing."

The jolly looking Tarven smiled, "I say! I would enjoy a bit of spice - Favour I insist that you add some to the banquet tonight! I've heard that over in Tarva they don't eat anything without some sort of seasoning or other."

Fav smiled, "But of course my lord," he then waved to a guard and gave him a money pouch, "Buy enough for the banquet." Then both Fav and the Tarven wandered away, while the guard approached Rage. Five minutes later and Rage had enough coins to live off of for two weeks!

*   *   *

The banquet that night, held by Lord Favour, was a tremendous success, and the Tarven man (who was only a rich land owner from further south) enjoyed the Anise spice so much and thought it so stylish, that he bought from Rage a small box full to take home to his manor. With that small victory under his belt and extra coins in his pouch, Rage had begun making plans of where they should go next to trade.

It was mid-morning after the banquet and Mise and Loy were making up a stew together. They both sat on little stools beside a fire with a large pot hanging over it, and were dropping in ingredients. It would be the best meal that they had had in a while. Between the two of them it was Mise who had learned to cook the best over the years. Loyal had done hardly any cooking before in her life, and found it hard to learn now. 'It just wasn't part of her upbringing to learn how to cook' Mise thought to herself. Cooking, sewing and farming were all things that Loy had not been taught how to do when she was young, there had been no need! She had been raised as a lady of Tarva - but Mise had learned all these things in the past five years. After all, she was just the daughter of a tradesman.

Beside Mise, Loy stood to her feet and brushing off her hands said, "This will be the first good meal we've had in two weeks!" She shook her head at the revelation. "At least out in the wilderness there was plenty of game to hunt!" Mise smiled at her mother's light hearted complaint. Across the camp, Rage paused from tending to the horses and looked up when he heard his wife's comment. He frowned.

"It will not always be this way for us," he said firmly. Mise and Loy looked up in surprise. "I did not bring us back to the west lands to beg for food and sit in the dust for the rest of our lives."

Behind him, Rage's horse Stream, gave a rude snort to remind him that he had not finished his rub down. Driving his wet nose into Rage's back, Stre shoved him roughly. Rage turned on him angrily, Stre only gave him a sheepish look. Cursing the horse under his breath, Rage went back to rubbing him down.

Mise wondered if it really would be better if they just gave up. Who were they fooling? Of course it would always be this way - a tradesman cannot advance in the ranks like a soldier can. This was their life. Would it not be better if they just returned home?

Home... where was home? Mise wondered, could their colorful gypsy wagon ever really become 'home'? Just then she heard the sound of a horse approaching. Mise looked up to see a Garatin guard riding up to their camp with a page boy running behind him. Courage stepped out to meet them, and Mise wondered if he had any weapons on him.

"Greetings from his Lordship Favour of Hawthorn," the guard said as he reined in his horse. Rage crossed his arms while Mise and her mother stood a little behind him. The guard dismounted.

"My master wishes to speak with you and bids that you come to the manor." The guard smiled. Rage was silent for a bit, his first thought was that Lord Favour had had enough of them and was going to run them out of Hawthorn! But, the guard seemed friendly enough. Rage glanced over his shoulder at Loy.

"The ladies are of course invited," the guard added. It all sounded fair and non-threatening...

"And what of our camp?" Promise asked suddenly before Rage answered. Everyone- including the page all looked at her in surprise. Suddenly Mise realized how unladylike that was, and shame burned through her as she ducked her head. What kind of a woman was she, that she couldn't even remember her place? There was an awkward moment's silence.

"The page will stay and look after your camp, good sir," the guard said carefully and only gave Mise a side glance as he did so. Rage gave a little bow.

"Very well, I accept his lordship's invitation." He turned and walked to Loy and Mise and spoke quietly.

"Favour might have summoned me to offer a trade route. We must make a good impression." He looked hard at Mise for a moment, and then motioned for Loy and Mise to mount up. Mise looked down at her half-finished stew, the page boy would no doubt enjoy it. With a short sigh she saddled her horse quickly. Butterflies danced through her stomach; they were going into the manor! Just before she swung up onto her horse, Loy, who was already sitting neatly on her horse, caught her daughter's eye. She mouthed the words 'side saddle' to her. Mise understood her meaning at once. Not wanting to make another mistake, Mise resisted the urge to swing one leg over the side of her horse and instead carefully lifted herself into the saddle. Once sitting, she straightened her back and nodded to her mother, who nodded her approval. But as soon as Loy turned the other way Mise shifted her weight with a grimace; she hadn't ridden side saddle for a very long time indeed - and it was most uncomfortable!

From the time it took for them to ride up to the manor, dismount and be shown into a room, Rage had worked out in his mind not only exactly what Favour wanted to talk to him about, but what he would say in response. But really it took so long before they finally arrived, Rage was rather bored thinking about it all! The guard led them through many halls and up many a stair before they walked into a cozy room, with a thick rug. Despite it still being in the middle of the day, a fire burned in a large fireplace. Several high backed wooden chairs were sitting in front of the fire. Three windows with colored glass panes let in the sunlight along one wall, while across the room stood a heavy wooden door; it was shut.

Without hesitation, Loy moved across the room to one of the chairs and sat down gracefully. Despite wearing a simple and frayed dress, she still managed to look lovely. Mise, who was feeling common and out of place followed her mother's example as best she could. Rage watched, and was pleased that his wife still knew how to act like a lady of Tarva. A deep pleasure rose within him; it would not be long before he would be a great and powerful man once again.

From across the room, the door opened and out came Lord Favour. Fav was wearing the same fine robes that Rage had seen him wear the day of the feast when he had been trying to impress the jolly Tarven, only now Fav wore them to impress Rage. Rage threw his shoulders back and held his head high, if this Garatin thought he could outwit him - then he would be surprised.

"Ah, here he is!" Fav said as if he and Rage were old friends.

Rage nodded, "My lord," he said softly, a head nod would have to do. He couldn't bring himself to bow.

Fav turned to Loyal and Mise. "My ladies, I trust you will make yourselves comfortable." Favour then stepped aside and smiled at Rage, motioning him to come into the room he had just stepped out of.

As they stepped into the room, Rage looked about it; in the middle of the room there was a large table with candelabras and carefully carved boxes sitting on it. To one side there were two cushioned stools on a soft rug. On a low table between them there was a platter of fruit and cheese. A large window on one wall had been opened and the light filled the whole room. Favour walked across the room with an air of confidence. Reaching the large table, he took from it a silver goblet. Turning he looked at Courage. Rage knew this game, and knew it well; Fav was trying to intimidate him by flaunting wealth and power - but Fav wasn't the only one who knew that game, Rage knew how to play both sides, and he knew how to win too. Instead of standing there like a humble peasant, Rage moved easily across the room and past Fav to look out of the window, leaving his back to Fav.

"Perhaps you know why I asked to see you," Favour said sounding rather indifferent to it all.

Rage answered with just the same amount of disinterest, "I would not presume to know your mind, my lord."

There was a moment of silence, Rage smiled to himself - he had already thrown Fav off balance.

"I have been pleased with the business you have brought to my village," Fav said suddenly.

Wiping his smile away, Rage turned to him with a raised eyebrow in question, "My lord?" Rage found he enjoyed toying with him.

Fav seemed nonplussed. He opened his mouth, but for a moment nothing came. "The spice you sell - it brings an air of uniqueness and respectability. It has proven to be of great gain," he said as if awkward about pointing out the obvious.

Rage couldn't hide a smile; it was time to tighten the noose. "Come my lord, enough of this dancing. You have something you wish to ask of me? Then ask it."

Suddenly Fav found that he had lost control. "I beg your pardon good sir, for I do wish to ask of you something," he said in an effort to regain control. "I wish to offer you a trade route."

"What are the terms?" Rage asked, stepping forward; he had Favour right where he needed him.

"I will provide you with means of travel to go between here and where you find the Anise spice… where ever that is." Fav paused awkwardly hoping for an answer.

Rage smiled smugly, "Yes, where ever that is."

Fav laughed weakly and continued, "As well as a few workers. The trade route will go from here to all the villages within a week's travel south and west of here. You will of course continue to sell here as well. You will travel under my namesake and protection, for all of this I will ask for fifty percent of your profits."

Rage stood still and watched Fav for so long that Fav became nervous. "If I accept this offer," Rage said as he stepped even closer and took up a second goblet from the table, drinking some of the wine before going on. "I will need your assurance that I and mine will be well looked after." He turned his back to Fav again as he began to wander the room. "Assurances that if I am harassed or arrested by another lord that you will intervene on my behalf - and let me make it clear that if I feel manipulated by you, I will leave, for surely there are many others who would be glad to have a spice trader." He finished and turned back to Fav as he took another drink.

Favour swallowed hard, his mind worked double time; who was this Tarven? If he was just a tradesman, then Fav would not allow him to bully him in this way - but what if he was a spy from Garason? Fav couldn't afford to take the risk of being wrong! He placed his goblet down, "I assure you, you will be protected while working this trade route." Fav was beginning to sound desperate. "I will go a step further to say there will be no reason for you to leave and sell elsewhere," he smiled.

Rage smiled as well - but he wasn't done yet. "Also, you do not offer me enough to justify fifty percent of my profits. However, offer me and my family lodgings in the manor and I will give you sixty."

Fav paused and looked as though trapped.

"No? Then I will have to turn you down-."

Fav interrupted quickly, "There is no need of that! You, your wife and daughter will live here in the manor, I shall have chambers prepared at once!"

Fav's blue, shifty eyes had a pleading in them that Rage found amusing. He smiled, "My lord Favour, I gladly accept your offer under the terms we have just agreed upon." Yes, things were just as Rage wished them to be, for at last, after five years he was moving up in the world. Turning away from Favour, Rage missed the small self-satisfied smile play on Fav's face.

Chapter 7   For Mercy

"These are good men Rizon! Good serfs - good workers!" The Earl of Fornor protested as a prison wagon was rumbled to a stop near by.

"These men are nothing more than rebel scum!" the Garatin with the pale eyes turned to look at the Earl.

"Fornor is a small town and I am a poor Earl - how am I to keep my land worked if you take five of my workers!?" the Earl argued reasonably. The pale eyed Garatin stared him down.

"These men have been proven to be Eternity rebels. I am arresting them under ambassador Sinister's orders - are you disputing his orders?" he asked. Behind them, the five Cokhawken prisoners were being lead in a line into the prison wagon. The Earl of Fornor clamped his mouth shut for a moment, then shook his head.

"No, I am not questioning his orders Horizon. But surely you could leave them here so that I can punish them - then I will send them back to work," he offered with a pleading tone. Horizon almost smiled.

"These men are rebels; by Garatin law their punishment is death."

*   *   *

Favour grimaced in pain as his finger nail peeled off too close to his skin, he had been chewing at it for quite some time now. As he looked down at his hand he realized it was his last nail that was long enough to chew; all the others he had already chewed away. Throwing down his hands in frustration he gave an impatient sigh. He was sitting in the same room where only a week before he had talked with the Tarven spice trader. Only now he sat at one of the couches in the company of three of his advisers. These men were the barons, the land owners of Hawthorn and the close by lands, the men that Fav turned to when he needed counsel and advice on things happening in his village. These men made up over half of the Garatin Council in Hawthorn, the other man who was on the Council was Trust (he was not a land owner). They all had worked alongside of Imagine's father, Obedience, for over a year, before he had died.

But on this day their thoughts were far from Dien the man who had followed Nity, instead they thought only of this new trader in Hawthorn; the Tarven.

"You worry yourself needlessly, my lord - he is a common trader, and a Tarven so by nature he will act entitled!" the first of the barons said to Fav reassuringly.

But Fav wasn't reassured. "Have you found out anything about him or not?" he asked in exasperation. The three men looked at each other, each waiting for the other to speak.

"Well!?" Fav demanded.

At last the second baron spoke, "No one we spoke to knew anything about him, my lord - even the other traders know very little about him; only that he had come from the east."

Favour ground his teeth in frustration.

The third baron, who was braver then the other two spoke up. "Could my lord be mistaken in thinking you have seen him before?"

The question irritated Fav. For the past week Favour had been bothered with the idea that this Tarven, Courage, was familiar to him, as if he had known him a long time ago. But he couldn't remember ever having known a Tarven trader before! And there was something else too; Rage didn't act like a tradesman, he seemed too high mannered and even too noble to just be a common Tarven. The way he had settled right into life in the manor suggested familiarity with the lifestyle itself. And his wife, Loyal, was so graceful she put the other court women to shame! Fav doubted very much that Rage was who he said he was, and if he wasn't a tradesman, then the only reason Rage would lie, was if he was a spy from Garason! And if the Tarvens were sending men to spy on him then Favour's position as lord was at stake!

But there were too many 'if's' to be certain enough to take action.

"None of you are of help to me - get out!" Fav dismissed them irritably. As they left, Fav raised his finger to his mouth, and tried to chew what wasn't there.

*   *   *

Promise smoothed down the skirt of blue and green trim, and spun about slowly so she could enjoy the full effect. The dress was the finest that she had worn in a long time; the waist dipped down low and the front of the skirt was cut away to reveal the under skirt of ivy green. The blue sleeves stopped at the elbow where a second sleeve of green continued down to her wrist. To her, she looked like a fair maiden - and what was more, felt like one too. She could hardly believe this was happening! A week ago she had been brushing dirt from her old skirt from where she had been kneeling outside, and now? Now her father had a trade route with Lord Favour, and for the past week they had lived in a lower part of the manor. Her parent's chambers consisted of three rooms, while Promise's one room chamber was across the hall. They were simple chambers but still they were in the manor. Now at last, Mise had a chance to become the maiden she was meant to be! After all, she looked like a fair Tarven maiden - surely everything else would follow.

"Only wear that dress on special occasions, and be careful not to dirty it," Loyal said.

"Yes, of course - it's beautiful!" Mise said spinning about again.

Loyal had also tried on a new dress that day, but it was a bitter sweet feeling; they had come so far, and yet were still so far from their former lives. 'But if we have come this far we will yet go further' Loyal thought with comfort. 'This is the first step to better lives, now there is a better chance at finding a good husband for Promise, and her future will be secure'.

"It's like a dream! Everything is just perfect," Mise said happily, Loy frowned.

"Yes, but it all can be taken from us again."

Mise stopped in surprise.

"Mise, you do understand don't you, that you must never speak of our past life - not to anyone. So too, you must never speak of your illness."

"You mean my death."

"I fear no one would understand."

Mise nodded, and they were silent.

"But you do look lovely!" Loy said pushing the seriousness of the moment away.

They were not the only ones enjoying this new life; that same day, Courage caught his reflection in a window pane as he passed by, he was pleased with the way he looked. The wild tradesman had been replaced with a sharp Tarven. This new trade route meant their lives were changing for the better, and it would not end here. He had only returned to the manor last night from his first trade route to a nearby village, and he had even sold a few things. He held his chin a bit higher as he turned a corner.

"My lord Favour!" Rage bowed his head.

"Ah - my tradesman Courage."

Rage winced inwardly at the idea that Fav thought he 'owned' him. This was the first time he had spoken with Fav since he had offered him the trade route, and Rage was put on his guard at once. Fav sounded too confident, as if he knew something. Had he remembered who Rage was, or was he bluffing?

"I trust your travels went well?" Fav asked.

Rage forced a smile, "Of course my lord."

"Very good then," Fav said with an insufferable tilt to his pudgy head.

Rage stood to one side as Fav moved to walk past him, and by an act of mere reflex Rage's right fist raised to his heart in a Tarven salute. He stopped himself just in time, but Fav saw the movement out of the corner of his eye and was just turning his head to look at Rage when a commotion broke out down the hall. It saved Rage from explaining why he almost gave a military salute.

They both looked up to see one of Favour's soldiers running towards them in a breathless manner. When he reached Fav he said with an alarming voice, "My lord! Your stallion - it's been stolen from the common!"

*   *   *

"YOU'RE AN IDIOT!" Mag yelled as he grabbed the front of Vanished's tunic. Van, although he was eighteen, was still no match for his twenty-year old brother. Mag shoved his brother backwards through their cottage front door and out into their dusty front yard. Van tripped and went down hard, and Mag stood in the now open door way with chest heaving and eyes burning. Van sprang to his feet and lunged at his older brother, the two of them tumbled about in the yard kicking up clouds of dust for a moment before Mag threw Van back. Thrown off balance for a moment, Van recovered quickly and rushed back at Mag like an enraged dragon.

Just then Ember appeared at the door of the cottage and rushed to them, when Mag pushed his brother back again, Ember was able to get between her older brothers. She threw her arms up as wedge between them.

"STOP IT BOTH OF YOU!" she snapped at them harshly.

Breathing hard the brothers glared at one another over their sister's head, a good deal shorter than both of them, Ember looked up at them with the face of a disappointed mother.

"You're both acting like children!" she turned and shoved Van on his chest with all her strength but he hardly moved. Turning her anger on her eldest brother she screamed.

"Nothing is to be gained by SHOUTING MAG!"

"What is going on!?"

All three of them turned to see their mother. Perilous and her youngest had been behind the cottage in the garden, when they had heard the shouting and both had come running. Dismay washed over Peri's face at what she saw.

"Imagine! Tell me at once what this is about," she demanded.

"This idiot son of yours is now a horse thief!" Mag said in disgust as his blood cooled a little. Peri turned fearful eyes on Van.

"Van what have you done?"

"Nothing those stuck up noblemen don't deserve!" Van said without missing a beat.

"Vanished you tell me right now what you've done!" Peri said.

"He's stolen Lord Favour's stallion - and endangered us all!" Mag spoke before his brother had a chance. Gritting his teeth, Van shoved past Ember and reached for Mag.

"NO!" both Ember and Peri said in unison. Ember grabbed wildly and caught hold of Mag and did her best to hold him back, while Peri darted forward and grabbed hold of her other son. With his mother so near, Van calmed down. After a moment of silence Peri looked about; to her relief no one was about to witness what Mag had just said.

"Mag, I suggest that you go for a walk. Van I want you to muck out the stables." Casting an eye about the street, she lowered her voice. "When you both get a hold of yourself we'll talk about this." For a moment the brothers hesitated.

"I said GO!" Peri said firmly.

Shaking loose of his sister, Mag turned and marched away into the street. Ember hurried to follow him. Remember followed her brother as he stormed his way out of Hawthorn. Just beyond the village walls was a little stream, over it was a little stone bridge. Here, Mag stopped and with arms crossed he leaned against the bridge and stared out at the fields.

Slowing her pace, Ember came to stand across from him. Mag avoided her gaze. Ember then lifted herself to sit on the short stone wall. For the longest time neither of them said a word. Around them the wind blew and bent the tall grass that grew close to the stream, and Ember's hair looked almost gold as the sun glinted down on them. From a tree nearby a bird sang out, but brother and sister didn't move.

"It's no use," Ember's voice was soft and was almost lost in the breeze.

But Mag heard her, he shifted his gaze to look at her. He took in a breath before asking evenly, "What?"

"I know you're more afraid for Van than you are angry with him." Her simple statement broke him like a twig. He sighed and looked down, the tension in his shoulders loosened.

"I am afraid," he lifted his blue eyes to look into hers. "Horse thieves are hung when caught." The truth spoken so bluntly made them both fall silent. Mag turned into the breeze and let it cool his face; it seemed to him that it also cooled his heart.

Ember watched him and felt a great weariness settle over her; the way Mag felt was more like what a father would feel for his son - instead of brother for brother. The day Mag had come home with an empty saddle it seemed he had left his childhood behind and had instead taken up the responsibilities of a father, protector and provider; it wasn't fair of Eloi. 'The villagers may still view him as a boy', Ember thought sadly, 'but he grew up long ago.'

Ember looked at her brother and thought about how he had changed; he was still slim, but his shoulders had begun to fill out. His blond hair was not quite long enough to touch his shoulders, and he always swept it away from his face, and his hands were rough and capable. But the real change was in his face- so much older, so much worry and grief around his eyes. Mag lifted himself up onto the wall to sit opposite of her.

"I don't know if we can get out of this one. Someone will find out sooner or later that it was Van - no matter how careful he was. And Lord Favour I am sure will be less than merciful when he finds out."

Ember swallowed hard and lifted her chin, "Did he really take Lord Favour's horse?" she asked.

He nodded and was silent for a moment. "Sometimes I wonder if it will always be this way for us - for all of us who follow Nity; one trial after another. Barely just surviving -" he shook his head. "How can Eloi do this to those who are just trying to do his will?" he finished in a whisper.

Ember looked at him in surprise; she had never seen him so hopeless.

"Father would have said that Eloi has not abandoned us. He would have said that Nity started something and that it is not finished yet." Her voice was shaky and frail, for she too was uncertain - but she went on. "And he would have said that maybe one day - when all this is finished, that we may just see why all this was necessary," she finished with tears in her eyes, she wanted so much to believe what she had just said.

"Yeah. Father would have said that," Mag said sadly.

Ember forced a smile, "Besides, Van stole the horse, not Eloi." Mag snorted a soft laugh, but that was all he could manage.

It took a moment more before Ember found the courage she needed to say what was on her heart, "I know you Mag - not like the villagers know you. Not like our sister and brothers do, or even mother. I know you like father did." Mag watched her and felt a calm take him as she spoke. "He always knew you were special - he loved us all the same, but he knew as I do; you are different from the rest of us. Eloi chose you Mag! You are going to do great things one day - you may not know or believe that, but I do! You have always been able to imagine a future that mere peasants have never even dreamed of before, you were born with the gift of hope... you've just lost sight of that for a time. Perhaps Eloi has made you go through all this to make you stronger, so that one day you can do great things - for all of us."

He sighed, then smiled, "You're much too young to be so old my little sister," he said it softly, hoping that she couldn't see the truth, the truth that he had forgotten how to even hope for better. Her words came close to scaring him; what if Eloi meant for him to give everything he had for this... new world, whatever that was.

Ember looked at him solemnly, "I was thinking the same about you, my big brother."

Mag's smile deepened, "What would I do without you?"

With a sly grin she replied, "Take a wife."

He shook his head, "No one could replace you, my little Ember."

*   *   *

The smell of horses, cow, hay, and dust was so thick that it could almost be seen in the air, but to Perilous it was a comforting smell, one she was well accustomed to. She paused for a moment just inside the stable door and let her eyes readjust to the dim light. She could see their poor old mule Stubborn and their brown musk cow Rose, at the other end of the stable; they stood as if they couldn't get close enough to the wall, and their large eyes were filled with mute terror. Standing in front of the little stall with half walls, with his arms out stretched was Vanished. He was trying to calm a beautiful dappled gray stallion. Van had tied ropes to the horse's bridle and secured them to the sides of the stall in an attempt to contain the horse. But it was as if the stallion knew he was a prince among peasants! The horse snorted and stomped with fury, his eyes were red and he was ill tempered as ever a horse could be! Peri wondered how Van had gotten the ill-tempered horse through the village without drawing attention to himself.

But as Peri watched, Van was somehow able to calm the horse. "So" she spoke, catching her son's attention, "This is Lord Favour's stallion."

Van looked at her, and from that look Peri wondered if she should have let him stew for longer than twenty minutes! But she couldn't wait another minute, every moment more they were at greater risk. As she returned her son's gaze she couldn't help but feel disappointment at him for sulking like this. She would expect that of her youngest son - but not of her eighteen year-old! It amazed her how grown up Mag was compared to Van.

"Well Van, why this horse?" she started slowly, trying hard to control her frustration. "Surely there must be a more important, more expensive horses in Hawthorn."

Van swallowed hard, "I wanted to teach Lord Favour a lesson - make him see how much the village hates him! Besides, we could really use a horse..." His voice trailed off as though realizing how childish he sounded.

Peri closed her eyes - she could hardly believe what Van had done.

"Van could you not have used your head?" her words stung Van and he was taken aback. But what he had done was foolish - and Peri needed to make sure he knew it. "Don't you think they'll be looking for him - even as we speak!?"

"Mother's right," Mag said before Van could respond. Mag stood at the open stable door with Ember beside him. Van scowled at his brother.

"You've put us all in danger." Mag came further into the stable and Ember let the door close, then went to stand close to her mother.

Peri looked at her older son, "Do you think we can fix it before they find him missing?"

"Maybe, if we're quick -"

He was cut off in midsentence when the door was burst open and into the stable came Survive and their little sister.

"There are soldiers coming!" Survive shouted with fear in his eyes.

Their frantic announcement didn't even take a moment to sink in. At once they all bolted for the door. Behind them the stallion screamed. Mag was the first out into the yard, the others poured out behind him. What he saw made him dig in his heels and throw his arms back to stop his family, to keep them behind him; safe.

At once they were surrounded by mounted soldiers, their horses pranced around them dangerously close as they snorted and screamed. The soldiers looked down at them with cold eyes and gripped their spears tight. Peri pulled her two daughters close while Survive stood by her side with frightened eyes. Van stood on her other side with defiance shining in his face. Mag jumped back out of the way of a soldier's horse that came too close, panic seized him. 'The horse!' his mind screamed. 'Release the horse- get rid of it!' But it was too late for that.

*   *   *

Favour had been livid at the realization of what had happened. His life was going wrong as it was- and now some peasant had stolen his horse! It aggravated him to no end that Courage, a Tarven, was there to witness this embarrassment and insult towards him. He felt out of control. He wanted Rage to know who was in control of Hawthorn, and that he wouldn't let a peasant steal from him - nor would he let a Tarven demand anything from him!

Fav had paced back and forth in the hall, shouting orders at his soldiers and nearly frothing at the mouth! When Rage had tried to leave, Fav turned his attention to him.

"Can you believe this - this audacity!? I swear, before the sun sets there will be a peasant in my dungeon - or blood on the streets!" It pleased him to see that Rage stayed put after that.

Rage felt as though an eternity passed before a soldier came with the news that the stallion had been seen entering a certain stable. Before marching out to the stables Fav insisted that Rage ride with him. Rage consented reluctantly, he felt like he was balancing a sword on his finger tip.

If he displeased Fav now the sword would fall and cut his hand off, and he would lose everything that he had gained. But as Fav marched down the hall Rage felt stuck to the floor. In his mind's eye he saw a Garatin peasant face down in the street in a pool of blood. The moment passed, and Rage swallowed hard, 'Don't get involved' he told himself as he followed Favour to the stables. 'Don't risk everything now.' He set his face and saddled his horse quickly.

Favour thundered out into the streets of Hawthorn with Rage by his side, and with them, ten mounted soldiers with spears. The people of Hawthorn were caught by surprise by this flurry of activity in the noon day, and they darted out of the way of the thundering hooves. As they rode, Rage mastered a face of stone- whatever happened he would not let it affect him. But as they rode further down into the village, his mouth became dry, and his brave heart quivered; how could he stand by and watch Favour slaughter people?

One of the soldiers led the way until they turned a corner, the guard pointed and there before them was a small fenced in cottage and yard. Rage's heart whispered that something was terribly wrong, yet still he did nothing. The soldiers went on ahead as Fav and Rage hung back. The soldiers poured into the hard packed dirt yard. As they did, three young men, a woman and two girls rushed out of the stable into the yard. The soldiers surged around the Garatin family, circling them threateningly. Rage gripped his reins as he watched - but still no words came to his dry mouth.

"Search the stable!" Fav thundered his order above the noise.

"Wait please!" the woman called out before the soldiers could follow his order. Rage looked at her, his unease growing by the second. The woman had grabbed her daughters and was holding them close to her sides in fear.

"Where is your husband woman?" Fav demanded, he seemed disgusted to have to speak to a mere woman. But before she could reply the oldest young man spoke for her.

"My father is dead."

Rage watched him closely - what he saw was anger and pain in the smoldering blue eyes of the young man.

"I am the man of this family."

Fav sneered at that. One of the soldiers directed his horse until he was beside Fav, he pointed to the boy who looked to be the second oldest.

"That was the boy seen with your horse, my lord."

Fav lost interest in the oldest boy and directed his full anger at the boy his soldier had pointed to.

"My stallion was stolen from the grazing fields this morning - NOW SEARCH THE STABLE!" he screamed at his soldiers. Two of the soldiers slipped off their mounts, flung the doors open and entered the stable. For a moment Rage dared to hope that the stallion wasn't there, and that Fav would leave the family in peace.

But it was not long before one soldier returned and reported. "The stallion is here, my lord, and unharmed."

"I took the horse - not my brother!" the oldest boy called out, almost desperately it seemed to Rage. Rage waited for Favour's response to this. Fav was still for an uneasy moment, then he spat as if he had a bad taste in his mouth.

"Take these Garatins to the dungeons to await punishment! Their lives are forfeit to me, their lands and all their possessions I now claim. Take them!"

"No please!" the woman cried out fearfully.

Rage flinched.

All of the soldiers dismounted and took hold of the Garatin family. The woman screamed as her daughters were taken hold of, and she too was seized. The youngest boy was taken without trouble, but the older two fought back, the younger of the two was over powered quickly. The oldest one pushed back the soldier who tried to seize him, the soldier raised his spear high and swung it about. The shaft struck the young man on the back of the head, he fell to his knees, stunned, then collapsed face first in the dust.

"For mercy's sake Favour - LEAVE THEM BE!" a voice boomed out; all activity ceased and all looked to Courage. He sat rigid and tense upon his horse, leaning forward, the veins in his neck bulged and his eyes were ablaze.

"The horse is unharmed Favour. It was an act of foolishness that will never be repeated. So for mercy's sake - leave them be!"

The anger faded from Fav's face as the colour returned. For a moment Rage wasn't sure what he would do, did he have Fav wrapped around his finger? Or did Favour have the backbone to defy him, a Tarven?

Fav's eye twitched as he stared at Courage, "As you wish," he said tightly. "Bring my stallion and whatever other horses or mules are there.

Leave the peasants." His lip curled in a half snarl then he turned his horse and trotted away.

After a moment's hesitation, the soldiers did as they were ordered. Rage remained where he was, and watched the soldiers as half of them went into the stable and came out with an ill-tempered stallion, the family's sad looking draft horse, and a pathetic mule. As they all rode away, the captain led his mount unnecessarily close to the family, gave Rage a defiant look, then left. The woman and the two girls knelt beside the young man as he pushed himself up. As he did, he raised his eyes to Rage, and for a moment Tarven and Garatin looked one another in the eye.

Chapter 8   Wrinkles

Loy took in a sharp breath as she pricked her finger, but it didn't draw blood. She closed her eyes and breathed slowly - there was no need to be worried. She went back to her embroidery with a calm that she did not feel inside. She concentrated on one even stitch after another, pausing only to pull the thread through. After a few quiet moments Loyal looked up at the hour glass sitting on the table beside her. She had tipped it over three times now, and as she watched, the last bit of sand fell from the top chamber.

Where was Rage? The question presented itself again in Loy's mind, she had been waiting for three hours now! Where was he? She leaned over and turned the glass over again, the sand began to fall. Loy frowned; what had happened to Rage? She sat back again, but instead of returning to her embroidery, she stared at the closed chamber door. Earlier that day she had heard the servants talking about how lord Favour's stallion had been stolen, but that the thief had been found. Loy had been shocked to hear that the servants said that Favour had not punished the thief - because 'that Tarven' had asked him not to.

It was now late into the afternoon, and she had not seen Rage since early that morning. Loy tried to tell herself that there was nothing to what the servants had been talking about - yet if that were so; where was her husband?

Just than the chamber door opened; Rage entered. Loy watched him until he looked at her. "Where have you been?" she asked softly, yet there was a note of irritation in her voice.

Rage went past her and removed his outer vest. "I had some business to attend to," he said without looking at her.

She turned in her chair to look at him with a questioning frown. He raised his dark eyes to her. She knew at once that he did not intend to tell her the truth.

"I heard it said that you counselled the lord not to punish a horse thief," she said evenly. "I intervened on behalf of one foolish boy to save his whole family," he said tightly. "I do not wish to speak any more of it."

She knew by his tone that it was not to be brought up - ever again.

She lowered her eyes.

They were not the only ones with wrinkled brows that night. Later that night there were others who twisted their thoughts over what had happened that day.

Favour's face was a mass of deep wrinkles, and his shrewd and shifty eyes were dark with thought. He stood in his private chamber with arms crossed. The one baron that he trusted the most was there also. Fav had called him to counsel him on a matter of great importance. The baron (who liked being in close counsel with the lord) had come at once, even though it was late in the evening.

"I do not understand why you let him control you the way he did today my lord." the baron spoke after hearing the story.

"I could not defy him so openly- what if he is a spy from Garason!? I dare not cross him!"

"I still say that you suffer this thorn needlessly, he is nothing more than an overbearing tradesman."

"I wish I could believe that - but I know he is not who he says he is!" Favour insisted. "It has been growing ever on my mind for the past several weeks, that I have known him before this."

The baron nodded. "It seems all that can be done is to wait till you hear back from Garason about who he might be."

Fav heaved a sigh, "I did not ask you to counsel me on the obvious!" he said in frustration, then he waved his hand. "Leave me."

The baron bowed then left the chamber. Favour chewed on his lip as he stared into his fire and pondered his next move.

*   *   *

The carriage jumped on the road and threw Thrive to one side, almost making him draw a black line across his letter with his feather pen. Raising his head, he sighed and wondered if he should finish his letter later. But he needed to clear his head, and writing he had found was the best way to do that. He went back to the letter.

'I am happy to say however, that two weeks ago we finally landed in Larsanne. I shudder even now thinking of the place, I doubt lord Contrast would do a good job of lording over anything. I left Larsanne a little over a week ago, and in that time have traveled north along the eastern shore of the Nennor Sea. I've passed through a number of tiny fishing villages and past many farms, but not one inn to be seen among them! I've never slept on the ground so many nights in a row before, I do believe I'm starting to feel my fifty-one years.'

Stopping with that, Thri read over his letter from the start. Although he had trimmed his beard back to a point, he looked rather travel weary; his clothes were rumpled and wrinkled, while his dark eyes had to try hard to hold on to their mischief. Again he was jostled to one side when the carriage hit another bump in the narrow road. With a groan Thri leaned forward to pull back the curtain and peered out the small window. All he could see was the dull countryside passing by, and even that was not clear, for the glass pane had a thick coat of travel dust on it. He tied back the curtain to allow the light into the dark carriage, he then reached across to the other bench and putting his letter and pen aside he grabbed a map that sat there. Carefully flattening out the deep creases, he angled it to the window and looked closely at it.

He glanced out the window again; as far as he could tell, they would be approaching the Cokhawk forest soon. From there they would turn east and travel through the great forest and on to the main city in Garatin. Thri slowly folded up the map, and gazed out the window, the carriage slowed and he saw a cottage pass by. He leaned forward and pounded on the wall of the carriage with the palm of his hand. "Where are we driver?" he called out.

"Just entering another village, my lord."

Pounding once more on the carriage wall Thri called out. "Stop here - I wish to unfold my legs," he said dryly.

"Whooa!" the driver called out, and the carriage came to a lurching stop.

Without waiting for his driver to open the door, Thrive stepped out and arched his back with a groan. Swinging his arms Thri walked around the carriage and took a look about him; about half a mile to the west he could see a sheltered cove of the Nennor, and sea birds flew about and screamed at one another. The village itself was a collection of cottages and shacks, the air smelled of fish. Inland he could glimpse fields of wheat. Breathing deep he turned back to the carriage - then he saw her. Crouched beside the road, on the same side he had gotten out on, was a little girl. Her dress was a nondescript color of gray, and her Garatin blond hair was dirty and matted, it hung over her face as though she couldn't be bothered to brush it aside. Her dirty and scuffed up knees poked out under her dress and she looked up at him with wide eyes as he approached. He expected to see curiosity in her gaze, but instead her blue eyes were filled with fear! It made him feel guilty for being so tall and menacing to a child's eyes. He was about to stoop down and speak with her, when a woman stepped out from around a cottage.

"Harmony? Come…" she began to call for the girl, but when she saw Thri she stopped, and her face looked stricken. Her eyes darted down to the child and back up again.

"Please don't harm her - she's just a child!" she whispered, it took Thri aback. He was about to explain that the girl hadn't done anything so of course he wouldn't harm her - but, the utter fear on both woman and child's face told him that such explanation would be lost on them. He stepped back and turned away from the child.

"Drive on," he said as he climbed back into the carriage. Settling back into his seat, he wondered sadly of the unjustness at the hands of the Tarvens that woman must have suffered to be so frightened of him. He picked up his letter and pen again.

*   *   *

The sky was filled with dark rain clouds, and it was just one of those wet dreary days where a fire and a warm blanket seemed so inviting. The dirt path that led into Hawthorn from the fields had turned slippery with mud, and water had gathered in pools and in the wagon ruts. A field mouse popped out of the tall grass onto the path and shook water droplets from his fur, he then rubbed his face with his little paws. With a sudden squeak he darted back into the grass. Further down the path came three figures, their muddy boots slipped and splashed in the puddles. They were tired from working all morning in the fields, and only now did they retreat from the rain. As they walked, the light rain began to fall a little more in earnest. Imagine pulled his thin cloak tighter around his shoulders, a water drop fell from his hair down into his eye, he blinked it away. Behind him he heard someone fall into the mud, looking over his shoulder he saw that Survive had slipped. Coming up behind him, Vanished pulled him to his feet and pushed him forward, anxious to get in out of the rain.

After a few hurried minutes the three of them reached the end of the muddy path and stepped out onto the main road into Hawthorn, from there they could go faster. Together they ran in through the main gate and along the streets, till they reached their fence. Van ran up to the fence and vaulted over to the other side, Survive, who was three years younger than Van, tried to do the same, and instead ended up slipping on the other side and falling yet again. Helping him up, Van laughed at him, then the two ran on to the house. Smiling to himself about it, Mag made his way to the fence gate, opened it and was about to close it behind him when his smile vanished; he had the sudden feeling that he was being watched by unfriendly eyes. Looking behind him quickly, he scanned the street; there was someone watching him! A street down from him, standing under an overhanging roof and half hidden by a wall, was someone watching him. And it was not the man who lived there! He was too far away to know for certain, but Mag thought he was one of the manor guards. Mag looked away and walked across the yard. Suddenly the rain felt warmer than his blood did…

"I think lord Favour is having us watched," he said as he closed the cottage door behind him. His mother and sisters looked up at him with round eyes, while his brothers paused for a moment in their wet cloaks, then they scrambled over each other for the closed shutter to look out. Cracking it open, Van asked with a frown as everyone looked over his shoulder. "Where?"

"Behind that cottage- I only saw him for a moment, but I know he was watching us as we came in."

"Well no one is there now," Van said.

But no one dismissed Imagines's suspicion, and all that day no one went outside at all. At nightfall Mag looked out the front door; it had been too dark to see, but he felt certain that the man was still there. The rain stopped after sundown and gave way to a lonely wind that wrapped the village in a cold cloak. Stray dogs curled up in corners and barn cats buried themselves deep in the hay. Up in the loft all five of Perilous's children slept - all but Survive. Vive lay awake listening to the wind blowing around the corners of the cottage, wiggling deeper into the blanket he shared with his other brothers, he tried to get rid of the chill he had had all day. Beside him Mag moaned restlessly in his sleep. Vive turned his head to look at his big brother, just then Mag rolled over and elbowed him. Vive pushed back - he wasn't about to give up bed space! Suddenly Mag awoke with a start, he half sat up and gasped as if awaking from a nightmare.

"What is it Mag?" Survive asked in surprise - since when did Mag have nightmares? Vive could see his brother's silhouette and the moonlight from the cracked open shutter shed a glow on his face. He was trying hard to still his breathing, and was staring with wide eyes into the emptiness of the cottage rafters. "Mag?" Vive asked uncertainly.

"It's nothing Van," Mag whispered. Survive frowned; surely his brother could see him! Yet he had mistaken him for Van. Mag lay back down with his back to him.

"Nothing's wrong," Mag whispered - if only it were true Mag thought. But how could he tell his brother the truth? The truth that he could in fact not see... he had been dreaming of the day his father had died - then out of the blue his vision faded to darkness! Waking up was worse though. It was sort of like what had happened in Shore - but instead of blurriness it was just blackness, as if it was getting worse. Mag lay awake for the longest time staring hard at what he couldn't see, after what seemed forever, he could see the window again, and the sliver of moon light. He blinked several times, what was happening to him?

Early the next morning Mag stood by one of the windows, he frowned and closed the shutter.

"What is it?" Peri asked as she stood by the newly made fire. He looked over at her.

"He's still there," he said in a low voice. Ember looked up from where she had been doing some mending, Van came over to look out the window.

"Why is he watching us?" his little sister asked in a little voice from where she sat at the table.

"Because of what happened with the stallion," Mag said shortly. From the window Van grated his teeth, but said nothing. "And now he's just watching to see what other trouble we get into."

Peri bit her lip and turned back to the fire. Over her shoulder she said, "Well, we can't let them find anything," she said firmly.

"What do you mean, mother?" Vive asked.

She turned back to her children. "I mean, that until they stop watching us, no more mischief," she said as she gave Van a hard look. "No public declaration of hatred towards the Tarvens - or any government." This time the hard look was directed towards Mag. She looked at the other three.

"And we mustn't be seen talking with anyone from the meetings, and until this blows over - we shouldn't attend any meetings."

"Why go through all that trouble?" Van asked. "Everyone knows that we've been a part of the meetings for years! Why try to hide that now?"

Peri looked a little uncertain. "Well," she said slowly, "If Favour has any kind of ear in the village then he will have heard that the meetings ended weeks ago. We must assume that everyone believes that. We have to believe that the meetings are still secret. And we must do all we can to keep them that way. With the new law, if Favour found out he would take our lands and this very cottage from us as he did our horse and mule!" Everyone cast their eyes about the room as if the cottage might disappear any moment. "And he would demand to know who the others are in the movement. We were saved from his wrath before only because of that Tarven. That won't happen again."

They were all silent for a time.

Mag spoke aloud what they were all they thinking, "How will we let the others know that we are being watched?"

Peri looked over to Ember. "Someone will have to tell Memory... without anyone hearing." She was quiet for a moment. "Today is market - Ember you are the one who usually goes into market - but you do not have to-" she was interrupted as Ember came to her feet.

"No mother. I will do it, remember? We're all in this together."

Peri nodded. "When you go into Mory's bakehouse, tell her that we're being watched and won't be at the meetings, and warn her not to come around here," Peri said to her eldest daughter.

"But be careful of who might be listening," Mag said, wondering if they should let her do it alone.

Ember nodded, "Don't worry," she said as if reading everyone's thoughts. "Whoever is watching won't think it strange that a girl will be going to market - they probably won't even follow me. I've done this many times before - I'll be fine," she assured them.

With determination and calm, Ember swung a gray shawl about her slender shoulders, then took the basket that Peri handed to her so she could fetch their bread. Everyone watched as she walked to the door, she paused for a moment, then set her shoulders and left.

"Well you had all best go about the day as normal, we don't want them to see anything unusual about this place," Peri said brusquely. Everyone all looked at each other, Peri raised her eyebrows.

"Go! And don't be acting strange like. The stables need to be mucked out, the garden needs to be tended too. Mag, you and Van go work in the fields... Go!" she said when they all hesitated. At last they followed her orders.

Across their front yard Ember walked with head held high, 'I've nothing to worry about' she told herself, quickening her step she made her way down the street. In a heart pounding moment she heard footsteps behind her. Her feet faltered only for a moment, she continued on her way, afraid that she was going too fast, she tried slowing down. Her ears burned - but she knew she couldn't look behind her. As she reached a side street, a friend of hers walked out and joined her, Ember was at once relieved; at least she wasn't alone.

"Good morrow, Remember," her friend said cheerfully.

Ember managed a smile, "A good morrow to you as well Gentle." Ember risked a glance behind her back; but the street was empty. She sighed, she had only imagined it. As they walked along Ntle gabbed on about one thing or another, but Ember couldn't seem to listen. Soon they entered the market square, and Ntle went on to talk to someone else.

Ember swallowed hard, then set her shoulders and walked to Mory's bakehouse. Stepping into the cottage, she was met at once with a warm wall of air created by the big oven. There was someone talking to the old baker, so Ember waited patiently. Just then something caught her eye from outside the open shutter; it was one of Favour's soldiers. She recognized him at once because she had seen him before, she drew in a sharp breath and jerked her head away - she was being followed! The soldier stood outside the bakehouse casually, and he was dressed in peasant clothing.

Just then Mory finished talking to the other woman. "Good morrow Remember, is anyone sick in your family?" Mory always asked negative questions.

Ember smiled as she stepped closer to the table that Mory stood behind, on the table all the loaves of bread sat cooling off. Ember hesitated till the other woman had left and the door was shut behind her.

"No, no one is sick, Mory," she said stiffly.

Mory didn't notice, she grunted then picked up the loaf that was marked with a 'P O'. "Here you are," she said gruffly.

As Ember leaned closer to take the loaf and hand her the coins, she whispered, "My family is being watched by his lordship." She darted her eyes to the open shutter and back.

Mory grunted as if that sort of thing was typical. "Tell your mother I said hello."

Chapter 9   Just A Talk

Favour licked his thin lips and reached for another pheasant leg, placing it on his already crowded plate, he then grabbed a handful of field berries. Dropping them on his plate as well, he paused while he took a drink from his goblet. He was interrupted from his evening meal when his man servant entered his chamber.

"Yes? What is it?" he asked impatiently.

The servant bowed and said, "The captain of the guards wishes to report."

Fav nodded and waved for the servant to admit the captain. The guard waited till they were alone before beginning his report.

"My lord, I have done as you ordered and the peasant family have been watched all day." Fav forgot his meal and sat up straighter.

"And?" he asked with raised brows. "Have you seen any suspicious activity?"

The guard frowned, "No my lord, not a member of the family was left unwatched at all, yet we did not see any activity suggesting a rebellious nature."

Fav cursed, "Watch that cottage - do not take your eyes off of it day or night! I am certain the trouble in this village is centered on them!" he waved his hand in dismissal. The guard left with a bow. Favour sighed in a frustrated manner. He was just about to take a bite of pheasant when he was interrupted again, by his servant.

"Forgive me my lord!" he said excitedly.

Favour frowned, "What is it?"

"A message has come for you from Garason!" he held out a message cylinder.

Fav grabbed it at once, he tore it open, and was so entranced he didn't notice his servant leave. He scanned the message eagerly; this was his reply about who Courage might be! He couldn't believe his eyes… the man he had wrote knew nothing of this Tarven Courage! With a hissed curse Fav crumpled the message and threw it across the room; he was back to where he had begun. Who was Rage? And where did he remember him from?

*   *   *

Promise lifted her simple skirt as she went down the five steps that led into the hall that opened up into the manor gardens. She had been practicing how to look graceful while walking, but her mother made it look much easier than it really was! Looking up Mise noticed a group of young maidens coming up from the gardens. Mise had seen them around before, they were about her age, and were the daughters of knights and land owners who lived in the manor. Their dresses were beautiful, and their hair always done just so, to Promise's eyes they were perfect, even if they were Garatin.

Mise straightened her shoulders and raised her head a little higher as she neared them.

"Are you really going to marry him?" one of the younger ones asked a golden haired girl.

"Yes of course, you silly goose! Did you know that he's almost the richest land owner in all Hawthorn?" the other girls gasped and giggled to one another as they went on in this way, but they stopped when they saw Mise.

Mise knew she should give a little bow, but she couldn't make herself do it. For a moment they all stood there awkwardly staring at each other, then the girls smiled and passed by her. As soon as they were behind her they started talking again, and Mise turned her head to listen.

"What a strange girl - and rude too!"

"Is she from Tarva?"

"I rather feel sorry for her," the golden haired girl said. "Unless she's lucky and marries well, she'll always be just a tradesman's daughter."

Mise looked behind her and watched as they disappeared around a corner, but their words stayed with her.

*   *   *

It had been two weeks since Lord Favour's stallion had been stolen. In that time Rage had been careful to stay away from Fav, it was a little too much like hiding for Rage and it pricked his pride to do so. But he knew that he had crossed a line that day with Favour, and Fav could at any time throw Rage out - or worse. Since that day, Rage had been in a foul mood indeed, what an idiot he was! Here he was playing a game of power with someone - then he went out of his way to offend him! What had he been thinking? The Garatin family had nothing to do with him, if he had just kept his mouth shut then everything would be fine.

But then the Garatin family would be in Favour's dungeons, if not dead. He argued with himself, and so round and round it went, until Rage had driven himself half mad!

"It is in the past," he murmured to himself. Nothing was to be gained by stewing over it. He straightened out as he stepped out of his wagon, and placed a crate down on the cobblestone. He had been on half a dozen trade routes in the past six weeks since coming to Hawthorn, even so the villagers were still wary of buying from a Tarven here and in the other villages. But almost all of the lords and land owners in the area had bought from him, further proving that Favour had much to gain by having him as his trader. And so as long as that remained, Rage and his family would be looked after within the manor walls.

As Rage placed a small box of handmade jewellery on the crate he noticed a Garatin man approaching him, Rage became cautious.

"Forgive me good sir," the man said politely.

Courage took him in carefully; he seemed to be of Rage's own age, tall and thin, with wispy blond hair, he had a good-natured and agreeable face, everything about him made Rage want to trust him.

"Say on," Rage said. It was obvious that this man did not intend to buy from him.

The man smiled pleasantly, "My namesake is Journey, and I couldn't help but wonder if you are the man who saved Dien's family?" Rage hardly had time to respond before the man nervously said. "I'm sorry, I must be mistaken."

He turned away, but something about him made Rage speak. "Do you mean the family who stole his lordship's stallion?" Rage asked.

Journ turned back towards him with raised brows, "Then it was you."

"I do not know 'Dien' or his family, but yes it was I who intervened on their behalf."

The man smiled, "Then, from all of us, thank you."

"You are their kin?" Rage asked.

"No, but we all look out for one another. May I ask…" he hesitated before asking, "Why did you do it?" The question made Rage pause; why indeed?

"I saw an injustice, I simply stopped it," he said quietly.

"Spoken like a true follower of Nity." As soon as Journ said it he looked frightened as if he hadn't meant to say it.

Rage looked at him hard, his heart beating in his ears; what should he say? "Perhaps." He hoped that Journ would leave it at that, and Rage turned back to his cart.

But Journ spoke again, his voice lowered ever so slightly. "I like to think that I have always been a good judge of character, the others may curse me for this later," he added under his breath.

Rage looked at him and waited with apprehension.

"There is a group of us here in Hawthorn who follow Nity's teachings - I understand if you would rather I do not say any more, what with the recent arrests." Rage's face changed; he had heard rumor of a rebel purge, but the reality of it came as a shock. Subtlety was not Courage's strong point and his interest must have shown for Journ went on. "You are one of us - aren't you?" he asked with wonder.

Rage looked about suddenly - this was not something to be discussed in the open like this! Grabbing hold of the front of Journey's tunic, Rage pulled him up the two steps into his wagon. Closing the door behind them, Rage glanced out between half closed shutters, no one seemed to have noticed.

"If you know what's good for you, you wouldn't discuss such things out in the open like that!" he said turning back to Journ. Journey's eyes widened and he looked slightly frightened.

"I'm sorry! I didn't intend to put you in any danger!"

"You endanger yourself when you speak so openly!" Rage glanced out the shutters again. "You had better leave before anyone notices, if asked what you were doing say I didn't have what you were looking for." He pushed Journ towards the wagon door. Journ nodded, but before opening the door he said.

"Look, the others will be coming to my cottage tonight after sundown. You are welcome to join us - we could use someone inside the manor." He pointed through the shutters to a cottage on the other side of the market square. Impatiently Rage leaned forward and opened the door for him, Journ still seemed oblivious to potential danger. Before leaving, Journ smiled and nodded his head.

Inside the wagon, Rage shook his head as he watched Journ cross the square; Journ had a few things to learn about being secretive.

"This is the LAST thing I need!" Rage muttered to himself when Journ was out of sight. One thing was sure, he wasn't about to blunder into a futile rebellion - again!

*   *   *

"Careful, don't pull so hard; you'll snap the thread," Loyal cautioned Mise as she was sewing up a tear in one of her skirts. Loy and Mise looked up at Rage as he came through the chamber door. His face seemed troubled. Mise took note of how Loyal was watching her husband with a questioning frown.

"Did something happen at the market?" she asked with a note of concern.

Rage turned to face them with a dark face. "Promise, perhaps you should leave," he said in a low voice, it wasn't really a suggestion.

A defiant look came across her face, "Why?" she asked boldly. "After all, you're only talking, I think I should hear whatever it is you have to say."

Rage frowned. "You would do better to hold your tongue and obey your father!" he said sharply.

But Mise held her ground. Loy looked at her husband beseechingly. "Rage, please - must we really withhold secrets from one another?"

For a moment Rage only stood there, at last he spoke, in a low voice. "I was approached by a man in the market. He's a Nity follower, he asked me to join them," he said bluntly.

Mise sat back and her look of stubbornness gave way to shock, beside her Loy only sat and listened.

"I had hoped to stay well away from such entanglements."

"Courage please, don't get involved! We've only just begun our new life here - don't risk it all now."

"Since returning to the west we have yet to learn of what became of Nity, if these Garatin's are Nity followers then they could tell me."

"What if you are found out? Rage, I've heard the talk; Nity followers are being treated like Garatin rebels for there is little difference between the two!" Loy said with distress.

Rage didn't answer her, and he went into the next room and closed the door behind him. Loy and Mise sat in silence for a long moment. Suddenly Mise threw down her sewing and stood to face her mother.

"It isn't fair! Why must father risk it all now by tangling with rebels?" her eyes were stormy and her face alight with fire of her own.

Loy closed her eyes and said in a firm but quiet voice, "That's enough Promise. You've already crossed the line; I don't wish to hear any more from you."

Mise pressed her lips together then stormed out into the hall to her own chambers. Loy sat in silence with a sad expression.

In the next room Rage paced the floor with a dark frown upon his face. Power, respect - that's all he wanted! That's all he had come back to the west lands for, so why would he throw it to the wind now that it was within his grasp?! 'You're already in the fire - don't pour oil over yourself!' he thought in exasperation. He would find out what happened to Nity some other way. He stopped suddenly as a memory came to his troubled mind; a Garatin family, seemingly deprived of a father, surrounded by guards on horseback ready to beat them into the dust they lay in. How many more like them would receive cruelties and injustices only because they aligned themselves with Nity?

Sitting down on a large chest, Rage closed his eyes and pinched the bridge of his nose. What was he to do? All that day he agonized about it. Yet it was nearly sundown before he knew in his heart what he must do. With shoulders held back and a set face, Rage went to tell Loy. She sat before the fire reading a small book. She looked up at him and even before he spoke her eyes told him she understood.

"I may not be able to get back inside the manor gates after sundown. If asked, say nothing of where I am." For a moment he wondered if he had read Loy correctly. Then at last she reached out and took his hand.

"Be cautious," she whispered.

Chapter 10   Outlaws

The gate keeper took no notice of him as Rage passed through the gates into the village. Rage began to silently curse himself for what would certainly turn into a misadventure. He pulled his cloak closer about and went over his options for what he would do after this meeting; the list was short. He couldn't stay at the Inn and risk Favour hearing about it, and he doubted if the Innkeeper would even let him inside the place. Nor could he ask the gate keeper to let him in when he came back; that would arouse questions of where he had been. All he could do was find an alley or a stable to sleep in and hope that no one noticed him. The more he thought about it the angrier he got with himself. All this risk and for what?

As he walked down the main street towards the market square the light of the setting sun began to dim. Every shutter he passed was closed tight and there were only a few people about. They all looked at him, it made him wince; what kind of secret rebel meeting was this? He reasoned that the whole village must know that it was going on!

When he reached the market square, he paused and scanned the cottages and shops, lastly his eyes rested on the cottage that Journey had pointed out. Sitting beside his front door was Journey. 'I should leave,' Rage told himself, yet still he made his way through the square and approached Journ.

"So, you came after all," Journey said with a touch of surprise as he removed a pipe from his mouth. "Mory will owe me a free loaf of bread," he said, chuckling to himself. Standing to his feet he met Rage's gaze.

"Yes I came - with no small risk to myself either. I'll have no way to re-enter the manor seeing as how they'll shut the gate soon." Rage wondered how Journ would respond. Journ was quick to answer.

"Don't worry - I know the gate keeper, and I'm sure I could convince him to let you back in."

'Oh yes' Rage thought, 'Favour won't find that suspicious at all!' Rage made himself relaxed, he was too touchy! "I came only because I am a Nity follower - however do not misunderstand me; I make no promises that I will support you in any way - not yet." He wanted that to be clear between them.

Journey nodded in an agreeable fashion, then he grew nervous.

"You didn't tell anyone of this... did you?"

"I assure you, neither Lord Favour nor his men have been informed of this by me."

Journ seemed to accept this and became calm again, stepping to his door he gestured for Rage to follow, but Rage laid his hand on his shoulder.

"Before anymore is said, I must know; do you know what has become of Nity? For I have long wondered."

"We don't know for certain," Journ said softly. "He was last seen in the Quy Lake region over a year ago." Rage was silent as he took in this news.

"I'm... sorry, I wish I could tell you more, but the truth is we have all been wondering where he is."

After a moment Journ opened the door and stepped in. With a moment's hesitation, Rage followed him inside. Journ closed the door behind them.

Just then, Rage froze as the tip of a long dagger was pressed against his chest. The hand that held the dagger was pale and bony, Rage calmly looked to his right and met the eyes of the old woman who held it; it was Memory, the bakehouse keeper with whom he crossed paths with a couple of weeks ago. She peered up at Rage with mistrusting watery eyes.

Journey sighed in exasperation. "Mory put that away! You have no need of it-"

She cut him off sharply, "Garatins will always have need of weapons when Tarvens are about! And don't you think to scold me, Journ! I'll not be told what to do by a boy just out of the cradle!" she snapped in her crackled and rough voice. Journ who had gray hairs of his own, simply looked down at her the way one would tolerate a child. Mory didn't seem to take notice however. Journ reached out and lowered Mory's hand with the dagger.

"Courage, this is Mory," he said wearily.

"We've met," Rage said looking at Mory with hard eyes. If he had wanted to, he could have snapped the old woman's wrist with the same amount of effort it would take to pull on his boots.

Mory made a loud 'humph!' before making her way to the back of Journ's cottage. Both Rage and Journ followed her. As they went Journ leaned closer to Rage and whispered, "Sorry about that, she treats us all like that from time to time." The edge of Rage's mouth turned up, and he decided that Journ was really a decent man.

"I must warn you though, most of the others will agree with Mory as far as you are concerned." Rage only nodded, but to himself he wondered if he was mad for coming here at all.

Journ had been unmarried all his life, and his cottage was quite small; a threadbare quilt had been hung from the beams to separate the one room cottage in two, giving a bit of privacy. Pulling the quilt aside Journ and Rage stepped through to the other side. In one corner was a bed and beside it sat a crate cluttered with a wash basin and other things. From the beams overhead herbs and flowers were hung up to dry, and that was it, there wasn't even a rug. Rage could imagine his friend Wilderness surrounding himself in such simplicity. Between themselves and the bed sat a table with several mismatching chairs and boxes. Around the table sat five men and women. As Mory sat down one of the men stood up nervously, he looked at Rage with open curiosity.

"He - he really did come after all."

Rage studied him; he was small and had a soft and even shy voice that stuttered every time he spoke. He blinked nervously and often, but still he had a look about him that said he couldn't be anything but honest. Journ stepped closer to him.

"Yes, I'm thinking it's a good thing Mag couldn't be here tonight."

Rage noticed how everyone seemed to understand the comment and they all exchanged knowing glances.

"Everyone, this is Courage," Journ addressed the whole group. "Rage is the man who saved Perilous, Imagine and their whole family from Favour's dungeons. I invited him here, he is a Nity follower."

Everyone looked at Rage, some with mistrust and others with curiosity. Rage swallowed his pride and let them stare.

Journ clapped his hands together, and around his pipe he said, "Save's cow is calving tonight so he and his sons won't be coming, there's no one else to wait for so let's begin." He shoved a small barrel over beside the table with his foot and gestured for Rage to sit, it was the last thing Rage wanted to do, but he did it anyway. One of the men sat up straighter.

"We can't begin yet- where is Imagine and Vanished?" he asked with a frown.

Journ answered him, "He and his family are still being watched by his lordship's men. They won't risk leading Fav to us," he said carefully. Nevertheless, they all turned mistrusting eyes upon Rage. Rage sat there with straight back and shoulders, and he weathered their gaze with dignity. Trus and Journ were the only two who did not look at him with a condemning eye.

"I give you my word; I had no part in the family's surveillance." Just saying it made Rage feel foolish! Why was he here? He didn't have to explain himself to the likes of them, yet still he stayed.

There was a moment of strained silence.

"And you think we can trust him?" one of the men asked Journ.

He hesitated only a moment, "Yes, I do."

Trust backed him up with a vigorous nod. Again there was silence.

"Well, that's good enough for me then," the same man replied. One of the women nodded as well. The others didn't seem as sure, especially Mory, who watched Rage with narrowed eyes.

"Let's put that matter aside," Journ spoke. "We need to decide how we can protect ourselves should Horizon come here. We've talked about this before, but we were interrupted last time. Realize, you said you had an idea?"

The man nodded and stood up, Rage listened but found it all so painfully childish it was all he could do to keep silent. He stood up half way through and went to a window and looked out of the shutter.

"I was thinking about how every time a meeting is called we send little notes to tell everyone where and when, or we do it in person. I'm afraid that Rizon, or Fav could easily find us out because of it. So my idea is that we pick one place and time to hold the meetings- say… once every twelve days? Then no matter what, it will always be in that place at that time!" Everyone nodded and smiled.

"T-That could work," Trus said, and Journ nodded in agreement.

"Yes that would safe guard us, Lize."

"You're all fools to believe that that alone will save you from this Horizon when he comes." The silence was stony as all turned to look at Rage. "I do not know about this man Horizon, but if he comes here he will most certainly find you all out. You couldn't be more obvious if you hung a sign on the door. The idea you have just suggested would be seen through instantly!"

"Yeah? And how would you know?" Lize said narrowing his eyes.

Everyone waited for his answer - it could be unwise to admit his past, but Rage was not one to hide. "I was once a captain in the Tarven army." The look on everyone's faces was almost disbelief. "I gave up that life for the sake of Eternity many years ago. So believe me when I say you will be easily found out."

They all became very sober, fear does that to people. "What do *you* think we should do?" Journ asked quietly.

Rage looked at them all and they were all watching him as if wanting to believe that he could help them. What was he to do? The only reason he had come was to find out about Nity. Did he really want to throw all his carefully laid plans to the wind by getting involved? He had dug his grave once before, had he really returned only to bury himself? A thought came to him suddenly; if he had been willing to take the risk then - why not now? Nothing had changed!

"Cancel the meetings," he said bluntly.

No one expected him to say that, and even Journ looked a little hurt.

"Or... you can trust me and take my advice. There are ways to hide from Favour and Horizon and I can teach them to you."

"Like what?" one of the women asked.

"Despite what you may have told your neighbors and friends, everyone in the village knows about these meetings, and I'd even go as far as to say that if anyone in the market square looks out their windows, then they'll know there is a meeting here tonight. To safeguard your location you must change it - often! Have nothing in your homes that could link you to this. If a message must be shared with someone don't risk sending notes - instead have a code that you all know; one open shutter means the area is being watched or a broom on the left side of the door means no meeting tonight and so forth. Never speak about Nity or the meetings while in public. And always have an exit plan should one of your meetings be interrupted." Rage paused to catch his breath, and was pleased to see that everyone was listening. "Those are but a few of the things you could do to remain safe and undetected."

Journ was watching him with a measure of respect, then he turned to the others and said, "If it is a vote of whether or not we accept Courage and his plans; I vote for him," he said boldly.

Beside him Trus came to his feet and peered shyly up at Rage. The man and woman stood also, they were joined by the other woman. There was a moment where all eyes turned to Mory and Lize, the only two still sitting. Then to everyone's astonishment Mory stood to her feet! Journ opened his mouth in surprise.

"Mory…" he breathed. "I-" he was cut short by her sharp words.

"Did no one teach you not to speak unless spoken to boy!?"

Journ closed his mouth and smiled in spite of himself, with a sour expression Mory looked down at Realize, and growled at him. "Get up to your feet Lize! I'll not stand for this group being split in two!" with a sigh the man stood to his feet reluctantly, he looked at Rage wearily.

"I'll vote for you - but if you stab us in the back; I'll be the first to repay you."

"AND," Mory said making sure Rage was listening, "don't think you're the only one with ideas in your head! My bakehouse would be the perfect spot for these 'codes' of yours. Everyone comes to my bakehouse, so I could arrange the pots and pans in certain ways, or even hide messages in the loafs! There - see, I got a few tricks of my own!" she said smugly.

Rage didn't dare say anything in reply, it was a good thing it was a good idea. 'Well' Rage thought to himself 'now look at what you've gotten into!'

*   *   *

Loyal stood still and let the slight breeze cool her face. Raising her eyes, she found a star between the dark clouds, the twinkling light held no charm for her though, not on this night. She stood before an open window, there was hardly any view but she could see a patch of night sky. Although the hour was late, she was still fully dressed. The light wind had a warm hug to it, and Loy closed her eyes and it seemed to her that she was taken away - taken back to that distant day so long ago on the deck of a great ship. She was just a child really, just turned sixteen - but still so young. She had sniffled as a tear had escaped down her tanned face, it blurred her sight of the shore she was leaving. She wiped her eyes and looked back at the carriage that sat near the docks. Just then a white handkerchief waved from the carriage window; it was her mother! Almost frantic Loy had waved her arm in response, then the carriage turned and the team of horses pulled it away.

The memory came back to Loy so vivid she could almost feel the sweat trickling down her back again, just the way it had on that muggy day, the day she had sailed away from the city and country of Tarva - forever. Loy recalled what her mother had said to her in their final embrace.

"Be strong and hold your head high, remember what you've been taught; you are a true lady of Tarva. You've nothing to fear, your father says that Courage is a fine young man, he has promised you will be well looked after." Her mother had paused as if uncertain. "And remember your place as his wife Loyal, you must follow his lead, do what you have been taught, and he will be good to you. He will protect you and do what is best for you - I'm so very proud of you." Her mother's words faded away, and Loy tried to remember what had happened next. Strange, she thought to herself, for she did not remember saying farewell.

Suddenly her face turned bitter; and now? She wondered 'am I to follow his lead even now!?' She thought briefly of just forgetting it all in sleep - but how could she just sleep when Rage was out there risking his life and THEIR lives all for the sake of a bunch of rebels! She breathed slowly, but instead it turned into a shattered breath as a sob tried to make its way out. Just then the door of the chamber opened and closed behind her, Loy spun about with a catch of her breath.

Rage looked up at her in surprise, he looked tired and weary, but unhurt. Upon seeing her, he glanced about the room.

"Loyal! Is something wrong?" he exclaimed.

Bitter tears threatened to spill over, and she wanted to lash out at him with 'YES something is wrong! You're risking everything!' But she bit back the harsh words.

"No," she said with a tight voice that he mistook for quiet. "I simply could not sleep." There was a moment of silence between them. She waited, then to her anger he turned away without a word!

"Rage what happened!?" she asked hurriedly. He turned back to her.

"They are not Garatin rebels, but Nity followers. They said that Nity was last seen near the Quy Lake… over a year ago," he said in small wonder. "Have no fear Loyal, they do not seek to overthrow Favour and they are far from violent. The rumors are true - laws have been passed in Garatin that forbid the following of Nity. They risk imprisonment and even death if found out by either Tarven or Garatin governments." He said it all wearily, as if telling her was a great burden. He moved to stand beside her by the window, but he didn't look at her, instead he breathed deep the night air. Loy watched him with apprehension, at last he spoke. "I pledged my allegiance to them and their cause."

Loy breathed out the breath she had been holding, and she thought it might be her last. But Rage did not seem to be shocked, or dismayed or even reproachful for what he had done! What was he thinking!? Her mind demanded, but again she bit back the words.

"One of the men there knows the gate keeper and he let me back in… say nothing if asked about it, if it becomes necessary I will deal with Favour's questions," he ended as if to himself.

Loy pressed her lips together. "I see," she said tightly. "You are now a supporter of rebel activity… again."

Rage turned sharply to look at her, she was glad that her choice of words had an impact. 'Supporting rebel activity'- that's what he had been arrested for in Garason five years ago. She met his gaze evenly, well, now he knew what she thought about all this.

"Things will be different this time," he said with a sharp edge to his voice. "This time it will not interfere with our lives."

Loy wanted to lash out angry words at him, but again she held her tongue. Rage turned on his heel and went into the next room, closing the door behind him.

A tear slipped down her check. "I am to follow his lead," she whispered. "Follow his lead."

*   *   *

Journ shifted his clay pipe, the red embers glowed and cast a light on his long face; he sat at his table, across from him sat Trust and Mory. Everyone else had left, and it was now late into the night, still they sat and talked in low tones of what had happened earlier. The whole cottage lay in complete darkness, except for a low fire that Journ had kindled.

"I was surprised that he came," Trust said, his stutter had calmed considerable. Journ raised his eyebrows and nodded in agreement.

"I was surprised as well - it won me a free loaf." He looked at Mory to see her reaction, but her face was unreadable in the darkness.

"Do you think he will prove faithful?" Trus asked uncertainly.

Journ hesitated to answer him, Courage had promised them a lot of things that night. Would all his ideas really keep them safe? He had made it clear that he didn't want to risk being seen with them. Was he just a prideful and arrogant Tarven, who liked to promise things?

"I don't know Trus," he answered truthfully, Mory grunted.

"One thing is certain though; if he should betray us, he'll not live very long!"

Journ nodded wearily. "Yes, and speaking of that," he looked up at Trus with a worried gaze, "How will we tell Imagine of this?"

Mory cackled. "Ha! Now there is a boy who has a healthy hatred of Tarvens! Leave it to Mag and that Tarven will not live long even if he does prove faithful!" she sounded gleeful.

Journ frowned, "Now Mory," he said reproachfully. "The teachings of Nity speak against hatred, one would think you know better than to say there is such a thing as 'healthy hatred'."

If Mory was ashamed, she didn't show it. The three of them were quiet for a time.

"Perhaps it-it would be best if I told him," Trus ventured. "I think he would listen to me."

Journ nodded, "It might be that the trouble will come from Van instead, he is the more impulsive of the two." Trus nodded sadly.

Mory sniffled. "If we're not careful those boys may go and kill that Tarven - and then we would have a real problem on our hands! We can't let that happen, now I want you two to show some cunning in handling this situation." She looked at them both like they were children who needed directing. Both Trus and Journ acted humbly, as if they had not already been discussing it.

"Now, young Remember comes to my bakehouse, she's a gentler one then her brothers, I can talk with her, and even talk to Peri herself." Journ put up his hands to slow her down.

"Don't trouble yourself with going all the way to their cottage - remember that they are being watched. I can talk with Perilous myself when I go to trade garden goods the way we've always done, and Trus can tell the boys while out in the fields."

Trus nodded, Mory gave a curt nod.

"And I'll have a talk with Ember!"

Journ sighed; there was no stopping this woman when she got going! He wondered briefly if she had the chance whether or not she would encourage Mag to kill Courage. It was a good thing Rage seemed like he could hold his own.

Chapter 11   A Tarven

Mag sat still as stone, as he stared at… nothing. The wind blew across his face, but he didn't notice. He sat on an old rotting stump out in the middle of his field, it was some time after sunrise and clouds had rolled in, but for the longest time Mag had just been sitting there. Van and Vive were off on the other side of the field, but they had not noticed their older brother's lack of work.

Mag didn't even know how it all started, but he had been thinking of his father, and before he knew it he had sat down and lost himself in old memories. They were distant and vague, and Mag had a hard time remembering when they had really happened. There was the time his father had first taken him out to the field, or the time his father had showed him the right way to deal with a mule who has up and sat down. But those memories suddenly gave way as he was thrown back to that day in Garason.

"How did it go?" Mag asked eagerly bounding up the stone steps.

Obedience sighed and placed his arm around his son's shoulders as he slowly descended the steps.

"They won't listen." Mag's heart fell, he had never seen his father so defeated. "I sat there for three hours before I was allowed to speak, and even then they disregarded my words!" Obedience frowned. "I thought that if I could just be on the Garatin High Council that I would have a voice in what happens in this country, that I would be able to bring about the change that Nity spoke of - but I was wrong! If Nity couldn't make them see reason, then how could I? They will hear nothing to do with him or his teachings. I told them that we have gone astray in our beliefs and that Eloi sent Nity to tell us how to make it right - but they would hear none of it!" Dien heaved a heavy sigh, but then he stopped and looked at Mag straight in the eye.

"But we must never give up! Someday Mag, someone will listen - someday. And when that day comes, don't miss it, this country needs to hear of what Nity did - nay, the whole world needs to hear!" Mag smiled; his father was far from defeated, and the battle was not lost. Together the two of them had walked across the square and onto a side street where they came across a fruit seller.

"Here, go and buy us something," Dien said giving Mag a few coins.

Mag took them excitedly and ran to the merchant. Mag looked over the different fruits that he had never seen before, and finally picked two bright orange, small melons. Handing over the coins Mag took a melon in each hand then turned and was about to return to his father's side, but he noticed that two men had approached his father and were now talking. It looked as though they were discussing something important, so Mag waited where he was and watched; his father had his back to him, and all Mag could see were the faces of the two men. Something about them looked wrong...

Mag was pulled from his thoughts abruptly when someone called out his namesake, the street in Garason faded away and he was back in his field. He looked up, Trust was making his way towards him.

"Good morrow, Trus," Mag said as he neared him.

Trus nodded, something about him alerted Mag; it must be something about the meetings! His eyes darted over to where his brothers were working. He could just see their heads over the rows of grain. They hadn't noticed Trus - perhaps that was best. Other than them, he and Trus were alone.

"I-I need to talk w-with you," Trus stammered.

Mag's heart beat quickened, Trus was nervous; something was wrong.

"What is it? What's happened?" Mag stood up and tried to get eye contact.

Trus kept his head down and only peeked up at Mag. "N-nothing has gone wrong," Trus said quickly.

"Then what is it?"

Trus hesitated. "Someone new has joined our cause..." he looked at Mag shyly.

'Who could it be?' thought Mag.

"This man is going to- to help us. He was a soldier before and he will help us h-hide from Fav and- and Horizon."

Mag frowned, it must be one of Favour's former guards - no wonder Trust was acting worried.

"Who is it, Trust?" he asked.

Trus hesitated and Mag felt something go amiss. "Trus... who is it?" he asked slowly and firmly. Trus lowered his gaze.

"The Tarven tradesman."

He said it so quietly that Mag thought he heard wrong - the Tarven!? His look of disbelief and outrage spurred Trus on to speak.

"H-he has promised to help us, and-and he is a Nity follower!"

Mag felt anger burn within. "'Nothing is wrong'?! With a Tarven in our numbers?" he spat the word as if it were poison, Trus winced, but Mag went on. "Do you mean to tell me that a Tarven was at the meeting two nights ago!?" his voice was getting louder - but he couldn't stop himself.

Trust's soft voice did much to calm him. "He saved you and your whole family's lives, Mag. You owe him a life debt; the least you can do is accept him." Mag clenched his teeth. "Journey and I are convinced that he c-can be trusted. He even pledged his allegiance to us, he gave us his word."

Mag breathed deeply before replying, "Eloi knows, I hold you and Journ in the highest regard - but you're both wrong! His word? Of what worth is a Tarven's word!?"

Trus hesitated before answering him. "I do not know, but we-we must put our faith in Eloi about this matter."

"Eloi!?" Mag burst in outrage. "Trust - Tarva is Eloi's worst enemy! Just look at what the Tarvens are doing to not only us - but the whole world! How can you suggest that this is the will of Eloi?"

For a moment Trus seemed at a loss for words, and Mag felt like he had won, then Trus spoke. "Your father believed that what Nity did was not just for Garatins - but for the whole world; for Tarvens too."

Mag felt his will break within him, he sighed and hung his head. His father did believe that - were not his last words about how the whole world needed to hear?

"You will n-not have to face this Tarven for a time yet, p-please, think on all this before acting," Trus said, then turned and went back to his own field, leaving Mag standing there with a heavy heart.

He stood struggling with his emotions, and then a thought hit him, and he couldn't shake it either; he had to see this Tarven! Narrowing his eyes, he thought quickly. The Tarven was a trader, so he would be in the market - looking up Mag determined that it was only late morning; the market would still be open. He looked over to where his brothers were working, Van noticed him and stopped what he was doing.

"I'm going into the village - I'll be back soon," he called out and turned, but Van called out angrily, "What do you mean 'you're going into the village!? We've work to do!"

Mag spun about and gritted his teeth, Van could be so tiresome at times! Without replying Mag continued on his way, while Van continued to yell at him. Mag walked quickly through the fields until he came to the little stone bridge, and across that he entered the village. Instead of turning right to the cottage he followed the street up towards the manor and the market square. At last he stopped short as he came to the edge of the market, he took a moment to look about, then he caught his breath; it was Ember! She saw him at the same time.

"Imagine - why are you in the village?" she asked as she came up to him. A dirty white apron was about her tiny waist and a basket hung off her elbow, half full of vegetables.

Mag tore his eyes from looking about the square to focus on her.

"I... came to help you carry things home!" with that he grandly looped his arm about her shoulders and turned back into the market. For a moment Ember was taken off guard, but she recovered quickly.

"You're lying," she said point blank. "Why are you here? It's not to meet a young maiden - that's for sure!"

He smiled down at her sweetly. "How did you get to know me so well?"

She only glared up at him. Meanwhile he had steered her into and around the market, looking this way and that way, looking for what was surely THE only Tarven in the village. Then he saw him, and stopped walking at once. Beside him Ember suddenly understood his visit to the market perfectly.

"Mag," she said quietly. His arm fell from her shoulders. "Mory told me about him. Mag, you need to leave! You know Lord Favour is still having us watched, don't give his men something to report!"

Without taking his eyes from the Tarven he patted her shoulder. "It's alright Ember - I just wanted to see him." Casually he stepped up to a cart where a woman was selling quilts and rugs, the woman was busy elsewhere and from there Mag had a clear view of the Tarven. Ember stepped up beside him and grabbed his arm, as if trying to hold him back, but for the moment he was calm and full master of himself. With cool blue eyes he watched the Tarven who had joined the movement.

Courage stood still beside his colorful wagon, his clothes were simple enough and yet he held his shoulders back and his head high. He was arrogant and prideful just like every other Tarven. Anger burned in Mag at the thought that he owed this man a life debt.

Just then Courage turned and looked right into Mag's eyes. For a moment Mag held his gaze 'how dare this man claim to be a friend to the cause?'

"Alright Ember, let's go," he said at last. He turned away from the Tarven's gaze, Ember breathed a sigh of relief.

*   *   *

"Where is it!?" Favour muttered to himself as he rummaged through old letters and parchment, he was hoping to find a letter of an agreement he had made with a man many years ago. Fav had gotten a message from this man, saying that he would not be sending anymore taxes to Favour - because their agreement of six years had expired. So Favour was now madly searching for the old letter where they had first made the agreement, he was certain that the agreement had been for ten years - not six. Favour was interrupted from his search when his head guard entered the chamber.

"My lord, I come to make my report," he said crisply. Fav sighed, but motioned for the guard to say on. "For the past five weeks my lord, we have kept our surveillance on the Garatin family day and night as you ordered, but have seen nothing out of the ordinary."

Fav sighed shortly. "Very well, continue your surveillance of them."

The guard looked less than pleased with that order, but he went on with his report. Fav tuned him out as he went on searching for the letter-that is until he heard the namesake "Courage".

"What was that?" he said as his head snapped up, the guard looked confused for a moment.

"The Tarven, my lord - we've kept an eye on him just for safe measures," he explained.

Fav frowned. "You said one of your men observed something strange about him the other day," he half asked.

The guard nodded. "Yes, my lord. The Tarven left the manor gates three nights ago near sundown, and did not return before the gates were closed." Fav frowned.

"The gate keeper swears that he didn't let him back in that night - but my men report that they saw the Tarven return to his chambers late that night. I punished the gate keeper accordingly."

Fav frowned; what did this mean? He dismissed the guard with a wave of his hand. Absently he looked down at the small chest where his letters were, then he noticed a folded letter, reaching for it, he hoped that it was the one he was looking for. Scanning it over, he sighed in disappointment, this letter was old, yes, but it was from Garason reminding him of taxes that he had to pay. He was about to toss the old letter aside when he noticed who signed the letter; in bold, large, black inked letters, was the namesake Courage…

Favour stared at it for a whole minute just letting it sink in. That's where he knew Rage from! Courage wasn't just a tradesman from the east! He was a high ranking Tarven soldier - or he had been. Favour squeezed his eyes shut as he tried to remember; it all was so long ago, and it took so long for news to reach him that by the time it did, it was old news.

But he did remember; it was something that the Tarven lord from the closest outpost had said, a long time ago. The lord had been talking about treason… and how some months before a Tarven by the namesake of Courage had been arrested for treason - but had escaped. The only reason Fav remembered that conversation, was because he had had dealings with Rage before. And now, some five years later, Courage had remerged, not as a spy - but as a fugitive.

Fav smiled to himself, and for the first time since Rage had arrived in Hawthorn, Fav felt in control again. There were still many unknowns, but now Favour had the upper hand, and there was much to be gained.

*   *   *

Courage let the sleeves of his white tunic fall back down to his wrists from his elbows from where he had pushed them. Looking up he paused; Lord Favour stood in the hall before him. Fav raised his pudgy head and bounced on the balls of his feet showing uncharacteristic confidence. Rage forced himself to bow his head in respect as he approached Fav.

"Courage." Favour said, his smile making his face dimple.

"My lord?" Rage asked tipping his head to one side.

"Walk with me along the ramparts," Fav said nodding to the entrance to a flight of stairs that led up and out to the wall surrounding the manor. It was an order, not an invitation. Rage felt the back of his neck prickle with concealed alarm.

"As you wish my lord." he said none the less - what else could he do? Shifting as he climbed the stairs after Favour, he made sure that the knife he always carried was still securely tucked into his belt and hidden under his tunic. Favour panted heavily as they reached the top of the stairs and stepped out into the open evening air, but Rage's breathing was still even. They walked alongside each other as they crossed the catwalk from the manor to the outer wall, 15 meters below them the manor court yard looked still and silent. Reaching the outer rampart wall Fav grabbed hold of it and took a deep breath to try and gain control of his labored breathing. Rage's heart pounded in his chest as he waited for Fav to speak.

"I've been watching you," Favour said. Rage turned to face him. "Just because you are Tarven does not mean you can do what you like whenever you like." He looked up at Rage with a nasty smile.

How much does he know? Courage's mind raced with questions, while his heart pounded, every move he made, any word he said could endanger him more. Narrowing his eyes, he turned his back on Fav, knowing it would irk him. Walking slowly, running his hand along stone wall, he looked out over the village below.

"So tell me, my lord; what can and can't a Tarven do?" he said turning back to Fav.

Favour shifted as though less sure of himself. "A Tarven soldier can't go against orders. A Tarven can't defy the Tarven Council and expect to live." He watched Rage carefully.

"Indeed there have only been a handful throughout history who have." Veiled pride could be heard in his voice as Rage returned Favour's gaze.

"Ambassador Sinister would pay a high price to have even one of those traitorous Tarvens in his prison - an even higher price if one such traitor had dubious dealings with the Garatin rebellion."

Now Rage understood. He had been careless and foolish to think that Fav would not take an interest in his late night activities. Favour licked his lips and continued.

"I of course would be duty bound to report it to Ister if I knew of where such a traitor could be found... however if said traitor were to give me information of rebels in the area, then I could overlook his past crimes." His voice faltered as Rage took a step towards him.

Fav was very much mistaken if he thought he could blackmail him!

"No," Rage said, his voice low, "Ambassador Sinister would not pay a high price. A handful of 'traitorous Tarvens' are less of a nuisance to him then a fly in his chambers! And that is what he would say in reply to you, if you were fool enough to write him, my lord. Take my 'friendly' advice, and do not pester the Ambassador of Garatin with so petty a thing."

Favour's round face went pale, as he realized that he had underestimated Courage, and perhaps chosen the wrong target entirely. Shifting his broad shoulders to one side Rage stepped past Fav, but before leaving him alone on the ramparts he turned and said to Favour's rigid back.

"I should be surer of myself next time before threating someone if I were you, my Lord Favour."

*   *   *

The ambassador Sinister had been in power for over thirteen years in Garason. Before that he had been a grand duke in the lands of Tarva, when the King, ever shall he rest in peace, appointed him ambassador to Garason. Since that time Ister had earned for himself a reputation that was feared throughout the land. Even though he was only into his fifty's, he made it well known that he intended to rule the country till he died. He had already outlived one king of Tarva, and it seemed as though he would outlive another.

Thrive had been preparing himself to meet the ambassador before he had even landed in Larsanne, and he had been dreading it for longer still. Even though the king had bestowed upon him great power before he had set sail, Thri knew that Ister was a man to be wary of. And he was not sure of what the outcome might be if Ister took a disliking to him. Surely the king would not stand for any misfortune to befall his right-hand man, one mission short of being THE Grand Duke of Tarva. But then the king was far away - what could he do to save him if anything should happen? Thri reminded himself that things did not have to go to extremes, if he could only spin his words with all the cunning he could master, if only he could be pleasant yet forceful all at once, then perhaps all would go well. He wouldn't let Ister take from him his chance to become Grand Duke.

Thrive smiled as though he had everything in his very grasp, little did anyone know that he was nervous. Sinister was powerful and ruthless, if he wanted to he could make life miserable. Talking with him would be like dancing with a long tailed dragon. 'I had better watch my step,' Thri thought to himself as he was admitted at last into ambassador Sinister's presence.

Thri stood with his hands behind his back, showing off the richly embroidered crest over his chest, his shoulders looked broad and his short beard was clipped to a point. With his feet wide apart in a confident stance, his boots gleamed, and the decorative dagger he wore at his belt shone in the sunlight that streamed in through a large window. He wore a crooked smile on his thin lips, and his dark eyes sparkled as though they too smiled. The servants held the double doors open and one announced in a deep voice.

"His lordship, the emissary of his majesty the royal King of Tarva, Duke Thrive."

Thri raised his eyes till they met those of Ister. Sinister stood across the chamber facing Thri head on, his feet were wide apart in an aggressive stance. He was tall and sturdy, broad of shoulder and stern of face, his black short hair had gray streaks through it, and his beard was clipped to a point like all Tarven officials. His dark eyes were shadowed by thick brows. Everything about him said that he was a stubborn and headstrong Tarven, from the silver embroidery across his chest to the gleam of jewels on his hands, which rested in tight fists on his hips.

Thri lowered his eyes and dipped his head respectfully, bringing his fist to his own chest, he saluted in the Tarven fashion. As he raised his eyes again he was pleased and relieved to see that Ister had done the same. With a confident smile, Thri stepped forward.

"My lord, I have traveled over sea and land to stand before you, and now at last I have that honor."

Ister raised a dark brow. "I have waited a long time to meet you as well, my lord," he said. "It was well over a year ago that the king, may his reign go on, wrote to me about this visit. I have prepared ever since for your coming."

Thri smiled pleasantly, but he wondered what exactly Ister had 'prepared', or whether or not it had mostly involved Ister sweeping things under rugs. Ister's face broke out in what was really a rather friendly smile, he snapped his fingers and a page brought forth a tray with two goblets filled with wine on it. Ister took one in his hand and Thri did likewise, but before he raised it to his lips, Ister raised his goblet in a toast.

"To the king; long life and few foes!" after drinking to that, Thri raised his own toast.

"To Garatin; may we follow the king's wishes for this country - and down to those who stand in the way." With a shrewd look at one another, both men drank deeply. After setting the goblets back on the tray, both walked leisurely across the chamber and sat down.

"I trust your journeys have been well in the country and that no one has prevented you from carrying out your orders," Ister said graciously.

A lazy smile spread widely across Thri's face as he looked about the room carelessly. "Nay, my lord! For what would a mission for the king be, if no one opposed you?"

Ister laughed as though he knew the feeling all too well. Then for a time the two of them talked the way only rich Tarven lords can. They spoke of the weather, of tax collecting, of the different problems with neighboring countries, till at last Thri felt it was time to speak of more important matters.

"As you know, my lord, I am traveling through the land gathering information for the king on the condition this country is in."

At the change in seriousness, Ister leaned back and pinched his eyebrows together.

"My regret is that my stay in Garason will be short. However, I will visit this fair city again before I take my leave of these shores," Thri said. Ister nodded.

"I trust you will find all as it should be in my realm, and should you not I assure you it will soon thereafter be put to rights." Thri smiled crookedly, but did not speak aloud his thoughts of whether or not Ister was above offering bribes. Ister continued.

"I will of course be sending out letters to the lords and captains you will be visiting to tell them of your coming."

Thri cut him off with a raise of his hand. "I pray you, my lord, do not send out these letters; I would rather my visits be as unexpected as possible."

Sinister smiled - it reminded Thri of the smile of a dragon. "Very wise of you. I assume you will allow me to supply for you travel arrangements? As well as a few of my guards to accompany you?"

Thrive nodded. "But of course, my lord, indeed I would be honored. I plan to leave by the new moon."

"Very well then!" Ister declared as he stood to his feet abruptly. "It is all decided, and I shall throw a grand banquet tomorrow night in your honor." He bowed his head to Thri. The two of them stood and walked slowly to the door.

"My page will show you to your chambers," Ister said waving to a page who had been standing in a corner. Again Thri bowed slightly to him, and turned to take his leave, when Ister called his namesake.

"Thrive." His tone of voice had changed to a more serious one, Thri narrowed his eyes. "It pains me to remind you of this… but you will of course remember, my lord, whose country you are in." There was a veiled threat in the ambassador's words. "And I hope you will keep it in mind when you make decisions."

Thri understood completely what Ister meant, yet bold as ever he smiled as if it was all a game. "And I hope my lord, that you will not forget who sent me."

Ister met the challenge with a smile of his own, Thri turned to go down the hall, when once again he looked over his shoulder for one last remark. "And I believe, if I remember correctly; Garatin is the king's country."

* * *

"-But I found out that he's betrothed already," Mise said with a note of disappointment. Loy shook her head and went back to her embroidery of the rose bush that sat across the path from where the two of them sat. Loyal and her daughter were out enjoying the fine morning air in the manor garden. Loy worked slowly and carefully on her handy-work while Promise told her about her search for suitable men to marry. Loy hadn't even realized that Mise was interested in such things.

"I am convinced now mother, that there is not one man in all of Hawthorn that I could marry!"

"Of course you realize Mise that you may not have any say in the matter. Your father has not had time to arrange a marriage for you yet, but when he does he will pick only the best of course." Mise sat there in stunned silence staring at her mother, her young face looked open with disbelief. Loy however did not look at her but continued on with her work.

"You mean to say that father will pick whomever he thinks is best for me to marry, regardless of what I think or even if I am unhappy the rest of my life?" there was a challenge in her voice but still a note of vulnerability. Mise was too worked up to see that a shadow had passed over her mother's face.

"Happiness is not promised to us in life." She paused for a moment as she gazed out at nothing. "When your father chooses a husband for you, you would do well to be pleased, for he will only settle on someone who can give you a good life." A bitter look came to Promise's face.

"Father has condemned his own plans! Being married to anyone of high standing is now far out of reach due to whom he has been keeping company with recently."

At last Loy put down her work and looked at her daughter sternly.

Mise went on nevertheless.

"I don't see how you can defend him in this, mother! He's risking OUR future with those-" She was cut off sharply when Loy threw her hand up in alarm in a motion of silence. Promise's heart leapt into her mouth and her eyes darted to their left where footsteps could be heard coming towards them. For a terrible few moments both women sat still as stone, with their eyes trained on the bend in the path where the footsteps came from. The high hedges hid from their view who approached till the last second, but no relief came to either of them when they saw who it was; Lord Favour himself!

Both Loy and Mise stood to their feet and curtsied as Favour came to stand in front of them.

"A good morrow to you ladies!" he said at once, and he made a shallow bow to them. "If I may, you are both the very image of beauty on this fine day." He rung his hands in a nervous gesture.

Mise did not know him well at all, and had hardly even spoken with him in the whole time since they had come to the manor. But even still she felt as though his kind words were forced and somehow unnatural. She looked at him suspiciously. Loyal however smiled becomingly and lifted her hand for Fav to kiss, after he had done so he stepped to one side and asked her in a pleasant way.

"I wonder, my lady if we could speak alone." He then looked pointedly at Mise.

Promise returned his gaze boldly and coldly, then without a word and only a nod to Loy she glided away, leaving the two quite alone in the garden.

Chapter 12   The Carriage Ride

"A fine daughter you have," Favour said as Promise disappeared.

Loyal smiled, "Thank you, my lord,"

"Please - sit." He said gesturing to the bench, she sat back down and he looked down at her with a smile that made her feel uncomfortable, she did her best not to show it though.

"I wonder if I may ask you a question, my lady?" he asked tucking his chin into his neck until it disappeared completely.

"But of course," she said returning to her embroidery.

"Where did you and your husband live before coming to Hawthorn?" he asked slowly.

Loy paused and her heart beat quickened. "Far away to the east my lord," she said at last.

"And before then?" Loy looked up at him with a frown.

"What are you driving at my lord?" she asked suddenly.

He swallowed before saying. "Have you and your family ever been to Garason?"

For a moment Loy only looked up at him blankly. What was she to do!? But before she could think of what to say Favour went on with new found confidence that made her weary.

"I know you have been to Garason before, my lady. You lived there over six years ago."

Loy lowered her eyes and stared straight ahead, her shoulders tense and her back straight. Her hands trembled ever so slightly. Fav slowly crossed to the other side of the bench, deep inside Loy felt trapped like a mouse before a cat. Suddenly the garden felt closed in and dark - what was she to do? She could almost feel his fingers beginning to pry away the mask that she wore.

"So many interesting things happen in Garason!" Fav said, but his words were fake and shallow.

Like a heavy load of snow falling from a tree branch, Loy stood as though breaking free of a spell, and faced him coldly.

"I grow tired of the morning air, my lord. Good day." She turned and walked briskly away, that man was revolting! And his words were empty, even though she told herself that, her heart trembled with unnamed fear.

*   *   *

"Hey! Watch it!" Vanished said suddenly, looking up at his older brother with a frown.

"Sorry," Imagine mumbled without even stopping in his work. Van's frown deepened; what was wrong with Mag? The two of them were working in the stable clearing away old hay in Ro's stall, while the docile musk cow waited patiently nearby, when Mag had shoved his pitchfork rather close to the back of Van's leg. Pitchforks were sharp! Van watched his brother with anger just waiting for Mag to notice, then he would tell him off. But, as he watched he noticed that Mag was working unusually slow. Van's frown turned to one of question rather than one of anger; what was wrong with his brother? Mag had worked in this stable all his life - and yet he was being clumsy, as if it was dark and he couldn't see...

Vanished looked about just to remind himself that it was still midmorning, and light was streaming in through the stable windows, and that although it was dim light in some places - it did not give reason for clumsiness in such a simple task of mucking a stall! Van watched him for a moment before hesitantly speaking.

"Mag...?" he asked quietly. Mag sniffled but did not look up.

"What?" he said.

Van stared at him - Mag didn't seem to notice.

"Nothing," Van replied, he knew his older brother found it irritating when he said things like that - but this time Mag showed no reaction. With a frown Van leaned on his pitch fork, then an idea came to him.

"You missed the corner," he said calmly. Then to his surprise Mag stuck his pitch fork into the corner and dragged it out again, like he would have done if the corner was dirty- only it wasn't. That corner had already been cleaned out, Mag could see that... couldn't he? Van stood with wide eyes trying to believe what had just happened, when suddenly Mag turned about to face him.

With a glare he said, "What are you doing just standing there for!? Rose won't do the work herself you know!" Mag then stomped out of the stall to bring in new hay. Van stood there for a moment in vague horror, for his brother's eyes had looked... black. Just then Mag came back and dumped a pile of hay down, and Van could clearly see, that now Mag's eyes were clear blue again. Going back to his work, he kept stealing glances at Mag, and he told himself that it really had happened, whatever it was. As if telling them to hurry up, Rose mooed.

*   *   *

"I dare say, his lordship does travel in style," Thrive said with one of his crooked smiles and dark twinkling eyes.

"How else would an ambassador of Tarva travel?" Sinister asked stiffly, then smiled as if the two of them didn't in truth hate each other. Thri had been in Garason for several days enjoying life in the city - it reminded him of home. Soon he would return home, and become the Grand Duke of Tarva, but first he must finish his mission. Ister had invited him on a tour of the city, and 'traveling in style' was hardly the way to describe it; the wood of Ister's carriage gleamed a rich brown and on the doors were painted Ister's coat of arms, four well-tempered dappled grays pulled while six guards on horse-back with polished swords, carrying the banner of Tarva on poles, called ahead of them to clear the way.

Sinister and Thrive had ridden about the city enjoying a cool breeze, and skillfully avoided any subject of importance. But that could not last for ever Thri reminded himself, there were still things that needed to be discussed.

"Ah, the Vase…" Thrive said in a hushed tone as their carriage entered a large square. Leaning towards the window Thri smiled as he took in the sight - for truly, it was beautiful. The square shaped fort looked strong and unmovable, it's stone walls reached up as if in challenge, the peaked towers on all four corners boasted long and narrow white flags that fluttered in the wind. Doors that matched in size to that of his majesty's castle stood tall and grim, their strange black wood shone in the midday sun. And last of all, a row of thin arched windows looked down at the square with colorful glass panes, depicting splashes of color around star shaped flowers.

Thri knew what this place was, he had heard of it many times, and truly the stories did it justice. Sitting across from him, Ister grunted.

"Yes, 'the Vase'. A mysterious place." Thri turned to him with raised brow. Ister continued. "They say that every Garatin heart beats there," he said.

Thri grinned. "What else do they say?"

"That 'Eloi' dwells within." he said with a measure of distaste.

Thri settled back into his cushioned seat. "Ah," he said. "The infamous 'Eloi', tell me are the Garatin people really as obsessed with him as I've been told?"

Ister sighed shortly. "Unfortunately; yes. HERE!" he shouted out to the driver. "Stop here in the square." For a moment there was silence as the carriage came to a halt.

"The Garatin people are obstinate and superstitious."

Thri laughed softly, "I believe that 'superstitious' has been used to describe Tarvens," he said with a devious smile. Ister glared at him in return. Thri never lost his smile.

"If you seek to convince me that the reason there is so little progress in the king's name in this country, is because the locals are 'troublesome' and 'obstinate', you are mistaken my lord," he said coldly and yet his smile remained.

Ister met his gaze evenly. "Perhaps when you have seen for yourself, and tried and failed at bringing about the change the king so strongly desires, perhaps then you will understand."

"Yes, perhaps." Thri left it at that. "So tell me," his voice changed to a lighter one, "What is inside this grand fort?" he said looking out the window once again.

Ister bit back his disliking for the man across from him and went on to explain about the 'Vase'. "Some ancient king or other in the old times, had a great vase crafted, it's worth unmatchable, so they say." He spoke with a level of contempt. "Then they decided they needed a protector (most likely because they are a snivelling and wretched people) and they decided that this protector would dwell inside the Vase."

"Ah, so that is where the legend of the great 'Eloi' comes from." Thri commented.

Ister went on. "So it would seem. It's disgusting, but it seems as though every Garatin centers their life on this one thing! I really thought more would have changed after what happened - but these people are like insects; they won't die."

Thri paid no heed to Ister's obvious contempt for every Garatin person. "What is this 'event' you refer to?"

"Some years ago there was a rebel who stirred up the people (he was quite tiresome) and well, one thing led to another and I had to execute him. The stories go that when he died the vase shattered."

Thri raised his brows.

"Rumors and superstitions flew wild, and- and," Ister laughed.

"The very same people who wanted him dead - wished that he was not! Well there is no telling what dirty rebellious peasants will do, as it was, they stole the rotting body of their would be king, and went to quite a bit of work to make it seem as though he still lives! And that in itself has very well near started a war between those who were glad he died and those who wished he hadn't. I had men search for the body for weeks after, but they hid it well. And so you have the cursed country of Garason, while the king eagerly awaits perfect reform and submission from the most stubborn and undesirable flea bitten GARATINS!"

Across from Thri, Ister sat with face red and eyes blurry with anger, his fists clenched and the veins in his thick neck bulged.

"Now the king sends a message that he is not pleased with me." Ister had regained a quieter voice, one that could make its very own chills. "I invite you, oh great emissary of his royal majesty the king of Tarva - I invite YOU to do in one year what I have been unable to do in thirteen! And when you return to the king choking on failure - to whom will the king turn to then?"

There was not a moment when Thri lost his nerve, or his grin. Waiting a moment after Ister had finished his threat, he spoke with calm assurance. "You paint an ugly picture indeed, my lord. Undoubtable the king would be disappointed if I failed to carry out his wishes. But... if I return to him in success - whom then will the king trust more; the man who carried out his commands in one year - or the man who failed to do it in thirteen?" The two men of power returned each other's gaze for a long moment. Then Thri spoke with a friendly voice.

"However rest assured my lord, I do not wish to be ambassador in Garatin, no my reward will be that of the Grand Duke of Tarva. Truly, if I please the king, his favour will fall upon you as well - will it not?" his smooth words worked on Sinister like oil, and the Tarven relaxed back into his seat.

"Driver, continue through the city."

Thri spoke loudly then, not giving Ister chance to say anything he went on. "So tell me, what did the Garatin people do? After all, this 'Vase' was THE center of their culture, what have they done without it? And where did their Eloi go?"

Ister grunted. "They recreated from the shards of the Vase a replacement, it is said it is likened to that of a large bowl, I have never seen it for they do not allow any Tarven inside. And the Garatin leaders say not to fear for although Eloi was angry he has returned to his people once more." He said in mock seriousness.

'Convenient' Thri thought to himself. "And what of the man? The one for which all the trouble was about - what has happened to the rumor he lives?"

Ister's face darkened before explaining, "After crawling out of his own grave, they say he went back to his home in the north. I will say this, those rebels who hatched this ridiculous rumor have done good work at convincing nearly every peasant in the Quy to believe that he lives. And what am I to do? You can only kill a man once - and I didn't want to even then! Thankfully those rebels never got anywhere, I think they got too nervous and dropped the whole thing, for now they say that the man was called away by Eloi because his work was finished- HA! They called him the 'king' and yet he abandoned them before reclaiming his country."

Ister was cut short for outside the carriage was a mob! Both men tensed in their seats while the driver was forced to stop the carriage because there were so many people in the street. Thrive watched as the people pressed up against the window. They looked to be all Garatin, and they held in their hands not weapons but strips of white cloth.

"Return to Eloi what is his!" "Enough of Tarven rule- we want freedom!" Thri could pick out several other things that the people were shouting out, but as he watched, Ister's mounted guards surged into the crowd and drove them away from the sides of the carriage.

"That," Ister said with contempt, "Is what the 'Eloi-man' left behind. He claimed his was a mission of peace, yet his legacy is discord. Four years since the man disappeared and more than that since he was executed- and his followers are more numerous than ever!"

"How 'numerous'?" Thri asked with a frown.

Ister sighed. "In the thousands, all throughout Garatin. It's become downright dangerous," he ended quietly.

"They do not appear to be violent," Thrive said thoughtfully, then added. "However if they are indeed as numerous as you say, then the country could be on the brink of a nationwide rebellion."

Sinister raised his head in pride. "The king has no reason to fear losing this country in rebellion, I have long ago taken measures to end this anarchy."

Thri raised his brow. "Of what measures do you speak?"

"This rebellion," Ister began slowly. "Based on the long since dead 'Eloi-man' is deeply offensive to the Garatin leaders. A convenient split indeed - they have come to me countless times about putting an end to it. However, as wearisome as these ever growing rebels are, they have showed no signs of violence, so I dare not touch them. But those pale-faced Garatin leaders don't see it that way, and protest saying these rebels are violating their ancient laws. So I gave them what they wanted; the right to arrest any Garatin guilty of rebellious activity and bring them back to this city for trial." He paused and sighed as though tired of the whole thing.

"In the past four years, thousands have been paraded before me, while the Garatin leaders beg me to sign for their death. It has dispelled the fever of rebellion to quite a degree I must admit. Even as we speak a man by the namesake of Horizon is in the northern villages rounding up suspected rebels to be brought back here for their trials. It is all quite amusing." Ister laughed to himself. "Why waste time and resources putting down a rebellion - when pale faced locals will do it for you!?" he laughed for a time, while Thrive looked out the carriage window and watched as the mob fell behind them. When Ister had finally stopped, Thri asked.

"What was the namesake of this 'Eloi-man'?"

"Eternity," Ister said with a slightly mocking face.

Thri smiled openly, "How fitting!"

* * *

Courage entered the room where he had been storing his trading goods and shut the door behind him. For a moment he stood there in the dark, and then he struck a match and lit a candle. On a few late nights he had laid out a blanket here and slept on the floor so as not to wake Loy, or like tonight when he needed to think. Going to a barrel where he had set a wash basin, he poured water into it from a pitcher. With a sigh he dipped his hands in the cool water and splashed his face. For a moment he let the water drip from his short beard, before drying his face with a rag.

"How did I get into this mess?" Rage quietly asked himself. It had been three weeks since he had gone to that first meeting with the villagers. And every time he went to another one it felt like he was getting himself deeper and deeper into a mess that he could not fix.

Earlier that day, at market, Journ had come to Rage and told him to go his cottage again that night. Journ hadn't said anything more and Rage had feared that something was wrong. But as it turned out, Journ and the others only wanted Rage to teach them more. At first he had been angry that they had pulled him out in the night for that, but his anger faded as he saw that they had (for the most part) accepted him! He had then proceeded to map out different places that they could hold meetings, again to his surprise they all listened and respected his suggestions!

Then when everyone began to leave Journ asked that he stay for a few moments longer. It was then that Journ and Trus had told him about one of their youngest members, and one of the more important ones.

"His namesake is Imagine, and it was his father, Obedience who first brought the story of Nity to Hawthorn." Journ had told him as Trus stood nearby looking sad.

"We all knew and loved Dien, even if some of us didn't understand him. It was a great loss when he died three years ago." Journ's voice was melancholy as he told the tale. "The story is that while in Garason with his oldest boy, he was attacked by thieves - and killed. Mag would not believe at the time that it was more than an accident. But we knew. And I believe he has come to accept it too, that Dien's death was a deliberate act by the Garatin leaders in Garason to put an end to him and his words about Nity." He had let the words sit there for a long time, before continuing. "Mag blames the Tarvens for not giving his father justice, he blames the Tarvens for overtaking this country, he blames the Tarvens for killing Eternity. He blames you... for being alive." Journ had paused before revealing the most damaging information.

"Mag and his family are the ones you saved from lord Favour's wrath. The fact that Mag owes you a life debt seems to have only made him hate you more."

Rage had gritted his teeth and said, "He can rest at ease; I have no intentions of forcing him or his family to honor their debt to me."

Hissing a curse between his teeth in frustration as he remembered the conversation, Rage wondered how he could have gotten mixed up in such a mess as this. He frowned deeply; why was he here!? Two months ago when he had left the Byla he had never thought he would be in such a position as this! Why? Why could he not just walk away from it all? Because. A voice seemed to say in his mind. Nity meant more for you than just a Tarven soldier. Nity meant more for you than just a tradesman. Nity meant MORE for you than what you are...

Rage did not know to whom the voice belonged, whether to his own mind or to Eloi himself - but he could not push aside the wisdom in those words. Nity did mean more for him. It was a simple truth that had been impressed upon him when he had met Nity face to face, a truth that had stayed with him ever since. A whisper in the back of his mind that he was not all that he could be - or all that he was meant to be. That was his answer as to why he could not walk away from Journey and Trust; that was the reason. Deep in his heart he knew that here was where he was meant to be.

A soft sound at the door startled him from his soul-seeking thoughts. The door creaked open, and Loyal's face appeared; he could not make out her expression in the dark - but something had to be wrong, why else would she come to him at such a late hour?

"Courage?" she said softly as she hesitantly stepped into the room.

"Yes, what is it?"

"Rage I must speak with you about something of importance." She walked into the candle light, he saw at once that her face seemed strained. Suddenly he grew weary; he knew why she was here, and he didn't want to listen to her questions of why he had to be involved with outlaws when he had already been asking those same questions of himself.

"Yes, Loyal. I went to another meeting tonight." There was an edge to his voice, if he had only paid attention he would have seen that his words hurt Loy. But he did not notice. "I have made my choice to aid them, I do not wish to hear any more of it."

"There is something else I must speak to you of, Rage."

"What is it?" he asked impatiently as he turned away from her. His irritation with himself was growing by the second, he just needed to be alone - why couldn't Loyal see that!? There was a moment of silence.

"Nothing - it can wait till later," Loy said briskly. Then she left quickly and shut the chamber door behind her. Rage sighed in relief; he was not ready to come to grips with the truth himself, he could not bear the thought of telling his wife his reasons for his actions of late, he had not even told her of Favour's empty threat!

On the other side of the door Loyal leaned up against it and breathed deeply; what was she to do? Even now Favour's words in the garden echoed in her mind, his meaning had been unclear, it could lead to danger - or Loy could simply be mistaken. All day long Loy had agonized over it, at last she had decided that she must go to Rage about it, to whom could she turn if not her own husband? But he had brushed her aside with irritation! As if she were a nuisance… how could she turn to him for help if he did not care? He would no doubt think she was a silly woman for getting so worried over something so small, he would probably not take her seriously even if he had listened!

Loy took a settling breath "I'll talk with him in the morning" she told herself, "When I've had a good night sleep, this will all look quite small." With a less than confident nod, she went to their bed chamber and tried to sleep, though she failed to put Fav's words from her mind.

Chapter 13   Deep Inside

It had been one week since Promise and her mother had sat in the garden together and been interrupted by Lord Favour. Mise had spent the time since in deep thought, and most of it in a black mood. She had done nothing but think of her future, or rather what she had thought would be her future. Over and over she replayed her mother's words in her mind, she had even muttered them bitterly to herself. "Happiness is not promised to us in life."

Now a week later she stood in front of a closed window - the only window in her small chambers, it was late morning and it was a fine day. Her chambers were positioned so that she did not have much of a view of the countryside, but the sun could still find its way in and it glinted on her hair. She had not dressed it yet that day and it hung down her back in long ringlets. The dress she wore was one of the simpler ones that Destination had given her. She marvelled that it had only been two months since they had arrived in Hawthorn. And less than that since they had come to live in the manor.

Her arms were crossed and there was a frown on her pretty face, her lips were drawn up in a tight line and her cinnamon eyes were stormy. For long moments she stood there thinking; her thoughts drifted here and there like the wind in the grass. Deep down she knew what her mother had said was true, the thought had eaten at her all week long.

"It's time you grew up Mise!" she whispered harshly to herself. But it was hard for her to leave childlike beliefs behind; all her life she had been cradled - first by her nurse, then by her parents after her 'sickness'. How was she really expected to grow up when those closest to her would not let her!? And then being isolated in the wilderness for five years was not the best way to leave childhood behind, Destination was a good example of that. Even after her experiences in Garason, Desti was still very childlike - in the best way! Mise thought, but still so much like a child at times. Chewing on her bottom lip, Promise's eyes filled with tears of uncertainty - life would be so much better if she could just stay a child forever!

Marriage? The word echoed in her mind dauntingly. Of course she had thought about it before - many times, only now, it seemed so… frightening! 'Only fools are fearless…' the words whispered in the back of her mind, those had been Desti's parting words to her. "It's all right to be afraid," she told herself in wonder. "But I can't let that fear control me…" she took a deep breath. Really she didn't have a choice, womanhood was upon her, she could not run from that, and with it, it seemed, that the whole world was watching - waiting for her to meet their expectations.

"This is what I want," she told herself, but the words were less than convincing. "I wanted to leave the Byla! I don't want to be just a tradesman's daughter anymore." A frown appeared on her face as she thought about the last few weeks in the manor. It was made clear every day that she was not like the other young maidens, her voice was too loud, her dancing too clumsy, her riding too manly. She just simply wasn't good enough.

"I want to become a true maiden of Tarva…" she whispered. "I want it more than anything!" To be silent and graceful, the perfect image of beauty. Held in honour, a lady who many would gladly die for if only they could claim her hand for their own.

"This is what I want!" she said in a strong voice, her eyes hardened, and the beauty in her face was met with fierce determination. "And I will create my own happiness! I'll marry whomever father picks if only it will mean I can be a true lady! This is what I want!" she said it loud and certain, knowing in her own heart that it was true. Everything else that got in the way of getting this would have to be put aside. Father had told her what he had learned of Nity, and she had wondered what had happened, only now finding out what had happened to Nity would have to wait. And really the movement didn't need her; what could she do to help, she was just a girl, and at last she would take her role in life.

*   *   *

As the sun sank lower, it seemed to Imagine's eyes as though it set the fields on fire, burning a path through the grain straight for him. His work done for the day, he sat on the edge of the chicken coop behind his cottage, watching the day die away. To him, everything was dying; the chickens beneath him would one day be on the dinner table, the vegetable plants in the garden would one day dry up, one day he too would die - even the day grew old and died. All these thoughts passed by in his mind without him thinking twice about them.

It had been three weeks since Trust had told him about the Tarven, even now the thought of that man left a bitter taste in his mouth. Sluggishly his thoughts drifted over the past few months. With mild shock he thought about how it had been almost two months since Witness had died, and almost a full month since Fav had sent spies out to watch Mag and his family. Vaguely he wondered if he was being watched even now. For two weeks he and his mother and Vanished had noticed his lordship's spies less and less; had Favour given up? With a weary sigh he hoped that he had, a month was too long to be away from the meetings, it was too long to be cut off from the others!

A noise behind him told him that someone was crossing the yard to stand behind him; instinctively he knew it was his mother. Perilous stood close beside him for a long moment in silence.

"It's times like this when I miss him the most I think," she said dreamily.

Mag looked at her in surprise, they hardly EVER talked about Obedience. Peri sighed and returned his gaze.

"Mag, I know it was hard for you, and living with the memories must be torture." Mag looked away, he knew what she would say. "And I understand if you're still not ready to talk about it. But I think it's time I knew exactly what happened to your father."

Pain shot through Mag; the less he was forced to think about that day the less he was faced with the truth, but he knew he had to tell her. Vaguely he wondered if it would make him feel better to tell someone about that day in detail after three years.

"Alright." He pressed his lips together, he was determined to hold his emotions in check. "We had been in Garason for four days..." he willed his voice to be steady. Peri watched him intently but did not interrupt him. "It was the third day we were there when the High Council began, it lasted all day. I remember waiting for him on the steps of the council chambers, watching the people in the square, looking at the 'Vase' across from me." He seemed to fade back into the past, and it was as if he could once again see the people in the square. "When he finally came out he was so tired, he told me that the Garatin leaders didn't seem to want to talk about Eternity at all, he said that they didn't see the need to change anything. He was so frustrated. But he was still hopeful that he could change their minds the next day." For long moments Mag was silent.

"Again I waited all the next day, it seemed to take forever, then at last he came. I asked how it went - he told me that they wouldn't listen." Mag frowned. "I had never seen him so... defeated! But then he told me that we couldn't give up, he was sure that one day someone would listen... We crossed the square, and he gave me some coins to buy fruit from a merchant across the street." Without warning Mag's voice broke and his eyes filled with tears, he was shocked by his own response. He had hoped to at last tell his mother the truth - but he couldn't get the words out!

"That's when it happened." He said at last, and it was as though he shut a door on his own emotions. His tears dried up, and his heart went numb to the pain again, it was such a hard thing to do that it made his heart heavy.

Peri opened her mouth to press him for more - what happened then!? But she stopped herself, she could see the pain rippling through her son, it had cost him so much to tell her.

There was a long moment when all Mag did was sit there staring off into the distance. At least that's what Peri thought he was doing, but the horrible truth was that Mag couldn't see into the distance - in fact he couldn't see at all! He struggled to keep his breathing even, all he could do was wait till his vision came back, and it always did after a few moments. But this was happening more and more, each time it got worse, and each time, it seemed to take longer till his vision cleared. Deep down a panic rose within him. What if it got so bad that one day his vision wouldn't clear? The more he thought of it the more it became clear that it only happened when he was angry, or more precisely when he was thinking of his father's death. But those thoughts always scared him and he didn't linger on them long. Slowly as he sat there, a red light penetrated the blackness, he swallowed hard, and waited till the red light faded and was mixed with a blue one, then different colors came back too, and quickly now, shapes. Soon he was able to see the fields of grain again.

With a sharp intake of breath, Mag slid off the chicken coop and faced his mother, with a grim smile he walked back to the cottage. After a moment's hesitation she followed him inside. As Mag opened the back door to their cottage he was met with a mouth-watering smell of soup. Eager to forget the sudden blindness that plagued him, Mag went to where his sister sat on a stool stirring a large pot over a hot fire.

Ember looked up at him and smiled. "Back off! You have to share this with everyone," she teased as Mag looked down longingly at the soup.

Smiling at her, Peri set what was left of their bread on the table. Just then the door burst open and Vanished and their youngest brother stumbled in. In exasperation Mag wondered if they could ever not burst into a room.

"Where have you two been?" Peri asked, but without waiting for a response she said hurriedly, "Make sure both of you wash up, we're eating soon."

"We went for a walk!" Survive volunteered cheerfully as he thumped across the room to the wash basin, energy seemed to bound from his skinny and lanky form even after a hard day's work! Mag wondered sadly if he had ever been that young. Van leaned on the table with both hands and looked at his mother.

"We went to see Mory, she says there is to be another meeting tonight." Everyone in the room paused; Ember looked up at their brother and Vive seemed to shrink back. Peri sighed heavily while Mag shot venom at Van with his eyes. Peri opened her mouth, but for a moment nothing came out.

"Van," she said in a low and weary voice but she was interrupted by Mag's low and calm voice.

"You're an idiot," he said it as a fact without emotion.

Van pushed off the table and glared at him. "It's been a month long enough! None of us have seen his spies for weeks now! We just can't hide forever!" Vanished exploded in true eighteen-year-old fashion. Peri closed her eyes.

"Van! Don't you see!?" she said, her voice rising only a little. "The past month of secrecy will all be for not, if we're found out now!" She sounded desperate and even afraid. Van seemed to soften a little.

"He can't have us watched forever! And I wasn't watched when I spoke with Mory - I swear it!" For a moment no one said a word.

"Regardless of what you think his lordship is doing," Mag said quietly, "You or anyone else in this cottage will not speak to any of the others until I say so."

Peri sighed. "In another week, if no one has seen any spies, then it will be safe to attend the meetings." She said it quietly and no one in the room even thought about arguing with her on the matter. "Now, it's time to eat," she said calmly. But Mag couldn't help but notice how tired she looked.

They all ate in strained silence for a long time, Ember looked around at everyone's faces, and she thought they looked calm enough to speak civilly to one another.

"Did Mory say why they're calling the meeting?" Ember's soft voice (as it often did) had a calming effect on everyone. Van reached out and ripped a hunk of bread from the loaf. He looked at their mother before answering.

"She said that they would be discussing safety with the 'Tarven'," he mumbled. Peri frowned.

"What for?" she asked cautiously. Van looked up at her.

"Mory said that Rizon is getting closer to Hawthorn." Everyone was quiet, ever since Witness had died they had all listened to the news of more and more men and women being arrested and taken to Garason. It was only a matter of time before Rizon came to Hawthorn. Beside her, Ember noticed that Mag had grown pale.

*   *   *

A fire glowed in the large hearth and sent out a pleasant smell of spice and pine; although it had been a warm day, the evening air was cool enough to enjoy the fire's heat. The sun had sunk away long ago giving way to the silver light of the stars, through a large gaping arch with no glass the night air carried in the songs of crickets and other little creatures who sing in the night. Loyal ran her finger tips along her embroidery with approval. She looked distant and cool, as she sat with straight back and shoulders. She wore a simple white cotton shift with a loose dark blue garment over top, and her dark hair curled back from her face gracefully, a strange contrast of grace and simplicity. Tired of her cramped chambers she had been enjoying the great hall, especially since no one else was there. Loy sighed and closed her eyes for a moment - but her trials had only just begun...

"You seem troubled, my lady," a smooth voice sounded from behind her. She stiffened.

Favour must have entered the grand hall some moments before, and now slowly he came to stand behind her, arrogance and self-confidence seemed to drip from him, leaving puddles where he stepped.

Loy turned her head to look at him, her face hard and unyielding, but inside shame scorched her; it had been a full week since Fav had spoken to her in the garden and she hadn't said a thing about it to Rage... why had she not just spoken with her own husband about Favour's threat? Why? In the past week she had convinced herself that Favour's words were empty, but now she felt her heart quiver with fear, and it was all she could do to keep her hands from shaking.

Fav walked in a wide circle around her till he stood facing her; he smiled down at her, but it was a cheap smile indeed. "Surely you are not surprised to see me again, my lady!" he said in a mocking voice.

Looking up at him Loy forced herself to relax. "You do me honor to speak with me, however I am afraid I do not understand your interest." Her voice was cool and calm - but she was bluffing, and they both knew it. Fav sighed heavily as though he was tired of the whole thing.

"It has come to my attention that word will be sent to ambassador Sinister himself, telling him of the whereabouts of Courage, the soldier and captain who defied Tarven rule and fled justice five years ago," he said in a detached voice, but it turned to a mocking tone. "Naturally I wish no harm upon you or your husband, I only wish there was some way that I could stop this information from being sent to Garason." He did his best to look innocent, but it made his wide forehead and shifty eyes look even more loathsome than normal.

Mastering the strength that she often hid away deep inside Loyal replied with dignity and a sharp edge. "The ambassador I am sure has other more important things to take care of, I suggest you leave him to deal with these matters in his own way." There was silence while the two of them looked at each other like warriors in battle. Loyal was the first to look away, and she began to gather up her things more than ready to be rid of this man, when Fav spoke, calm and sure of his words.

"Do you think that the ambassador would be more interested if he were to learn that this same Tarven was once again deeply involved in rebellious activity?"

Favour had aimed well, and this time he had indeed hit his mark, for Loy seemed to be frozen where she sat. Her neck ached, her back felt strained, and the hairs on the back of her neck seemed to stand up on their own. Her throat felt thick and her hands shook, she was certain that if she tried to stand that her legs would give beneath her, and her heart... her heart felt so heavy.

"What do you want my lord?" she asked weakly. Fav licked his lips in a nervous gesture.

"I want to know what the rebels are doing."

Loyal caught her breath and looked up at him in fear; he was deadly serious. She lowered her eyes and nodded her understanding.

Fav stepped back and smiled, "I expect to hear from you shortly then." Fearing that her shaking legs would not hold her but wanting to escape, she picked up her embroidery and stood to her feet. Turning her back to Fav she walked as quickly as she could without breaking into a run, but as she neared the archway that lead out of the great hall she became aware of one of Favour's guards standing to one side. Shrinking inside, she tried to pass him, but he shifted his shoulders and side-swiped her hard.

Loy nearly lost her balance and spun about to look at the guard with a mixture of surprise, outrage and fear. The man's face was impassive.

"Keep this conversation to yourself, my lady." Favour said from inside the hall, his voice echoing off the walls. "I wouldn't want anyone to fall into harm's way." Loyal looked first at Fav then the guard in unbelief. The guard shifted his eyes to look at her, and Loy swallowed hard; she had never felt so surrounded and alone at the same time before - but she did now!

*   *   *

Favour smoothed out his bed sheets and patted them down awkwardly, then looked about his dark chamber, with an impatient sigh, he laid his head back. Hardly a minute passed by before he lifted his head back up again, his eyes didn't look the least bit sleepy and he had a nervous energy about him. Only an hour ago he had delivered his devastating news to Loy, but now his restless mind went over his carefully laid plot over and over again.

Loyal was scared and unsure, he had her right where he wanted her - he hoped. She had not argued with him or shown any resistance. The only thing that could go wrong was if she told Courage about his threat - then all would be lost. But he didn't think she would tell him - or would she? Fav continued to agonize over it all.

Fav laid his head back down again, and forced his eyes shut. His plan would work; Loy would bend to his will. And through her, he would find every last rebel in Hawthorn and snuff them out. Then Tarva would have no need to come marching into his village, he was still in control... wasn't he?

Chapter 14   The Dark Horse

Courage ducked through the low doorway into the bakehouse cellar, this was perhaps the safest place for the meetings to be held. There were three ways to get into it; one was through a hatch door behind the bakehouse, another was down a ladder from a nearby shack, and the last was through the bakehouse floor itself. Mory had been proud to show off her ideal cellar, and pointed out that it was oversized, so there was enough room for everyone. The people on the street wouldn't be able to hear voices or see lantern light through windows; it was indeed perfect! Rage had been teaching the group to flee the meeting within seconds and without a sound, in case Fav's men should interrupt.

On this night however, Rage wasn't certain if there was to be any training, Trus had not said much other than that he should come. Rage almost hadn't come, but it was like he couldn't stay away. Even after four weeks of attending the meetings, he still was the target of suspicious glances and mutterings among the small group of Garatins. It was a great thorn in his pride to have to bear the brunt of these people's suspicions and ill thoughts. Yet somehow it only made Rage want to try harder to prove that he was trustworthy. Perhaps that's why he had come.

"Courage I'm glad you're here!" Journey called out. He was standing in a tight group with the others, near the table that had been brought down. Truly Journ did look and sound pleased to see him as he walked to him to clasp his hand, his blue eyes sparkled in a way that Rage did not expect.

"Rage there is someone here who you must meet," he said. Rage frowned; who could it possibly be to make Journ so excited? He looked sharply to the group of villagers gathered about, there were three Garatin men who he didn't know, but he forgot about the other two when one of the men slowly walked out from the middle of them and stood before him and Journ. The man was average height and build, blond and blue eyed - in fact there was not much about his appearance that made him notable, rather it was his sprit that stood out from others. At this particular time, he was calm and cool, but one could see almost at once a liveliness and passion hiding just beneath the surface.

"This is Courage - the one I was telling you about," Journ said warmly. Then he turned to the other man and said, with as much warmth.

"And this man is Quest. A close companion and confidant of Eternity himself." Rage felt himself fill with astonishment and surprise - for he knew this man!

Est smiled and exclaimed, "Courage!? Well why didn't you say his namesake? I know this man!" he said happily.

Rage tensed, what would Est say about him? All the others knew about him was that he had once been a captain.

Est frowned and asked, "You do remember me - do you not sir? We were never introduced in this manner, but we have met, however it was under strange circumstances!"

"You two have met in the past? How is that?" Journ asked. Everyone else was watching closely.

"You were there with Eternity when he woke my daughter," Rage stated.

"Woke her! Yes, that is one way of describing death."

Journ's eyes widened. "Eternity did the impossible for YOUR daughter?!" Journ asked with bewilderment.

"Do you mean to tell me that Rage has not told you his story? Why this is the man who stood up against the Tarven Council itself and refused to arrest Nity. He was arrested himself for this very thing - I heard it told that you were rescued by rebels, and then were forced to flee the country," Est said.

There was shocked silence throughout the cellar. Whatever pride that Rage might have felt was overshadowed, as he thought of the months he had spent planning the assassination of Nity - if these people knew that part of the story - if Quest knew and told them; they would kill him. Est was watching Rage with a mysterious air. Who was Rage fooling? Est knew all about that part of the story! In fact, Rage was surprised that Est knew anything else other than that part. But… if Rage wasn't mistaken, Est wasn't about to tell anyone.

"Well…" Journey said gaining control of himself again, "This is a story I should like to hear more of!"

"But we didn't call this meeting to tell stories, did we now," Realize said.

Journ took a deep breath and put his pipe in the corner of his mouth. "Right then, that will have to wait for another time," he said with a bit of reluctance. "Mory, are we all here?" Mory, who sat at the table gave

Rage a sour glance, then nodded.

"Everyone but Mag and Van!" one of the men spoke up. "Really, how long until they can come back!?" he asked impatiently. Journ looked weary, while Mory just looked annoyed.

"As long as it takes!" she said sharply, with a piercing eye she surveyed the group. "This meeting has been called to discuss the coming danger of Rizon, real or not - so I don't want to hear any grumbling about who isn't here and who is!" she glared at Rage as if he was a naughty child.

Beside Rage, Journ smiled with warm affection for the sharp woman. Everyone then sat down around the table, perched atop barrels that cluttered the cellar. Quest had been given the place at the head of the table where everyone could clearly see him - and everyone stole admiring glances at him throughout the meeting.

"Well now," Journ seemed nervous to speak in the presence of greatness, "We all know that there have been many arrests in the past two months in southern and western Garatin - we all heard what Imagine saw happen in Shore. Although it would seem that Witness's death was an accident. But we know that men and women are being taken to Garason to face trials…" Journ paused and a shadow passed over his face. "There have been reports that most of the Garatins arrested and taken to Garason on trial - have been executed."

There was a collected gasp about the room at this news, Est's face looked very grim as he spoke, "I can confirm this, many have died."

"But we aren't rebels! What have we done wrong?" one of the women said quietly.

"W-who has authorized th-these a-arrests?" Trust's stutter was painfully pronounced.

Est was silent for a moment. "The Garatin High Council requested the papers to make the arrests, and the ambassador Sinister granted them full authority. Begging your pardon miss, but we are rebels."

Everyone was silent at this news, at last Journ spoke again.

"The arrests have been largely handled by one man. You have already heard of him; Horizon. He is Garatin, and I think he holds a small position on the High Council." Trus shifted in the uneasy silence that followed, Rage studied the faces of the others and was relieved to see that none of them were looking at him in an accusing manner.

"These are dark times for us, my friends," Est said. "However, I have lived through worse." Instantly Rage was reminded of the night he had been arrested, two days after Nity had died; indeed, those had been dark times. Est continued with an excitement that was contagious.

"Many of you have lost hope, you think that Nity has deserted us… and it is true that he is no longer here." There was a collected gasp through the room. "No - I did not say he is dead! They did execute him, but he lived again, as you all know. And after spending many months with us, Nity told us that it was time for him to leave, that he had finished what Eloi had intended him to do- I don't have the words to describe how…" Est's voice softened in uncertainty as he tried to explain, "His body faded away… as if he was going to a place where he could not take it with him." He was silent for a moment as everyone tried to understand what he meant, then he continued on with vigor.

"But he has not deserted us! He is here in the hearts of those who love and follow him, I know this beyond doubt! We have been able to do the impossible - things that only he could do; by this I know that he is still here." Est pointed to the ground, as if Nity was standing beside him. "The last thing Nity told me and the others was that it was now up to us to continue on - and we have. You here in Hawthorn are most certainly not alone! The followers of Nity have grown to great numbers - and are still growing. My brother, Finished, is working hard in the villages along the Quy lake, and the others who were with Nity are traveling into Garason, the Cokhawk, across the plains to the Arrow Sea, and along the eastern shore of the Nenor itself! The word of Nity - the impossible story has been told in every corner of Garatin! People who never heard of Eternity before are now ready to follow him - we are not alone!"

Sitting there watching the passion flow out of this fiery eyed man, Rage felt a stirring in his heart - one that could not be denied!

"My brothers and sisters, do not lose hope. This battle is far from lost! What Nity set out to do IS being done, thousands already believe that Nity was - and is THE Eloi man." Est's voice became soft. "I know that you are all willing to lay down your own life for this cause… but take hope, your lives are much more valuable than your deaths," he finished with a smile.

One or two others were able to return the smile. Rage noticed how the emotions in the room had changed from fear and despair to determination. Again he wondered how Quest could be so good at moving people. Est rose to his feet and stepped over to stand by a hand drawn map that he had pinned to the wall, everyone's eyes followed him wordlessly. The map showed a large portion of northern Garatin, including all the tiny villages normally overlooked.

"For three years now this man Horizon has been arresting and harassing the followers of Nity," Est began. He was facing the map, holding his hands behind his back. "He started in Garason itself, but since then has moved north. The High Council was completely behind him, but I think he was forced to move north by the High Council and the Tarvens because he was causing too much fuss in the city."

Rage felt the mood change, even Trus seemed to take on a hostile air where this man Horizon was concerned. Rage, who was not Garatin, couldn't help but wonder what kind of passion this man must have, to be able to turn against his own people.

"Now I come to the part of my two friends." He gestured to the two new men. The two who had yet to speak looked tired and worn out like they had been through much recently. "This is History and Transform, for many years now they have led the movement in Garason itself, and now they are fleeing for their lives. Horizon has been searching for them for weeks and he knows they have gone further north." He paused and looked about the room. History spoke next and he sounded even more worn down than he looked.

"Transform and I have been running for four weeks now, and Tran has fallen ill - we need a place to hide. It will not be safe for you, but we plead with you to help us."

There was silence and Rage wondered if they would be turned away, but then Trust spoke.

"I- I will take you in, you b-both can stay in my c-cottage for however long you n-need." Est looked at him.

"Be warned; Horizon's next stop will be very close to Hawthorn - if not Hawthorn itself. If you are found harboring them, you and your family will share their fate," Est warned. Everyone looked grim, but Trus nodded, and the two men thanked him. Est went on.

"If Rizon does come here, you all know that you cannot count on protection from Lord Favour. From what I've heard he'll be only too happy to have you all arrested - and believe me some of you will be arrested." His words hung in the air like vapor.

"We all knew that risk long ago," one of the men said in a low voice. The others nodded in agreement.

Est continued, "You have the beginnings of a good system here, I am told that is thanks to Courage. There is a chance that you will not be found out - however Horizon has found many who were thought to be 'safe'. I urge you; be ready."

*   *   *

Rage slipped into the storage chamber later that night, the moon lighting his way. His heart beat like the wings of a butterfly. He went to the wash basin and splashed his face, the water was icy cold and smelled stale, but he found it most refreshing! As the water stilled again he could see his reflection and it surprised him; he looked animated, his eyes glowed like that of a young man - he looked so alive!

Just then the room was filled with the golden light of a candle, he turned to see Loyal standing at the door. She looked at him in a bewildered fashion.

"Rage - what happened tonight?" she asked. Worry filled her soft voice and her face open as she waited for his response. Suddenly Rage smiled and swiftly went to her in three long strides, he took the candle that she held and put it aside, and then he took both her hands in his. She looked up at him with wide cinnamon eyes.

"Yes Loyal!" he exclaimed without noticing that it didn't make sense. She frowned up at him.

"What is it Rage!?"

"He was there!"

"Who?" she asked, her heart beat quickened.

"Quest... The man who knew Treasure, is here in Hawthorn! One of the men who was with Nity from the very beginning!" his eyes shone. "Can you imagine it!? A man as important as Est here in Hawthorn - he was one of Nity's closest friends. He has answered the question of what became of Nity!"

For a moment Loy said nothing. "Is that why he came? To answer questions?"

In the back of Courage's mind, it bothered him that Loy wasn't excited and again he failed to note the strange expression on Loyal's face. He stepped away from her.

"No, he came to warn us of danger - that man, Horizon, is coming closer. He will try to arrest all those who follow Nity... Est also brought two fugitives from Garason. One of the local leaders, Trust, invited them into his cottage, it could mean his arrest if they are found - but he did it anyways," he said in a faraway voice.

Loyal swallowed hard. "What are you going to do?" she asked in fear.

Even still Rage misunderstood her. "We are all well prepared - Rizon will not find us, nor Favour. Not a single one of us!"

Loyal nodded in a sudden and jerky movement. "Good night, Rage," she said and turned to leave.

Rage hesitated only a moment then called to her. She looked at him and was surprised at what she saw; his face was open... undisguised by pride - open with nothing to hide. He walked to her slowly and cradled her long face in his hands.

"This is a good thing for us, Loyal. A very good thing." He then leaned close and brushed his lips on her forehead, the tenderness he showed her in that moment made her heart feel lighter than a lark. For a moment she stood absolutely still, then turned and closed the door behind her, she leaned against it and gasped for a breath.

What was she doing!? How could she spy on her own husband like this? She held her breath and blinked rapidly, sudden tears spilling out, her beautiful face was twisted in an inner pain she had never felt before, and her heart.... Her heart was so heavy, even the news of Nity did not lighten it. I must tell him! The thought was loud and firm in her mind.

But doubt is a powerful force, and even as she straightened and turned back to the door, doubt flooded over her. Favour's threat was real; his guards were always there watching - there was Promise to think of! What if they harmed her!? Favour had threatened imprisonment for rebel activity... What if Rage challenged Favour to a duel for his threats? She was not worried that Rage would lose such a fight - but what would happen to them all after he won!? Scenes of being run out of the village by soldiers flashed across her mind, then there was blood; if Rage killed a lord, they would not survive ...

She drew her hand back from the door. The only way to save Rage and Promise, was to do as Fav had asked. She bit her bottom lip. "This is the only way," she whispered.

*   *   *

Thrive sighed and looked out the carriage window with boredom, his driver was going at a comfortably slow pace so that the bumps in the road were made softer. The countryside was of sloping grasslands and gentle hills. Thri could smell the sweet fragrance of wild flowers, and he inhaled gratefully. With some difficulty he turned back and tried to focus his attention on the tiresome lord sitting across from him in the carriage.

Two days ago Thrive had arrived in the village of Dahin overlooking the mouth of the Quy River where it emptied from the Quy Lake. The lord of the manor of Dahin had welcomed Thri with open arms (it had made Thri wary of him at once), and for the past two days had endeavored to keep Thri busy with anything but business! However, Thrive had managed to invite the nervous lord out on a carriage ride, with high hopes that he could get down to serious matters with him. Despite all his careful planning though, the lord (whose namesake was Consider) had talked non-stop for a whole hour now. He talked of everything and nothing, and kept up this prattle without exhaustion, giving Thri no chance to get a word in edgewise!

Thrive however, was a much wiser man, and he knew better than to try and cut in on Consider's mindless chatter and snorting laughter, instead he kept his dignity and sat silently. One would think that he was smiling politely every now and then - but really he was smiling in amusement at this rather small and irritating lord. When at long last Consider had stopped to take a breath, Thri spoke.

"I am sure that the price of eggs in Tarva will be very useful to me at some point in my life, my lord, but at the moment I am more interested in the price of eggs in your own village." His voice positively dripped with sarcasm, but he added a note of deadly seriousness. Consider took a deep breath to reply but stopped short and frowned at Thri in confusion. Thri grinned, showing his even white teeth.

"Yes, my lord," he said in mock reassurance. "I have noticed some rather shocking things about your neat little village of Dahin." Sid looked at him and gulped. Mercilessly Thri went on, with private amusement.

"I had hoped that this problem was a rare one - but it has become ever common in this region. Almost everywhere I go, nobility live in splendid wealth, while the villagers they are meant to protect and nourish, live in poverty and filth, begging for the right to live!" A heavy silence hung in the air between the two men. A disdainful look crossed Thri's handsome face.

"I expected such from pale Garatin lords - but of Tarven lords?!" Consider opened his mouth with a pleading expression upon his face.

"No, no, don't speak," Thri said raising one hand with impatience. "I've heard the explanations before and I have grown tired of them. You and too many others have gone unchecked for far too long," he said with emphasis. Across from him Sid appeared to be speechless.

"But really I would like to know, after you raised the serf's taxes so high, leaving them with scant to live on, then claim half of all sales made on all their livestock and fowl (so really it does come down to the price of eggs). But what I would like to know, is after you've bled them dry... what more do you expect to get from them!?" Thri kept his cool through it all, and watched Consider rather like a little boy watching a fly with torn off wings try to fly.

"My lord, I- I, well I..." Consider stammered.

"The question does not require an answer, my lord. You may remain silent," Thri said as though talking to a child. Sid's mouth shut with a snap, while his eyes widened. Thri smiled.

"I have decided to continue on in my travels," he said airily. "Send my things to Lord History's manor." He was cut off when Consider (who had regained his composure) spoke with insufferable arrogance.

"My lord," he said with a smug and over confident smile. "I am the Lord of Dahin, the villagers are MY serfs, unless the king - may his reign go on - has passed a new law, I may do what I please with my serfs. I have the right to control their taxes, in whatever way I deem." He smiled deeper, the effect was not pleasant.

For a moment Thri only watched him with lazy indifference, the smile he wore was matched in laziness. Something caught his eye from outside and when he looked he saw a beautiful horse prancing about in the field, his coat was a glossy black. A good ways behind him Thri could see a cottage.

"My lord Consider, have you ever heard the tale of the dark horse?" Sid frowned in confusion, but Thri went on. "The story is of a knight who captures and tames a horse - a dark horse." Silence stretched between them broken only by the sound of the carriage and horses. "The knight was cruel to this great beast, and soon forgot that this dark horse was once wild. One day the dark horse was offered sweet oats to eat, fine oil for his mane, silver for his bridle, and the chance to run free again, and the price for all this, was to betray the knight. Needless to say the dark horse did betray the knight, and was at last free from his cruelty. The knight lay dead, but the dark horse ran free with a silver bridle gleaming, his mane bathed in fine oil, and sweet oats in his saddle bag." Thri ended in a bitter-sweet voice.

"Yes... well," Consider said awkwardly. "We all love old tales, I am sure, however." He paused and raised his eyebrows in a gesture that said 'need I say more?' Thri's handsome face lost the bored indifference and he replaced it with bored disgust.

"The Garatin people would be much more willing to serve the king of Tarva if their stomachs were full," he said in a flat voice. "The King sent me to bring back reports on his lords, and to quiet rebellious whispers." He let it sink in before going on. "I will be returning here soon again, by then I hope to see your 'dark horse' better fed. DRIVER!" he called out sharply. The carriage slowed to a stop.

"Get out," he said quietly and strangely good-naturedly. Sid looked at him with wide eyes, it made Thri smile broadly. "I believe you heard me correctly, my lord."

Consider nodded, then with almost dumb movements he opened the carriage door and stumbled out. Almost at once the carriage started up again, this time at a faster pace. Outside the carriage, pounding horse hooves could be heard from the escorting guards from Garason. Thrive settled back into the bench seat, and sighed as he soaked in the sweet silence. Then he smiled as he thought of the embarrassment that Consider would have to endure at having to walk the mile and a half back to the village. The man had frustrated him to no end, and he was quite glad to be moving on. Outside in the field the black horse broke out in a reckless gallop and screamed.

* * *

"There is one other thing, he mentioned a man who is one of the leaders, his namesake is Trust..." Loyal paused.

"Yes? What about him?" Favour asked impatiently, Loy glanced past him to his guard standing nearby, like a hunting dog, waiting for his master to release him onto his prey. She looked away and continued. "He's the one hiding fugitives from Garason, in his cottage I believe."

Fav raised his brows, "Trus? That stuttering peasant? I should have known." He paused for a moment, his mind buzzing with this new information.

"And that's all you found out?" Favour asked.

Loy nodded, "Yes, that's all he told me," she said quietly.

Fav looked surprised for a moment, he then said mockingly, "Oh, he told you all this! He must really trust you."

Loy winced and Fav could see the shame burning her up.

"Don't worry now," he said as he patted her shoulder like she was a small child. "This really IS the lesser of two evils." He smiled, then he and his guard left her alone. Only when they had left did her face crumple, she covered it with her hands and wept.

Chapter 15   Castles of Sand

"They won't follow your advice or methods until they are convinced that they can trust you, a Tarven," Journey explained. Rage nodded his head slightly.

"We've never known a Tarven who wanted to help us before," Journ said with a raised brow.

Still Rage didn't speak. It had been two days since Quest had come to Hawthorn, and he had left only that morning to travel on to Shore leaving his two friends in the care of Trust. He had left the rebels of Hawthorn feeling strong and confident that all was not lost. Journ had told Rage at market that he must speak to him. So after market, Rage had taken out his horse Stream for a leisurely ride and had 'happened' to run into Journey out in the fields. Now Journ led Stream by his halter as if he was a stable boy, while Rage rode Stre and the two of them talked in quiet tones.

"You're suggesting I travel to Fray and meet with them face to face?"

Journ looked over his shoulder at Rage. "No, but I am asking you to," he said carefully.

Rage nodded. Just then Stream halted and pulled back on his halter, Journ lost his grip and turned in surprise to look at the horse, up to this point he had decided that Rage's horse was well mannered. But now Stream leaned forward and bent his front knees, Rage breathed a curse and jumped off his back. He did it just in time too, for just then Stre rolled over onto his back! His back legs stuck up in the air and he tucked his front legs in close, he then thrashed his head about, both Journ and Rage stepped well away from him. Stream laid still for a moment and looked up at Rage with large bored eyes.

"Fool horse," Rage said. Almost in response Stre snorted and began thrashing about with renewed vigor. The two men watched him, Rage with dry irritation and Journ with ill-hid amusement.

"You want me to teach the rebels in Fray what I taught you here?" Rage asked suddenly.

"Yes, it could save their lives if Rizon should travel that far north. The codes and escape plans you have taught to us, could save them from the lord of Fray just as they have saved us from Favour. They, like us before you came, have no idea how to protect themselves. They will of course have a mistrust of you at first, but I will send a letter with you vouching for you." There was a moment's silence, even Stream stayed still.

"Is the lord of Fray Garatin?" Rage asked at last.

"No, he is Tarven, by the namesake of Esteem." For a moment Journ watched Courage's face change as he thought it all over. Journ knew better than to try and hurry the process up.

"It will prove hard to convince Favour to let me go there, with no other reason than to trade; it's outside of my trade routes."

"I think he will allow it, he's afraid of you," Journ said shrewdly. "If I know him at all, he is afraid that you have more power than you have said you have."

Rage sighed, "He has no reason to fear that. Despite what I was in the past, I am a tradesman." Again they were silent, Stre seemingly having had enough of a roll, had begun the awkward process of standing up again.

"Why are you so hesitant to do this?" Journ asked suddenly.

Rage couldn't answer that - not to Journ at least. The truth was that he didn't want to risk his personal life in all of this, like he had in Garason; he was afraid of losing everything in such a risk as going to Fray would be...

For long moments the three of them stood there; Stream standing there blinking in boredom, Journ slowly brushing the dust off of the horse, and Rage looking off over the fields battling within himself against forces that couldn't be seen.

Courage was a man of strength, a man with a sharp mind made for battle. Very few times in his life had he ever come up against a problem that he could not fix on his own. He could fight men twice his size and still come out on top. Fear was something he despised, but at that moment Rage could see plainly that he was afraid. Afraid that Favour would see right through him - afraid that Favour knew all about him. Afraid all he had built would be lost again. Afraid...

Suddenly Rage tightened his jaw: since when had he let fear control him? "Yes I will go," he said suddenly.

Journey smiled, he had had a feeling that Rage would help. He was still far from understanding this Tarven in all his complexities. Although, he did have a nagging fear that when it came down to it Rage was not fully committed to the cause of Nity. Journ pushed the thought aside at once, Rage was trustworthy.

*   *   *

Loyal stood before her window with the panes opened wide, and the wind blew in her face. The tears streaming down her long face felt cold as the wind blew across them, but she didn't try to brush them aside; more would only come. In her heart she felt a dull ache - but it was not quite pain, more like emptiness. She took in a shuddering breath, and wondered how it was that she felt so suddenly old.

Just then Promise entered the chambers, her dark eyes took in the room in one sweeping glance. When she spotted her mother she took a step forward and opened her mouth to speak. But she stopped short in surprise. Her mother's shoulders shook and Mise was certain that she could hear her sniffling! For a moment Mise stood absolutely still - paralyzed almost, what should she do? Very few times had Mise seen her mother cry, and those times that she had seen her cry, the reason for her mother's tears had been clear - but why in the king's namesake would her mother be crying now!?

Promise knew that she ought to go to her mother and comfort her as best she could... but she didn't want to. Whatever her mother was upset about, Mise didn't really want to know... No, Mise did not want to know. In that moment Mise felt like she was holding a castle of sand to stop it from crumbling away. Mise was comfortable where she was, silently she backed up and shut the chamber door softly, as if by closing it she could protect her castle of sand.

Loyal never knew that her daughter had been in the room; she stood there allowing her mind to go blank. For a few sweet moments she didn't know who she was, or what she had done. With a deep breath she forced her mind to focus on reality - it was not a pleasant thing to do, but she had no other choice. Behind her she heard the chamber door open and close.

"Loyal, Fav has granted me my request to go north - I didn't think he would, but he did," Courage said with a touch of astonishment.

Tell him the truth! A voice seemed to shout in Loy's mind, her heart pounded to an erratic beat, and the words formed in her mouth.

"I had almost hoped that Favour would not allow it..." Rage sounded unsure- a strange thing for him indeed. The words of confession died away on Loyal's lips; Rage was being so... open and honest with her! It was a feeling like no other, to know that her husband trusted her, and respected her and even loved her enough to tell her private things about his life. 'How would he react if I told him the truth?' The question gnawed at her and the seeds of doubt grew. Quickly and gently she brushed the tears from her face and turned to look at him. His face changed as he took in her red rimmed eyes.

"Let me go with you!" she whispered fiercely. He frowned in confusion.

"I will return in a short time."

She took a step towards him and spoke pleadingly, "Rage please, let me go with you to Fray."

His face softened and he moved to stand in front of her, he took her hands in his and was surprised; they were trembling.

"Loy… there is no need to be afraid." His voice was low and calming as though talking to a frightened child. "I will return from Fray in little more than a week." He stopped short when she shook her head.

"Please, Courage - let me go with you," she said it slowly and beseechingly. He frowned a little.

"I want to be with - and help you." She choked on the words, but they had the right effect on Rage, he looked surprised and touched by her words.

Gently he touched her face with his fingertips.

"Alright Loyal," he said soothingly. "Yes you will come with me to Fray." She looked deeply relieved, vaguely he wondered why. "But what of Mise?" he asked.

She looked surprised, as if she didn't know of whom he was speaking about, but the moment passed almost too quickly for him to notice.

"There is no need for her to come."

He nodded, "Alright, I will ask Favour to take her as a ward of the manor."

'Fav would surely agree' Loyal thought and she dismissed the issue quickly, leaning forward she rested her head on his chest, in return he placed his arms around her. But she found little peace.

*   *   *

Favour bounced his booted foot slowly, the fire's light made the boot shine. He sat comfortably in a low backed chair with his feet up resting on the arm rest of another chair. His private chambers were silent and dark except for the fire's glow. Cool night air drifted in through slightly opened windows. The only sound was the fire cracking the wood, and Favour's slow even breathing. For the first time in several months he was free from nervous uncertainty, but never-the-less his Garatin face was dark in thought. One of his hands held up his round chin while the other carefully traced the deep carvings in his arm rest with his fingertips.

His mind worked slowly but methodically over his plans, he had always been devious and sly - but never before had the stakes been this high! It was a few hours after sundown, although it felt like a life time had passed by since the sun had risen that morning - so much had happened that day. And, he thought with pleasure, all of it had been good - for him. As long as he kept Loyal scared (and he was certain that he could) he didn't think she would tell her husband the truth.

"She doesn't have the backbone" he muttered. He was also certain that he had Courage completely fooled! When Rage had come to him earlier and requested an extra trade route to Fray - Favour had told him that he would think on it. As soon as Rage had left, Fav had sent for Loyal. He had been quick and to the point with her, and with only a little hesitation on her part, she told him all she knew on the matter of Fray. Then he had quickly made his plans. And Loyal had gone along - quite nicely at that! Everything was just as he had wanted; Rage would travel to Fray with his wife, and would meet with the rebels there. But while they were still on the road Loyal would find out all she could from Rage about the upcoming meeting, then send a letter back to him reporting all she had found out. Rage would be completely blind to it all. Then Fav would have the information he needed to not only expose the rebels in his own village but in Fray as well! In so doing proving to Tarva that he was very much in control of the entire area, and perhaps they would reward him.

Favour paused for a moment in his thinking… he had not given thought to the young maiden though – was it Secret? No, her namesake was Promise. He had not even considered what Courage and Loyal would do with their daughter, and had been surprised when Rage had asked if she could stay in Hawthorn as a ward. But now, as Favour thought it over, he began to like the idea very much. The young maiden was not betrothed to anyone, so no one was looking out for her…

'Of course' Fav thought with a cruel smile, 'no harm will come to the girl - so long as Loyal cooperates.' Yes, it was perfect, one last thing he could fling in Loyal's face should she begin to have second thoughts. And if she proved to be helpful after all - then she need never know about this little back-up plan.

Favour went over his plans one last time, then he turned his thoughts to his future - and a bright future it was beginning to look! He closed his eyes and indulged for a moment in dreaming about what his life would soon be like. He surveyed these thoughts and plans much the same way a child would look over a city he had just built, only unlike a child, Favour didn't realize that this future was just castles of sand. One day, the wind would blow and Favour would be left with nothing.

*   *   *

Remember looked up at the manor walls wondering if any of Favour's men were watching her. If there were, she didn't see any. Readjusting the basket on her arm Ember passed under the manor gate into the courtyard. She nodded once or twice to the few people about as she made her way to the kitchen side door. Standing by the door was the manor's head cook talking to a woman from the village.

Pausing beside them Ember waited patiently for them to finish talking. But as soon as they saw her, the head cook and the other woman stopped talking and stared at her. Ember felt a little embarrassed, she supposed they had been talking about something private.

Clearing her throat Ember spoke. "Good morrow Vision, Cherish." She addressed both women warmly. The head cook, Cherish, forced a smile and nodded but the other woman made no such attempt at pleasantness. Ember shifted her feet, 'what have I said wrong?' she wondered nervously.

"I just came by to sell our radishes and spinach... since they're ready to eat..." she said awkwardly, when neither woman said anything. Suddenly both women looked very uncomfortable themselves, the head cook looked at the other woman who shifted the basket hanging off her arm but she said nothing. Finally, the head cook cleared her throat.

"You're a few moments too late Remember. I've already paid Vision for her radishes and spinach," she said as she took hold of Vison's basket and gave it a slight shake as if to prove her words. Ember frowned.

"But... you've always bought from me before too - surely you still need more." She smiled, but her eyebrows were still pinched. The head cook huffed a sigh and the other woman looked at her with sharp disapproval.

"Look Ember," the head cook said heavily. "Your brother...well,

148

let's just face it, your family is the cause of all trouble in Hawthorn, and has been for years. When Van stole his lordship's stallion - you see I have no choice - his lordship has ordered me not to have anything to do with you and your family." Ember looked from her to the other woman in shock, it had been a month since the whole mess with Van, she hadn't thought it was still an issue.

"But... you've always bought from me before!" she repeated - this wasn't fair! "Who will I sell to if not you!? Please we need the money!" her voice betrayed her panic, the head cook shook her head and turned away without a word, while the other woman gave her one last disapproving stare, then she left too.

Ember stood in the courtyard alone with a look of shock and panic on her long face. She wandered back through the village slowly running it over and over in her mind - how could Favour do this!? Wasn't it enough that he had taken their horse and mule? What would she tell her mother?

Reaching the fence that enclosed her cottage yard she looked up and paused. Imagine was just coming out of the stable, the two of them were the only two in the front yard. For a moment Mag stood in the open door of the stable, he looked troubled and didn't seem to notice her. Then Mag, with recklessness that was not his own, turned on his heel and began to march to the cottage. From where Ember stood she could see him plainly, however the stable door was opened and sat right in Mag's way. With a swiftness that stunned her, Mag walked straight into the door! She heard the sickening thud of his head against the wood, and the whole door shook on its hinges from the impact. Almost comically Mag fell backwards, his legs crumpled awkwardly against the door while his arms sprawled out beside him; Mag lay motionless.

After a moment of shock Ember dropped her basket and ran to her brother, falling to her knees beside him, she called out his name and shook his shoulders. After only a few seconds Mag groaned and with much effort sat up. Ember stared at him with fearful eyes.

"Are you alright Mag!?" she asked frantically. He shook his head as if to clear it, he then grinned weakly.

"Yeah of course - I just didn't see it, that's all." Her gaze turned to astonishment.

"Didn't see it!? How could you see anything else?"

"I didn't," he said quietly, a very somber look on his face.

Ember frowned, and noticed at the same time that Mag's eyes seemed to be a darker blue than normal - maybe it was just the lighting.

"What do you mean?"

He shook his head, "Nothing! I'm alright."

Stubbornness took over her pale face, "No, Mag! Tell me - what did you mean 'you couldn't see anything'!?"

Slowly he looked at her, and she felt a dread take hold of her - but she needed to know. "Mag…" she said quietly but firmly, "You're not telling me something, what's wrong?"

With a look of defeat mixed with weary relief he stood to his feet and pulled her up with him. Then with a tender hand to the bump that was already beginning to swell on his head he went back into the stable. Ember followed him. Seated on over-turned crates, there was no one else besides Ember who heard Mag's low and halting words.

"It started a little while ago… I don't know why, but I keep losing my sight!" the fear and panic could be clearly heard in his voice, Ember didn't know what to say. "At first, it was blurriness for just a few moments - but now…" Ember swallowed hard, and Mag looked at her almost pleadingly. "It's gotten worse. For minutes at a time now I can't see a thing. Ember I think - I think I'm going blind!" he whispered in horror.

Remember felt stricken, she could only hope it didn't show on her face. Blind… the word seemed to whisper in her head over and over in a mocking voice. What would they do if Mag went blind!? How would they live - how would he live? The sun would set that night - but Ember was not at all sure that it would ever rise again.

"Ember - you can't tell anyone! No one knows - no one has to know, you understand? Please…"

Numbly she nodded her head. Gently Mag pulled her close and hugged her.

"It will be all right," he whispered to her, and she clung to him.

"Favour has forbidden the head cook to buy anything from us…" she whispered after a moment. He pulled back and looked at her. Ember shook her head.

"She won't have anything to do with us." Mag clenched his teeth and turned away. Putting his hands on his hips he said with a voice that wasn't quite steady, "We had better go tell mother then."

*   *   *

Down the streets of Hawthorn on that same day, far from the lives of peasants, in the courtyard of the manor, Promise bid farewell to her father and mother. She stood and watched as her father drove their wagon out of the manor courtyard, their riding-horses tied to the back. Mise stood perfectly still as a Tarven maiden should, only raising her slender arm in a final wave as they exited the Manor gateway. She stood still for a moment longer after they had disappeared, then with a tiny smile she turned on her heel and glided back into the manor. She hurried through the hallways - much too quickly to be lady like - until she reached her own chambers, where at last she closed the door softly behind her and smiled broadly.

Her parents would return in one - maybe two weeks' time - but until then... Mise left the thought unfinished. She felt high-spirited and free, able to fly if only she had a mind to try it! Going to stand in front of a looking glass she gazed back at her own reflection and was pleased with what she saw. She wore her best dress, and her dark hair was tied up in complex twists and curls - it felt strange, and normally she would have tugged and pulled at it till it all tumbled down. She would rather wear her hair down or tied back with just a simple ribbon - but a true lady always had her hair done up - and for that reason, so too would she.

With a sudden burst that seemed to come from deep within, she turned about and spun. First she hugged her arms to herself then she let them fly out, closing her eyes she giggled, half at herself, and partly for no reason at all! Stopping abruptly, she watched as her deep mauve skirts spun tightly about her legs.

"Who knows father," she whispered mischievously, "Perhaps when you return, I'll have taken care of the matter of my betrothal myself, since you seem too preoccupied to bother about it." But in truth she really couldn't make herself be angry at her father - not today, even if he had asked her to go to a rebel meeting - after all that was only if someone contacted her, and Mise was sure that that wouldn't happen. Even after her father had shared the news of Nity, Mise had failed to feel much excitement. There was a time when she would have asked a thousand questions, but now it didn't seem that important.

Chapter 16   A High Tide

Favour sat back suddenly with shock, and with a touch of wonder he ran his thumb over the seal of ambassador Sinister of Tarva. The seal was large and weighed down the paper that Fav held. Rizon's arrival upset his plans... 'but perhaps' he thought, 'some good may yet come of the situation.' He looked up at the man who had so abruptly disturbed the night. He stood still and unmoving, his pale Garatin face and cold blue eyes gave away nothing. Favour smiled suddenly, and truth be told it was a genuine smile.

"If it is rebels you have come for - Hawthorn is indeed afflicted with them! You have my full permission to make arrests here." The words were just for the sake of courtesy, Fav had no choice but to cooperate, and they both knew it. "I will provide you with escorts and a prison wagon at once. I wish you success."

Horizon bowed his head respectfully, but he didn't move his hands from behind his back, as if he found it too much effort. "I assume, my lord, that you can also provide me with information on where I might find the rebels. And please do not misunderstand, I am not here for just any rebels, but for the Nity followers."

Favour chewed on his lip for a moment. "I do have an informant who tells me there are two Nity follower fugitives from Garason hiding here with one of the rebel leaders; his namesake is Trust."

*   *   *

Remember pulled the needle through her little brother's tunic sleeve, until the thread was tight again, she sat up straight and sighed. She liked doing the mending in the daytime when there was lots of light, but there were so many other chores more important to be done in the daytime! And so, she was forced to do the mending at night by firelight. Ember looked up and watched as Mag chipped away at a stick, he carefully collected each curled chip to later use as kindling. He was slow and precise with his knife; Ember was put at ease; there was nothing wrong with his vision at that moment. He looked up at her, the fire lighted a flame in his blue eyes, his face was dark, and he knew what she was thinking.

With a sigh she went back to mending the hole in Survive's tunic. Just then Perilous, looking tired, opened the door from her bedroom.

"Van?" she called up the ladder to the loft. Her youngest daughter and son poked their heads out and peered down at their mother.

"Vanished isn't up here," Vive said quietly. Both Ember and Mag sat up and looked at Peri, she frowned and looked about the room.

"Where is he? It's late," she said almost talking to herself.

After a moment's hesitation Mag stood up and said, "I'll go out and look for him." Stepping to the door, he had it half open before Ember jumped up and said hurriedly, "I'll go with you!" Taking up a brown shawl and tying it in a knot about her slim shoulders, she went to stand at his side. He opened his mouth to protest, but the look she gave him stopped him. She was worried that he would lose his sight.

"Alright," he said. After checking the yard behind their cottage and in the stable and finding both empty, they went out into the street. They walked quickly; Hawthorn was much too small of a village to have a curfew, but still, it was frowned upon to be out late without good reason. And more trouble with Lord Favour was the last thing they needed!

"Do you know where he is?" Ember asked as she worked to keep up with his quick pace, and pulled her shawl closer against the night air.

"No, but his friend's cottage is this way, he might be there - he should know better than to be out now though!" He glanced about at the dark cottages, and said in a hushed voice, "Look, keep your voice down - I don't know what he's up to, but I would rather not have to explain it to anyone - whatever it is!"

Ember frowned. Van! She thought in frustration, what are you doing!? They hurried down one street then another. Mag looked around suddenly, something told him that all was not right. He stopped abruptly, behind him Ember bumped into him, her bare feet making an eerie slapping sound on the cobble stones. For a moment they stood still, then Ember grabbed hold of his arm in fear - for they both heard it.

Low voices with an edge of demand, restless horse hooves, the soft roar of torches and the clink of chains... Mag and Ember looked about themselves with wide eyes, but the sounds were muffled - they were coming from the next street over - all but one sound. Just then Van jumped out from between two cottages and nearly knocked them down. Vanished looked wide eyed and frightened.

"Mag!" he exclaimed in an odd hushed tone. Mag grabbed hold of him.

"What's happening!?" he demanded in the same tone.

"He's here - he's come to take us all away!" Van replied in horror. "Who!?"

"Horizon."

For a moment no one made a sound. Ember watched Mag's face and she saw something change, a hardness seemed to settle into his very being. Wordlessly Mag turned and disappeared between the two cottages from where Van had come. Without hesitation Ember followed him. For a moment Van stood there panting, then he swallowed hard and went after them.

On the other side of the cottages the three of them hid in the shadows and looked at the procession that was moving down the street away from them. There were several men on horseback, most seemed to be Favour's guards, and following close behind was a wagon - a prison wagon. Even as they watched, the guards came to a halt in front of a cottage.

Mag grabbed Van's arm with surprising strength, "Trust lives there! Those two men from Garason are staying in his cottage!" His voice sounded hoarse and panicked - but there was nothing to be done.

The guards pounded on the cottage door until a frightened and bewildered Trus opened it, and the guards rattled off a well-rehearsed order of arrest. Mag turned to his brother and sister.

"Listen!" he whispered fiercely. "Go - warn the others! Van, tell Mory to lock up her cellar, then warn everyone south of here - then go home. Ember run! Run as fast as you can home…" he turned away from them to look at Trust. He whispered barely loud enough to be heard, "Mother will know what to do."

"What will you do?" Van asked.

"I'll warn everyone to the east, and return back home as soon as I can - now go!" After a moment of hesitation both Ember and Van turned tail and ran. Mag stayed where he was and watched as Trust was shoved roughly into the prison wagon. What happened next, Mag would never be able to forget, and he would have never been able to prepare himself for the shock and horror of it all. He had steeled himself to the possible arrest of the rebel men, but he had not considered that their families would also suffer their fate.

Seemingly without feelings the guards pulled from the cottage Trust's tiny wife, five daughters and young son as well as the two rebels from Garason… Trus's wife crumpled in a corner of the wagon and wept while holding their young frightened son close. Trust's daughters, ranging from sixteen to eight years, all wept and cried out in strangled and panicked voices.

No! Mag wanted to cry out - this wasn't right! He had grown up with Trust's daughters, and they were not strong enough to survive this! It wasn't fair - not fair at all that this should happen to such gentle and meek folk! But despite his righteous anger, Mag could find no courage to voice it. He watched with his heart in throat as the guards ransacked the cottage for anything of value. One guard was left outside, but he paid those in the wagon little heed. Mag needed to get to Trus - he had to. Darting from shadow to shadow he was able to draw near to the wagon without being noticed. With the wagon between him and the guard, he crept up and grabbed hold of the rusty bars.

"Trust!" he whispered.

Trus looked up and around till he caught sight of him, two of the girls gasped softly and even gazed at him hopeful - it tore him up inside. One of the two rebels looked very sick while the other one kept an eye out for the guards as Trust crawled across the wagon, casting frightful eyes on the lone guard's turned back.

"Trus - I... how?" he felt as lost as a small child. Trus shook his head and reached out a trembling hand and touched Mag's shoulder through the bars. Mag fell still as he gazed up into Trust's pale and fearful blue eyes, the man shook like a brown leaf in the wind. Mag felt overwhelmed by guilt, and a deep sense of unfairness. His eyes traveled over the young women behind the bars, they huddled in the dirty straw and only breathed in tiny panicked animal breaths. Their eyes already held an empty glazed-over stare of people who had forgotten how to live without fear. If only they hadn't taken in the two men!

"This shouldn't have happened!" Mag whispered in a fierce yet despaired voice.

"W-we knew wh-what it meant to-to follow Nity. We u-understood the-he risks of it-it all." His stutter had never sounded so halting before, but somehow it commanded that Mag listen like he never had.

"W-we knew the r-risks, as d-did your f-father."

Mag felt like he had been hit hard in the stomach! What was Trus saying!?

"Imagine- y-you have lived t-too long running f-from the t-truth.

Obedience- Dien; I d-do not believe that h-he would have done anyth-thing differently if he had known- and neither would I."

Mag seemed to be having a hard time drawing breath - even more than Trus seemed to be having. Trus raised his shaking hand and brushed Mag's face.

"Your eyes-" he breathed, "It's time you opened them!" The din of the guards ransacking the cottage stopped abruptly. "Run!" Those were the last words that Trus ever spoke to the son of his long lost friend.

*   *   *

When she had been very young, someone had told Ember about the Nennor Sea and of the tides... it had given her dreadful nightmares as a child! Of running along so fast and for so long that her lungs felt as though they would burst - but no matter how far she ran or for how long, she would never escape the rising tide. Never once did she ever look back in those dreams, but she had known that the high-tide water gained on her swiftly, until it lapped at her heels, then the sand would begin sucking at her ankles!

It had been a long time since Remember had had such nightmares - or had even given thought to them - but now they came to her memory fresh and frightening as ever - because now, it felt as though it were really happening. After leaving her brothers she had slipped through the village easily as a cat, and she had only been but one minute from her cottage when she had taken a chance and stepped out in the open street. Next it had felt like her heart exploded inside her! For of course there was more than one group of guards sent out to arrest the rebels. Ember was spotted by five of the manor guards and ordered to halt, it was like her nerves gave way at their order and she bolted! The guards began chasing her at once, but she had a good head start on them, big enough so she could think clearly. She was so close to home - but she couldn't lead them there, she darted down the street that lead up to the manor - and away from the cottage.

Her feet pounded on the cobble stones and her breath seemed to labor to keep up with her. She could hear the guards clamoring after her and shouting at her to halt. But just like in her childhood nightmares, she couldn't bring herself to look back; the tide was rising, and Ember feared that they would all drown. In that moment all she wanted to do was give in - but her feet wouldn't stop, and they carried her fast away, until she turned a corner. Then she ducked behind a great big crate and huddled there till the guards ran past.

She remained in her hiding spot for what seemed a long time, her face buried in her arms and her eyes shut, while her lungs dragged air in... and back out again

"It's alright little Ember!" Dien shifted so that he was closer to her in the loft, she looked up at him with wild eyes and whimpered. He reached out and held her close against him. "It's alright, it was only a dream! I'm here now," he whispered softly. Ember wrapped her little five-year-old arms around his neck and held tight.

Then... she breathed.

*   *   *

Remember paused at her cottage front door to look over her shoulder at the empty street and felt immense relief, she had lost the guards! But as she stood still a noise came to her ears... it was distant and unclear, but it was the sound of an unsettled village; horses' prancing, the dull roar of torches and sharp voices. Ember caught her breath, then hurried inside.

Her children could never understand how a simple village maiden had ever become so strong in times of trouble, but they would never truly fathom just how much of a warrior's heart Peri really had. Mag had been right to put his trust in his mother. For the moment that Ember told her what was happening, Peri sprang into action like she had been waiting for this her whole life!

"Ember go up into the loft with your sister and brother and all of you pretend to be fast asleep!" her voice was calm and commanding all at once. Ember flashed her a look of astonished confusion, but did as her mother said. Up in the loft she found her youngest brother lying in his bed; stiff and flat, with eyes wide in fear, but it was her little sister who demanded Ember's attention. She sat in their bed hugging her knees and rocking back and forth, panting in panic. Ember pulled her close and hoped that her little sister couldn't sense the fear and panic that was in her. A shiver ran through her and she realized; she had lost her shawl! It must have come off when she was running away. Ember felt a nagging fear take her, she couldn't think of a good reason as to why, but she didn't want to leave her shawl out in the street for anyone to see. But there was nothing to be done - she couldn't go after it now. Biting back her fear she laid down and continued to hold her sister close.

Down below, Peri moved about quickly and without hesitation. She blew out the large candle on the table that she had left lit while waiting and she also poured a little water on the fire. It steamed and hissed, she stopped when it was small and it's light not so bright. It was then that Van came bursting into the cottage. He looked at his mother in surprise.

"Why are you still here!?" he half exclaimed, half demanded.

Swiftly Peri moved to close the door that Van had left wide open, she then turned to him.

"Keep your voice down Vanished!" she whispered fiercely.

He looked around almost in wonder then (much quieter) he stated, "We need to leave Hawthorn now! Before they come for us too!"

Peri grabbed his arm, "Listen to me Van, we don't know that they will come here. If we try and run, we will be caught for sure and they will know why we were running. But if we stay here there is a chance that they will not come here - no one who they arrest will betray us! We must believe that they do not know of our involvement - in which case we must lay low! If they hear us talking at this hour or see too much activity, then it will all be for not!" She looked hard at him to make certain that he understood. Van blinked then nodded his head.

"Good - now get up in the loft and don't make a sound!" she told him, not unkindly.

He climbed up and thought (not for the first time) of how smart and level headed his mother was. He lay down and was surprised to find that he was out of breath! Across the loft he heard Ember's soft voice.

"Van..." he looked over and in the dark he could make out her pale face.

"Where's Mag?" she asked fearfully.

It gave Van a start as he realized that his oldest brother was not in his bed. He had just assumed that Mag would be here when he got back... had something happened!?

It was a full half hour later when Mag crept in through the back door of the cottage, he felt emptied of every bit of strength that he had. Peri jumped up and ran to him at once and he held her close and found comfort.

"Are you alright!?" she whispered looking him up and down.

He held a brown shawl in one hand. He nodded wearily.

"I just had to hide for a bit before I could get back here... what are we going to do? Trust and his whole family were taken along with the two men from Garason, and who knows who else... what are we going to do?" Peri laid a hand against his face, after a moment she said in a voice of steel.

"We *will* survive this, Mag. And should the day come when we can't, then we will give ourselves over to Eloi - but! Until that day, we will trust him to carry us through!"

How could she have such stalwart faith? But Mag nodded just the same, even though his heart still felt heavy as lead. Peri gripped his shoulder.

"If they were coming for us they would have done so by now. You did well."

With that Peri went into her room and Mag climbed up into the loft. Even as he went to his bed he could feel Ember and Van looking at him. Bending over he spread Ember's shawl over her (he had found it on the street and recognized it as hers), she reached up and touched his hand as he turned away. Finding his and Van's bed in the dark he all but collapsed onto his side and breathed deep. He was a little startled when Van laid a hand on his shoulder, he turned to him and saw that his brother was half sitting up looking at him.

Mag lay still waiting for his brother to say something, but Van only gazed at his brother with intense eyes.

Mag managed a weak smile, and whispered, "I'm alright Van. I'm alright." Suddenly Imagine's heart didn't feel quite so heavy knowing that his brother - Van of all people - was looking out for him.

He lay back down and Trust's last words played over in his mind, he shut his eyes; the truth was unbearable! Trus knew what he was doing, and was willing to give up everything, just like his father. Mag pushed the thought away.

*　　　　*　　　　*

Promise sat on a stone bench in the garden reading an old Tarven book of poetry. She sat straight and looked elegant with the manor rising behind her and the garden spreading out in front of her. She had been sitting outside enjoying the sun and trying hopelessly to understand the poems. Each poem went on for pages and pages; the words began to slide into each other until Mise couldn't remember what the whole poem was even about! She had lost the rhythm of the poem long ago and now it only seemed to be a mess of ill planned words. She sighed and concentrated on the poem again hoping to at least finish it!

It was then that voices invaded upon the silence. Mise tried to block them out, but her wandering mind seemed to work against her. Before she knew it, she was only looking at her book and was listening to the conversation that was going on somewhere behind her. She recognized Lord Favour's voice almost at once but the other was unknown to her; they were speaking on a low open terrace.

"... I had really hoped for more, my lord. Striking at night has always thrown the other rebels into a panic making them much easier to find. But it was as though the village slept last night." The voice she didn't know sounded (although polite) disdainful. Favour spoke with a confidence that was sickening.

"Fear not, after all that happened last night, the rebels that are left will call a meeting tonight. I have not been able to find out the location of their meetings. But, I know they must be either in the Inn, the bakehouse or one or two cottages that are big enough in the village. I will send guards to each of these places tonight. And... if we find no one, well, then we can rest assured that all that is left of the rebels have given up."

Mise didn't move a muscle, she only stared down at her book - she didn't dare look behind her! Her heart beat fast and she felt a strange sense of excitement rising within - mixed with danger. Mise sat still as could be for what seemed a very long time. Slowly the voices began to grow faint, at last she stood up and turned about to look at the terrace; it was empty. Then like an arrow being loosed, she broke out into a quick walk, her face was set and her eyes determined. She walked so fast that people began looking at her all through the manor, but that didn't deter her from reaching her chambers as quick as she could. Only then did she realize that she had left her book behind in the garden - oh well, she thought, she didn't like the book anyways!

Her mind worked quickly trying to form a plan, she paced and frowned to herself. At last she forced her mind to think clearly.

"One of the rebels is the bakehouse keeper - that's what father said," she said to herself. "They have to be warned! They need to be warned..." She could hardly believe what she was thinking - it all seemed unreal to her, but just the same she knew what she needed to do. Even if she didn't want to be involved in the movement - she had to warn them! Her face held in determination, she flew open the lid of a trunk from which she pulled out a plain and simple dark blue skirt, a baggy light blue tunic and a braided belt of leather. After she had changed into it, she picked up a small looking glass and tried to decide how best to wear her hair. Finally, she pulled it out of the net that held it close to the back of her neck. She shook her head until her dark wavy hair fell about her shoulders, then she tied it back simply with a ribbon. She was satisfied with the result, when a thought struck her; her face was clean… if she was trying to look like a common villager - shouldn't her face be dirty? She thought it over, but it would be so undignified to smear dirt over her face!

With that she left her chambers and quickly made her way out of the manor. On her way she noticed several people giving her strange looks, and it occurred to her that she should leave by the servant's hallways. She was disgusted with herself to find that she didn't know how to get to the servant's hallways! It took her much longer then she intended to leave the manor, but at last she made it out into the village. She walked down the main street with head held high, and was slightly disturbed to notice that people were staring at her! That's when it hit her like a thunderclap; she was one of (if not) the only Tarven in Hawthorn.

She was glad that she didn't have anyone with her to experience her embarrassing oversight - but with determination born of her father she made her way to the bakehouse. At last she turned a corner and stopped as she looked over the little cottage. Over a little porch hung a sign that read "Mory's bakehouse". Suddenly she felt nervous about the whole thing. She looked around the street, she could see one or two other people about but they didn't seem to be watching her. She then squinted her eyes to try and see inside the cottage, but of course she couldn't see anyone. Licking her lips, she whispered something to Eloi about giving her strength, and then almost marched to the door of the bakehouse.

*　　　　*　　　　*

Journey carefully rubbed the deep creases in his forehead with his middle finger, his whole face spoke of worry and loss of sleep.

"Yes I believe that Trust and his family are being held in the manor," he said heavily. "But Mag… listen to yourself! You sound like Vanished, there is NO way that we could rescue anyone from the manor dungeons. And even if we could… what would we do then? We would only be hunted down, and then we all would be arrested."

Mag listened without trying to interrupt. He felt hopeless, he knew that there was nothing that could be done to save Trust, and yet he couldn't make himself accept it. He had asked Journ to meet him at the bakehouse. Journ always treated him with respect, and although he had enough to deal with already, he had come and listened to Mag's desperate idea and now that Mag had spoken it aloud he saw himself how impossible it was. Mag felt like he had been betrayed by Eloi... how could he let such a terrible thing happen?! How were they to go on?

Imagine and Journey were sitting in the private room of the bakehouse while Mory moved about in the front half of the cottage finishing off the day's business. Mag rested his head in his hands and heaved a sigh, he resented the idea that they could do nothing. Even as he sat there he felt anger take over and replace his hopelessness with seething rage. From the front of the cottage came Mory's sharp voice, it sounded like she was surprised and displeased. With a weary frown Journ got up from the table and passed through a doorway to see what the matter was. Mag stayed where he was, too consumed by his emotions to trouble about getting up.

But Journ's voice came to him; it sounded... troubled. Mag got up, with a dark frown marring his face, as he passed through the door he made an effort to calm himself. But what he saw rekindled his anger like a roaring fire!

Mory and Journ stood on either side of a stranger, Mory's face was set into deep suspicion and mistrust while Journ's kind face looked somewhat perplexed. And the stranger? Was a Tarven maiden! Everything about her instantly outraged Mag to the bone! She wore the simple clothes of a villager - but the way she held her head screamed superiority and arrogance. Her dark eyes flashed with challenge and defiance as if she was astonished that the whole world was not bowing down to her - such was how Mag first perceived the maiden. He marched toward her in unmasked resentment and fury.

"She does NOT belong here - GET OUT!" he thundered pointing an offending finger at her. The maiden held her ground and only stared him down with mild distaste. Mag felt like throwing himself at her in a lunge for her throat - but Journ quickly stepped in his way and all but held him back.

"Stop Mag! She's a friend!" Mag looked at him like he had just lost his mind, he had a great deal of respect for Journey - but, a 'friend'!?

"She is the daughter of Courage - the man who has proved to be a great friend to us," Journ said.

His voice was compelling Mag to believe - But the realization that this was the daughter of the Tarven trader - the one whom Mag owed so much - only made him even more furious. He almost flung his fiery gaze at the maiden.

"Tarvens will never be trustworthy!" he spat in contempt. In return the maiden seemed to shoot poison at him through her flashing eyes.

"It seems as though you need friends now more than ever - whomever they may be," her voice was smooth and brittle all at once.

It made Mag cold inside, and he instantly veiled his hatred to match her cool challenge. He stepped back and grated his teeth; it did little to reassure Journ.

"What proof do you have that you are Rage's daughter?" Mory asked with narrow eyes. The maiden looked at Mory rebelliously, and Journ quickly interrupted with his smooth and calming voice.

"Please my lady! We have proven rude and unfriendly to you, accept our apologies, I am Journey. This is Memory and... Imagine." His manners had the right effect on the little spitfire, Mag noticed. She looked at Journ and made a tiny bow.

"My namesake is Promise; I am the only child of Courage." She then pulled forth a small vial from around her neck. "I believe that the Cers'aren is your secret sign of allegiance." Inside the vial crumpled and yellowed Cers'aren petals could be seen. She looked back up at Mag with raised brow, she then tucked the vial away again. The Cers'aren was a sign of allegiance to the Garatin rebellion not Nity followers, even still Journ smiled.

"No more proof is needed Promise, who else could she be but Courage's daughter?" he said to Mory.

"So that's it? You're just going to trust her?" Mag asked in a low voice. It irritated him when Journ turned to him with a measure of impatience.

"Yes Mag, as I said, her father has proven a great and helpful friend, and is even now working for the cause. She will be welcomed at tonight's meeting and any other meeting," Journ said firmly.

"I'm afraid that there will be no meeting tonight," the girl said.

Everyone then turned a suspicious and astonished eye on her, she bore their gazes well.

"I have come to warn you," she gave Mag a hard glare. "Favour knows that you will be having a meeting here tonight; his men will search until they find you then Horizon will arrest you all." Mag felt his heart miss a beat in the silence that followed.

"You know this for certain?" Journ asked.

She nodded, "I heard it with my own ears, not one hour ago."

Journ turned to Mory, "We must get the word out not to come tonight."

Mag interrupted him, "And how would Favour know where we meet?" Journ looked at him, and Mory pursed her lips and looked at the girl.

"There is only one person that could have told Favour about our meetings." He looked meaningfully at the Tarven. She narrowed her eyes and opened her mouth in outrage.

"Are you suggesting that my father is a SPY?!"

"Are you suggesting that he is completely trustworthy?" he didn't miss a beat and he made sure that his voice had a calm mocking tone to it. "How else could Favour have found out about our meetings, and how else could Trust and the others be found so easily?" She opened her mouth to deliver what was sure to be a stinging remark, but Journ spoke first.

"That's enough! The only thing that matters now is that everyone is warned before sundown, that doesn't give us much time. Mory, hang your red carpet out your window to warn everyone in the town square like Rage taught us… We can't plan for another meeting until its safe. I'll go the way I came, through the back…" he then looked at the maiden as if he had forgotten her.

"Don't worry about her," Mag said suddenly in a cool voice. "I'll see that she gets back to the manor."

Promise glared at him, and Journ stiffened at once.

"Imagine- I." but Mory interrupted him in her stout voice.

"That's a good idea Mag - wouldn't want her getting lost."

Mag moved to the door and turned to give Promise a challenging stare, she met it with raised brow, and then she pranced out the door.

"Mag…" Journ said in one last attempt, Mag gave him a hard 'end of discussion' look, then followed the spitfire out into the street. He set a quick pace, and was slightly surprised when she kept up to him. She gave him a hard side glance.

"You need not escort me, I can find my way back just as easily as I found my way here."

A muscle in Mag's jaw twitched as he tried to suppress his anger. "Oh but I insist," he said. But he knew he sounded less than courteous, he could feel her murderous glance. Her mocking voice took him aback.

"And I thought gallant Garatins were as few as trustworthy Tarvens." Her sting found its mark.

Mag stepped into a narrow side street and roughly pulled her with him.

"You listen good now!" he gritted between clenched teeth, "You do NOT belong with us! Not you - and not your father!"

Her cinnamon eyes flashed hot anger, "How dare you?! I risked everything to warn you - people I have never met! I have as much right to follow Eternity as any of you - MORE in fact." She stared up at him daring him to say more, she then added in a much calmer and even reproachful voice. "And I will not be told what I can and cannot do by a pale faced boy." With that she walked back out into the street and continued on her way to the manor.

Mag stood there a moment longer almost in shock; how dare she? An insult like that was unforgivable! He may take that kind of thing from the villagers- but not from that Tarven GIRL! He hurried after her, disbelief written on his face, but once he reached her all he could do was fall into step beside her again. If she had been a man, a glorious fight would have followed... but Mag had no idea what to do when a woman insulted him! He glanced at her face; she wore an unbearable smug little smile.

His astonishment at being insulted by a woman had made him forget about his anger - but her smile made him remember at once. Together they strutted down the street both seeming to hold in check a great deal of hatred. Those who saw them couldn't help but notice the vast contrast between the two (and the oddity), some might even have likened them to night and day.

As they neared the manor gate, she made as though to go on through without so much as a glance at him - he couldn't let her have the last word! He reached out and grabbed hold of her arm, she swung around to face him - her eyes burning holes into him.

"I want you to understand one thing," he said quietly. "You may have Journey fooled but I know what you are. No matter what Journey said - you are NOT welcome at any of the meetings."

She returned his gaze for a moment before jerking her arm loose, she then flicked her hair in his face and turned on her heel and left.

Imagine jerked his head away as her hair whipped across his face, he took a levelling breath; never in his life had he met such an infuriating female before!

Promise collapsed into a chair as soon as she reached her chambers, took in an unsteady breath and closed her eyes; never in her life had she met such an arrogant and insufferable mutt before! The moment he had marched up waving his arms and pointing his finger, her legs had gone weak and tears had fought to spill. He made her feel so unwanted and little... she had wanted to run away - but knew that she would never have forgiven herself if she had! Even when he pulled her into the side street she had wanted to scream and run as fast as she could away from him... ah, but pride is so strong.

But, it gave her great pleasure to know that she could render him speechless in one biting comment. Pushing those thoughts aside she wondered at the change in her, just knowing that she had warned the rebels, and more than likely saved lives, gave her... a thrill!

Chapter 17   Eyes Open

Courage glanced up to where the manor sat half a mile away on a hill overlooking the village. Fray was really a nice village, the three dozen cottages were scattered about in a pleasant way, with worn dirt paths leading from door to door. It was hard to really see it in the dark but it had the feeling of a well lived yet remote kind of place. The manor was built as a military outpost of the Tarven army, and as such was small, compact and practical, without any rich foolery that Favour's manor portrayed. Rage instantly liked the village and manor of Fray, it was just his kind of place.

He glanced behind him at the little window that looked out over the driver's seat, but the shutters were still shut. Rage frowned in worry, on the first night on the road north, Loyal had retired into the wagon early saying she had a headache, by morning her head hurt so much that she couldn't even stand. For three days now she had been like that, and Rage hadn't the faintest idea of what could be wrong with her. All she had done was sleep, and she ate hardly at all.

Now it was well past sundown on the fourth day since they had left Hawthorn, and since they had slowed their pace to ease Loyal's pain, they had only now reached Fray. Rage was relieved; now Loyal could have the rest she needed and would soon get better. He shouldn't have let her come!

They left the tree line and the wagon bumped its way along the narrow road, Fray didn't seem to have as many fields as Hawthorn, but he could see fenced in pasture fields for cattle. In a few minutes he passed the first cottages of the village - the streets were empty and quiet. He slowed the two nameless draft horses down when they came upon the only building that could be the Inn. He looked about restlessly and wondered how soon he could get in contact with the rebels, for the sooner he did that the sooner he could take Loyal back to Hawthorn where she could really rest. But with an inward sigh he reminded himself that meeting with the rebels in Fray would take some work - after all they thought he was a Tarven spy! And between all that, he had to find time to trade; he couldn't go back to Hawthorn empty handed. He turned his attention back onto the Inn, and to his surprise, sitting under the porch of the Inn was a young Tarven man. Rage could tell by the way he was dressed that he must be a page or a squire. He sat on the top stone step leading up to the door, his shoulders were slumped over and his chin rested on his chest. The corner of Rage's mouth turned up, as the young man's slow even breathing turned to a soft snore. Rage wondered why someone from the manor would be waiting on the steps of the village Inn at such an hour.

He climbed down from the driver's bench quietly then made his way up the stone steps. The young man came out of his slumber with a start just as Rage was stepping around him. Rage stepped back as the young man jumped to his feet and snatched his feathered hat from his head.

"Good sir!" the young man exclaimed. "Forgive me I pray!" Rage raised one brow.

"You're forgiven," he stepped past him to knock on the Inn door- but before he could, the young page spoke on.

"Good sir... you are Lord Courage traveling from Hawthorn, are you not?" Rage turned sharply back around and glared down at the young man. Standing one step higher than the youth, Rage stood head and shoulders above him. A streak of annoyance and irritation ran through Rage and he said sharply.

"No! I am a tradesman." Disdain could be heard in the way he said it.

The young man's face went red with embarrassment, and he quickly tried to amend for the mistake.

"Of course, Courage - ah Lord Courage - I mean…. Good sir." He swallowed hard and tried again.

"My tongue slips." He made a little bow. "I am Justice, page to Lord Esteem of Fray, and because of his benevolent hospitality, he has sent me to escort you to his manor." He seemed relieved to finish his memorized invitation as he swung his arm in the direction of the manor.

Rage blinked in surprise; how would Lord Esteem know that he was coming?! Rage did his best to hide his suspicion and surprise from the page; he couldn't answer anything. Instead Rage nodded and said. "My Lady, is in the wagon- she is ill and tired from the road, she will need rest immediately." Justice smiled, and made an elaborate bow.

Rage should have felt pleased knowing that they would be staying in the manor instead of the Inn… But instead he felt a sense of foreboding, how had Esteem learned of his coming and why invite a tradesman into the manor?

*　　　　*　　　　*

Thrive's handsome face was drawn into a troubled frown as he stood leaning against the archway that led out to his own private balcony. That morning he had arrived at Lord History's manor, and for the first time he had liked what he had found. Thri had found that Lord History was an honest man and a good lord. His manor was small and its village was even smaller, but he was the lord of a large area and several other villages nearby.

Thri had been so relieved at finding an honest lord that he had decided to stay for a few days, but even still he was troubled. History's manor was (in some ways) no different from any of the others; in the face of every peasant - every Garatin had the same look. A look of fear, hatred, and bitterness. Always the same, never was there any change.

Garatin was not like the other countries under Tarven rule, the Garatin people had not accepted their new king. They lived like slaves waiting to be freed, choosing to fight rather than give in… the whole thing bothered Thrive terribly. Why did they have to fight? Why couldn't they just accept Tarva? Thri turned back to his writing desk and sitting down he began to write another letter.

'Young Dese, perhaps one day you will read all these letters that I have written to you, but I sincerely hope that you never fall prey to the unjustness and brutality that I have seen in this country. Even at your tender age you have already seen how Tarvens treat one another, but the way Tarvens treat the Garatins, is shameful.' Thri paused in his writing, and to look at him then, it might break your heart. For he was beholding the truth about his nation, and he found it ugly indeed.

'The Garatins treat us like barbarians, and it is well deserved for we act like barbarians. I didn't want to believe my people could be so brutal, but we are. My King (may he reign forever) has done little to win the hearts and loyalties of Garatins. Sixty years ago we marched in as victors taking our prize. Since then I had thought that Garatin had merged with Tarva and had become Tarven - but that is far from true.

The king will dub me Grand Duke upon my return should he be pleased with me. But I will have little peace of mind, for I see little that I can do to change this country.' Thrive looked up and evened out his face, that night there would be a banquet and he would have to smile and make pleasant conversation, as if all was well, for it seemed as though he was the only Tarven who looked at this truth with eyes wide open.

*   *   *

Courage felt the sweat forming on the back of his neck from the heat of the forge, as he waited for the blacksmith to say something - anything. At last the man looked up at Rage, and handed back the letter of introduction from Journey.

"Journey speaks highly of you," he said shortly.

Rage wanted to burst! 'Yes! The rebels in Hawthorn trust me - and you should too!' But Rage held back his frustration - it was the last thing that would help.

After a moment of hesitation, the blacksmith stuck out his thick, coal stained hand and said, "I'm Realize, and that's my apprentice, Earnestly."

As Rage took Realize's hand in his own he glanced at the younger man, Earnestly. Both rebels were weary of him, and Rage was certain he could see veiled hatred in the eyes of the younger man. But at least he had met with them - that was the first step, hopefully they could leave in a week's time. In two weeks, Rage thought with relief, all this would be over - he will have proven his worth and trustworthiness to both those in Fray and in Hawthorn. He would do whatever it took to prove he was on their side… then his life would continue the way it was. Rage never considered that maybe this would cost him so much more.

"To begin the training Journey mentions in the letter you will need to call a meeting. I can't train everyone - a group larger than six would draw attention, I will leave it to your judgement whom I will train, for family by family they must teach everyone else," he said, hoping to get the whole thing over with by the end of the week.

The blacksmith and his apprentice exchanged glances. "We can call a meeting together in a few days' time," Lize said.

Again Rage held back his frustration.

"I'll make sure to let you know when and where."

"Very well," Rage said tightly, then left. He wondered if Loyal would have recovered by the time they could leave - for she was still bedridden with fierce headaches.

The subject of rebels was foremost on Promise's mind that same night, she couldn't stop thinking about them, especially that boy! Just thinking of him and how rude he had been to her made her mad. It would take something catastrophic to get her further involved with the rebels - no matter what her father did. She tried to push those thoughts away, after all there was a banquet in the manor that she was to attend that night! Here was her chance to show off how lady like she was to the court. But she couldn't help but wonder if the rebels were still safe.

She looked at herself in her looking glass, the dress she wore was not one of her favorites but, it was the style for Tarven ladies to wear. And that's all Mise wanted to be that night; a true lady of Tarva. She would be as quiet as a mouse unless spoken to. She would remember all the steps to the dances, and would only dance a few times as a true lady should. She would be as graceful as... well as graceful as her mother!

True indeed, Promise did her Tarven name proud that night. She ate tiny little bites of food, she walked slowly and spoke little - and found herself bored to tears! No one seemed to notice her, the women wouldn't speak with her and when it came time to dance, she was left alone in her seat. She felt useless... very different from how she had felt after warning the rebels a few days ago. She tried to keep her face from betraying how she really felt, but she couldn't help it. Mise let her eyes wander the room, lingering on the dancers. Then she noticed a group of young maidens including the golden haired girl she had noticed before. They were whispering behind their hands and every once in a while they all looked at her!

Tears stung her eyes - she knew what they were saying, they thought she was just a common Tarven girl, pretending to be a lady - playing dress up, and wasn't it true? She had tried her hardest that night to be a true lady, but had gone unnoticed. She didn't belong here. Mise bit her lip, who was she fooling?

*   *   *

"My lady?" Loyal turned her head to see who had spoken. A handmaiden stood there watching her with anxious eyes.

"Is my lady feeling any better today? Do you think you could try eating something?" she asked hopefully.

Loy lay on a large bed, her dark hair fanned out beside her and her face had lost its glow. Even though it was late morning she still wore her bed clothes. She turned her head away as if it was very heavy.

"No, I do not wish to eat anything," she said in a dull voice. "Do not disturb me again today." The handmaiden nodded and turned away looking forlorn. Loy waited till her chamber door closed before she let a tear slide down her face. It had been a week since they had arrived in Fray, and Loyal had never felt so miserable in the whole of her life!

That first night on the road she really had had a terrible headache… but it had only lasted a day. Since then she had been pretending to be ill. But truthfully, she was ill, deep in her heart - how could she spy on her own husband!? How had her life come to this? Loy felt that she was at the end of all her strength. Even if she could think of a way out, she would never get there. Loy closed her eyes. She hadn't written Favour the letter that he had wanted. She told herself that she was ill and hadn't found the information that Fav had wanted. She couldn't tell Favour anything if she didn't know anything!

It was a weak defence, and deep inside Loyal knew it. She knew that one day she would have to face Favour again… But it was easier to forget her troubles, easier to let her mind wander away from reality, that way she could also forget her shame - her burning shame. The longer she pretended to be ill, the longer Rage was safe from her spying eyes, and the longer it would be before he found out the truth, and hate her for what she had done.

The truth was that it wasn't her head that was so very heavy - but her heart.

* * *

It was a day later, in the late morning, when Imagine, Remember and Vanished stood together in their stable, all wore the same grim face. At last Mag looked at his sister and brother and spoke in a low voice.

"There's nothing else to be said, they need to be warned."

Ember looked at him, concern shone in her wise eyes. "What good would it do? We knew he was coming and he still made arrests!" Ember said.

"But they don't know Horizon is coming!" Van argued.

"He's right, the village of Fray is so far from the rest of Garatin that they may well know nothing of Horizon."

Ember bit her lip, Mag had the look of unstoppable determination, and Van was little better! That morning she had come back from market with the piece of news that Horizon had left that morning traveling north; in four days the rebels in Fray would be helpless against his arrests - unless they were warned.

"But Mag!" she tried to talk sense into him, "There is no way you could get to Fray ahead of Horizon now - even if you went through the Quy marsh! Or have you forgotten that Favour took both Thicket and

Stubborn!"

Van screwed up his face. "Ember's right, even if we still had Thicket and Stubborn neither old Ket or Stub could go faster than a quick crawl even when they were young!"

They all were silent for a few moments. Ever since the incident with the stallion they had been without their trusty, if old and tired draft horse and mule. They all missed the old things, it was yet another memory of their father taken from them. The only thing Fav hadn't taken was Ro. They all looked over at Rose, but of course the idea of riding the musk cow was ridiculous. Ro mooed as if to confirm this. 'That will put an end to this' Ember thought. But Mag was silent for a moment, and he looked deep in thought.

"I know how I can get a horse," he said quietly. Both Ember and Van looked at him in surprise.

"How!?" Van demanded, "The only people we know who have a horse fast enough, wouldn't let you have him!"

But Ember knew her brother better, and she could see that Mag knew of someone who could get him a horse, it made her feel nervous.

"Who is it Mag?" she asked.

He raised one hand and rested the knuckle of his pointer finger against his lips, and still he did not speak. Both Ember and Van waited and watched him with weary eyes.

"The Tarven tradesman would have access to horses," he said at last. Ember blinked in surprise.

"But hasn't he gone to Fray himself!?" Van more stated than asked.

"His daughter is still here," Mag said. Ember could see a shadow of displeasure cross his eyes.

"And you think she'll help?" Van asked unbelievingly.

"I don't know, but we don't have another option."

"What about mother? What about Journey? You haven't even talked to the others in the movement about this! Don't you think they'll have something to say about you riding off!?" Ember asked franticly.

"There's no time to call a meeting over it; I'm doing this. Van you will have to look after the fields while I'm away." Van nodded. "And please Ember," Mag said turning to her, "Don't tell mother till I'm gone. This has to be done."

Van grinned in excitement as he slipped out of the stable. Mag went to follow - but Ember was not done yet.

"Mag you can't go," she whispered. "You can't go off on a wild race against time - and what will be waiting for you on the other end!? Mag you could go blind at any time... you can't go alone!"

Mag's face softened as it often did when speaking with Ember, but he was determined to go. He took her gently by her upper arms.

"Ember... little Ember, you worry far too much for your older brother! If I don't go, who will?" he sighed. "Ember, this is something that I must do." He smiled and brushed her hair back from her face. "I will return - at the most in two weeks, you'll see." But then she only looked frightened.

"Two weeks!? Mag what do you intend to do!?"

He sighed again with impatience, "Remember, I am going and I will return."

Ember closed her mouth; wherever this path led, there would be no turning Mag from it.

Chapter 18   Two Horses

Promise leaned as far out the window as she could, then she closed her eyes and took in a deep breath; the air was fresh and cool. Opening her eyes, she sighed, "I've had enough of this musty old manor!" Jumping back from her window she looked about her chambers, the whole place had lost it's magic. Ever since the banquet four days ago she had felt restless, and now that feeling had grown till she very well itched with it! Never before had she felt so... useless! She wanted to do something of importance, and more still she wanted to be free of all the expectations she herself had made. She longed to run through the long grass of the Byla - strange, she had not thought of the Byla in a long time.

With a sudden frown she remembered that there was a banquet tonight and she was expected to attend! She grimaced, the thought of going through another banquet with people looking at her and talking about how common she was, made her feel sick! All she wanted was to escape - just for a little. She had spent the past two months striving to be the best she could - and still she was only a common girl. She wanted to be a great woman one day - a true lady... but could she not escape for a time before trying again? To run barefoot out in the open! To ride bareback! She bit her lip and smiled; yes, that is what she wanted to do.

Just then a knock sounded at her door.

"Yes?" Mise called out. In walked her handmaiden, an old sour woman to be sure. She breezed in unannounced.

"I'm here for your wash," she announced. All joy faded from Mise's face, as she watched the woman walk to the other side of the room and begin to strip her bed. More than everyone else, Mise was sure that this woman thought of her as just a commoner from the wilderness.

"This came for you," the woman said holding out a small folded paper, she looked like she disapproved of it. Mise's curiosity was kindled at once. She took it from her quickly and made sure to walk away so the old woman couldn't read it over her shoulder. She unfolded it and read it quickly.

'I must speak with you at once. Manor courtyard. Imagine.'

Promise blinked in surprise, it had been almost a week since she had met with that insufferable Garatin. And now he had sent this note. What was she to think? She had half a mind to throw it away - but... she smiled, the whole thing sounded exciting, and after she met with Imagine she could get her horse and go for a ride! It was perfect. Looking down at herself, she was glad she had put a simple and practical dress on that morning.

"I'm going out," she announced suddenly and walked to her door.

"Where are you going!?" the handmaiden asked in outrage.

Mise turned to look at her with disgust, "What business is it of yours?" She then glided out into the hall. It irritated her to think that her whereabouts were kept track of by others!

When she reached the courtyard she looked around until she found him, then with a short sigh she steeled herself and walked up to him. He looked the same as when she saw him last, and it occurred to her that he probably didn't have any other clothes. Mise swallowed hard; this time she wouldn't let him make her feel like a child! As she neared him he turned to her, it gave her pause - he looked so angry and determined!

"Well? Why is it you wish to speak to me?" she looked away hoping he wouldn't notice her trembling. There was a moment of silence, but she couldn't bring herself to look at him, instead she searched the courtyard for something - anything to watch. His silence unnerved her.

"Horizon is traveling north to Fray - they must be warned before he arrives. Prove you are a friend to the cause and provide me with a horse." His voice sounded flat and demanding.

Mise knew Rizon had left - but she hadn't known where to. She looked at him for a moment, at first he did not return her gaze but when he did it made her nervous.

"The people in Fray are in danger?"

"Yes," he sounded downright impatient! She pressed her lips together.

"When and where shall I have this horse?" she asked trying hard to sound as grown up as she could.

"Outside the village on the north side, in one hour," he replied.

"Shall I load it with provisions?"

"I can provide my own food thank you!" he snapped.

She glared at him in outrage; how dare he!? She had offered him help - and he threw it in her face!

"Very well then." She looked him up and down. "Don't be late!" She turned on her heel and walked away, as she did she felt her ears burning - wasn't he going to say something?

Unseen to Promise, Mag stood with mouth hanging open staring after her. How dare she!? Every chance she got she was insulting him! Suggesting that he was too poor to pack his own food! The whole time acting like she was superior over him - not even looking at him! Mag turned away with a fierce frown, "Don't be late indeed!"

Promise closed her eyes and breathed; she needed to calm down. Something about that - that Garatin just made her angry! Just then her handmaiden came into her chambers.

"There you are! I need a message sent to the stables to have two horses saddled at once and ready for me."

Mise was stopped when her handmaiden spoke in her flat and sour voice.

"His lordship Favour thinks you should remain inside today, my lady." Her face looked downright pinched as she said it. Mise stood there looking at her in stunned silence, the woman nodded and walked right back out muttering about why she should need two horses.

"His lordship thinks I should not go out today..." Mise said into the empty room, her face was blank as a white page. She couldn't have been more shocked if the woman had smiled at her! Slowly her eyebrows came together to form a perfect look of outrage. What gave Favour the right to tell her if she should go out or not!? As if she would let herself be controlled like that!

*   *   *

"You will be careful won't you?"

Mag laughed at Ember, "How is it a little sister can worry so much for her older brother!?"

"How is it that an older brother could need so much looking after?" she returned without missing a beat.

Imagine's smile faded a little as he looked down at her. "Promise you won't tell mother until I'm away?"

With a heavy sigh Ember nodded. Mag stepped closer and hugged her, pulling away he smiled firmly. Ember wanted to say something more but he turned away before she could. She watched as he walked away down the street, a sack thrown over one shoulder and his cloak hanging off the other. Ember stood there for a long time letting her mind wander here and there. She remembered what she had once said to Mag, about him being able to see a bright new future, and she wondered if he remembered her telling him.

"Ember - I just heard - tell me it isn't true!"

Ember turned suddenly to see Journey standing there, he had just come from working in the fields and he was breathing hard from running. She grimaced.

"Did Van tell you?"

He nodded then said almost in despair, "He's already left...hasn't he?"

"Yes... he'll be alright though. There was no turning him from this."

Journ sighed. "I'm not sure for whom I'm more worried; Mag, or Horizon," he said darkly.

Ember's mouth opened in dismay - she hadn't considered what Mag might do to Horizon... what if her brother came back a completely different man? She spun about to look where she had last seen him; but it was too late, the future was already in motion.

Imagine walked quickly as soon as he left the village walls. He followed a foot path that led northward through the fields. At first he saw a few villagers out working in the fields. Mag was careful not to make eye contact as they looked at him with open curiosity. At last he got beyond the fields, here the land seemed to billow out into rolling hills and patches of trees. When he topped the first hill he looked down to the bottom and there under a great willow tree stood the Tarven maiden, and two horses...

Mag frowned; why had she brought two horses? He looked around and was relieved to see that there was no one else about. He then took a closer look down the hill - but he didn't find any peace of mind! For he saw that BOTH horses were loaded down with saddle bags and packs!

He started down the hill at a quick pace, with equal parts confusion and anger. As he neared she looked up at him, and he was surprised to see that she was dressed for travel!

"Ah, there you are. I was beginning to wonder," she said briskly. "We need to leave at once!"

For a moment Mag only looked at her. "We?" he said at last. He must have sounded abrupt for she blinked in surprise before speaking.

"Yes, we."

For a moment neither said a word. Mag stared at her, at a loss for words, but slowly he felt muted outrage rising in him.

"No, you're not coming with me," he said, narrowing his eyes.

She in turn lost her momentary pleasantness, she placed her hands on her hips and cocked her head to one side. "My father and mother are in Fray - and they are in as much danger as any! I am not asking you to take me with you, I'm going."

For the first time in his life Mag felt tempted to backhand a girl, he opened his mouth to speak but she beat him to it.

"And since these horses were provided by me, I really don't think you have any say in it - do you?"

Mag closed his mouth firmly; how dare she!? "All right," he said tightly, taking a step towards her (he hoped it would intimidate her) "You're coming - but we do this MY way - understand? I don't want any arguments from you - and don't lag behind. I have to get to Fray before Horizon does, and so if you slow me down, I will leave you behind. Do you get it?" he held a hope that she would get scared and decide to stay but to his horror she raised one brow and said calmly.

"Well then, if we're going to get there ahead of Rizon we should stop wasting time."

And from that moment on Mag fought the feeling of admiration for her.

Promise bit her lip as she turned her back on Imagine - was she really doing this!? Taking a short breath, she stood before her horse and told herself that this was what she wanted to do. 'I can't stay here with my handmaiden watching over my shoulder every second, and Lord Favour telling me what to do and what not to! Besides mother and father are in danger- I'm not sure I could trust Imagine to warn my parents.'

That was as much thought as Mise would allow at that moment. With a firm nod to herself she grabbed hold of her horse's reins in one hand then with one foot in the stirrup she swung herself up onto her horse. Almost at once she was hit with the immense relief of NOT riding side-saddle! 'How long has it been since I've ridden astride?' She wondered. Then like a flash from a diamond, she remembered the time when she had first gone bareback riding with Destination... now that had been when she was young, just a child.

Oh what Mise would give just to be that child again! She closed her eyes for a moment, life had been so much simpler when she was a child. She opened her eyes again; now life was different. Now she must race across a marsh with a man who despised her very existence, to warn her parents and a whole village of coming danger, in so doing risking her own life to the possibility of arrest. She looked over her shoulder to see Mag mount his horse, she paused in surprise to see that he didn't use the stirrup. Instead he jumped and struggled until he sat in the saddle. She looked away quickly, and blinked as she considered the thought that maybe… maybe Imagine had never ridden in a proper saddle before!

Mise turned her head to sneak another look hardly believing this new revelation, to her embarrassment Mag caught her looking! For a moment she stared wide eyed into his blue eyes. Fearing her face had turned red Mise looked away and said tightly, "Shall we be off then?" with a smart kick she started her horse off into a trot. And she was certain she heard Mag say something under his breath; these next three days would be horrible!

*   *   *

Favour sighed impatiently and patted his round middle and once again turned to walk to the other side of his chambers. At last a knock came at the door.

"Enter!" he called out. In came the page whom he had sent to the gatehouse hours ago.

"Well?" Favour asked with raised brows. The page shook his head.

"No, my lord. No messages have come from Fray - or any other place. The sun will be setting soon - there will be no messages coming, not this night."

Favour collapsed into a chair, his face gone pale; what was he to do? He had given all he had and now Loyal hadn't sent the information… she wasn't scared of him; he had lost his hold! Suddenly his face hardened. No, he still had a hold on her, and he would make her pay.

"Page!" he said sharply, "Have guards bring the maiden Promise to me! And prepare a room for her - in the tower."

The page bowed out of the room, and left Fav alone. He let out a breath, and closed his eyes - he had a terrible headache. He sat there in silence as the evening shadows filled the room, all the while his head pounded. At last he stood. 'I must lie down' he thought to himself. He even smiled at the thought of condemning the maiden to the tower dungeon from the comfort of his own bed - then he could close his eyes and rest while the pretentious child screamed all the way to her new 'chambers'. He reached the side of his bed but just then his chamber door burst open, he turned with a smug smile- but his face was wiped clean at what he saw! Four of his manor guards stood there, in front of them was the handmaiden he had told to spy on Promise. The handmaiden and the guards alike stood with wide-eyes and frightened expressions.

"Where is the girl!?" Fav demanded in outrage. The handmaiden shifted uncomfortably, her sour face pinched in fear.

"The girl left the manor this afternoon with two horses - she has not returned... she was seen heading north... I, I was going to report this to you, but..." her voice faltered off.

Favour's legs gave way and he sat down on his bed with a great whoosh of breath escaping him. His face looked whiter than a ghost! All that he had stood to gain - was gone. If the guards and handmaiden had been looking, they would have seen a great sand castle, blowing away in the wind through Favour's shaking fingers.

Hoping to be forgotten the handmaiden slipped to one side.

"What are your orders my lord?" The guards asked, "Shall we go after the maiden?" Fav looked up in surprise, and suddenly with new hope.

"Yes - go after her at once! Bring her back - unharmed, but do not let her escape!"

The guards bowed their heads then marched out, but they would not find the maiden. They rode their horses along the road north, and never once looked at the roads leading into the marsh. They returned to their master several hours later with empty hands, but Fav had one last hope. If he threatened to hurt Promise then Loy would send the information not knowing that her daughter was in fact safe, it was his last hope. But the message must be sent swiftly to arrive before the girl!

*   *   *

The Quy Marsh started on the most northern border of Garatin and stretched away east above the Byla wilderness, and its soggy hold on the land did not end till it reached the strange Mayfren Forest. It was said that no man had ever traveled the whole length of the marsh - and it was quite possibly true! The marsh was mild and livable in the west and eastern sides and along the edges, but in the center was a 'no man's land'. Bottomless pits of quicksand, stagnate lakes of mud, and green water that disguised itself as dry land. Low shrubs and sad trees that sheltered swarms of bugs. Low sloping hills of swaying grass that hardly looked like they belonged. This land was home to only jack rabbits, sparrows, snakes, four-horned deer, idercoons and the dreaded marsh wolves.

However, for miles along the edges, the Quy Marsh held a lonesome beauty that filled the heart with quiet and peace. The song of the sparrow and cricket blended together in a calming melody, and it was easy to see why the Quy Marsh folk called this place home. The Marsh folk didn't build castles or keeps, nor did they have a king or lords, they didn't belong to a country because they were hardly a nation! Marsh folk villages were no larger than twenty-five people and they were isolated from each other by miles. There were two kinds of marsh folk; there were the villager folk and the gypsies. The villagers were farmers and hunters, they kept to themselves, and did not welcome strangers, however it was next to unheard of to have an argument with the marsh folk. The gypsies were traders and craftsmen; they were known to have trade routes beyond the marsh. They were lively and colorful amongst themselves but shy and quiet around strangers.

By all accounts the Quy Marsh folk were a mysterious people. Imagine knew all this well. Growing up, Mag had known a number of Marsh folk, and he had explored the northern tip of the marsh with his brothers when they were young - before Mag had become the man of the house. He knew that there were paths all through the marsh, the path that would take them to Fray would not take them anywhere near the center of the marsh, or any marsh folk villages. It was a straight shot to the other side, really just skimming the borders of the marsh, just three nights. He glanced over at Promise. From the moment they had started there had only been a couple of words spoken between them, Mag was more than fine with the silence - but he found himself growing curious about this maiden.

This strange Tarven maiden who rode horses astride, and who shot fire from her eyes, who acted like a princess but who took to the wilderness like a soldier! He glanced over at her again, she looked cool and comfortable on horseback. When they had started five hours ago, Mag had been annoyed by the thought that she would need frequent rests. But she had not even tried to slow their steady pace! What kind of a maiden was she? Suddenly she looked over at him, he looked away quickly, embarrassment making his face heat up. He swallowed hard and spoke, his voice sounded hard and angry- he hoped it hid his embarrassment.

"The sun is going down; we need to find a place to camp."

She nodded then looked around, "There," she pointed off to the right where there were several birds flying about low in the grass. "Those are River Sparrows returning to their nests, they only nest in the embankments of swiftly moving rivers. If we camp there, we will have fresh water." She turned to look at him, her dark face free of any expression.

Mag's mouth opened slightly in surprise; how did she know all of that? Mag closed his mouth and frowned. 'Pull yourself together!' he told himself as he dismounted. He then looked to where she had pointed, the ground was higher and there were some low bushes. Mag led his horse up the incline all the while holding the frown on his face. Out of the corner of his eye he could see her smiling smugly to herself, his frown darkened.

Mag stood at the edge of the river bank and looked down at it; the river was a couple feet wide and it had cut a channel through the marsh two feet deep. And sure enough, Mag could see the River sparrows flying into little holes in the banks where grass and twigs stuck out. The water was clear and flowed quickly past.

Mag dropped his horse's reins and looked around. There was space enough between the low bushes to lie down and make a fire. He smiled when he thought of the high and mighty Tarven maiden sleeping on the ground hugged by bushes on all sides. She would complain all night long! He looked over at her; she sat on her horse and looked about with prim satisfaction.

"I'll go and find some fire wood," he said.

She dismounted and reached into her saddle bag, "You would have to go a fair way to find any here, we can use the coal I brought." She handed to him a black sooty bag of charred wood. Mag stared at her.

"Well you think of everything," he said bluntly. He took the bag and he could feel the resentment rising in him. 'She thinks she's so much better than me!' He fumed to himself as he knelt and began making a small fire. After a moment she came up beside him with a neat little frying pan and several strips of dried meat. He couldn't stop himself from glaring at her.

"Don't worry," she said innocently. "I packed enough for both of us."

But even still Mag was certain he could see venom in her eyes. They cooked and ate in silence. Mag envied the horses; they seemed to be having a pleasant time grazing together. By the time they had finished eating it was almost quite dark, they both stood to their feet and walked to the horses and unsaddled them. Then with a grin Mag took an apple from his bag and bit into it loudly. Mise looked up.

He pushed the piece of apple into his cheek and said with a spiteful smile, "Sorry, I didn't pack two - I thought I would be traveling alone."

With that he walked back to the fire and spread out his blanket. A moment later she followed and disappeared behind the bushes where her own blanket had been carefully laid out. After finishing his apple and throwing away the core, Mag shuffled deeper into his blankets.

Closing his eyes Mag tried to hold back a smile as he called out, "Good night, careful of the swamp spiders."

Mise didn't say anything but he was sure that she made a small squeak, Mag broke out into a silent boyish grin.

Both slept deeply that night, while a lone carrier pigeon flew over them, silently making its way northward, the message it carried would steal the last frayed bit of hope that Loyal had left.

*   *   *

'NO!' seventeen-year-old Mag cried, *as he clutched at his father's tunic and tried to pull him up. But it was too late... Dien was gone. His Garatin blue eyes had gone dull - unseeing, and his last shallow breath seemed to echo in Imagine's ears. Mag heaved his strength into pulling his father up, but his body was dead weight, his arms hung down and his head fell back unsupported. Mag's strength gave way and he laid his father back down with a thump on the cobble stones. Dien's eyes gazed up at Mag, empty and lifeless, Mag sucked in a breath but choked on his tears instead.*

'Father! No...' he sobbed and fell across his father's chest. The blood from Dien's several stab wounds soaked into Mag's clothes until they dripped. 'Help...' he thought numbly, he needed help. He remembered seeing Tarven soldiers nearby - they would help! They would catch those men - they would help...

Mag sat up and clenched his teeth, his breath hissed in and out. The night was silent around him except for the wind moving the bushes around him. Crickets buzzed in his ears, and he could feel his blanket under his tense hands... but he could see nothing. Not the bush beside him, not his feet in front of him and not the stars above. He sat as still as he could, waiting. 'Just wait' he told himself over and over. With a streak of panic, he heard Promise sitting up and sighing - it was morning! What would she do or say if she found him like this!? His panic raced through him as he strained his eyes to see - to see anything!

Chapter 19   Unlikely

Promise sighed and looked about at the world with new eyes, then she jumped; the sun was up! She threw off her blanket and stood to her feet - oh, Imagine would be down her throat for sleeping in! She looked around over the bushes, she could see the horses down the river a bit, and the fire was nearly cold - but where was Mag? She frowned as she smoothed down her skirt and quickly tucked her tunic in, then ran her finger tips along her hair. Still nervous she pulled on her boots, and began rolling up her sleeping things.

Just then Imagine popped up from behind the bushes, and walked over to the fire, he didn't look at her but she could see that he looked… Mise wasn't quite sure how he looked.

"Good morning," she said, hoping she sounded chipper yet aloof. She watched him carefully, he didn't seem to respond to her, but he stepped too close to a bush and it scraped past his legs - still he seemed unaware of it. Her dark brows pinched together, as she watched; this Garatin confused and intrigued her all at once. She knew that most Garatins didn't like Tarvens at all - but he went beyond dislike! Who had so wronged him that he had so much anger? As she watched he stood looking down at the fire with his back to her, suddenly he looked up and around.

"It's late, we need to get moving, we'll eat in the saddle," he said with little emotion.

She bit her lip; good, he had over slept too. He turned around, and looked at her; for the first time she noticed his eyes, she had always felt a little envious of Garatins for their bright blue eyes - but his were a strange black blue color! She was certain that they were a brighter blue than that… but then his eyes seemed to clear into a light blue, it must be the early morning light. Afraid he would notice how she was staring at him, she smiled. She wanted to get past this misunderstanding they seemed to have, whoever he was angry with - it wasn't her fault! But her smile was wasted on him, he winced as if disgusted by her, he then went to pack up his sleeping things. Mise shifted her bottom jaw to one side, and blinked several times; apparently he wasn't interested in finding common ground.

Ten minutes later and both horses were ready for the day. Mise climbed up in the saddle easily, she felt more than ready for a long day. She watched out of the corner of her eye to see Mag struggle up into the saddle again. Then he pulled from his bag a large piece of flat bread, she stared at him as he took a bite, then he noticed her watching. With a sigh he reluctantly tore the flat bread and handed her half. She took it grudgingly, and so began the second day of their journey in the race to Fray.

For the next couple hours, they traveled in silence, sometimes riding beside each other and sometimes riding one in front of the other. They had to keep the horses at a slow trot for the most part, for fear of stepping off the narrow path and sinking into the marsh.

After a few hours of traveling through tall grass that made a scraping sound when brushed past, and nothing but puddle after puddle of swamp, Mise was sick to her teeth of the whole thing - but she dare not complain. Just the thought of Imagine's smug face made her sit up straighter. But to her relief when they came upon one of the few clear, fast flowing rivers of the Quy, Mag stopped his horse.

"It's midmorning, we'll water the horses here."

He slid off his horse and dropped the reins. Mise did the same, those maidens back at the Hawthorn manor (especially the golden haired girl) would feel stiff and sore after riding for a few hours. But thankfully, Mise thought, she had traveled much in the saddle before this, she wouldn't have to give Mag the satisfaction of watching her hobble around. Still she sighed in relief at the cool breeze that came down the river.

Mise turned her back on Mag and walked slowly along the river. Her horse followed her until it found a place where it could get close enough to the river, then she dropped her head and began to drink. Mise turned to watch her horse, timidly she peaked over her to see what Mag was doing - just then her horse jumped down the embankment into the river. Her hooves splashing water and her reins dragging, she plunked across to the other side where she stood in the knee high water and began eating leaves from a bush on the embankment.

"HEY!" Mag called out sharply in alarm, "Those leaves are poisonous for horses!"

Mise jumped forward, "No!" she cried out. But it turned into a tiny scream, for the ground gave way beneath her and she fell down the embankment into the river! She landed with a splash on her feet but lost balance and fell forward, she threw her hands out in front to stop her fall, and they splashed water into her face as they hit the surface of the river. Next she felt a sting on the palms of her hands as they hit the river bed.

Reeling to her feet she shook her head and sputtered the water from her face, she then forced her way across the river, stumbling on her wet skirt. As she reached for her horse's reins, the horse mischievously sidestepped away. Mise leapt forward and snatched the reins in a wet grasp. One of her feet stumbled and she went down on one knee with one last splash.

At last she stood, knee deep on the far side of the river, wet head to toe, water dripping from her chin and from the tips of her hair. She hunched her shoulders as a shiver ran down her spine, gasping for breath she blinked water from her eye lashes and looked up at Mag on the far embankment.

When Mise had fallen, Mag had frozen in place and all he could do was watch like it was some kind of gypsy play. But when at last Mise stood still, dripping and panting looking at him with wide eyes, he at last found himself again. As a grin spread across his face, he tried at once to hide it, but he couldn't hold back the chuckles that bubbled out. Promise's wide eyes changed to that of outrage and embarrassment.

"The river's shallower than I thought it would be," he straightened out his face as much as he could.

Mise gasped one last time before shivering, then slowly she sloshed her way back across the river, horse in tow. But as she crossed the middle of the river, the river bed deepened and she sank up past her knees. She gasped, but doggedly continued. Sadly, it was not meant to be, for just then her horse stumbled, and shook loose Promise's sleeping roll.

Mag jumped into action at once, with a splash he landed in the river and with one last jump he landed on his back, arms out stretched, and by some strange fortune, he was able to hold the bed roll above the final splash.

Mise squeaked and turned away from the splash, and Mag found himself floating face up holding Mise's bed roll above his head. For a moment he and Mise stared at one another in perfect shock. Mag blinked in surprise and Promise's dark face of outrage broke as she burst into laughter! She pointed a finger at him and giggled, her eyes and nose wrinkled. Shaking the water from his face he stood to his feet and half grinned. He fastened her bed roll back to the saddle, and glanced at her. He was surprised to see that she really had a pleasant face when she was smiling, in fact... she looked even likeable!

Mise sniffled and pushed back her wet hair. "Well," she said, her voice still full of laughter. "We make an unlikely team don't we!"

Her words cut to his heart, and the joy and carelessness died at once from him, and he felt his heart grow even heavier. A bitter taste came to his mouth.

"A team?" he said looking her up and down. "Unlikely is the word for it, Tarven."

Her face went blank and she blinked in surprise. Mag sloshed past her, and climbed back up the river bank. Mise stood still, and she was certain that she had felt a chill from Imagine's cold shoulder as he walked past. She stared blankly at the river, the water pulling at her skirt as it flowed past; how? She wondered in faint outrage. How could anyone be so hurtful!? She swallowed, and blinked quickly for fear the tears in her eyes would spill out. Her outrage faded as she realized how hurt she was by his words; why couldn't he accept her? Was it really so terrible to entertain the idea of a Garatin and a Tarven making a good team? She pressed her lips together and determined to not let her wounded heart show. Turning about she led her horse to the river bank, impatiently she scrambled up, tripping on her wet skirt as she went. At last she stood on dry ground, and she pulled on her horse's reins until her horse reluctantly jumped up. In ill temper she tied the reins around a bush branch.

"We don't have time to dry off," Imagine's voice sounded hard. She glared up at him - he looked just as hard back. He glared at her, his blue eyes looked brittle. "We can't waste time with a fire now - or have you forgotten whom we have to get to Fray ahead of?"

Mise fought the childish impulse to stick her tongue out at him, instead she sharply grabbed her pack from her saddle. Then the two of them stalked off in opposite directions to change into dry things. Mise darted one last glance at Mag, up till meeting him she hadn't been aware that anyone could be so rude! After going behind a little hill she changed quickly into a dry tunic and skirt and grudgingly rolled up her wet things. A short five minutes later they were both back in the saddle, shooting each other murderous glances as they went. Mise would have liked nothing more than to ride off and leave him there - but she couldn't let him have the last word!

The bright morning changed through the afternoon into a thick close day, with dark clouds gathering to the east, and from time to time they could see the flash of lightning. But the wind blew to the east, and it didn't look as though the storm would come to them - still Mag felt edgy and cross, but to his surprise - he was cross with himself! His sharp words to Mise after the river accident still rang in his ears. He wished he could have taken back what he said - but he couldn't bring himself to apologise to her. For the past half hour, they had been walking along leading their horses behind them. Glancing over at Mise, he couldn't help but take notice of the way her hair curled down her back. Her long wide skirt flared out around her legs as she took long determined strides, she held her shoulders back and her head high. To Mag, she looked removed and untouchable. Just then she turned her cinnamon eyes on him - he looked away.

"I didn't mean to fall into the river, you know."

Mag swallowed hard, "I know." After a moment, he found the courage to say what was really in his mind. "It's just that we don't have time to waste - we need to get to Fray ahead of Horizon... we need to get there." Suddenly the image of Trust and his wife and daughters huddled in a dirty prison wagon, hopeless and doomed, flashed across his mind. Mag gritted his teeth - he wouldn't let that happen in Fray!

"What if this whole journey is in vain?"

Mag stumbled over a bush and stopped to look at her in faint outrage.

She stopped too and said quickly, "No - I didn't mean that we won't get there in time. But... what if Horizon isn't even going to Fray? What if he doesn't intend to make any arrests there?"

With a shake of his head Mag went on walking. "Exposing 'rebels' is what this man does. When he arrives in Fray, he will arrest anyone he can find connected with the namesake Eternity - just like he did in Hawthorn," he said sadly.

"I'm sorry," her voice sounded sincere. "Did you know the people who were arrested in Hawthorn?"

Mag closed his eyes and again heard Trust's last words to him... 'Your eyes... it's time you opened them', a bitter taste came to Mag's mouth, and he pushed the truth that his heart was trying to believe deeper. One day maybe he would face the truth - but not now.

"I know a bit of what that's like."

Mag smiled cruelly, "Yeah, I bet you do." How dare she try and empathise with him! As if she had any idea of what it was like to be hunted, ostracized and persecuted, to be made on outlaw in one's own country! As if she had any idea!

"I know what it's like to be cast out." Her voice sounded hard and challenging, it shocked him that she seemed to know just what he was thinking. Looking at her he dared her to go on.

"Five years ago, my father stood up against the Tarven High Council and refused orders all because he chose Nity over his own king. He was arrested and sentenced to death for his treason. I and my mother fled from the city knowing that if we were caught we would be killed too."

It was all Mag could do to meet her gaze, he could hardly believe it!

"Through selfless friendship between Tarven and Garatin," she stressed the words, "My father was rescued from his fate and we were all able to flee. That was five years past, since that time I nor my father and mother will ever be accepted back into the Tarven culture." She raised her dark brows. "Why do you think we chose to live in such a small village like Hawthorn?"

Mag looked away and frowned, the last thing he would ever let himself feel for a Tarven was sorry. He stopped walking and threw the reins back over his horse's head; he had had enough of walking - and talking. With a jump and a heave, he pulled himself into the saddle, out of the corner of his eye he watched Promise mount her horse - she did so with such ease and grace... it made him feel like a fool!

The rest of that day passed in relative silence, both Mise and Mag kept a close eye on a storm gathering in the north but it did not threaten to come any closer. They had to pass through a low spot and it was there that the bugs became unbearable! Both horse and rider were driven nearly mad with it, but after a quick trot and a few hissed curses from Mag they left the low wet spot behind. They rode and walked all through the afternoon and into the evening and said little to one another - Mag wondered what Mise was thinking of. As for himself he couldn't get the thought out of his head that he and Promise were not quite as different as he had first thought. But that only made him cross!

When at last dusk snuck up upon them, they made a mad scramble to find a place to sleep. When they did, they had to scramble even more to set up camp before the darkness settled down on them, for dark clouds covered the sky and hastened the night on. The night found them on a low flat hill top, surrounded by high growing grass and a willow tree grew not too far away. The horses were tethered by the tree a short distance away and were happily settled in. Mag knelt over the pile of willow sticks that they had gathered and worked to get a spark from his flint stone, anxious to ward off the coming cold, but he was having a hard time of it. On the other side of the would be fire, Mise was setting out the cooking supplies for dinner, something about the way she held her face made him want to talk... somehow she looked unguarded and open.

He opened his mouth to express his frustration with his flint stone, when he heard the fall of a heavy foot... Both he and Mise froze, their hands stopping in mid movement. Mag held his breath and suddenly the beat of his heart was very loud. His ears pricked and the hair on his neck stood on end. Off in the dark the horses nickered uneasily. Mustering all his self-discipline, Mag calmly put down his flint stone and steadied himself with his hands. Like opening a stiff door, he turned his head - but all that he could see was darkness.

Mise started at the sound of what she imagined was a large animal shifting in the bushes at the edge of the clearing. She swallowed hard; something was out there... she looked to Mag with wide cinnamon eyes. His face looked grim as he searched the darkness. She watched as his right hand slipped to his hunting knife and gripped it till his knuckles went white. They both stood slowly to their feet without a noise, and waited for something more. But the night went just as still as before, as if breathing in relief.

Reaching down Mise grabbed the flint stone and without trouble struck a flame. She blew on it till it burned on its own. Standing up again she met Mag's gaze. He shrugged his confusion of what they had heard. She half laughed and opened her mouth to speak.

With a heart exploding roar, out of the darkness sprung a great marsh wolf! Its thick gray/ black fur stood on end all down his spine. His great wide, powerful front paws were hooked with the sharp long claws of a bear, and his barrel chest was wide and powerful. Mise looked up into a face as dark and hideous as ever she would. Its ears pointed up like cruel horns, while his muzzle was curled back in a snarl to reveal jagged yellow teeth, and the light of her small fire glittered in his eyes. A deep heart-stopping roar split the night, as the marsh wolf took a step towards Mise. She stepped back and tripped over the food pack. Falling back, she hit the ground, screaming in terror she kicked and struggled to get up and away. In a single leap the beast was over her, and turning his great head to one side, roared in her face. But the roar changed to a grunt of pain, and the beast lost its balance and fell to one side!

Mag kicked hard and stabbed with his hunting knife over and over, but the marsh wolf's fur was thick, and the stench of it filled his lungs. Mag felt totally lost, after he had hit the beast from its side at a dead run, he had fallen over with it. Suddenly Mag felt ground beneath him, he raised himself to his knees just in time to see the mighty clawed paw swing about and catch him on the shoulder. He flew to one side, and hit the ground hard, face down. Pushing himself up with his hands, he shook his head trying to clear it, and tasted blood in his mouth. With horror he felt the ground shake, and he knew that the beast had made one long stride on all fours and now stood behind him. Mag rolled over as if time had slowed down, and watched in morbid fascination as the wolf lifted itself onto his hind legs, his thick lean muscles rippled as he brought back his head ready to feast.

With a sickening thud an arrow entered the Marsh wolf's chest, the beast threw his head back and roared in pain. It took an unsteady step back. Another arrow flew and struck the hairy throat. The beast fell back - his roar dying. The ground shook under his weight as he fell on his back, the body quivered. Mag looked back and like a tiny warrior, Promise stood, her whole body shook, and her eyes looked wild. In her out stretched arm she held his bow, she gasped and tears flowed from her eyes. In desperate and uncontrollable panic, she raised another arrow to the string and loosed it before drawing it back far enough, the arrow landed harmlessly beside the still, hulking body of the marsh wolf.

Without knowing how, Mag found himself up on his feet, as he stared at Mise, she dropped the bow and sobbed. With unsure footing and shaking legs she walked to Mag, when she reached him they stood staring at each other in bewilderment. Then both of them fell into each other's arms, weak with fright they collapsed to the ground and clung to one another like children. Mise gasped and choked on her tears while Mag struggled to just breathe. When they at last pulled away, his own face was wet with tears. Together they turned to look at the horrible body beside them. Even laying down, the marsh wolf's body loomed over them. Swallowing hard Mag stood and looked at it. Suddenly the still carcass twitched and shuddered, Mag jumped back and Mise squeaked.

"It's alright!" Imagine's voice sounded strange and hoarse to his own ears. "It's dead... it's dead."

Mise covered her face with her hands and gasped for breath, while Mag went quickly to the small fire. Lighting a torch he had already prepared, he returned to Mise's side. Together they peered at the dead beast from the fire light with new found horror at its mere size!

"What is it?" Promise's voice shook even in a whisper.

Mag took a step closer to it, and winced as he saw that his hunting knife was still buried up to the hilt in the coarse fur. "A marsh wolf," he whispered the answer.

Mise gulped with new fear. "Do they travel in packs!?"

For a moment Mag shared her panic as he looked about into the darkness, but he grabbed hold of reality. "No... they hunt alone."

They were still for a long time and just gazed at the hairy carcass, then they looked at each other, as if just realizing that they had indeed survived the attack.

Chapter 20   Laughter

Two sparrows hopped about on the ground foraging for seeds and small insects to bring back to their full nest of hatchlings. Their tiny delicate legs hardly disturbed a single grass blade as they hopped along. Their little wings would flutter from time to time as they few from perch to perch. They chirped at one another like they were talking about how they would pass the day. Like dancing, they made their way along until they came upon a huge mound. Much as curious children, they poked their heads here and there, and tilted their little heads to the side with dark sparkling eyes. At last they moved on from the large, still and hairy carcass, and they instead found interest in two other still objects. One sparrow was courageous enough to hop up onto one of them; he gazed up at it. But at a slight movement from the formerly still object, both sparrows took wing, and fluttered away.

The moment Imagine shifted his body, his back and neck protested at their long endured upright position. He froze at the pain at once and winced. Slowly, like crawling out of a small box, he straightened out his one leg that he had kept bent - it was so stiff it hardly felt like his own! That was the last time he'd ever fall asleep sitting up! Vaguely he wondered if his neck would ever forgive him for sleeping with his chin resting on his chest. He shifted his shoulders- but again he froze, for he suddenly became aware of Mise...

His mind snapped out of its sleepy bumbling, and he remembered what had happened the night before. Like scenes from some half-forgotten dream full of fear, he remembered the horrible fight with the marsh wolf- Promise's scream and the beast's roar. For a moment panic seized him again, then his eyes fell upon the still mound of coarse fur and sharp claws; it was dead - they killed it. After that they had been too frightened to finish making camp! With a fire blazing beside them they had sat down back-to-back hardly daring to breathe. The last thing Mag remembered was listening to his heartbeat. He didn't recall it - but Promise's head had fallen back and now rested on his shoulder.

Mag looked about himself, the sun had only just risen, and its golden light was restricted to the southern horizon, for covering the north sky and stretching out, were dark gray and blue clouds. Beside them the fire had died down to a few glowing coals - again he glanced nervously at the hulking form of the marsh wolf. He had to get up.

Awkwardly Mag cradled Promise's head over his shoulder and lowered her to the ground, then he stood and suppressed a great moan as his whole body seemed to stiffen against stretching. He caught his breath when a shot of pain went through his shoulder, nervously he turned his head to inspect. Four deep gashes marred his shoulder from back to front where the marsh wolf had cuffed him. Mag winced; animal hair and dirt clung to the wound, and his torn tunic was stuck to his skin. He wondered how much it would restrict his movements, he tested it out by rolling his shoulder; the pain made him gasp, but it wasn't unbearable. On the ground, Mise seemed to melt into a deeper sleep, but suddenly she opened her eyes, then closed them again as she yawned. Sitting up she frowned and scratched her head - and just as Mag had, she froze when she saw the Marsh wolf.

"I have to bandage up my shoulder, then we need to be on our way," Mag said.

Mise, still looking at the Wolf, said in a little voice, "I didn't think that I'd ever fall asleep."

Mag nodded, he knew that feeling all too well! He looked about their camp, their bed rolls were still neatly sitting on the other side of the fire where they had put them the night before. Cooking supplies and their food pack were carelessly strewn where Mise had helplessly kicked them in her panic to escape. Wearily Mag went to find a bandage amongst the scattered supplies. There would be no breakfast this morning - he had a feeling that like himself, Mise was strangely not hungry.

Promise sat for another moment fighting to wake herself up. Under different circumstances she would have been embarrassed to know that she and Mag had fallen asleep back-to-back. But she would have had no peace otherwise - she had been so frightened after the attack that just being close to someone else had given her comfort. Still unable to take her eyes from the beast, she stood to her feet.

"I'll go and saddle the horses." She turned and walked a little ways away (luckily, the marsh wolf had approached from the other side) to where they had tethered the horses. Looking up she paused in horror - one of the horses was lying on his side in the grass! Just then both horses looked at her. Mise closed her eyes and scolded herself for such wild imaginings - of course the horses were all right! It was Imagine's horse who was lying down, but he struggled to his feet at once, while her horse went to her quickly. She rubbed her nose and neck with affection. They had hobbled both horses as well as tied their leads to a low willow branch, but the branch had broken and the horse's leads were horrible tangled. Suddenly Mise felt very sorry for the poor beasts - she didn't recall hearing them scream in terror the night before, but they must have been terribly frightened!

"You poor things!" she whispered. With a few extra pats than she normally would have given, she untangled and saddled them both. Mise led them back to where Mag had just finished packing up, he had already cleaned and bandaged his shoulder. Together they added the packs to the horses. Then anxious to leave that place Mise mounted her horse and waited for Mag to do the same. He stood looking at the dead beast.

"Think we should take some of the meat?" he asked quietly. The very thought of staying close to that... that thing made Mise feel uneasy.

"No - Mag please - let's just go!" she said pleadingly.

With a grim look on his pale Garatin face Mag seemed to not hear her and took a step towards it.

"Mag!" Mise called out almost in a panic. "Please - let's just go!"

"Yeah..." he said walking right up to it, "I have to get my hunting knife though."

Mise felt downright sick as she realized that his hunting knife must still be buried in the marsh wolf's flesh. Screwing up his face, Mag leaned over to look, but he didn't seem to find it. Mise watched, unable to do anything but screw up her own face with distaste and fear. Gingerly Mag placed one hand on the wolf's sloping back and leaned over it - Mise remembered that he had stabbed the beast's underbelly. She swallowed hard as he reached out with his other hand and withdrew his sought after knife. Taking a deep breath, Mise steadied herself with the knowledge that soon they would be well away from that nightmare. After cleaning off his knife, Mag came to his horse, he glanced at her briefly before jumping and struggling into his saddle - he had slightly more difficulty in doing so with his wounded shoulder.

And so they started out on the third day of their race to Fray, one more night and they would reach their destination.

All through that morning and into the afternoon of that day, the dark clouds from the north continued to build and stretch out towards them, and with them they brought a cool wind. Mag and Mise almost felt as though they were being swallowed up the closer they got to Fray. Still, despite the oppressive weather, there was no more snapping, or death glares between the two. They even talked to each other without finding fault with what the other said!

Indeed, they both knew that things had changed between them - the change could even be felt. They knew it was there, but neither wanted to talk about it, in fact they didn't even want to give it thought. But the change was there.

Suddenly two people found themselves very much the same, words like 'Tarven' or 'Garatin' no longer held sway over them - the only thing that seemed to matter was reaching Fray in time!

It was some time after midday when they came to a shallow clear river and stopped to drink and water the horses. Careful not to repeat their earlier mistake, they watered the horses first then secured them some way off. Only then did they themselves kneel on the riverbank and quenched their thirst. Perhaps it was the change between them that spurred Mise to ask - for she had wondered about it ever since Mag had first mounted the horse she had brought for him. With all the bluntness of her father she turned to Mag as they knelt on the bank.

"Why don't you use the stirrups when you mount your horse?" If Loyal had been there she might have blushed at how tactless the question was.

Beside her Mag hesitated before looking at her with a rather vulnerable looking frown. Fleetingly Mise wondered if he would be offended. Instead Mag matched her straightforwardness.

"Never had stirrups before - I don't know how to use them."

Promise blinked - somehow she hadn't even considered that answer! She felt a lump come to her throat and a flood of guilt and shame nearly overwhelmed her. Again it must have been the change between them, because the first thing that came to her mind was 'you're that poor!?' but to her credit she held her tongue, indeed she couldn't think of what to say. For a moment she returned Imagine's blue eyed stare. She blinked once.

"You just put your one foot in the stirrup and swing your other leg up and around," she said simply, feeling a little foolish.

Mag stood to his feet, still frowning in confusion, Mise stood with him. Together they started moving slowly back to the horses.

"I just don't see... why people need them." he said simply.

"Well - it's easier (especially with a wounded arm) and faster to use stirrups."

Mag gave her a sideways glance, and there was a mischievous look in his face, "Faster?"

"Yeah- faster."

"I guess I could give it a try."

Mise looked at him quickly - and was surprised at what she saw; it was the look only a carefree child has. Then suddenly he broke out into a run for his horse, a squeal escaped Mise as she too broke into a run. Like children remembering how to play, the two of them raced for the horses. Mise felt the competitive spirit of her father break forth as she breathlessly reached her horse. Nervously her horse shied away from her, taking no heed of this she grabbed hold of the reins and yanked them free of the bush she had tied them to. In one smooth motion she slid her right foot into the stirrup and swung her left foot up and over. Out of the corner of her eye she saw Mag pause for a moment before awkwardly stepping into his own stirrup. Excitedly Mise spurred her horse, at the same time she looked over her shoulder. The look on Imagine's face must have been comical - even priceless! However, Mise never saw his expression, for when she turned to look, she saw Mag sitting backwards!

Promise doubled over in laughter, almost losing hold of her reins, her laughter even bringing tears to her cinnamon eyes. As if being cruel in not releasing her from her stomach cramping laughter, Mag twisted in the saddle and looked over his shoulder at her. His face was perfectly blank - except for one eyebrow that was raised ever so slightly. That and his eyes, he seemed to be begging her to help him make sense of his awkward position. Through her laughter she managed to speak.

"You- you mounted w-with the wrong foot!"

Mag accepted this with raised eyebrows and a slight nod of the head, he then turned back around. This did nothing to help Mise stop laughing.

The embarrassment that Mag felt was drowned out by Promise's laughter… it sounded musical and even sweet to him. The idea that he could bring her joy was more exciting then he would admit to even himself! It had been a long time since he had made anyone laugh - suddenly he remembered a time when laughter had been a common thing for his family.

He had been no more than twelve and little Remember had been just seven… and they were working in the garden when Mag had found an earthworm. Little Ember had screamed and squealed, it had made his little brothers Van and Vive laugh, and even his mother who was holding her three-year-old daughter had laughed at her daughter's overplayed fright at such a helpless thing. And his father... he could hear his father's laughter, he could feel the comfort that he gave Ember as he explained that it was just a worm. He could see his blue eyes - sparkling and alive, suddenly they changed, the life drained from them and the laughter died. Obedience was dead.

But Mise was still there.

The day passed on with many glances toward the gathering ominous clouds ahead of them, Mag predicted that the rain would catch up with them later that night. Neither of them looked forward to the thought of spending the night huddling under their blankets in a downpour, so they pushed both themselves and the horses hard all that afternoon. They weren't sure of it when at last night found them - but they had made very good time that day. Come morning there would only be a few short hours till they came in sight of Fray.

*   *   *

Loyal lay on her bed, forlorn and forgotten, wiping her mind clear, hoping to forget the pain, all the while a storm raged outside streaking the window panes with rain. It was evening when a knock sounded at her door.

"My lady?" it was the handmaiden. Loy opened her eyes, with weary determination, she sat up and slipped out of her bed, lifting her head high she willed her tears to dry.

"Enter," she said. The girl looked very relieved to see her mistress standing. She bowed, then held out a tiny letter cylinder.

"This came for you yesterday morning - I wanted to let you rest before delivering it. It came by carrier pigeon no less," she sounded quite excited. "It was one of the birds from Hawthorn."

Loy felt a dread take hold as she took the cylinder in hand. She nodded and waited till the girl once again left the chambers. Then with foreboding she took forth the small letter. At first she determined to read it slowly, but as soon as she laid eyes on the first couple words panic seized her! The letter read:

My Lady Loyal,

You have proven less than trustworthy in sending reports on your husband, and I am displeased. I find that you are no longer of any gain to me - however if you send the information now I will yet forgive you for your... disloyalty to me. I hope you do; it would

199

be a shame if anything happened to your 'valuable possessions' in my care.

His lordship, Favour.

The letter fell from Loyal's trembling hands and fluttered to the ground. She stood staring down at it like it was the dead body of someone she loved. Horror and disbelief were stamped on her dark face and her breath came in short quick animal like breaths. Reality had found her, and her time of hiding from it was over.

Promise...

Her mind echoed over and over - how could she have been so blind!? She left Promise behind, and she was now in mortal danger!! A gasp escaped Loyal's anguished lips, almost as if she had been stabbed. What was she to do!?

Promise...

It was like Loyal had forgotten where she had come from, and couldn't remember where she was going, she wasn't even sure of whom she was. She had lost so much already... and now she had lost it all. Then with one last ribbon of strength she remembered one last thing that she still had: Courage!

As though in a craze she spun about and stumbled to her chamber door - she had to tell him! Even as she came through the door, she realized that to tell him of what she had done would mean that she would also lose him... it didn't matter, she had to tell him. Her heart beat in her ears and her vision seemed to blur around the edges as she went down the hallway between their chambers.

The whole manor seemed to have up and turned over or else she was walking down the hall on her hands, for they were always out in front of her grabbing hold of things, pushing and pulling herself along. The back of her neck suddenly felt sticky and her hair felt unbearably warm and stifling around her face. Everything seemed to be falling around her and crashing to the floor. To her eyes the hallway had grown and was even longer than when she had started. At last she reached Courage's chamber door (she could never remember if she had run there or crawled).

She pushed past the door and stumbled into his chambers. Courage sat at a small table, but he at once jumped to his feet and ran to her side.

"Loyal!" he cried, as he took her in his arms and all but held her up. "Loyal what is it? Are you all right!?" Loy turned her tear streaked face up to him, and marveled at how his gaze was filled with love for her; he would never look at her like that again.

"Courage - Forgive me!" she breathed. His eyebrows pinched together. He still doesn't understand, she thought numbly.

"Loyal, what is it?"

"I have betrayed you!" she sobbed. A shadow crossed his face. "And now Promise is in danger! I've betrayed us all…"

"Loyal what have you done!?" he demanded. Loy cried out. Her heart, it was in such pain - It was so heavy.

"Favour told me he knew you were involved with the rebels! He demanded that I spy on you!" she choked the words out with a sob. "If I didn't, he would inform Ambassador Sinister of you - I had no choice! But now he has Promise!" she collapsed against him sobbing. But Rage offered her no comfort. Now she had lost everything.

"Loyal!" he demanded, "Tell me everything - NOW!" she choked and sobbed until she had said everything, and then pointed to her chambers.

"The letter is in there."

Rage then pulled her to the chair he had been sitting in and pushed her into it. Then he ran to her chambers, leaving her alone. She sank from the chair onto the floor and held her face as she wept. After all she had come through, through Eternity's death, and her husband's arrest. After escaping into the wild, and finally finding a new life - this was how it would all end.

Rage read the horrible letter over three times before he threw it away. How could he have been so blind!? He should have known Favour would not give up! Then he clenched his teeth and threw himself into finding a way to save his daughter - there had to be a way! Favour must still fear him, and if Fav still feared him then there was a chance that he had not done anything to Mise yet! Rage had to believe this - it was madness to believe otherwise.

Loyal raised her face, and as the tears streamed down she breathed. "Eloi… I've been such a fool!" she sobbed again, "I didn't trust you enough to protect us… and now I've lost it all! Please! Nity - don't let her die! You woke her once… save her again."

Rage burst back into the room and went to his travel trunk and began pulling things out. "There is a chance that Favour has not harmed her yet." His face looked hard as stone.

"You will go to her!?" she half pleaded, she could hardly believe what he said.

"The storm will have made the roads impossible to travel fast on, my horse could be injured trying and then I would be further delayed; I'll have to wait till the morrow to leave," he said without stopping his packing. When he finished with his bag he then left the room with long strides, never once did he look at her.

*   *   *

In anticipation of the coming rain Mag and Mise searched for a large tree to make camp under, once they found it they made quick work of setting up camp. While Imagine took care of the horses and tied them down so they couldn't bolt in the coming storm, Promise laid out both of their sleeping rolls, and began their dinner. But before they had a fire, the storm clouds hastened nightfall a half hour before its time.

Mise worked quickly and tucked their packs and saddles (there was nothing worse than riding in a wet saddle) away as best she could in a little hollow that an uprooted tree had left. While she did this, Mag wandered off into the darkness to find as much firewood as he could for the cold and wet night ahead of them.

"Promise…" Mise looked up and out into the darkness at the sound of Mag calling out her namesake - he sounded unsure. Mise felt a measure of alarm rise within her. She stood to her feet and tried to judge where Mag was.

"Promise where are you?" Mag called out, he sounded to be only two dozen steps away, but he sounded… quite frightened!

"I'm still by our camp - what is it Mag!?" she answered with a spike of panic - was it another Marsh wolf!? Mise waited and was surprised when Mag seemed to hesitate.

"I… I can't see," he said at last.

Mise sighed and pushed her heart back into her chest. Mag had just gotten lost in the dark - that was all.

"Wait… I'll light the fire," she said turning about and squinting down at where she knew Mag had dumped an arm full of fire wood and his flint stone.

Mag didn't say another word as she fumbled about for a moment and at last lit a twig aflame, carefully she fed the small fire till it was big enough to care for itself. Pleased she stood to her feet and expected Mag to come looming out of the darkness - but he didn't... with an uneasy frown Mise searched the darkness beyond the fire light.

"Where are you?" she asked.

Like a frightened child Mag spoke after a pause, "I can't see." He must be standing in a low spot, Mise reasoned, and a hill was hiding the fire from him.

With a touch of impatience, she called out, "Just follow my voice - you can't be that far away!" she paused for a moment, and heard his hesitant footfalls. "Really though!" she laughed. "This is almost funny! Just think of the both of us wandering about in the dark - we would be lost till sunrise..." her voice trailed off.

Out of the darkness Mag came slow and unsure, but he stopped dead in his tracks as soon as she stopped talking. She felt a chill run down her spine. For he stood there, half bent over as if afraid of hitting his head on the sky. He held his hands out in front to protect himself against running into anything while he stared wide-eyed and unseeing. He was looking right at her - but it was as though he couldn't see her!

Mise froze in disbelief and a vague sense of dread; Mag really couldn't see anything!

"Promise?" he called out, the look on his face was close to panic! For a moment Mise could only stand there - what was wrong with him!?

"I'm right here Mag," she said softly, almost in a whisper but still he heard her. He began walking slowly towards her again. When he was just a few feet away, Mise stared up at him in horror and disbelief: it was like his blue eyes had been covered by an inky black mist!

"Mise?" this time his voice was quieter, the panic ebbing from him. Like reaching out to hold a delicate butterfly, Mise put out her hand till it touched his outstretched trembling hand.

"Mag, what's wrong with your eyes?" she whispered. He grabbed hold of her hand with both of his.

"I don't... I don't know," he whispered, but still the fear could be heard plainly.

Steadying herself, Mise swallowed, "Just - come and sit down by the fire here," she said softly. Together they sank to the ground, never once did Mise take her eyes from his face - she had never seen anything like his eyes at that moment - and it shook her to the core. With strength born of her father she asked him in a low voice.

"Has this happened before?"

Licking his dry lips, he hesitated before nodding his head.

"How many times?"

"Too many to remember…"

Despite her fear she felt relief, "Then you will see again! And once in Fray you can see an herb man to help you!"

Despair filled his sightless face, "Since when has any herb man ever been able to help?"

Mise swallowed hard, with gentle fingers she touched her wrist, although old and faded the scars were still there. Her memories of her sickness when she was young were dim and muddled between dream, nightmare and reality. But she did remember when the herb man had bled her - or at least she thought she remembered it, at any rate she couldn't argue with Mag that herb men were any good at healing.

"But you will see again," she offered this small comfort.

"Yeah…" he spoke, "My sight always returns after a time - but I will lose it again… and again. Each time it gets worse! Each time I wait longer for it to return."

He didn't speak it, but Mise knew that he feared that one day - his sight would be lost completely. "Does it happen often?"

Again he nodded.

"Has it happened before… on this trip?" she found herself afraid of this answer.

He blinked several times before whispering, "Yes."

"Why does it happen - do you know?" but even as she asked the black mist cleared from his eyes and he blinked rapidly, and she knew that his sight had returned. He looked at her and she watched his face harden.

"It's personal." Then like giving up his hold on a rope he had been climbing, he released her hand that he had been holding oh so tightly. He stood and went to his pack.

Mise sat there seething at him - what was wrong with him!? She had just helped him - offered him comfort when he was near well shaking with fear - and he couldn't even tell her what was the root of this problem!? She wanted to lash out at him - but she didn't, instead she pushed her anger away. She knew that speaking her anger to him would not make him open up. Instead she sat there and bridled her anger and frustration, and truth be told it was the wisest thing that she could have done at that moment.

For Mag - although his secret was dark and painful, he longed to share with someone - anyone! He longed to tell someone the truth! He had spent too many years bearing the pain of his father's death alone, now at last he wanted to talk about it. And if Mise had spoken her mind Mag would have buried his feelings deeper still. Instead after a moment of silence he returned to the fire and sat crossed legged, leaning his elbows on his knees with his fingers interlaced, he gazed into the fire with a dark face. Mise watched him, and was surprised when he spoke.

"Is your father still living?" he asked quietly.

To Mise this sounded very odd, and she was quick to respond with a sharp edge, "Of course!" she realized her oversight at once, for a streak of pain crossed his face. And as clearly as if the words had been spoken aloud, she knew that his father was dead.

"It happened when I was young," his voice was rough with pain. "He was beaten to death and I could do nothing! I ran to help him but was held back by a man... it was Horizon."

A coldness settled in her, as Mise came to fully realize what this meant. Mag's face twisted in hatred.

"That man is responsible for the deaths and arrests of many that I loved! He saw my father - he knew that he would die - and he did nothing!" he breathed for a moment. "And now, when I remember my father - when I relive that day... that's when I lose my sight!" he confessed, again he sounded fearful, and Mise wondered if that was the first time that he had ever told anyone that.

Suddenly she knew exactly what to say, it was time to tell a secret. "I know what it's like to face death."

Mag turned his brittle blue eyes on her in a challenge, "Have you lost a mother or father?" he asked harshly.

Mise didn't move.

"Then no! You don't know what it's like."

Mise knew she had made a mistake, but she wouldn't back down! "I've lost everyone before!" she replied heatedly, Mag only stared at her. Slighted by this, she said impulsively, "I died!!!"

His face changed to contempt, "Don't mock me," his whisper held an edge.

"When I was but a small girl, I became very ill - there was nothing that could be done, I died!"

Mag narrowed his eyes, "How is that possible!?"

Promise felt a calm come over her, "Because Nity woke me," she said simply.

But that name changed everything - as it always did. Suddenly the scoff left Imagine's face and he looked at her demanding more with his eyes. She turned to look into the fire, forcing herself to go back in time.

"My memories of that sickness are sharp...but not clear. Even then I was not sure what was dream and what was true. Those who were there tell me that I would cry and beg for things, but I don't remember. I do remember the horror though, the fear that I was lost, beyond hope of being found, the panic of knowing that something terrible was happening to me - and there was nothing that could be done to stop it! And the pain, the loneliness, the certainty that I would never see my mother... or my father, ever again. I died. I stopped breathing and died!"

She turned to see Mag's reaction. He seemed unsure of what to think.

A smile tugged at her lips at her next memory. "Then Eternity - he came to wake me... he called my namesake, and I had to answer him."

"You knew Eternity!?" Mag breathed in wonder.

"My family's history is intertwined with him," she said dryly - she could imagine how murderous Mag would become if he learned the whole truth.

"After he woke me, he helped me water a flower that I had been growing. That same flower withered up and died when he was executed."

By the look at Mag's face, Mise knew that she had made him a believer.

"The very day that same flower put forth new growth, we received news that Nity was alive... I still keep that same flower's petals with me." With a tender smile she pulled out the vial that she wore about her neck. Mag remembered that vial from the first time they had met, but now he gazed at it in wonder. Then he noticed tiny scars on her wrists. He leaned forward and lightly touched one. She smiled and held out her wrist so he could better see.

"The scars from when I was 'bled' before I died." Mag looked up at her, although he wanted to disbelieve her, he couldn't... he surprised himself - for he believed every word!

They sat in silence - for there was nothing more to say.

Chapter 21   Fray

A light breeze of early morning drifted through the open window and unsettled the wispy canopy around the large bed in the center of the room. Two large tapestries hung on the walls, one depicted fields ready to be harvested under a gray sky. The other was a wooded pathway lined with spring flowers, both told of new beginnings, of hope. But hope was gone for Loyal. She lay on the bed like a body without life. Tears slowly made their way down her face and her breath came slowly - sometimes it seemed as though it would not come at all.

What a horrible fool she had been! How had it come to this? How had a few simple words from Favour led to her daughter's endangerment?

'You let it happen...' The voice was her own, constantly tormenting her, dragging the biggest mistake she had ever made in front of her with all its ugliness. If Promise survived she might forgive her mother, Rage might even love her again someday. But never, as long as she lived would Loy ever forgive herself. She squeezed her eyes shut and held her breath, for it was moments like this when the emptiness inside her was replaced with a very real pain - but it never lasted long. The pain would drift away and leave her empty again, denying her even the punishment for her actions. A soft sound came from behind her.

Courage had been standing there for what seemed forever - just watching the still body of his wife. He knew he had to leave soon but he couldn't tear himself away. Several times he almost jumped to her side in fear that she had indeed stopped breathing. Of all the plans he had made as a young man- all the dreams he had dared to dream, never had he perceived such pain and suffering in his own family. How had all this happened?

'You let it happen...You should have seen it! You should have been waiting for your past to catch up - instead Loyal had to go through it alone. You should have been strong enough...' Rage clenched his teeth, as much as he believed this mess was his fault he couldn't help but think of how Loyal hadn't come to him - of how she had betrayed him - and the villagers in Hawthorn!

Why had she not come to him? What had he done to make her believe that she couldn't come to him for help? How had he been so blind!?

'You let it happen,' echoed in his mind.

Just then Loyal rolled over and looked at him, but he turned and walked away quickly. He couldn't face her - not with all his shame and broken pride. He made his way to his private chambers, his face in a dark frown. In his life Rage had faced many a hardship, so what he felt was no strange thing - but it hurt none the less; it was the weight of a heavy heart. Courage's army-trained mind was not often subject to panic, but he feared he may soon lose his calm.

Entering his chambers, he was surprised to see a man waiting for him. He was average height and build, his black hair was smoothed back, and his eyelids seemed heavy with boredom. Despite the warm air, he had wrapped about him heavy furs. He was Tarven: it was Lord Esteem. Rage knew it was him because he had seen him several times since they had arrived in Fray but he had not met him yet. It had bothered him ever since they had arrived that although Lord Esteem had sent a page to escort them to the manor he had not welcomed them himself, nor had it been explained why he was showing them such hospitality. Those troubles had been pushed to the back of his mind of late. But now - here he was! Rage wanted to blast out the question of what in the king's namesake was Esteem doing in HIS chambers! But, Rage knew well his place as a tradesman, and he held his tongue.

"My Lord Esteem," he said with a respectful bow of his head. Esteem turned to face Rage slowly.

"Oh, good - we both know one another, no need for introductions then." His voice was low and slow and he spoke almost breathlessly as if about to laugh softly about some hidden joke. The man made Rage feel uneasy.

"Of course my lord, we are grateful that you have allowed us to stay in your manor."

A strange emotion flitted across Esteem's face, "Where else would you have stayed?"

Rage frowned, "At the village Inn, my lord."

At this the corners of Esteem's eyes crinkled and he almost smiled. Courage's urgency to leave was stifled by Esteem's strange behaviour.

"The Village Inn!? A Tarven of your standing staying a night in a village Inn!" he seemed to find this funny.

Rage threw up his guard at once - 'a Tarven of his standing'!? What had Favour told Esteem about him? Or worse... what did Esteem already know?

"I am but a tradesman." Rage said quietly.

"Oh yes... of course."

'He knows...' Rage braced himself for what may come next.

"And why would you, Courage the tradesman, have ordered that your horse be saddled and ready for a long journey on this morning while your wife is so ill?" his eyes narrowed as he watched Rage for his reaction. Rage was careful not to show any.

"I am a tradesman my lord, I must go where I can trade."

"You would leave your wife here alone?" was that a veiled threat? Or was Rage over reacting?

"I am confident she is safe in your manor," he said, but now he wasn't certain at all.

Este look pleased, "Very well then..." He slowly walked past Rage for the door as if dismissing him.

As he went past, Rage withheld the urge to hold his breath, for the furs that Esteem wore smelled like they had not been tanned correctly. Courage swallowed hard, he had recently thought that they had escaped from Favour and were (or almost) now safe - but now Rage had the uneasy feeling that this strange Tarven lord was worse - much worse than Favour. What was he to do? Go to save Mise and leave Loyal unprotected from Esteem?! He couldn't do that.

'There must be someone in the manor whom I can trust - or at least pay to look after her', his eyebrows pinched together as he tried to think of who he could go to. The page Justice? Perhaps - but that was a risk. One of the rebels in the village? No, they wouldn't do Rage any favours. Who could he turn to?

*   *   *

The night had been truly horrible for Imagine and Promise. The rain had pelted against them, soaking them through and through until their blankets were dripping from the corners. Their poor horses had screamed whenever thunder roared through the night, hot on the lightning's heels. And when at last the storm had ended it was deep into the night - and both Mag and Mise dropped off to sleep as soon as the rain stopped. Truth be told, a chill set into their bones that night and it took them weeks to be rid of it!

When morning came, Mise and Mag were reluctant to get into the

saddle too early after their wet night but were spurred on by the idea that
Fray was only a few short hours away. So they spent a (much too short) half
hour by a small fire to dry themselves as best they could, and Mag redressed
his wounded shoulder. Then with the stale water in his water skin Mag put
out the fire, he then looked up at Mise with raised eyebrows.

"Ready?" he asked simply. To his surprise she smiled brilliantly at
him and nodded sweetly. When she turned away Mag tilted his head to one
side: he had never fully understood girls. Up till now Mise had been
standoffish at the best of times and stuck up at the worst - but now after a
horrible night and a cold morning she was as sweet as sugar water! He put
the puzzle aside in his mind - there was no use trying to figure it out!

The storm had moved on overnight, and it was as though it had
never come. The early morning clouds disappeared leaving a clear blue sky
and a golden sun. The two unlikely travel companions rode side by side and
took note of the countryside beginning to change. The marsh was giving
way to solid ground, cattails turned to grass and trees started growing in
fives and sixes instead of ones and twos. Rivers were no longer flowing in
all directions - instead they only flowed south, into the marsh. What had
been the haze of forests on the horizon the night before, took form and
shape before them.

As they went along they talked from time to time, not about any
one thing, for Mise couldn't bear the silence so she kept finding things to
say or ask. This might have annoyed Mag before, but now he found he
really rather liked talking with her. Climbing a hill, they entered a forest, and
picked their way through the trees. After a lapse in the conversation, Mag
decided to ask a question of his own.

"How long will you be in Fray?"

"Oh, I don't know - depends if father has betrothed me to anyone
here or not." Mise didn't really think that her father would have betrothed
her in two-weeks time. In the back of her mind she hoped that piece of
information would impress Mag - but she was half startled by his response.

"Your father would betroth you without telling you!?" he turned to
look at her. She returned his gaze.

"Yes of course," she said flatly. He blinked and looked back ahead
of them. There was a moment of uncomfortable silence between them.

"And you would just accept it?"

She detected a measure of unbelief in his voice; it irritated her.

210

"Yes. I would," she said quietly. "My father would not give my hand to any man - he will only choose the best, someone who can ensure my future." She repeated her mother's words, but to her further irritation he smiled cheaply.

"So you would be happy to spend the rest of your life as the wife of some Tarven lord with a gray beard, giving him children and running to do his every bidding!"

Mise pulled up her horse in front of his and stared at him in outrage - how dare he!? "Yes. I would be happy to be a wife and mother - happy to be a lady of Tarva! That is what I want."

His smile was replaced with a confidence that infuriated her.

"No Promise," he said quietly, "I don't think you know what you want."

"And I suppose that you in fact know what it is that I want!" she raised her voice - and he matched it.

"I think I have a better idea of it than you!"

She opened her mouth in perfect outrage - but he went on.

"You seem to have a low opinion of yourself Promise - to lash yourself to a perfect stranger and call him your husband. Resigning yourself to the lot of a blind, speechless and simple-minded 'lady of Tarva'! In fact, you seem to have a low opinion of Eternity himself! To suggest that he woke you from death so that you could be a social tool in the hands of your father, is putting a cheap price on the gift Nity gave you!"

Silence followed his bold and reckless statement. No further words did he require to drive home his point, indeed truth rang out of every word to defend him.

Promise felt thunderstruck, all she could do was sit there staring, her eyes wide and vulnerable. Never before had she considered what Mag now said - could it be possible that Nity had woke her for a reason far beyond what could have been grasped at the time? Could she possibly play a role beyond what was imaginable? But then... Mag seemed to believe it. Could Nity have saved Mise the child, so that in time, Promise the woman could do great things???

No, like the flashes of lightning the night before, the word struck her firm and steadfast. She was but a woman - a Tarven woman, her only hope of worth was to marry someone of importance. It was not possible for her to do any great thing for Nity. Her face hardened.

"I know who I am." Her voice was like stone. "I know what I want. Never again tell me what you think of my life. Never again dare to tell me what Nity could have planned for me!" With a yank of the reins she pulled on her horse and broke out ahead of him.

As Mag watched her go he felt the heat drain from his face, a cold certainty took its place.

She was wrong, he thought instantly. He didn't know why, but the thought of Mise marrying a Tarven lord in Fray - was wrong!

It did not take them long to ride through the wood, and Mag caught up to Mise on the edge of the forest. Together they paused to gaze across a clearing at their destination; Fray. And beyond that sitting on a hill overlooking the village like a sentry, stood the keep. Promise clenched her teeth together and glanced over at Mag - she hoped he could see how angry she was with him. He had no right to tell her what she should and shouldn't do - he had no right to assume he knew what Nity had planned for her! She spurred her horse into a gallop across the clearing, while Mag kept pace behind her.

When they reached the village, Mise expected Mag to turn aside and go his own way. But he rode beside her as she made her way to the village Inn. She wanted to coldly inform him that she did not require an escort. But she couldn't bring herself to even look at him to tell him this. Stopping in the Inn courtyard, Mise looked about for her father's wagon but she didn't see it. Before they could dismount a boy ran up to take the horses.

"I'm looking for the tradesman Courage," Mise said stiffly. The boy frowned.

"You mean the Tarven? He's staying up in the manor."

They both looked to where he pointed, if they hadn't been so angry they would have stopped to consider how strange it was that her father was staying in the manor. But as it was they rode on till they came under the shadow of the keep. Holding her head high, Mise passed under the open arch of the portcullis into the courtyard beyond.

She stopped her horse in the center and proudly looked about, sure enough she glimpsed the colorful gypsy wagon beside the stables. She found herself annoyed that Mag sat there glaring at her as if shouting out at her 'YOU'RE UNBELIEVABLY STUPID!' She tilted her head even higher and looked away. Just then two stable boys ran out and took the reins of both horses. They waited expectantly for Mag to say who they were, but instead Mise spoke with as much superiority as she could master.

"I am the Lady Promise. Send word to my father, Courage the tradesman from Hawthorn, that I have arrived." The boy holding her reins nodded and dashed off, Mise then turned what she hoped was a chilling gaze on Mag.

"Goodbye Imagine, I wish you all the best in your quest here." Mag's smile was dim with ill humor, and his eyes crinkled as he said in return.

"Goodbye Promise." Then he yanked the reins from the stable boy and swung his horse about without kissing her hand the way one should when a lady was about - Mise felt sure he did it just to irk her!

Two days ago Mag was waiting for the moment when he could run away from her, but now he felt reluctant to do just that. As he rode back into the village he looked back over his shoulder several times. He couldn't get it out of his head that Mise was making a horrible mistake!

"Why should you care?" he mumbled to himself half-heartedly, again he looked over his shoulder, the castle gate was out of view now.

"You'll break your neck like that," a gruff voice spoke from Imagine's other side. He looked down, the man who spoke was tall and thick looking. He looked up at Mag with piercing blue eyes, he seemed to carry a challenge with him. Mag at once felt as though he had seen this man before. He dismounted and rounded his horse's head where he stood to face this man.

"My namesake is Imagine; I've come from Hawthorn."

The man looked him up and down. "It seems to me that I knew a man who lived in Hawthorn once... he was a man with some radical ideas. It has been many years since I have seen him. I seem to recall this man had a son of your same namesake." The man narrowed his eyes shrewdly. Mag turned his head to one side - he must be careful at all times.

"Do you still know this man?" he asked.

The man smiled faintly, "No... I had word that he died."

He knew it was coming but the spike of pain hit Mag and nearly overwhelmed him. He swallowed hard and before his eyes flashed again the narrow street, the fruit seller, those men - and Horizon.

"That man was indeed my father."

The man bowed his head in respect, "Obedience was a good man, and I called him friend. I am Transform. I would be honored to call you friend as well." He offered his arm and Mag grasped it, but he still felt uneasy about how much he could trust this man.

"Stay in my house, my wife will be happy to have you."

Mag considered it only a moment, "I would be honored to stay with a friend of my father."

*   *   *

True to his word Mag had indeed been welcomed into Transform's house. They all sat around their rough little table - much like his own, and enjoyed the noonday meal. Tran and his wife had three sons and one daughter, the girl was about Mag's age, but the boys were all older, and they all had their father's roughness. Nearest to him sat one of the sons who was closest in age to him, his namesake was Earnestly. He was an apprentice to the blacksmith. Mag had been surprised because Tran had directed him to sit at the head of the table; it was a place of honor, a place given to respected men and women when they visited. Almost no one in Hawthorn treated him with that kind of respect, maybe Tran and his family didn't know how old he was.

Mag couldn't help but fidget and tap his foot impatiently, he knew time was short - Horizon could arrive anytime now, but he couldn't just say that; what if Tran and his family weren't part of the rebellion, what if they couldn't be trusted? But before he could think of how to broach the topic, Tran spoke with surprising openness.

"How goes things for the movement in Hawthorn? We hear dark rumors."

Mag leaned back and frowned, 'that was sudden!' he thought.

"You speak openly with a man you have only just met. You trust me?" The whole family seemed to blink in unison.

"You're Garatin! Of course we trust you - there is no need for whispers and secrets when amongst our own kind!" Tran said.

"Who can we trust if not our brothers?' Earnest said, as if it were a common fact. "Save your suspicion and mistrust for the Tarvens."

Mag felt a great weight lift from him - as though all his problems melted away in the noonday sun; he was - at long last, amongst friends. Now to say what he had come to say.

"Dark indeed must the rumors be, for danger and peril are close to us all."

214

"I knew something was going to happen," one of the brothers muttered darkly.

Mag paused a moment. "I have come here to warn of the coming of a man who would see us all imprisoned! He is Horizon - a Garatin who has turned against his own people. He has terrorized the countryside for months, arresting all he finds involved in rebellious activity - and killing those who resist for even a moment. He is under orders from the Garatin High Council and he carries the seal of Ambassador Sinister himself."

There was silence for a long moment.

"Apparently even our own brothers can't be trusted," the wife said darkly. All the young men seemed stunned by this news while Tran swallowed hard.

"We knew something like this would happen one day - following Eternity is a crime too horrible to be left unpunished!" he said bitterly.

"And you say this man is coming here?" the girl asked.

Mag nodded solemnly, "Word must be sent out at once to go underground - into hiding, make no mistake, my village was ready for him, but he still made arrests… a massacre is coming." Once again there was silence in the cottage.

"Why must we hide when we have done nothing wrong?" Transform said quietly. Mag narrowed his eyes. One of the sons spoke next.

"We have been the hunted too long - the time has come for action!"

"There are enough of us to fight Lord Esteem's men!" Earnest said.

The men were on their feet now, and Mag stood with a dark smile. His family was safe in Hawthorn, there was no one to protect; it was time.

"Rely on my sword," he said. How could he have known that he had just sealed his own dark fate with this deed? Truly, he had added the last heavy load to his heart of lead.

*   *   *

"Promise!" Loyal called out as she ran down a flight of steps and captured her daughter in a staggering embrace.

Mise frowned over her shoulder; what kind of greeting was this!? Her mother couldn't have possibly known that she had traveled through the Quy and been in danger! Loy stepped back and looked at Mise like she was some sort of vision! Mise hoped her face was clean.

"Oh my child! You are safe!" Loy sobbed and it startled Mise - safe from what!? She looked at her father who had been only steps behind her mother, his face looked stricken and renewed all at once! He placed his hand gently on her head and only gazed at her like he had not seen her for years.

"Mother? Father what is it? You act as though I have come back from the dead... again."

"You have dear one!" Loy whispered, Mise felt her stomach tighten - what did that mean?

"This is not the place to discuss it," Rage said, as he looked up and around - they had gathered several onlookers. Loy pulled Mise close once more and Mise felt her mother's tears rub off onto her own face. Then her mother began leading her away, but it was as though her mother had to stop and look at her every two steps before going on. Promise walked beside her supporting her with an arm around her waist - what had happened? Her mother was so weak!

Rage was steps behind them when he became aware that Lord Esteem had walked slowly up and was watching with a peculiar gleam in his black eyes.

"What a lovely daughter!" Esteem said in his breathless manner.

Rage stiffened.

"And such a heartfelt reunion!"

Rage knew that he must make some sort of explanation, but he must be cautious. "She was to join us here a few days ago... she and her guardian must have been delayed by the storm my lord."

"And yet she is here now," Esteem smiled. "And such a lovely thing - she is your only child?" Rage heard warning bells go off; why was Esteem so interested in Mise?

"Yes, my lord, our only child."

Esteem's eyes crinkled at the corners, "How precious!" He watched Promise and Loyal for a moment before turning and walking away.

Rage wanted to feel relief, but somehow he could not dismiss his lordship's strange behaviour so easily.

Promise watched as her mother composed herself. It unsettled Mise to see her mother so distressed - but it unsettled her more to think that her mother would not tell her what exactly had caused her to worry so. Mise sat beside her mother, watching her closely, it was as though Loy cast off a robe of distress and gathered a new robe about herself - one of self-poise and dignity.

"I am so very glad to see you Mise," Loyal said touching Promise's chin with a still trembling finger. Mise held her mother's hand and looked at her with worried eyes, Loy smiled weakly.

"Mother... what is this is about! We have only been parted for two weeks! What has happened?"

"There are many questions that must be answered," Rage said as he closed the door to Loyal's chambers behind him. He then knelt before Mise and looked up into her face for a brief moment before rising and standing before them. Mise swallowed hard - she always felt guilty when her father talked about questions being answered. She noticed that her mother looked suddenly pained and she turned her face away. This confused Mise and she looked at her father with a question on her face.

"Before anything else is explained - Promise you must tell me what happened in Hawthorn."

Promise had prepared an explanation of why she had left Hawthorn - but she had expected her father to be cross with her for leaving.

"Nothing..." she said softly, wondering what in the world her father had expected her to say. "Nothing happened, father. I had just grown tired of Hawthorn and wanted to be with mother and you."

Beside her Loyal raised her eyebrows in disbelief, and Rage again knelt before her and this time took both her hands in his own.

"Do you mean to tell me that no harm befell you by Lord Favour's hand?"

"Of course not." Even as she said it she remembered her handmaiden's strange behaviour the day she had left. Rage hung his head and breathed as though for the first time, while Mise frowned.

"Why should he have harmed me? What has happened!?" Mise was growing impatient, she reached out and grabbed her father's hand. "Father! Tell me, what is this about!?" To her surprise Rage hesitated, and looked at Loy. Her mother stiffened.

"Favour sent a message... to me shortly after we arrived here, he demanded information on the rebels here - he... guessed that I was involved, he threatened your life if I did not comply," he said with a strangely halting voice, as if searching for what to say.

Mise sat there blinking in surprise - she felt like the wind had been knocked out of her! All that time that she had been alone in Hawthorn, she had been in danger! She thought of the time she had warned the rebels of Rizon - if she had been caught... the thought near well made her sick. Why... she had left Hawthorn perhaps hours from her own death! Unless her father had indeed given Favour the information he had asked for - instantly she thought of Mag, had he walked into a trap!?

"Father - did you give him the information?" she asked in a hush - again Rage looked at his wife before saying.

"No, I was preparing to leave for Hawthorn this very morning to get you instead, had I been quicker about it - I would have missed you completely." All three endured the silence for long moments, then Courage spoke with the power of his very namesake.

"We all of us have escaped danger by a breath, Favour also threatened to send word to Sinister of me. However, I am confident that he will not do that," he paused. Mise took note of how he again looked at his wife. Loy touched her forehead with her finger tips and closed her eyes as if in pain.

"The risk is great all the same, and we can never return to Hawthorn again. We cannot risk someone important taking an interest in me, it seems the past is not as far behind as I had hoped."

Fear and uncertainty sprang up in Mise. "Where will we go from here?" she demanded.

Rage looked uncomfortable, "I don't know."

Her father didn't know!?

"I fear that Lord Esteem can be trusted only as much as Favour." There was silence.

"What are we to do?" Mise felt her voice was very small indeed.

"We will remain here for now - I do not want to abandon the movement. I was to meet with the rebels but they have failed to contact me, they do not trust me. If we left now it would be as though I had betrayed those in Hawthorn."

Promise thought of Mag - he would truly never forgive her if she up and deserted him and the movement - strange how that suddenly mattered to her. Suddenly she remembered!

"Father!" Rage looked down at her with one raised brow. "I came here with one of the rebels from Hawthorn - we rode only a day ahead of the man Horizon… he's coming here!" Rage's face became grave.

"You are certain of this?" Mise nodded. "Yes, he came to Hawthorn, and arrested many…" Loyal's face went deathly pale and she opened her mouth but no words came out.

"Who? Do you know who was arrested?" Rage asked.

"No - but I met with the bakehouse keeper, and two men, Journey and Imagine. Mag is the one whom I rode here with, he has warned his friends by now." Rage looked slightly relieved.

"And you say Horizon will soon be here?"

"Yes very soon."

Rage nodded gravely.

Chapter 22   A Twisted Game

"Yes there are several roads from the south, but only one by which Rizon would travel by - and that's this one," Transform said pointing to a dark smudge on the poorly drawn map. Mag nodded.

"Who knows this road best?" he asked looking up at the group of fifteen Garatin faces gathered around in the little barn. Again he was struck with the thrill that they all listened to what he had to say with respect. For a moment the men and women looked around at one another. Tran patted a tall and skinny young man on the shoulder.

"Devotion travels that road almost every day." Devo smiled eagerly. Mag looked him up and down.

"You can run fast?"

Devo's smile widened, "Faster than anyone!" Devo was younger than Mag but was taller than him by far - Mag did not doubt his claim at all.

"Good, then pick a spot on the road - far from town, a place where you can't be seen. Wait there for Horizon and his company." Mag was cut off by one of the older men.

"And when you see the brute, you run boy! Run fast - we'll need a warning of his coming if we are to survive." Everyone seemed satisfied with this, but no one did anything - they just stood there...

"You had better leave now," Mag said. Everyone looked at him slightly surprised, and some even offended.

"Now?" Devo asked.

"Yes. Now - he could be on the other side of that door for all we know!" Mag pointed at the barn door, again everyone looked shocked. "We could all be arrested where we stand! The only chance we have is knowing when he comes! You stay there all night if that's what it takes! We've wasted enough time as it is!"

Devo nodded, and with all the awkwardness of his age he stumbled from the barn. Everyone watched Mag with a mixture of disbelief and fear.

"When Rizon arrives he will begin arresting whomever he can find! Believe me - I have seen it happen! We must be ready for him!" Most of the women and some of the men still looked doubtful, but never the less they began making hurried plans.

*   *   *

Devo squinted his eyes and looked down at the road a half mile from where he crouched on a ridge. The ridge was well sheltered from view by thick pine trees. Satisfied that he had a good view, Devo sat down on the knotted roots of a large tree. He shifted until his spine fitted the tree trunk, then settled his still heavy breathing from running the two and a half miles out of Fray to this spot.

Soon the birds forgot he was about and began singing as before, he listened for a time while keeping his eyes on the path below. Then a bit of movement caught his attention, with a smile Devo realized that it was a four horned deer not two hundred meters away - if he had brought his bow with him he would have brought home fresh venison! Time slipped by and Devo grew bored with his scouting. It was well past dinner, his belly reminded him often, but he would be surprised if his four brothers left him anything! Why had he been picked for this job anyhow? And why all this fuss for one man!? He wondered in frustration, but he knew that no one would listen to him or take him seriously if he spoke his doubts.

Suddenly movement below jolted him back to his responsibilities; it was Horizon.

The light had all but gone and left the village of Fray with only the shrouded light of the stars and a half-moon, still Mag ran his sharpening stone down the length of his hunting knife. He sat behind Transform's cottage and was well sheltered from the street. Tran had hardly a sliver of ground between his cottage and stable. It was here that Mag had settled down in wait for word from Devo. Again and again he ran the stone down his short blade, the metallic sound gave him discomfort at most times - but now it seemed to calm him and prepare him. He needed to be comforted when the blindness took him. He had just been sitting there waiting for Horizon when his eyes went dark! Panic fought to take over but he couldn't break down now! He must be strong! Slowly the blackness left him and he could breathe again. He became aware of Tran walking up behind him. For a time, he was silent.

"Looking at you…" he said quietly, "One would think you are looking for blood." A heaviness entered Mag's heart, all he could do was look up at Tran. Mag was almost certain that an understanding passed between them.

Suddenly Devotion burst in, behind him came Tran's sons and several others. "He's coming!" Devo said excitedly.

Mag jumped to his feet, "How long before he arrives?"

221

"An hour," Devo said.

Mag frowned, "Why so long?" he asked confusedly. Surely Devo couldn't run that fast!

"He travels by carriage." There was a silence.

"Mag…" Tran spoke quietly, "What is it?"

Imagine shook his head, "Rizon and his company left Hawthorn by horse back."

Devo looked lost, "What does that mean?" he asked.

Mag felt sick, "It means that Rizon sent word to Lord Esteem while on the road. They may have made plans to make arrests tonight!" Mag spoke aloud what everyone else was just beginning to realize.

"What should we do?" someone asked, the fear on their face was hidden by the darkness.

"We hold to the plan!" Mag said firmly. "It doesn't matter when he comes just as long as we are ready for him." Looking around Mag sensed fear and uncertainty - why couldn't they see the opportunity!?

"I'm not sure this is worth it; Esteem's men will crush us." Mag couldn't see who had spoken but there were many who grunted in agreement - he was losing them, Mag thought desperately. He had to do something - what would his father do?

"Not worth it!?" Mag spun around to try and find who had spoken, everyone watched him and he felt his face heat with passion. "Whatever you do - fight or hide - he will take whom he pleases! Then he will go on to the next village and more innocents will pay - we can end it here and now!" His fist grasping his knife trembled in excitement as he spoke, "Yes Esteem's punishment will be swift - but we will be rid of the plague of Horizon! So tell me; is our freedom not worth the risk!? I can see a future where we are free, and it starts tonight!" His voice was full of emotion, and his passionate words kindled a fire in the hearts of the villagers. Doubt was forgotten, and reason left behind; the Garatins of Fray would fight!

"Everyone go to your own homes - and wait till he makes the first arrest - then he will know the point of his own sword!" At Trans' words everyone dispersed into the night, each grasping a weapon. Mag stayed behind, and he felt the blackness fight to take his sight again - biting his lip he waited till his sight was clear again. Now they would just wait for Rizon - and then, then Obedience would be avenged.

An hour later, the sound of carriage wheels played upon the

listening ears of the still village, Mag closed his eyes and felt a coldness settle in him; soon very soon now.

But the carriage and six riders passed by and rode up to the manor, the whole village waited for Esteem's soldiers to come marching down the hill with torches in hand...

They waited deep into the night and still nothing. Imagine could feel the villagers resolve fading. Stepping out into the street and looking up at the manor, Mag felt uncertainty take him; why did Rizon wait? What twisted game was he playing!?

*   *   *

"I don't understand it father," Mise spoke in a hushed voice late the next morning. "Why has he not made any arrests?"

Courage shook his head; he couldn't understand it either. He had watched from his chamber window the night before and had seen Horizon arrive. Rage had braced himself for a horrible scene below... but it never happened. He had waited half the night, but the village hadn't been disturbed. Early that morning he had walked the streets to be sure - but there was no sign anything had happened the night before. If Wilderness had been there he would have disagreed and drawn attention to the many footprints about the houses, furthermore he would have seen that these footprints were not made by any soldiers. However, Rage had no such subtle skills, instead Rage wandered the manor court and talked to many people. In this way he learned that Rizon had indeed arrived the night before, and yes Lord Esteem had opened his hospitality to him, but no one in the court, noble man or serving girl had seen Rizon. And from what Rage could gather, Rizon had not yet had an audience with Lord Esteem.

His concern for the villagers of Fray was matched only by his confusion over Horizon's actions.

"Do you know what the rebels plan to do?"

Mise shook her head, "No, Imagine only said that he had to warn everyone." She looked up at him beseechingly, "What is Rizon doing father? Why does he delay?"

"I don't know. But I intend to keep a close eye on him." He turned to go but suddenly he had a thought, turning back to his daughter he said, "And stay away from Lord Esteem as much as you can." She nodded her head, and they said no more.

*   *   *

"And your friend, he had no warning?" Earnestly asked, as he and Mag walked along.

"None of us knew what was happening - Horizon didn't care that Wit was unarmed, they just ran him through like it was part of their job."

Earnest shook his head, he was rough and hard to read, but Mag could tell that his words and stories had left an impression on him. A hatred had been kindled in Earnest's heart for Rizon. It made Mag feel... better, to know that there was someone else who hated Rizon as much as he.

"Horizon travels under Garatin laws, he makes arrests in the name of Eloi and for the sake of justice, but he doesn't know the meaning of the word! Instead he kills whomever he pleases."

Mag had to stop because his emotions were overwhelming him. Beside him Earnestly seemed to understand and he remained silent. It had been three days since Horizon had arrived in Fray, two days of tense waiting and watching, never knowing when he would come - and Mag was convinced that he would come. Everywhere he went he carried with him his hunting knife, and Transform and his sons (whom Mag had stayed with) also carried knives with them. They had committed to never going anywhere alone, and staying in large groups as much as they could, always casting their eyes up to the manor expecting the worse. Now it was late morning, Mag was walking with Earnest who was on his way to the smithy to begin his work for the day.

"How many would you say Horizon took from your own village?" Earnest asked as they neared the smithy. Mag felt a darkness take him as he remembered that fateful night.

"Nine," he said, his voice thick and low. "Four of them were mere children." Earnest's face turned ugly with hate, and Mag felt a sense of comradery.

Together they entered the open door of the smithy, the atmosphere was vastly different from outside; the smithy had once been a small barn, and the back wall was completely gone with just the waist high stone foundation left. One entire corner was taken up by the oven and the giant bellows used to work the fire up to a fierce heat. Close by was a barrel full of cold water and a work table cluttered with different tools. And over every flat surface was a thick layer of brown dust.

Gathered about in a tight bunch was the blacksmith, Realize, and several other of the rebels; they all stopped short when Mag and Earnest entered.

"And there he is!" Realize said pleasantly. Earnest looked annoyed.

"I'll start working right away sir," he said.

"I was speaking of our friend from Hawthorn." Mag gritted his teeth; he could feel his welcome wearing thin even as he stood there.

"It seems your journey here was in vain, our scare of a couple of nights ago was just that; a scare." The blacksmith was suddenly quite menacing.

"I agree," said another one of the men who had been there three days ago, he sounded less hostile. "Whatever danger this man Horizon brings is hardly enough to concern ourselves over." The others all nodded in agreement, they acted as though it was a trivial matter, as though Mag was just a foolish boy. A helplessness entered him; Rizon was going to come for them at any time now - and they didn't believe it!

"We can't be certain he isn't a threat," Earnest said. "This man has terrorized the country - we just can't dismiss that!" To Imagine's relief this gave the men pause, but what was said next made his heart skip a beat.

"He's right, we would be foolish to believe we are completely safe..." someone said with a frown. "What about the Tarven - he is in the manor with Horizon." Mag blinked in surprise; of course! Promise's father - but they couldn't turn to him in this matter! Suddenly he saw Promise's face staring at him, accusing him of being unfair and childish - but he pushed the thought away. The man went on.

"If he could be trusted, perhaps he can shed light on Horizon's plans. Then at least we will know what the danger is." The men considered it for a moment, then Lize turned to Mag.

"Wait - the Tarven Courage was sent by you and the others in Hawthorn!" Mag swallowed. "So tell us; can the man be trusted?" Everyone waited for his answer.

What an opportunity! Just a few words from him - and they would never accept Rage... who knows he might never bother him and his friends again. Mag could rid the movement of a troublesome Tarven! But then there was Mise... he had no right to condemn Courage solely for the fact that he was Tarven. But he couldn't make himself say so.

"He has not done anything to prove himself untrustworthy." Surprisingly everyone seemed to accept this.

"Can you speak with him about Horizon?" Again everyone waited.

Well one thing was certain - he would meet with Mise not Rage… but to face Mise after what he had last said to her? Would she even agree to meeting with him?

"I can try."

*   *   *

"This is the Garatin's chambers my lady," Justice the page said waving his arm to a door. He looked at Promise and smiled. "Is there anything else I can do for you?" he asked eagerly.

Mise shook her head, "No thank you Justice, that will be all." She offered him a smile and was sure that she saw him blush before he walked away.

Mise tightened her grip and felt the thick paper of the note crumple in her fist. Both her hands were sweating, and there was a weakness in her knees, as she waited for Justice to turn a corner and slip from view. She forgot about him at once, then she turned back to the door.

'I'm being foolish,' she thought to herself. 'I should wait for father and show him the note, let him deal with this.' It made perfect sense in her mind, after all what did she owe Mag? In truth he owed her! It was she who had provided him with a horse for the journey here - a horse that he had still not returned. It was a good thing she was never returning to Hawthorn again; she would be accused of horse stealing! She had half made up her mind to turn around and leave- just standing there pricked her pride knowing that she was doing Mag a favour, especially after what he had last said to her! Why should she put herself in danger like this for him? But… there was their danger to think of too. How many in Fray were waiting for Horizon to come for them? The information that she could gather behind that door might still save lives.

Suddenly Imagine's face sprung into her mind; smug and cold, self-righteous as he dared to presume he knew better then she what she wanted. She could see him there, shaking his head in disapproval, as if to say 'I knew I couldn't trust you with something important'. Mise would prove him wrong if it was the last thing she did. Her jaw tightened and she threw her shoulders further back, with the pride of her father she opened the door and stepped in closing it behind her. For a moment she stood in half darkness and took in the small room, a small bed, chest and thick rug filled the otherwise empty room. Opposite the bed was an archway to another room where the crackle of a fire came from. Slowly, quietly, as if her shoes were made of fur, she stepped out into the chamber and glanced into the second room, there with his back to her, sat a Garatin man.

Promise's heartbeat quickened - she was here, in the same room as Horizon! The man who had caused such strife throughout the land was only a few steps away. It only vaguely crossed her mind that she could be in danger, alone with a man who apparently had no heart. Now what?

"My lord?" she called softly, and wondered if it wasn't like calling death closer. The shaking returned to her knees as he cocked his head to one side, then stood to his feet to face her. With the fire to his back and only dull sunlight coming from a window Mise had a hard time seeing his face - but she could see strange dark blue eyes.

"Who's there?" he asked. Mise felt a streak of surprise; his voice sounded kind! But then not all evil was plainly seen, she surmised. Now it was time to discover the truth.

"I am Promise, daughter of Courage the... the tradesman." She stuck out her chin. He stepped to one side and in so doing the fire lit up his Garatin face - again she was surprised, for although his face was sharp and had a hard look about it, the malice she had expected to be there was strangely void and his eyes had a strange color to them. Childlike curiosity took her; what kind of man was this? She stepped closer.

"He said you'd come," he breathed, "I've been waiting." He gripped the edge of the mantelpiece.

Mise frowned in alarm. "Who?! Who said I would come?"

"Eternity. He told me you would come," he answered quietly.

Mise blinked in surprise; Nity!? What was he saying?

"I met him on the road, on my way here."

"That can't be!" she said slowly.

"Can't it?" he asked, "you are a Nity follower, aren't you? Don't you believe in the impossible."

Her frown deepened in distrust, how did he know that about her? "I might be... what happened?"

"A day short of reaching Fray, my company was attacked by bandits, in the darkness and confusion I was separated from the others. I was lost and disoriented, when a man came out of the darkness towards me. I thought him to be one of the bandits, but he was unarmed. I asked him who he was... I had no idea what was to follow..." Rizon paused and seemed lost in the memory.

"He said that I should know him, that he was my bitter enemy! I had never seen him before, but he said that I had hunted him all my life!"

Still skeptical, Mise asked, "And it was Eternity?"

Deadly serious he replied, "He told me that I had closed my eyes on the truth... He took my sight away and said when I was ready to see the truth that a girl – Promise - would come and my sight would be restored."

"What else did he say?" Mise asked in a hush.

"Things for my ears alone..." he replied solemnly. "Soon he disappeared, and I found myself in the midst of my camp. Day was breaking, and my companions had been searching for me all night. But I had gone completely blind."

For so long Mise had been plagued by the question of what had become of Nity after Treasure spoke with him. The things her father had learned had hardly been satisfying, and she had not cared (why was that?). She had thought that Nity would be at the front of the rebel movement - if he could defy death... no one could stand in his way! But instead he had disappeared and had not been seen for over a year - until now. This man, this Rizon had seen him! Spoken with him even! Promise's hand went to the vial about her neck with the remains of her flower. Impossible indeed.

"He said that I would come? He spoke of me?" She asked in wonder, he nodded. A breath of excitement escaped her; Nity remembered her!

"He said that I would restore your sight when you were ready to see the truth..." she said quietly and looked up at him. "Are you? Are you ready to turn from your ways - or are you still an enemy to Nity?"

Horizon was silent before her - he looked weary as though struggling with an inner battle. Mise stepped closer to search his face.

"Eternity... was right, I have hunted him for what feels like my whole life. When first I heard of him and his teachings seven years ago, I was confused and torn; how could a Garatin uphold Eloi and yet cast down everything we know about him? I rejected him and his ways. Then I began what I thought to be a righteous purge in the name of Eloi, ridding Garatin of imposters who had forgotten the truth." He paused, and Mise could see the battle waging in him.

"Never had I considered that it was I who had closed my eyes... Nity made me see the lie that I believed. Now I understand; Eternity held up the true Eloi, and cast down the lies that we as a whole nation had come to believe as true. He did so because he was – is - the Eloi-man. Death did not stop him from opening my eyes to the truth."

Mise felt her throat grow tight, and she knew what she had to do, even if she didn't know how she knew. She stepped close to him and reached out her hand to touch his, but before she did she looked up into his eyes and was surprised; they looked just like Mag's eyes did when he went blind!

The next moment her hand had touched his and he closed his eyes as though in pain, and he cried out. Mise stepped back in fear - what had she done!? Gripping the mantelpiece with one hand and the chair arm with the other, his face crumpled in pain. A moment later when the pain passed, he opened his eyes and blinked rapidly, and Mise could see that his eyes had changed to a bright cold blue.

"It worked!?" she asked in surprise; had Nity just done the impossible through her!?

He covered his face with his hands then looked about the room. "Yes... I see now."

Mise let out her breath in relief. She wasn't sure of what had just happened; it seemed so unreal.

"I don't know if you or any of the others will ever believe me when I say this, but I have changed!" He spoke after a moment, "I have not made any new arrests because I do not intend to."

Mise looked at him for a long moment; she knew people could change - her father was an example of that! But so much could be lost if she trusted Rizon, and he proved to be lying to her...

Rizon narrowed his eyes. "Will you believe me?" he asked.

Mise glanced down at the hand she had touched Rizon with; the impossible didn't happen without reason. "Yes..." she said at last, "I believe you."

"Will you tell the rebels who are here in Fray and plead my case?" he asked.

"They will have no reason to trust you," she said thinking of Mag's hatred.

Rizon nodded, then looked to the fire mantelpiece, stepping up to it he picked up a folded paper. Unfolding it he handed it to her, a heavy seal made one corner hang down. Mise took it from his hand, it was his authorization from Ister himself, granting power to make arrests. The wax seal held the crest of the Tarven ambassador. Mise raised her eyes to meet Rizon's, he then took the paper from her and stooped to the fire. Making sure Mise had full view, he held one corner to the flames and the heavy paper blackened at the fire's touch. Promise watched as the yellow flame licked along the paper leaving a blackened trail behind it. When the paper was half aflame, Rizon let go of it and it floated down into the full fury of the fire. The blackened paper came apart in the air as it fell, and the heat currents sent the crisp ashes floating upward.

Mise watched for a moment as the paper was consumed by the flames, leaving the wax seal to bubble and melt. Mise glanced up at Rizon's face, but he wasn't watching, instead he held in his hand the wooden handle of an official seal. With a small knife he pried off the bronze crest, it came off with a pop. Stepping to the mantelpiece again, he pounded the intricate crest with the handle until it was flat. He looked up and returned her gaze. He then handed her the bent out of shape bronze plate that had been an unstoppable seal.

"Let that stand as proof of my intentions."

*   *   *

Imagine scuffed the cobbles with his boot, again he ran his eyes over all the windows that were staring down at him in the manor courtyard, he couldn't see anyone, but he was certain people were watching him. He turned back to the cart of hay that he stood beside and hoped that no one would question why a Garatin peasant was waiting about in the manor courtyard. But out of everyone walking here and there, going about their daily chores, no one seemed to notice him. He looked up and there coming down the manor steps at a leisurely pace was Promise. She wore a red tunic that came just above her knees and brown pants with little boots. Her hair was pulled back from her face and tumbled down her back. Even from where he stood he could see how her thick lashes framed her cinnamon eyes. She looked about until she saw him, but instead of walking to him she stood where she was and waited.

Mag clenched his teeth, he knew what she was doing. Her face was unsmiling as she stood there: this was payback for his parting words three days ago. She was going to make him walk across the courtyard in plain view and talk to her, and risk drawing attention to himself. Just then Promise's stormy face gave way and she walked towards him. This surprised Mag, that she was the first to swallow her pride - and so quickly too! Not a word was said as she came to stand beside him; she reached up, removed a thin stick from the hay cart and held it in her small hands.

"Hello Promise," he said tightly.

"Good morrow Imagine; I hope your wound is healing well."

Mag subconsciously rolled his shoulder and managed a tight nod. He waited for her to speak further.

Mise was silent for a long moment - much too long for Mag. "What were you able to learn?" he asked.

"I don't think that Rizon is a threat anymore," she said suddenly, there was another silence, but this time on Mag's part.

"No longer a threat?" he asked, his eyes narrowing; he couldn't have heard her right!

"That's what I said," she replied, not looking at him. Again Mag was silent, this time he shifted his weight so he could look directly into her face. She returned his gaze, she was sincere. He let his breath go - what could this mean? What kind of trickery was this - what kind of game was Mise playing at? And he hadn't missed how she dispensed with the formality of calling Horizon by his namesake.

"Mag I know how you feel about this - I do, but," she spoke before he could clear his mind. "He's changed," she said firmly.

"And you know this how? Because he gave you his word!?"

She snapped the stick she held in half and tossed it away. "It was more than that!" Taking from a pocket of her tunic she held out to him a bent out of shape bronze disk, no larger than the palm of her hand. He looked down at it suspiciously.

"What's that?"

"Ambassador Sinister's seal," she said simply.

What!? Mag frowned as he took it from her hand and examined it.

"Even if he wanted to - he can't make arrests, not here." Mag looked up at her, still unbelieving.

"He burned his papers of authorization from Sinister - I watched him do it, then after, he pried that seal off of the stamp handle and he pounded in the crest. Mag! Don't you see? Our troubles are over - he has changed... he's harmless."

Imagine's head reeled with this information, and in all the chaos he realized what all this implied; Mise had spoken face to face with Horizon and had put herself in danger! He was somewhat startled when she stepped closer and laid her hand on his, lifting his eyes he saw that she was looking intently up at him.

"Mag... don't you see? The people of Fray are no longer in danger from Horizon - the whole country is safe! He's one of us now."

"Harmless?" he did not whisper the word in reference to Rizon- but rather, himself. If Mise had realized this, perhaps much would have been different.

"Are you saying..." Mag asked softly, "That he... has asked for us to accept him as one of us? Because it will never happen Promise!" Mise swallowed and looked down.

"He has not asked for forgiveness, Mag, he just wants us to believe him."

"And you do?"

She bit her lip, "Yes; I do."

Mag stepped away shaking his head, breathing seemed hard to do. Again the flashback came clear and strikingly vivid.

Young Imagine's foot slipped out in front of him as he ran, just barely catching himself, he looked back with tears streaking down his face. The man who held his arm in an iron grip looked down at him with eyes like ice.

Suddenly the memory went black and Mag gasped as his sight failed and the world went dark. He stumbled on an uneven cobble stone. 'Calm down!' he told himself - but he couldn't, all he could feel was hatred as cold as Horizon's eyes. He clenched his teeth, heat rose up into his face, and he gripped the deformed seal until it's sharp edge cut the palm of his hand. The pain did not shock him back but rather drove him deeper. Behind him Mise reached out and grabbed his good arm, from her foot-steps he knew she had stepped around to face him.

"Mag - it's happening again isn't it?"

He couldn't answer and instead gagged on his own breath, the way his tears had choked him so long ago.

"Mag," Promise lowered her voice until it was calm and reassuring. "You need to calm down, thinking about your father and how he died is doing this to you - so please, calm down..."

Slowly he gained control of his breathing and closed his unseeing eyes, again he buried deep his anger for another time. The two stood there for a long time, until Mag felt Promise's hand opening up his clenched fist and carefully removing the seal. He opened his eyes and was surprised to find his sight had returned. Mise looked up at him, in her hand she held the bent seal - it dripped with his blood.

"I know," she said simply, and somehow it touched his heart. "I know Horizon is responsible for so much heartache, but he has changed. He has done great wrong to you - don't let that blind you! Please, let's give him a chance and then judge him." Gently she placed the seal in his other hand.

"Show this to your friends and tell them what he said. If it's true, we are all safe - if he lies, then he will have to obtain new papers before arresting us, either way we are safe for the moment." She smiled and then left him standing there.

Chapter 23   Dark Plans

The heat from the forge made it near well impossible to tell whose faces were flushed with the heat and whose faces were flushed with anger. The little blacksmith shop was crowded enough without tempers running high. There was Realize, Earnest and Mag. And there was Earnest's father Tran and one of his sons, the other was outside acting as a lookout in case of a trap. Along with one of the other rebels, who had spotted the excitement, there were six men in the little smithy, and every single one of them held untrusting eyes on the seventh and eighth men who stood in the center of them all; Courage and Horizon.

The night before Mag had hesitantly told Tran and his sons what Mise had learned – they had been confused and wary. After some discussion they had agreed that it was some sort of trap and that they must be careful. The news had traveled surprisingly quickly and by late the next morning everyone who had been in danger of Horizon had heard the news, and it seemed they all had their own opinion on what it meant. When the Tarven had been seen accompanying Horizon to the blacksmith, in the late morning, they had been shadowed closely by Tran and his three older sons.

Now the group of men stood about in a close knot, casting nervous eyes to the windows and doors, wondering if at any second they would be overrun with Esteem's soldiers. It was one thing to make light of Rizon the day before, and a whole other thing to be face to face with him. Realize was the only one who remained calm, and he mindlessly pounded away on the bent horse shoe that Rizon had brought in as an excuse for his visit.

"Again, I tell you that I believe Rizon *can* be trusted." Courage said, he tried hard not to let any of his frustration over the whole thing be heard in his voice.

"So you say," Transform said with narrowed eyes. "But who's to say we can trust you?" Rage looked to Imagine, but the young man didn't look up at him, and Rage gave a short sigh. He realized that he had been foolish to believe that Mag would vouch for him. Horizon spoke then, and he offered up the palms of his hands as he spoke in a pleading gesture.

"I know I have done great evil to you and many others - but I denounce my past actions. I swear to you in Eloi's name; I have changed. I have seen Eternity face to face - and I have changed. I would not come here in this way if it were not so." He paused and looked about but could see that his words had no impact. In the back corner Mag gritted his teeth with distaste.

"If you will not take me at my word then let me prove my sincerity through my actions," he offered. Still no one spoke. "Will none of you give me the chance to prove my words?"

The stony silence was broken harshly as Realize pounded the horse shoe one last time. Rage looked about uneasily, the tension was so thick Rage felt as though he were buried in it! Rizon closed his mouth firmly in disappointment.

"I will soon depart from Fray, to leave you all in peace, but before I do - please consider my words."

He was a passionate speaker, but his words fell on deaf ears. The people of Fray were too wary of lies; they had listened to Imagine's stories of hatred and treachery all too well. After a moment of silence where Rizon looked beseechingly at everyone, Lize held out the repaired horse shoe.

"No charge," he said gruffly. Rizon looked at him but before he could say a word Lize continued just as gruffly, "Just get out." Tran and his son parted, making a clear path to the door. Rizon hesitated but Rage laid a hand on his shoulder.

"Come, there is nothing more to be said here." Rizon nodded and the two of them turned, and as they left, Tran's son bumped shoulders with Rizon roughly - and not entirely by accident. Every eye watched the two men leave the smithy, but when they were gone the atmosphere did not lighten a shade, rather it darkened.

"First a Tarven seeking friendship, now a turncoat Garatin," Tran said in an ugly manner.

"Next it may be the King of Tarva!" someone said.

"Someone would find a knife in their back long before then, if I had my way," Earnest said passionately.

Lize shook his head, "Horizon should be driven out of town!"

"That's too good for him," Mag spoke for the first time. Ever since yesterday morn they had lost their respect for him, but they listened now.

"Makes me downright furious how he talks about Nity - claiming that he spoke with him! As if Nity would come from the grave to speak with a murderer!" Tran said.

"Nity would more likely run him through before speaking to the likes of him!" the other man said.

"Well he hasn't, has he?" Earnest said sourly.

"Perhaps we're the ones who are meant to do that," Trans other son who had stepped in from outside said, with a dark look in his eyes.

"Why not?" Earnest's other brother agreed. "That imposter needs to pay for all he's done!" Everyone stirred and muttered in agreement.

"Call him back and let's do it now!" Earnest said hotly grabbing hold of one of the blacksmithing hammers.

"No!" Realize said in alarm, "Not here!"

"He's right - we must be cautious, or we could end up in Esteem's dungeons or worse, remember he is a Garatin official!"

"We'll get him on the road when he leaves town!" the other man said excitedly.

"Aye! We'll ambush him! And that will be the end of him and his treachery!"

"We need to be certain of when he leaves," Tran said, "We wouldn't want him to miss our farewell."

*　　　　*　　　　*

Courage knew he should be angry with Promise for confronting a potentially dangerous man, but instead his heart had swelled with pride. There had been a time when he had wished she had been a son instead, thinking that she would never take after him - how wrong he had been!

Rage had been hesitant at first to believe that a man such as Horizon could make such a drastic change, but then Rage was a man who believed in such things. Had he not once been a different man too? It had been Wilderness who had believed him, shouldn't he in turn believe Rizon? And then there was also what Mise had said about his eyes - that she had done the impossible! To Rage it seemed unreal that it could have happened at all.

After Mise had told him everything, he had gone to meet Rizon himself. After he did, all his doubts vanished. Impossible or not, Rage knew what a recently changed man looked like, he had once looked the same way. He had then offered to accompany Rizon and speak for him when he met with the rebels. He had really hoped things would go better than they did.

Now he and Rizon were back in Courage's chambers to discuss what was to be done next, along with Promise and Loyal, who sat apart from them.

"None of them would listen?" Mise asked with concern after hearing what had transpired at the smithy. Rizon shook his head.

"Was Imagine there?" Rage noticed how her concern seemed to grow, he spoke when Rizon hesitated.

"Yes, I believe he was, but like the others he gave us no quarter."

"Imagine has a lot of bad blood towards you," she said looking at Rizon. "But he'll come around!" Again Rage noticed how distressed she appeared about this.

After a moment Rizon spoke. "I should have known how deeply they would hate me - but I had to try. If I could only make them understand my shame over my actions, then they would believe me."

"It is no use agonizing over it - their minds will not be changed," Rage said.

Promise looked deeply dismayed at his words. Beyond them and clearly apart from them sat Loyal, upright and regal as ever. But there was a brokenness about her face that Rage could plainly see. She remained silent and only listened, her eyes lingering often on Mise, and sometimes Rage could feel her lonely gaze settle on him. He longed to call her closer. He knew that Mise would find comfort from her mother, but Loy seemed to distance herself as though afraid that she might do further harm to her. (Rage could only imagine what Mise must think). But no matter how forlorn Loy might appear or how strong the stirrings in Rage… his pride would not allow himself to even speak to her.

Indeed, he didn't know what to do; she had betrayed him, yet was clearly devastated by her actions. Real harm had been avoided. But Rage couldn't make himself speak words of forgiveness to her, indeed she begged him to forgive her every time her dark eyes fell on him. But pride is a powerful force, and he could not put away his pride - even for his wife. He turned his back to her - he could never forgive himself should he bend his pride for her! He was a man of Tarva, some things just were not done.

"I'm afr…" Mise was interrupted as a knock was heard at the door. Rage waved for Rizon to move out of sight, they didn't need it to be known that Rizon was there.

"Enter," Rage said after a moment. Justice the page boy stepped in and held out his hand.

"A message for the maiden Promise," he smiled shyly.

Mise took the note from him, and was surprised, it was from Mag!

Mise murmured her thanks and Justice went to the door and gave a little bow before leaving. As soon as the door had closed behind him, Rage asked eagerly.

"What is it?"

"It's from Imagine - he wants to speak to Rizon as soon as possible!" they all looked to Rizon - perhaps they had been wrong! Quickly they called Justice back and sent him in search of Mag, instructing him to bring Mag to them. Rage gave Justice a hand full of coins and 'suggested' that he keep all this a secret, it made Justice smile all the wider. The four waited for the page to return with Mag.

Mise found herself nervous and unsettled. First, there was the unanswered question of what exactly had happened when she had touched Rizon? She had restored his sight certainly, but how!? Was it Eternity's doing? And why could she not heal Mag's eyes when she touched him!? did he suffer from something different? Or was her 'healing touch' a onetime thing? Until she knew the answers she didn't want to tell Mag anything, and she hoped it didn't come up in the coming conversation.

And that lead to the second thing she worried about; what on earth was Mag going to say to Rizon!? All she could think of was his story of what Rizon had done to his father. Looking at Horizon now, she found it hard to believe that he could be cruel at all. Suddenly Mise felt guilty for not explaining in full Mag's hatred towards Rizon. This unexpected meeting could become more than a little hostile.

And that was the third thing fluttering about in her head and worry sickened heart. Her parents and Mag in the same room… there were so many ways that could go wrong!

A knock was heard at the chamber door. Mise opened the door; Justice stood there with his incorrigible smile. "Found him!" he whispered excitedly. Beside him stood Mag who was looking over his shoulder nervously.

"Yes thank you Justice - remember don't tell anyone!" Mise said hurriedly hoping he would leave. She reached out her hand to grab Mag's arm.

"Is he here?" he asked almost in a whisper. Mise nodded and quickly pulled him inside, leaving Justice in an empty hall. Mag hunched his head down as if embarrassed or afraid, his eyes fluttered about the room till they rested on Horizon who stood at the far end of the chamber. Promise's heart beat quickened as she watched Mag's face grow paler, and his lips grew tight as he swallowed over and over. Across the room Rizon shifted as he sensed the tension. Promise reached out and touched Mag's arm gently, she could feel his muscles corded up ready for... what?

"Mag?" she whispered, "What is it you needed to speak of?" Mag ducked his head suddenly and averted his eyes from Rizon.

"Promise I... I couldn't just pretend not to hear them - I wish I could have..." he sounded torn and his eyes kept half darting to where Rizon stood, then back away again.

"Mag what do you mean?" she became aware of Rizon and her father watching them closely. Mag gasped softly.

"The others.... They're planning to kill you!" he made himself look up at Rizon for a half moment. Mise blinked in surprise, in the back of the chamber Loy gasped and Rage's face darkened.

"You heard them say this?" Rizon was the first to speak. Still Mag couldn't look at him fully, but he nodded. "As soon as you left the smithy - they... they want your blood. They plan to ambush you on the road when you leave." There was silence, and Mag met Promise's gaze.

She couldn't believe it; he had betrayed his own to warn the one man who could make him - literally blind with hatred! She smiled faintly.

"I should have seen this coming," Courage spoke. "The rebels here are mad with hate, for the sake of your life I bid you do not leave the safety of the manor walls!"

At once Rizon shook his head, "I must. Remaining here would not appease them, instead they would find a way to come to me, manor or no. I am not welcome here, you said it yourself 'their minds will not be changed'. I must leave."

Mise was struck with wonder that there was no anger or resentment in his voice towards those who would see him dead. Rage nodded.

"Then you must depart today - now, while there is yet time."

"No!" everyone looked at Mag, the single word was spoken almost desperately. "It's too late, they're already waiting. They sent me to watch inside the court yard. You won't find any man in the fields today, they're all out waiting... for you." Again there was silence.

"But there must be a way out!" Mise burst with a touch of panic. "There must be a way to slip past them!"

"I tell you there is none!" Mag said to her. "They will wait until the

moon falls into the Quy before leaving their posts- it is blood they seek!"
No one spoke for a time, everyone knew that they couldn't ask Lord
Esteem to send soldiers to escort Rizon. Esteem was more likely to boot
Rizon out and watch like it was a sport rather than round up the rebels.

"I will see that you make it out!" Rage said impulsively.

"No, I told them I've changed. Leaving in a blood bath would not
convince them of that. Besides you couldn't possibly hope to go up against
that whole village and come out alive."

Rage hissed under his breath and turned away in thought.

"Tomorrow," Rage said suddenly. "There is a banquet tomorrow
night. That is when you must leave!"

Rizon frowned, "How?"

A smile spread across Courage's face as his idea took form.
"Esteem will send out wagons of food for the villagers as part of the
banquet celebrations..." there was silence, as comprehension came to
everyone's faces. "You will walk out through the manor walls past your
would-be assassins along with the wagons disguised as one of Lord
Esteem's men!" Rizon nodded, and Mise felt her heart grow light again.

"My packs can be hidden on the wagons, and once in the village I
can slip away in the crowd unnoticed... but what of my horse?" Rizon
wondered aloud, Mise stepped forward.

"You can have your horse hooked up to one of the wagons." Both
Rage and Rizon nodded, then Rizon sighed.

"I could never get this all done myself without being noticed."

"Leave that to my daughter and I. We will see that you escape
Fray." Mise felt a surge of excitement and pride at her father's words.

"But what of Esteem? Surely he will notice if you disappear from
the banquet, then all of these subtleties will be for not."

"Have no fear my lord." Everyone turned their heads to Loyal who
had spoken for the first time. She sat still at the far end of the room as she
returned their gazes.

"It is time I did something of help, and if keeping Esteem's
attention elsewhere is all I can do, then that I shall."

Rizon bowed his head, "My thanks to you my lady, and to you
Courage. This I know, if I escape Fray it will be because of you. And to
you, young man." He turned to Mag who had been silent. "I owe you
much."

Mag made himself look up at him, and Mise was certain he trembled.

Promise felt a change in the room that day, the strange rift between her and her mother was still there, but… something was different.

They made their plans carefully and made sure everyone knew their part. Then fearing that the rebels would be looking for him, Imagine slipped from the room. With a glance behind her, Mise followed him.

"Mag!" she called softly, he stopped and looked at her, his brows raised; she smiled. "Thank you, I know this wasn't easy for you."

Something flickered across his eyes, he opened his mouth but instead only returned her gaze for a moment before smiling grimly then slipping through the halls, and a tender smile touched Mise's face. Everything would be well.

* * *

Imagine paused and looked over his shoulder. This was unexpected, this guilt… turning back, he hurried through the manor until he stepped out into the courtyard. It had been a risk to go through the manor. If the right person noticed him he could have been thrown into the stocks for the day - and that would have ruined everything! But it had been necessary.

"Mag!" Earnest called out from the street, with him was Tran and his two other brothers. Mag went to them at once.

"Well?" they urged, "What did you learn?" Mag looked at them.

"He leaves tomorrow morning for the south."

They frowned, "You discovered this by just asking around?"

Mag swallowed, "I told you I would get the information."

Earnest slapped him on the back, "Then tomorrow morn it is - then at last we will rid these lands of him!"

Long before the light of dawn began to show and while the owl was still hunting, Transform, his three sons and Mag all found places to sit and wait out of sight near the manor gate. Tran and his oldest sons smoked pipes while Earnest shaved at a stick of wood. The gate would not open until after dawn, and they knew that Horizon was not likely to leave before then, but they did not want to risk missing him. And so they waited, soon the streets became busy as day broke - and still there was no sign of Rizon. Tran and the others grew restless and worried, while Mag sat still, and hoped that they wouldn't guess the truth behind his lie. And so they waited.

Chapter 24   Bitter Revenge

Promise looked at herself in the small misted looking glass, and should have been pleased with her appearance. She had worked for hours to prepare herself for the banquet. Each lock of her dark hair was carefully curled and gleaming. Her dress was of a dusty rose hue, the sleeves were tight through the shoulders and the wrists pointed to her middle finger. The sleeves turned silver and puffed out at the elbows allowing for movement. The skirt was full and heavy, but it hung straight and trailed behind her. About her hips was a silver corded belt that hung down the center of her skirt.

She looked truly elegant, like a true lady of Tarva… she sighed in impatience, why did beauty and impracticality always go hand and hand, she wondered. Grabbing a silver cord, she pulled back her hair - but was careful to leave it framing her face, and wrapped the cord about her hair at the back of her neck, so that her long curls tumbled down her back. For a moment she considered how she was more excited for this banquet than any other! At last satisfied with how she looked, and a bit nervous, Mise turned about to see her mother sitting watching her.

Mise went to her. Ever since she had arrived in Fray, from her mother's tearful welcome to her wistful glances, Mise could see plainly that something was wrong with her mother - she seemed ridden with guilt for a crime that Mise knew nothing of.

That night her mother looked as beautiful and delicate as a Cres'aren flower. Her dress was of a dark blue and her hair was perfect (unlike Promise's). But her face was void of something… perhaps she was only worried about that night, but Mise couldn't push the feeling aside that her mother was hiding something dreadful. Kneeling down in front of her mother she took her hands in hers.

"Mother… are you alright?" she asked intently, to her surprise tears glistened in Loyal's eyes - this only confirmed Mise's fears.

"Of course child, I only worry that something will go wrong tonight." Mise smiled.

"Nothing will go wrong mother- Rizon will get away safe and nothing can harm me or father - really it is you who will have the hardest part; keeping Lord Esteem distracted."

Again Loy looked saddened, "It is time I did something of help."

Promise frowned, "You have done much to help, you have been by father's side through it all!"

Loy blinked back tears, "It is you who your father is proud of," she whispered. Just then their handmaiden entered the room.

"My ladies? The banquet begins," she announced from the door. Behind her they could see Rage waiting in the hall. Like putting on a mask Loy brightened.

"Then let us not miss the festivities!" Together they rose. Mise followed her mother into the hall, she watched as her father greeted her mother with a stiff bow and a passionless kiss to her hand. He then turned to Mise and she noticed his face soften as he spoke to her in hushed tones.

"You are ready and know what must be done?" She smiled and nodded. He nodded in return and then offered a stiff arm to his wife. The three of them made their way through the hallways to the banqueting room.

Promise's heart thumped in her chest and the palms of her hands sweated, despite what she had just said to her mother there was so much that could go wrong. Rizon could be noticed by the rebels outside or Esteem could notice their strange activity - and who knows what he might do!

Rage and Loy stepped out into the well-lit banqueting hall, but Mise paused on the threshold, and she swallowed hard. Music drifted out to her along with the murmur of voices and laughter. To her it seemed as though all the loud noise knitted together and faded, and she could hear little sounds like candle wax dripping, servants whispering, the flutter of flags outside - and the beating of her own heart. What was she doing? She was just a girl! Was it possible that Mag was right about her? That she was meant to do great things? In that moment she hoped so, for tonight, much depended on her. Her red lips parted and she closed her eyes, with one last breath, she stepped out into the hall.

The hall was filled with benches and tables laid down with platters overflowing with food of every kind, and pitchers of red wine. Candles flickered along the tables and quivered every time someone bumped into a table. Silver goblets gleamed at the head table where Lord Esteem sat with several richly dressed knights and dukes. Candelabras hung from the stone ceiling, and cast strange shadows on the walls. The long tables were set out in a U-shape with a roaring fire at the open end, where several spits of venison and beef roasted. Along one wall standing in front of the windows were half a dozen musicians playing a lively tune. Behind them and through large open windows the evening sun sank into the fields. Along the other wall were a row of trumpeters who would call for silence for announcements or toasts from the head table, or announce important guests.

Promise made her way through the crowd of glittering gowns and billowing capes. She smiled absently at different people but her mind was filled with other things, there was no desire in her that night to impress the noblemen and ladies. After a time, everyone was seated to begin the feast. Promise sat down with the trumpeters to her back, along with all the other unmarried women and the unmarried men sat facing them. On the other side of the U sat her parents. The people Esteem saw as more important sat closer to the head table, and so both Mise and her parents were sat almost in the middle of the tables. Courage sat with his back to the windows, and so throughout the feast Mise met his gaze often; she was comforted and strengthened by how calm he appeared. He believed that she could fulfill her task... she would indeed make him proud.

How little she ate was the only thing Mise did right by Tarven standards, and really Mise was hardly hungry at all - she was too nervous! So nervous that she paid no attention to the young women around her and stared right past the young man in front of her. The girls whispered about her behind their hands and the young man went so far as to laugh at how vacant she was. Any other night she would have been deeply hurt and embarrassed - but not this night, this night she didn't even notice!

Promise's breath caught as she realized that the servants were clearing away the food trays, the feast was over and the dancing would begin: it was time. Standing to her feet she glanced out the windows, the sun was gone and darkness would soon claim the village. Sweeping the room with her eyes she saw her father and mother parting ways. Her father was making his way to a dark hallway while her mother glided gracefully towards Esteem who was now standing and looking about the room. Now everyone was on their feet waiting for the tables to be cleared away for the dancing. Despite Promise's vacancy, every young man who had sat near her had made up their minds to dance with the beautiful maiden. But when the tables were cleared away, the dark haired beauty was gone.

Loyal's dress of dark blue off-set her dark skin and eyes. Gently she touched her hair where it was held at the back of her neck in black netting.

Sweetly she smiled and nodded to people as she passed them. One would have hardly known she was wracking her brain thinking of what to say once she reached Esteem. Whatever happened she must stay by his side - but he would wonder where Rage was, since a wife should always be accompanied by her husband. But she couldn't say that she couldn't find him for then Esteem would search for him.

"My lord," she said softly upon reaching him, he turned about and bowed.

"Ah! My lady Loyal!" he said in his breathless way. Loy forced a smile and nodded in return. "I trust the first of many banquets here in Fray has been to your liking?" Loyal was shrewd enough to perceive the true question behind his words, 'the first of many banquets in Fray' but Loyal also had enough social graces to skirt the question.

"Indeed my lord you outdo yourself! But I pray you - all night I shall wonder what instruments your musicians are playing if you do not tell me!"

"My Lady! You have been in the East too long!" Esteem said, then proceeded to name each instrument to her, much to the amusement of the noblemen around them. Loyal, who knew the instruments better than Esteem would ever, and could have told HIM where and when each piece had been invented, endured the noblemen's chuckles with grace. All the while she kept glancing past them to where Rage had disappeared. All was going as planned.

*   *   *

Courage crossed his arms over his chest and impatiently shifted his weight; why was Horizon late!? Again he glanced down the hall where he had come from; it was a small hall that the servants used, but Rage was alone for the moment. Where was Rizon?

Just then out of the darkened hallway loomed the Garatin - but something was wrong, he had no packs with him. Mise was to pack his food - but where were his personal things?

"What happened!?" Rage demanded in a hush.

Rizon looked about them before speaking, "Esteem has guards watching me."

Rage was silent as his mind took in the news. "What do you mean?" he said glancing behind Rizon.

"Early this morning I awoke to guards outside my chamber door,

Esteem had ordered them to prevent me from leaving Fray."

"What!?" Rage asked in astonishment.

"That's all I know - Esteem has it in mind to keep me here, he expected me to leave this morning of course, but none the less he does not want me to leave at all."

It made no sense! Courage's logic based mind complained, what reason would Esteem have to keep a small Garatin official in Fray? Perhaps he knew of Rizon's planned assassination and wanted to avoid trouble in his village. Could Esteem really be credited with that much foresight? Rage shook his head, whatever Esteem's motives, Rizon was escaping Fray that night!

"How did you elude the guards?"

"With promise of wine from the banquet when I return."

"Those men will be thirsty all night - come it will not take them long to grow anxious." Rage led the way to the courtyard.

Outside in the chilled night air Mise scanned the dark courtyard before stepping out and shutting the little door behind her. Picking up her skirts and clutching the food pack for Rizon, she went quickly to the stables. Inside the torches were ablaze, making her pause to blink in the sudden light. Just then voices sounded outside. She froze.

"Just be sure to sober up long enough to have that horse ready boy!" an angry voice said not far away. Mise dashed to a stall that she could see was empty, her ears burned as she ducked behind it and closed it just in time.

The stable door opened and shut and she heard the unsteady steps of the stableboy making his way past her. Mise thought rapidly; this boy was here to ready the horse who would pull the banqueting wagon out into the village. She had hoped to arrive long before him. Gently she eased herself down until she sat on the stall floor, placing her foot up on the stall door she took a steadying breath. Then hissed, "Hey!" Sure enough she heard a surprised grunt from the stableboy, then slowly he made his way closer. Mise closed her eyes and held her breath. Reaching out with a sixth sense she waited until the stableboy had bent close to the door to listen.

Bracing herself and gritting her teeth she kicked the stall door open! It swung out with a jerk and impacted with a thud against the stableboy's head, the door swung back and slammed shut. Promise's eyebrows were arched and her teeth clenched shut as she heard the stable boy's surprised grunt of pain then heard him fall into the hay.

Slowly Mise stood to her feet, and hesitantly she pushed the door open and peeked around it; there flat out on the hay was the stableboy, no older than herself. Under one arm was a brown jug, a red welt was beginning to rise on his forehead, a snore rose from his gaping mouth.

Mise had to be quick, looking about she saw there was a pile of hay at the end of the stalls - she just had to drag him there. Bending over with her back to the stable door Mise didn't hear the foot fall behind her.

A hand was laid on Promise's stooped shoulder, with a strangled squeak she jumped around and struck out, her attacker ducked and grabbed hold of both her wrists. She struggled a moment more while he tried to hush her.

"SHHH!"

Looking up she gasped; it was Mag!

"Mag! What are you doing here!?" she yelled in a whisper.

"Calm down Mise!" he said releasing her hands. "I came to make sure everything was alright." She gasped as if to say 'oh! You've got a great technique!'

"Well just don't stand there! Help me move him over there," Mise returned her voice to an appropriate whisper.

Mag shouldered the stableboy and dumped him on the hay, while Mise grabbed the jug and carefully nestled it under his arm again. Biting her bottom lip, she gently spread his hair over the worsening bump. Then she retrieved the food pack that she had dropped in the stall, and went to work preparing Rizon's horse. Looking up she noticed Mag was watching vacantly, she paused.

"Mag?" her fear that he was having another blind spell diminished as he looked up at her; his eyes were clear. "Are you alright?" she asked none the less.

"I will be," he said softly with a faint smile.

She smiled in return, "We're doing a good thing here; I know."

As soon as the horse was ready, Mise took the saddle and the food pack in hand. Both those things had to be slipped into the banqueting cart itself. She paused and looked about the stable. Rizon's horse was standing in the open area waiting, while the stable boy 'supposedly' snoozed in the corner. Mag patted her on the back to assure her that all was as it should be.

"Alright Mise, this is where I leave again," he said softly.

She smiled up at him, "Thanks Mag." Then they slipped out together; Mag darted out into the courtyard and vanished. Mise hugged the wall and turned a corner, there stood the wagon waiting for it's horse. Two men walked back and forth between it and a side door, filling it with baskets of food. She waited until both their backs were turned and then ran low across the yard until she reached the side of the cart. Quickly she tucked the saddle and pack inside. She looked about at the different little doors and arches leading to stairways into the servant's side of the manor. In one of those doorways waited her father and Rizon for her signal - there they were, crouching in an archway watching her.

Promise stood to her feet, and evened out her shoulders and tilted her head high. This was perhaps the hardest part of the plan for her. The two men turned back to the cart and froze in surprise. Mise smiled and stepped forward.

"Good sirs, I pray you, I have lost my way. I stepped outside for a breath of air and..." she said sweetly and made a helpless action with her hand. The two men looked at each other with frowns; it was next to unheard of - but then she looked like she belonged at the banquet. For a moment Mise was afraid it wouldn't work - then they both bowed and offered ready smiles.

"My lady! We are at your service!" the corners of Promise's lips turned up with her mother's smile, and she offered her hand, and one of the men took it and bowed over it.

"Allow us to escort you back to the banquet, my lady," he said leading her to one of the doorways while the other man followed. He told her, with concern, that the night air wasn't good for her. Her smile was out of amusement as they escorted her, one on each side, to the nearest door.

Before they had even disappeared from the courtyard, Rage and Rizon darted to the cart. Upon reaching it they paused, and Rizon turned to Rage.

"I can think of no reason as to why you should have helped me Courage, my words are not enough to thank you - but I swear on my honor, if I ever can, I will repay you." Rage bowed his head and touched his right fist to his heart.

"If ever I have the chance to help you again - I would do no different than I have done today. May the wisdom of all go before you, to guide you as you discover Eternity and his plans."

With that Rizon nodded then pulled his hood over his head and went to the stables to retrieve his horse. He would then hook it to the wagon and lead it out into the village. Rage watched for a moment before disappearing the way he had come.

*   *   *

Thrive flung out his cape behind him and sighed with impatience, another village, another corrupt lord who believed he could fool the king of Tarva himself. Thri's outlook on Garatin - on life in general had been dampened in the past two months. All he had seen was Tarven brutality and Garatin corruption; this was not what he thought it would be. He had thought that the world was a much better place than this, he had seen the ugliness of war, and he knew the pain of defeat, but he had believed in his country, in his people. But they had proved themselves unworthy to carry out the dream that Thri had once thought possible.

Taking a deep breath, Thri put his lazy smile on and straightened his shoulders, now was not the time for despair, he must fulfill his duty to his king. He waited in the shadows, flecking travel dust from his fine tunic as a nervous page announced his arrival; this if nothing else would be amusing to watch the surprised lord stumble about trying to accommodate him.

"Presenting the King of Tarva's emissary from the city of Tarva, his lordship, Duke Thrive!" the room was quieter than a tomb as Thri stepped out into the light. Thri was about to make his way into the interrupted banquet when he hesitated, careful to keep his smile intact he leaned towards the page and whispered.

"Quick, what's the namesake of this lord?" the young man smirked as he replied in hushed tones.

"He is Lord Esteem, of the manor and village of Fray, my lord."

"Oh, is that where I am?" he whispered before making his way slowly through the crowd towards the only man who looked arrogant enough to be Lord Esteem. All around him were dukes and knights with mouths a gaping. Thri winced inwardly at the thought of embarrassing a lord in front of his noblemen, but then, from Thris's past experiences this lord deserved it like all the rest. Thri was conscious of everyone's eyes on him, but even so, he was not nervous. His rich embroidered tunic of dark rusty brown bore the crest of Tarva, and his flowing cape of scarlet gleamed. Not a hair was out of place on his dark head or beard, but his eyes had indeed changed, the mischief that had once been there was almost replaced entirely with weariness.

"My Lord Esteem, forgive me the rudeness of my sudden appearance." He smiled and watched with faint interest as Esteem's mouth moved open and shut without any noise. At last he spoke.

"My Lord Thrive!" he seemed to burst and he bent low. Thri, waiting for Estee to right himself, blinked with pleasant surprise. For standing next to Estee was a lovely Tarven woman, her cinnamon eyes seemed to cast beauty where ever they looked, and now they gazed at him. Over Esteem's bowed head he shared a subtle nod with the silent woman.

"My Lord Thrive! You have caught me completely off guard! Had I known of your coming, my plans would have been different!" Esteem had a breathless way of speaking that was unnerving, Esteem waved his arm to the side of the room, and said loudly, "Bring back the head table - his lordship Thrive will feast with me!" Thri bowed his head in thanks, while Esteem sputtered on. "My lord, this is my head knight Realize, and my duke Save… and this is the lady Loyal -" At this Thri paid attention. "From eastern lands."

Thri reached out and gently took her hand and bowed over it, looking up again he met her gaze. "I would be honored if you would join me my lady," he said gesturing to the table that was being hurriedly set up. Esteem looked outraged (obviously this was not an important woman.) Thri didn't care, and he waited for her response.

She handled the awkward moment well, smiling she nodded her graceful head. "I assure you my lord, the honor would truly be mine." Her voice was calm and self-poised, she had the elegance of a true lady of Tarva - and yet she was from the east!?

A moment later all three of them sat at the head table, while the servants madly tried to set out a little feast for the mysterious and powerful man of Tarva. Thri had sat down in the center of the table leaving Esteem on one side and the lovely lady on his other side. He hoped her presence alone would make this whole thing bearable. As Thri began to eat, the rest of the banqueters began the first dance.

While Thri ate his fill, beside him on his right Esteem was so nervous that he ate his second feast that night. While on his left side he noticed Loyal hardly moved, but he was almost certain that she was paying careful attention to Esteem's mindless and breathless prattle.

"Oh yes my lord! All is quite well in my little village of Fray, as isolated as we are here, my subjects know who their king is and they follow my rule without question!" Thri frowned; he didn't like the way Esteem referred to his lands and people as HIS subjects and HIS rule... as if he thought of himself as... king!

"You find no trouble with rebels then my lord?" beside him Thri could have sworn that Loyal leaned closer.

"Rebels? Oh well, there is the odd one here and there my lord, but I have recently taken action to put an end to all of that." Thri's hand paused as he reached for his goblet and he looked at Esteem with a question.

"Actions that will put an end to the rebels, my lord?!"

"Ha! Wish I that there were such actions that could put an end to all rebels! Rather I speak of a certain strain of rebels that plague these lands. Perhaps his lordship has heard of a man named Eternity?" Thri sat up straighter.

"Indeed I have." Again he noticed Loyal paying close attention.

"Well," Esteem said smugly, "A few days ago a Garatin by the namesake of Horizon came to Fray with papers authorizing arrests of any found connected with Eternity." He lowered his voice as if telling a great secret, "At least that's what Rizon was meant to do - but I have learned otherwise! He has really been conspiring with Eternity himself!" Esteem dared to poke Thrive in the shoulder in excitement.

Thri shifted away from him and frowned, "But the man Eternity is dead," he said flatly, slightly amused by this backwater lord's misguided information.

"So we have been cleverly told!" he continued boldly in spite of Thri's disbelief. "But I believe the man is yet alive and in these very lands! Those men in Garason have been lying to us to cover up their blunder," he leaned even closer to Thri vigorously shaking a chicken leg at him. "They never really did catch him!" Esteem paused to take a bite of his chicken leg. He then calmly wiped his mouth and sat back as if nothing had happened.

Thri shifted uncomfortably, but Esteem went on breathlessly. "Now I believe Horizon is here to meet with Eternity. I have made sure that this man Rizon cannot leave and tomorrow I shall make him tell me where Eternity is hiding. And so my lord I will put an end to these rebels forever, they will be helpless without Eternity."

Thrive watched Esteem with unmoving face, in his heart he felt a sinking feeling; the lordship of the King's country of Garatin was left in the hands of fools… there was nothing else to be done - nothing else to be said; Esteem was a fool, or more likely even worse than that. It was yet another unsavory report that he would have to give to the King on his return. Thri looked away, two months ago he would have dealt with Esteem and his foolishness - but now there didn't seem to be much point, Esteem was just like the other lords in Garatin, power hungry and bent beyond repair.

Thrive made up his mind right then to leave on the morrow - early, there was nothing he could do here.

Loyal struggled to stay outwardly calm, there was no telling what would happen if she seemed too interested in what the two men were talking about. She turned her head slowly to look over the hall; oh where was Rage? Had Esteem truly prevented Horizon from leaving? Were all their plans made the day before going amiss? Suddenly she saw her husband entering slowly into the banqueting hall. She wanted to get up and run to him - she wanted to tell him that things had changed, that there was double risk involved now! But even as she thought this, Rage turned his gaze on her; his dark eyes were so cold - would she ever win his love back?

She breathed and settled back in her chair - she must prove to him she was worthy of a second chance. How could she get to him and warn him of Esteem's plans? As she watched, Rage nodded and looked away, Loy let her breath go; Rizon was safely away! Loy made herself relax, all they must deal with now was Esteem and his loosening grip on reality.

Promise leaned against her heavy door and breathed, it had worked she told herself. They had gotten Rizon out of Fray, and out and away from the rebels blood thirsty grasp. Or so she hoped.

The fear sprang up in her suddenly and without warning. She pushed away from her chamber door and went to her window, swinging the glass open, she leaned out. Below she could see the village beyond the manor walls. At this time of night, it should have all been dark, instead lights were ablaze in the market square and she could faintly hear music and laughter. It was the villagers having their own feast and enjoying the wagon of food that Esteem had sent out. Mise strained her eyes but try as she did she could see nothing clearly, it was too dark and too far away to see the cart and if the horse was gone yet. Nothing below spoke of danger, but she couldn't shake the feeling that something had gone wrong, and over and over one name went through her mind. Each time it did, she feared all the more though she didn't fully understand why: that name was Mag.

Earnest angrily kicked the crate he had been sitting on.

"Earnest! Quiet!" Tran hissed harshly at his son. Earnest stomped along the wall of the cottage to his father and whispered hotly.

"I'm done waiting! We've been here all day! Wait through the night if you like but I'm done, I'm going to go get something to eat from the banqueting cart before it's all gone. Imagine are you coming..." Earnest's grumpy speech died on his lips as he looked around for Mag - and didn't find him. All the men sitting beside the cottage, even the ones sitting near the street keeping watch, turned about and looked at where Mag had been sitting only one hour ago... but he wasn't there!

"Mag!?" Earnest dared to raise his voice to call out for him but there was no reply, Mag was gone.

*   *   *

The scream of a rodent followed the hunting cry of an owl as it swooped through the night. All noise of the village's festivities had died away and the night was still and dark indeed, but not as dark as when Mag's sight failed him. But this night his sight remained strong as his long awaited revenge drew near. All the noise to be heard after the owl cry was that of Rizon's horse hoofs, and Rizon's own feet. Mag couldn't even hear his own heart beat - perhaps he didn't have one. If that thought had crossed his mind, it wouldn't have bothered him. Truly it would have broken both his sister's and his mother's heart if they had have seen him then.

At last, Mag knew his time had come. He rose up onto the dirt road from the ditch, a metallic ring cut the night as he drew forth his dagger. Ugly hatred marred his Garatin face, too long had he been pretending to Promise. Now it was time to avenge his father.

Again like a streak of lightning across the sky he saw his father's battered face and heard his last breath. Again he saw Rizon's cold face as he held Mag back from helping his father. Again he watched him die.

Ahead of him Rizon stopped, his horse stopped beside him and nickered uneasily. Mag didn't hesitate, he walked forward, head lowered and eyes blazing, his right hand gripping the dagger was eager to stab. Rizon dropped his horse's reins and turned about to face him. Mag stopped and took a wide stance ready to fight until revenge was his - but first he wanted to look at Rizon one last time. Even more so, Rizon needed to know why

Mag was going to kill him - he needed to remember what he had done!

"You're here to kill me?" Rizon's voice was calm and without contempt.

"It's what you deserve!" Mag said darkly.

Rizon's face turned suddenly very sad, "Of that I am certain!" he breathed without a hint of mocking, just simply speaking truth.

Mag was taken aback. No! Horizon was evil! He had watched his father die without guilt - how dare he show remorse now!? Mag shook his head rejecting Rizon's words.

"Do you know me?" he asked, his voice tight. Rizon was silent. "Don't you remember me? I was the boy three years ago." Mag choked on his emotions. "I was the boy you held back while thieves beat MY father to death!!!" Mag waited as Rizon's face changed with remembrance.

"WHY!?" Mag's voice broke like it had on that day so long ago. "Why did you let my father die? Why didn't you stop them? Why did you stop me?!" Mag waited for the answer that had haunted him, while tears streaked down his face.

"Your father spoke the truth; he spoke it when no one wanted to hear it." Rizon's words were quiet but Mag heard every one. "That day your father spoke to the Garatin High Council, and he challenged them and their laws - I was there, he meant to change the way Garatin was that day. He pointed out how corrupt we had grown, he wanted to place Eternity in the throne, he wanted to turn the world upside down. None of us wanted to hear it, we were all too comfortable with the way things were. I thought of his words as a crime against Eloi himself. The Council gave him a choice; give up Nity, or die. Your father said nothing would silence him. After your father left, the High Council arranged for those men to attack your father."

Mag gulped in air, at last... the truth.

"I was wrong; I see that now. I have killed many - too many, all in the name of what I thought was right. But what I told everyone in Fray is true, I came face to face with Eternity. His presence proved my life work wrong, he told me that I had closed my eyes to the truth, and that in it's place I believed lies."

Mag was startled by the significance of those words. Rizon paused as though unsure of his next words.

"I was blind literally! Nity took my sight away... I was blind for several days, and my sight did not return until I faced the truth. After years of hating and turning people over to their deaths my heart was heavy enough to be lead, but now I do see the truth. I hope that one day you too will open your eyes to the truth, and find a way to forgive the wrongs I have done you. But if this is not that day, so be it. Do what you must."

Mag heaved his breath in and out, instead of his father's last moments he saw Trust and heard his last words to him. Mag gritted his teeth as his eyes went blurry with tears, words were beyond him now - it was time for action. With a strangled cry Mag raised his dagger and threw it, it hit the dirt road off to one side where it raised a cloud of dust. Rizon jumped a little and let out a nervous breath. Imagine dropped to his knees with clenched fists, the cry from his own mouth was much worse than his father's death cry. Rizon took a hesitant step closer.

"GO!" Mag screamed raggedly, "Leave!"

Rizon stumbled back and mounted his horse. After another pause Mag heard him ride away, and Mag was left alone with his tortured mind, broken spirit and bitter revenge. After three years of planning and waiting for this moment - Mag couldn't do it... Rizon was a changed man. Mag raised his head to see the stars - but he couldn't see them anymore! He was blind. Panic had become common to him but fear would forever have the power to paralyze him.

After three years of denying the truth Mag saw it plainly at last. His father had died for his words, he had *chosen* to speak out against injustice and take the risk, he *chose* it. He *willingly* died for what he believed in.

What did Mag believe in? Hatred? Revenge? Were these things worth dying for? He wanted to avenge his father - but his father had believed in peace. Mag had once believed in peace too; he had once imagined a world where the laws of Eloi were followed by every man. A world where hatred was buried and wrongs forgiven. Where Garatins, Tarvens, Cokhawkens, Quy people and every man lived alongside each other and had no differences. Had he truly traded that world for bitter revenge?

Mag felt an empty hollow inside where his heart of lead had melted away forever. Stumbling to his feet Mag stood and gasped, taking a few blind steps Mag felt the ground give way beneath him and he fell down an embankment, tumbling head over heels, he hit the ground with a thud and lost consciousness.

Chapter 25   The Witch

The silence in the room was enough to drive a weaker man to
insanity, but Rage remained silent as he waited for Esteem to speak. But
Estee only stood there at the far end of his council chambers as if stepping
out into the light would burn him. Courage's topsy-turvy hair spoke of the
early hour from which he had been summoned by Esteem. The hour alone
would have warned Rage that things were terribly wrong, but Esteem's
bloodshot eyes and shaking hands bespoke of a danger yet to come. The
man was crazed. Rage stood with arms held behind his back, one could
have been fooled into believing that he was calm.

"Where?" Estee's voice was unsteady, "Where did you hide
Horizon!?" Estee hissed.

Rage was taken aback - of course he knew Esteem had intended to
keep Rizon in Fray - but how had he guessed that Rage had helped him
escape!? Still Rage didn't speak. Esteem bared his teeth like some sort of
wild beast.

"Do you seek to deny what you've done? As if I can't see the
truth!?"

"Horizon is gone, my lord. And well away from here." Prideful to
the last, Rage would not feign innocence. Esteem's face twitched into a
smile then faded as he demanded with a rising voice.

"Where!? Where did you hide him?" Rage frowned.

"He is gone my lord."

"Fool!' Estee breathed, "You don't know what you've done! None
the less, I will have what I seek!" Estee stepped forward. "Tell me! Where is
the rebel Eternity?" Courage's lips opened in shock; this is what Estee was
really after!? The whereabouts of Nity? And he thought that Rage could tell
him!? How did he even know that he was involved with the rebels? Esteem
laughed - it was far from joyful.

"HA! Nothing escapes my eye! Not in my manor. You are one of
those cursed Nity followers - so tell me where is the man?" Rage felt an
iron will enter his heart, a reassurance of who he was, and he smiled.

"No my Lord Esteem. If I knew where Eternity was - I would not
tell you."

Estee looked beaten - with his eyes wide, he turned his back on
Rage and walked back into the shadows. Rage was about to leave when

Estee spoke again.

"There are many ways that I can make you talk." Rage paused. "Your daughter - Promise... your only child." He looked over his shoulder, and Rage felt his strong heart quiver within him. "It must have been... terrible when she fell sick five years ago, how unbearable it must have been for you." Rage narrowed his dark eyes as panic began to seep in; how could he know this? Esteem went on in his breathless manner. "I have heard it tell that the daughter of a Tarven soldier with the namesake of Courage, fell ill five years ago... and died! And yet she is here! Some have said that there was witchcraft involved." Rage swallowed hard, and Esteem's face hardened.

"Tell me where Eternity is."

Rage was silent, the horror of it all sinking in.

"So be it. Guards!" instantly two soldiers entered the room at his sharp command. "Arrest the maiden Promise and hold her in the dungeon!"

"NO!" Rage shouted and lunged towards Esteem. The two guards grabbed hold of him before he got far. The three of them struggled for a moment before Rage was overcome. One of the guards held him in an arm lock.

"You have until sundown to tell me where Nity's hideaway is, if you still refuse then your daughter will be burned at the stake - for the witch that she is!" Estee left the room, and Rage went limp. The guard dropped him and he fell to his knees. The guards left the chamber to follow out their orders. Rage kneeled there and heaved his breath in- then out again. Promise!

*   *   *

Promise stretched out her arms and moaned, then went limp in her bed, turning her head to the window she saw that the sun was only now just rising. After the late night she had had, she should have slept till late in the day. But for reasons she could not explain she was wide awake. Suddenly without thought of the early hour, she felt an irresistible need to speak with Mag. Getting up she went to her trunk at once, and for a moment considered what to wear. She chose a long red tunic with a black belt and black pants. She dressed quickly and looked at her hair in her little mirror. Impatiently she braided it half way so that her hair was free past her shoulders. With one last stretch of her arms she opened her chamber door and shut it behind her.

Walking down the hall she frowned when four of Esteem's guards came down the hall towards her - it was strange to say the least! She was about to step aside for them when they stopped before her.

"You are the Maiden Promise, are you not?" one of them asked. Mise's frown deepened.

"Yes, yes I am - why?"

"By order of Lord Esteem you are under arrest for witchcraft! Take her." Two of the guards stepped closer and seized her by the arms. She tried to step back and leaned away from them as panic and unbelief washed over her. They started to pull her back the way they had come.

"WAIT! Please - I don't understand! I am no witch!" she shrieked in fear. Ahead in the hall her father turned a corner.

"Father!" she called out, just then a door opened behind her and her mother stepped out in her night gown.

"PROMISE!" she reached out and would have run after her, but her father (who didn't seem to be surprised) ran to her and held her back.

"It will be alright Mise!" he called after her, but Mise felt no reassurance.

*   *   *

The first morning light filtered down through the pine and spruce trees, chasing away the shadows of the night before, lighting up the forest with the light of a new day, bringing hope and the promise of life reborn! A four horned deer with her almost grown fawn walked together on delicate hooves through the forest. An owl, perhaps the one who had been hunting in the night, flew up to his tree and nestled into a hollow for the day. Bursting through the morning air a bird put forth her song to be admired by all.

His eye lids opened slowly and with reluctance. For a moment everything was a blur of green then, slowly a single plant came into focus. It grew hardly a foot from his face, and a beam of weak sunlight shone down upon its tender leaves; it was a Cres'aren.

Even as his blue eyes watched, the little plant uncurled itself and opened a flower to offer to the sunlight. The five pointed petals were of pure white, it could have been a star for all its simple beauty. Imagine's cluttered mind focused on the flower; to think about this flower. Its ivory star shape could be found on any number of Garatin flags; it symbolized everything that Garatin was, but it had also become a symbol for Nity. It meant new life.

Mag groaned as he raised his head, and found it hardly possible that the world could continue on when his life had been turned inside out. He tried to move his legs but his whole body was so stiff it hurt. Going limp again Mag closed his eyes as tears filled them, new life? How could he find a new way to live? Revenge had powered him ever since he became fatherless, was it even possible to give that up? How would his life look without his burning hatred? What would there be left to live for...?

Like the gentle beat of butterfly wings Mag opened his eyes with a thought he had never considered; there was still beauty in this world without his father beside him, there was yet love in this world without his father's embrace. There WAS reason to live. His father had died fighting for a world reborn. Imagine would live to see that world!

* * *

Loyal pressed her hand to her mouth and closed her eyes; Esteem asked the impossible! It was now an hour after sunrise, and Loy had dressed hurriedly, but now after hearing Rage explain what had happened she saw no way out.

"Oh my Promise..." why must she suffer every time? She wondered in agony.

Suddenly Rage knelt down in front of her and looked up into her face; it made her take pause. It had been so long since he had looked at her without contempt, since he had offered her anything but coldness.

"We will get out of this Loy!" he said firmly, "Estee will not harm our daughter!" Determination shone in his dark eyes as he reached up with his hand and gently touched her chin. A single tear slipped from her cinnamon eye, and for the first time in what felt like forever, her husband kissed her.

Rage stood to his feet and pulled her up with him, then Loy was surrounded in his strong embrace. There was still something between them - it was pride, but in that moment she felt certain that one day, they could overcome even that. Pulling away, Rage went to the door of her chamber. Pausing, he said to her, "I will speak with Esteem, I think he can yet be made to see reason." Then he was gone, and Loy stood there holding on to the comfort that his touch had given her.

Loy waited for Rage to return with news that Mise was safe and that Esteem had renounced his rash actions. She waited, and waited. She paced through her chambers, she gazed out of her window, and she sat and worried the fabric of her skirt. More than once she considered going and finding Rage herself - but she was afraid of Esteem, he was acting unreasonable and there was no telling what he might do next. But waiting for Rage near well drove her mad! She waited for three hours, and was worried sick the whole time for Mise.

Then at last Rage returned, her heart hollowed within her at the look on his face, he shook his head as the chamber door closed behind him.

"I tried..." his forehead was riddled with wrinkles. "He wouldn't let me see him, and when he did he demanded I tell him where Nity is... he won't see reason!" Loy watched as his face hardened again with determination.

"If Estee will not release her then we must rescue her." He walked to a trunk and threw it open, searching through it, he grabbed his sword. He held it for a moment - it was his sword from the old days, the sword of a soldier. He had not touched it since packing the trunk upon their departure from the Byla. But now there was cause to wear it again. He strapped it to his back in the manner of a traveler. He also grabbed an unstrung bow and tucked it into the strap on his back along with half a dozen short arrows. Taking a little pouch, he opened it to make sure that the bow string was there, then tied it to his belt. Then he swung a light cloak over his shoulders to conceal his weapons.

"Where are you going?" Loy asked.

Turning to her he said, "To ask the rebels for help."

Loy gasped, "but Rage!"

"I know - but not all of them could have been involved in Rizon's planned assassination, there must be some good men among them."

"But Rage they never contacted you, they could not see past your Tarven face - why would they risk their lives to help you now?"

"There is Imagine, who warned Rizon, he will help..." he paused a moment to consider who else might help. "There is no one else to go to."

Loy paused, "Yes. There is," she said quietly.

Rage frowned as he tucked a dagger into one boot, "Who?"

"Thrive. The Tarven Duke! He left at sunrise, he cannot be but three hours down the road!"

"How do you know he will help?"

"He will... he must!"

After Rage had armed himself and Loy had slipped her riding cloak over her shoulders they hurriedly made their way through the manor. Coming to a cross hallway they heard voices, and Rage grabbed Loyal's arm and held her back from stepping out in the open. Loy looked at Rage with a question in her eyes. Almost in answer, a voice from around the corner spoke as if to several other men.

"You have your orders then; the Tarven must be kept inside the manor, if he tries to leave, you are to arrest him." Then there were many footsteps going down the hall and towards Rage and Loyal's chambers.

Rage was glad that he had thought to use the servant's hallways to leave their chambers. Otherwise they would have come face to face with Estee's soldiers. As it was, they had gone around them, evading them only by seconds. After a few more close calls, they made it to the stable without being seen. The stable hands were not around. Rage quickly saddled his horse Stream while Loyal kept watch at the stable door. As Rage finished saddling Stream he whispered close to his twitching ear.

"For once in your pathetic life - ride hard!" the horse looked at his master with one large, challenging brown eye. "Useless thing," he muttered.

"Alright Loyal," he said holding out his arm to her.

She turned away from the door and came to the side of the horse. She paused, placing her hand on Stream's shoulder, she held her breath.

"I can't lose her again!" she breathed. Rage reached out and placed his hand over hers, but he quickly removed it.

"You can not tarry here," he said tightly, "Your swift return may be the only thing that can save her." Loy swallowed hard and nodded, then with his help she jumped up into the saddle. It perhaps, was THE only time in her life that she rode astride! Looking down at her husband she felt an ache in her heart that she could not explain.

"You are certain of the path he took?"

She nodded, "He spoke of traveling south to Hawthorn last night." Loy watched as he seemed to momentarily lose control of his emotions.

"Then ride swiftly!" his voice was thick.

Loy nodded and Rage opened the stable door wide for her, urging Stre forward, she paused beside her husband.

"He will return with me... I know he will." Then she broke Stream into a canter into the courtyard and out into the village. Rage hesitated a

moment, he knew he did not have much time, but he needed a moment…
reaching out he leaned a hand against the stable wall and covered his mouth
with his other hand. He closed his eyes and wished that it was he who was
riding away. Rage allowed himself only one moment of weakness; there
wasn't time for any more.

*   *   *

Loyal had heard it said that riding astride was easer then riding side
saddle, but as she entered the south woods she nearly lost her seat as
Stream bounded over a little incline. Leaning forward Loy gripped the reins
tighter and made herself forget her lady like posture - for once, good
breeding would not save her daughter.

Loy pressed Stre hard - she had to, for she must reach Thrive and
return with him to Fray before nightfall. Although she and Rage had not
said it, they both knew that it would be nearly six hours before she could
possibly return with Thrive… and it would certainly be nightfall by then.

But Loy also knew that no horse could gallop hard for six hours
straight, it was a wonder that Stre could gallop at all! And so Loy was torn
between pushing him hard and riding at a slow trot. Every time she allowed
Stream to slow down, she glanced up to try and glimpse the sun through
the trees. Each time she did, the sun had moved further to her right, into
the west.

On and on she went, till her hair came loose and fluttered behind
her, and sweat dampened her neck and back. Still she rode on. It seemed
strange to her that she and Rage had traveled on this road only a week and a
half ago; things had been so different then.

After a time, Loy had to slow Stre down almost completely so she
could catch her breath - her mouth was so dry but she had not brought
with her any water skin. Breathing hard she closed her eyes and allowed a
few tears to slip out, they were not tears for herself - although they could
have been; she had come so far from what she had once been. But rather
they were tears for Promise.

Suddenly Loy opened her eyes and held her breath. Ahead of her
on the road she heard a voice - the first voice she had heard since leaving
Fray - for she had not crossed anyone on the road.

"A horse approaches from the north my lord."

"Relax! Not every rider is an assassin intent upon my death!"

The scornful voice filled with culture couldn't possibly be any other

262

than Thrive! Loy spurred Stre on around the bend in the road. But at once she pulled him back, Stre reared at the sudden stop, Loy paid no heed. She slipped off his back before he had even touched the ground again and fell to her knees. Around her Thri's six guards spread out to surround her and cast glances from where she had come, two of them gripped their sword hilts. In front of her Thrive sat on his horse and cocked his head to one side as he watched the road weary woman.

Loy lifted her face, and Thri opened his mouth in surprise.

"At ease! It is the Lady Loyal!" he jumped off his horse and knelt before her, he tried to pull her to her feet, but she spoke before he could.

"My lord! I beg you to hear me for I am in great need of your help!"

"Speak it my Lady - I swear on my honor whatever it is I will help."

Loy felt a thrill at his words. "It is the Lord of Fray, my lord - he has gone mad and means to burn my own daughter at the stake for witchcraft!"

Thrive rolled back on his heels and let go of her hands, Loy mistook his shock for unbelief. She reached out desperately and grabbed his hand. She clung to it as if afraid he might run away.

"Please my lord - she is innocent," Loy's voice shook, "if you do not come now my daughter will perish! My lord - would not the King of Tarva seek to end such injustices in his own country?"

Her words were bold and spoken out of rank, if it had been any other duke he would have struck her for such impertinence. But Loy was right about Thrive, he would come.

"Guards - we passed a cottage not two miles back, was there not a horse tethered nearby?"

"Yes my lord, there was."

"Very good, ride ahead and pay the peasant whatever he demands." He tossed the guard a coin pouch from his own belt. "The lady must have a fresh mount!"

Loy turned about to see that Stream was indeed spent, his flanks were frothy with sweat and he hung his head low. Loy did not remember passing a cottage, but then she did not remember much of the road she had come down. The soldier Thri had spoken to, thundered down the path the way Loy had just come.

*　　　　*　　　　*

The cottage door opened a crack in the middle of Courage's insistent pounding, a woman's face appeared on the other side. She gasped and tried to slam the door shut again, but Rage shot out his hand to keep it open. He could have pushed the door open and forced his way inside had he chosen to, but instead he spoke through the partly opened door.

"You are the wife of Transform are you not?" the woman didn't answer, but Rage was fairly certain that she was. "I am Courage of Hawthorn."

"I know who you are - what do you want?"

"Please - I need help." It wounded his pride just to say the words. "My daughter has been falsely accused of witchcraft, she must be rescued tonight!" the woman ducked her face behind the door as though trying to escape his intense plea.

"You'll get no help from us." She tried to close the door again but couldn't, "Now please leave!"

"Wait - where is Imagine?" Rage braced his shoulder against the door, he reconsidered forcing his way in. "He was staying here, was he not? Where is he?"

The woman looked genuinely concerned. "I don't know, the boy disappeared last night - now please, just leave!" she begged again.

Rage stepped away from the door in despair, the woman slammed it quickly. Now what was he to do? If Mag was not to be found - then he was on his own… But there was no time to despair for long, it had only been a few minutes since Loy had left, even so he must hurry to find a way to save Mise - or it would be too late! Looking up the street he saw eight soldiers run from the manor courtyard. They were searching for him.

Chapter 26   Sundown

Imagine had laid still for what seemed ages, he had rolled over on his back and gazed at the blue sky, marvelling at how clear it was. The more he thought of it, the more he couldn't remember when he last looked at a clear sky... but then he remembered. It had been with his father one night on the road to Garason, perhaps a week before he had died. They had sat gazing at the night sky - it had been so clear Mag had felt certain that they would fall into it. That was the last time he remembered looking at a clear sky, it was the last time his heart had been so clear... so light.

The same way it felt now. Clear of hatred, anger, revenge; clear of heaviness - clear as the blue sky! As he looked into his heart he found that there was still pain over his father's death, there was still emptiness over his loss and there was still anger about how he had died. But the burning need to avenge his father... was gone! In its place was a realization that his hatred had turned him into something ugly, something his father would have been ashamed of... it had to end!

Rolling over Mag pushed himself onto his knees, he had to shut his eyes at the pain, his wounded shoulder felt worse. He forced himself to climb to his feet. Grabbing hold of a nearby tree he leaned against it, then he looked up from where he had fallen the night before. It was a three-meter drop from the road above. Well, that explained why he was in so much pain! From there Mag stumbled on through the woods until he could climb back up onto the road. Then he made his stiff way back the mile and a half into Fray, his progress was very slow - but he can't be blamed for that, how could he have known that Mise was in danger?

When at last he cleared the woods and saw Fray in the light of a setting sun, he paused. What was he to do? He could not stay in Fray - he did not belong here. He thought of Transform and his sons so full of hatred, a hatred that Mag had fuelled. Mag couldn't stay. What if he sunk back into the anger and hate? He must get away... but where?

Home.

Yes, he must get home, he did not know what would happen once he got there or how his life would go on, but this he knew, he must get home! He felt a weariness enter him. He must go into Fray, to fetch his belongings and the horse Mise had gotten him. He could then return it to Hawthorn. But that brought up another thing, how was he to face Mise!?

He had lied to her - deliberately deceived her! How could he say farewell to her and not mention that little fact?

No. He couldn't face her, not yet. But he would - someday.

*　　　　　*　　　　　*

"I have more planned for you than this Promise." Mise opened her cinnamon eyes and jumped, the back of her head hit the stone wall with a thud. She looked around the dungeon quickly - but there was no one there. The words she had heard a moment ago had seemed so real, like she had spoken them herself, but she was alone. She looked towards the dungeon door, it had a little barred window at head level, but there was no one there who could have spoken the words. No, and that voice... she had heard it before! It was the same voice who had awoken her so many years ago - it was Nity!

But that was impossible! Nity was not here, and how could he have used the same words that Mag had spoken to her in private? That was impossible - but could it also be true?

Mise wasn't sure how long she had been waiting in the dungeon. The light that trailed down through the little barred window had been feeble since she had been left here and the window was too far up to look out of. But she knew that it must be drawing near to nightfall by now. At first she had been afraid when the guards had closed the dungeon door leaving her alone in the dark musty cell. But it had not taken her long to get over her fear. She had sunk down against one wall to sit. Once a rat had poked its little nose into the cell from a hole but it had disappeared soon thereafter. Mise didn't think she could, but she had drifted off into sleep, and then she had heard the voice.

Pulling her knees up and wrapping her arms around them, Mise sat still and wondered what was to become of her. Over and over the word 'witchcraft' played in her mind. Unless there was some sort of horrible mistake, Esteem had found out about her sickness - and her death. But why would he bother about something that had happened so long ago? Witchcraft had been outlawed in Garatin for many, many years, but the fear of black magic was strong none the less. Witches were burned at the stake - it was the only way to be sure that their magic died with them.

A certainty sunk into Promise's heart until it was heavy; for whatever reasons - whether he believed it was true or not, Esteem was going to burn her as if she were a witch...

When he reached Tran's cottage. Mag still had not decided what he would do. While he thought about it he went to the little stable behind the cottage and saddled his borrowed horse, then he went to the cottage. It was not yet sunset, and perhaps Tran and his boys were not yet home from their day's work; Mag hoped so. Slipping into the cottage he found no one about, he quickly packed his few things - just then he heard a sound behind him, he spun about. It was Tran's wife and daughter! They gasped as they recognized him.

"Imagine, it's you!" the young girl said in relief.

Her mother added, "We thought you were that Tarven again!"

Mag frowned, why were they so nervous and who was the Tarven - Mise!? "What Tarven?" he asked.

"The one you said you knew, Courage. He came here looking for you a few hours ago." Mag paused, why would Rage be looking for him?

"Where have you been? We were worried about you," the girl said.

Mag hardly heard her, "Why was Courage looking for me?"

The wife frowned, "Where have you been? He wanted your help; his daughter has been accused of witchcraft - they're burning her at the stake tonight!"

Mag went cold... witchcraft - Mise!? What had happened? - wait! "When did you say they would burn her?!"

"Sundown - in the back meadow."

Mag spun about to look out the window, the village had been cast into shadow; the sun would soon set! He turned and ran out the door.

"Where are you going!?" they called after him.

"To save Promise!"

Imagine felt as though the world had slowed down as he dragged the horse from the stables - he had to get to the far side of the manor - now! Like Mise had shown him, he stuck his foot in the stirrup and swung onto the horse. Then like the leading rider in a fierce horse race, Mag thundered down the streets of Fray.

Mise turned her head to the door as she heard a key turning in the lock. The door swung open and Lord Esteem entered with the air of a king. Mise rose to her feet with her face set, she looked confident and strong in her rough clothes. She leveled Estee with a glare that spoke volumes, whatever respect she had for him because he was a lord, was gone.

"Ah my lady Promise!"

She frowned, he made it sound like they had just bumped into each other. Mise glanced to the open dungeon door, standing there was a stone faced Tarven guard, but she saw his eyes flicker towards her - almost with pity.

"I am sorry that this should have to happen, it will all get quite ugly before the morrow," he added softly looking about the cell.

Mise remained silent.

"There is however no need for harm to come to you, child. If you will tell me what I wish to know you will see another dawn."

Mise tried hard to remain strong and unmoving but her heart quivered as the thought settled in her - this could be THE last night she would ever have... but there was yet hope - Esteem only wanted her to tell him something.

"What I wish to know, and I'm sure you will tell me," he paused, "Where is the rebel Eternity?"

Promise's stomach turned over and she heard a faint buzzing in her ears, she blinked several times trying to find reality. He wanted Nity... Mise could hardly believe the horrible position she was in. Die, or turn Nity over to Esteem. It surprised her that Estee even believed that Nity was indeed alive (why, he seemed to have more faith in that than she!) Her eyes had become wide with fright; she didn't know where he was! She shook her head in a tiny motion of desperation.

Estee smiled as if he found it amusing.

"Of course child, a young maiden can hardly be expected to know where such a man would be hiding. Yet fear not, there is something else I think you will tell me." His face darkened, "Tell me the namesakes of the rebels in Fray."

Mise went truly cold, for this she did know. It would be so simple, trade in Transform and his family and Mag for her own life. She didn't owe them anything. They wouldn't think twice about it if they were in her position. Why should she care about a few Garatins? Suddenly Mise felt a steadfastness enter her.

"No." Her voice was almost startling in the silence, and both Estee and the guard at the door were surprised as she set her shoulders back and raised her chin. "I will not tell you! I am a Tarven maiden and I know the meaning of loyalty. Of this be certain, my lord, I will never trade in someone else to save myself. Nity and the people will not be betrayed by my lips - I will burn before telling you anything!"

Esteem's face went white for a moment then turned red with anger.

"Guard! Take the witch out, and prepare the stake!" he turned on his heel and nearly tripped in his rage.

The guard at the door stepped aside for him, then took a step towards Mise. She shot her eyes at him like daggers, then with head held high she walked out of the dungeon with the guard steps behind her, not daring to take hold of her arm. As Mise climbed the stairs up out of the dungeons of the manor with the guard following close behind, she felt a despair take her - but she was not afraid.

Out into the courtyard they came, and Mise was made to climb up into a cart. Her wrists were bound to the edge of the cart with a bit of rope. The whole time Promise held her head high, and kept her eyes averted from Esteem's gaze. He watched from the courtyard steps as his horse was brought to him. Mise cast her eyes about in search of her parents - but she could not see them. The courtyard was dotted with curious and horrified onlookers. But her father and mother were not among them, it was then that fear seized her; where were they? Didn't they know what was happening? What had Esteem done to them!?

Promise raised her head to the darkening sky and blinked back tears as the cart lurched forward. The words she had heard must have been her own imagination, for there were no further plans for her, she would die this night.

The cart went out into the village and circled around the manor walls until they reached the far side. Many people had come to watch, and Mise was astounded by the fear on their faces. But it was not fear of her, the supposed witch, but of Esteem. Although there were many who watched, none followed the cart into the meadow.

Mag rode the horse hard up the path towards the manor, and he passed through a small crowd returning to the village. Glancing over his shoulder he saw that it was just moments before the sun would be gone below the tree line. Just then he heard a voice, he was rounding the manor and the meadow was in front of him, but the voice had come from one side.

"Imagine!" it was Courage! He stopped his horse short and his hooves slid on the cobbles.

"Rage! Mise - where is she!?"

"They've taken her out now!" he pointed towards the meadow, where a cart and several figures could be seen.

"Mag there is yet time to save her - will you help me?!?" Rage flung his cloak back and Mag could clearly see his weapons.

"What can I do?" Mag asked breathlessly.

The sun set as the cart pulled up beside a stake that had been driven into the ground. Mise couldn't take her eyes from it, but she knew Estee was watching, so she held her head high. The guard unbound her from the cart but left the rope tight around her hands. Because of this she had difficulty getting out of the cart. Surprisingly the guard picked her up and lifted her down. She looked up at him and was sure she saw a deep sorrowfulness in him, as if trying to apologise for her fate.

Estee rode up close on his horse and looked down at her, "This is your last chance witch; tell me what I asked."

Mise with all the grace of her mother tilted her head higher and walked past Estee toward the stake without even looking at him.

Everyone was slightly shocked when Estee's face crumpled and tears sprung to his eyes! He punched his horse's neck and muttered through his tears, "From the cradle to the throne, into fire we all must go!" his guards paused and glanced at one another in astonishment at his crazed behaviour. Estee pointed to the stake, "Prepare the witch," he ordered. His six guards hesitated a moment. Then the same man who had lifted her off the cart gently tied her wrists behind her back around the stake.

Mise hardly knew it, but she was so noble looking, it was as though she were a queen about to be crowned. The other guards began to pile bundles of sticks and hay about her feet. Looking to the cart Mise realized that the driver had carried with him a torch, he now walked towards her.

Off to one side Esteem's face had gone stern, his earlier outburst forgotten. He called his head guard over (the one who had lifted Mise off the cart) "After the witch is burned and dealt with, I want you to take your men into the village and round up the villagers." The man frowned, and shock shined in his Tarven eyes.

"My lord?"

Esteem smiled - it was not at all pleasant, "Eternity must be close - I can feel him. The rebels will know where he is, and they WILL tell me. And if I cannot learn who the rebels are, then the villagers themselves will turn them in- even if I have to kill every last one before they do!"

The guard went pale, "My lord - my sister and her family live in the village!"

Esteem looked outraged that the guard would speak out of turn.

"Then she should have turned in the rebels long ago! You have your orders - follow them, or you will be the first to die after the witch!" He flung his arm to point at Mise, "Set the witch to flames!"

The man with the torch stepped towards Mise. She closed her eyes, and it was as if Nity was bound to the stake beside her, for again she heard his voice 'Promise, wake! I have so much more planned for you than this!' Promise's breath shuddered and her eyes fluttered open as they had when she was but a child. But instead of Nity's face she saw the face of Esteem's guard about to bend over and light the fire!

The sun was gone and clouds rolling in had stolen it's light from the sky. The torch burned brightly in the guard's hand, it could be seen clearly in the otherwise dark night. Everyone's eyes were on it and all saw it was suddenly knocked from his hand to the ground. The man jumped back in surprise, for only he had heard the whistle of the arrow that had knocked the torch from his hand.

"What!?" Esteem's outraged and astonished cry was ended short as another arrow thudded into the chest of a guard standing nearby. He fell over and was lost in the confusion that followed. For out of the darkness arrows were landing all around them - two more guards dropped with arrows in their chests. Then a galloping horse was suddenly on top of them, the four guards left standing drew their swords and looked about wildly for the attacker on horseback. But as they turned their backs Rage broke out among them on foot from the darkness, swinging his great broadsword about and one more fell. Before he knew what was happening, the others surrounded Rage. Again and again they advanced to try and bring him down but none could get an opening, as Rage wielded his sword like the warrior he had once been.

Behind them, forgotten, Mag had ridden up and slid off his horse beside Mise. As he did she gasped in fright for the torch that had been knocked to the ground suddenly licked flame across the grass and the hay around her went up in sudden flame. Behind her, Mag cut the rope with his hunting knife while beside them the sound of steel against steel could be heard as Rage fought. Mag grabbed Promise's arm and swung her away from the fire, and in one smooth motion she mounted the horse. The horse screamed with fright and broke away taking Mise far from danger.

It all happened so fast Mise hardly had time to realize what had all passed. When she did, she turned the horse about, but the darkness hid her father and Mag from sight. She could hear the noise of a mighty fight though! Fear struck her again, what if her father fell in that fight?

Rage wheeled about and heard his sword strike against one of the guard's shoulders, there was a grunt of pain, and the man fell back. For a moment Rage was left wide open! The other guard took the chance and brought his own sword down on Courage's back. Rage arched his back and swallowing his own cry of pain, he fell to his knees, and felt sure that this was the end. But Mag had come up behind his attacker. Being weaponless, he jumped onto the man's back and heaved his weight so that the man fell backwards atop of Mag. Rage rolled over on the ground and saw it all. Just then the head guard flashed his sword down. Rage deflected it with his own, and the man's sword tip struck the ground only inches from Rage's face.

Standing well away from the fight, Esteem watched, fright and astonishment written across his face. Just then there came a frighteningly loud horn blast from the village!

Everyone turned, and there riding towards them, torches like beacons in the night, and horse's hooves thundering along, was a group of seven riders. Five were Tarven soldiers with swords drawn, one was a Tarven woman with hair fluttering about her, and the seventh was a grand Tarven man.

Confusion broke out among the group about the stake. The head guard suddenly disappeared into the darkness along with Estee, while Mag suddenly found himself struggling against a limp guard on the ground.

"IN THE NAME OF THE KING OF TARVA; CEASE THIS MADNESS!" the Tarven's voice fell upon them as they were surrounded, their faces were lit up by not only their own torches but also by the sticks and hay that were now ablaze about the stake.

"Promise!" Loyal called out in panic, before realizing that there was no one amongst the flames. Thrive's men dismounted and took hold of four of the six Guards, two were lying still, and the head guard had suddenly reappeared.

To his two remaining men Thri ordered, "Find the mad man responsible for this!"

They remounted and went off into the dark meadow in search of Esteem. Meanwhile Loy had slipped off her horse and near well flew to Courage's side, helping him to his feet she asked breathlessly with eyes wide with fright, "Where...?" she never finished for Mag called out into the darkness.

"Mise!"

She came out into the firelight atop Mag's horse, her hair had come loose and her face was smeared with black fire smoke. Before coming quite close enough she slipped off her horse (it was more like falling) into Imagine's supporting arms. She lingered there as if drawing strength from him, then stumbled to her parents, where she was surrounded by her mother's embrace. Loy sobbed and looked into her face making sure she was quite unharmed. Rage placed his hand on her head, and if one had looked they would have seen tears sparkling in his dark eyes. Mise reached out and grabbed hold of the front of his tunic and rested her head against him.

They were safe.

Chapter 27   Plans of Eternity

Promise watched as the light of first dawn streamed in through her open window and shone golden on the stone floor. She had fallen into an exhausted sleep the night before, even before her mother had closed her chamber door. But she had awoken before dawn and had watched it break forth from the confines of her own room. It was so much more beautiful than ever she remembered mornings being. She laid there just watching, there are so many things to see when you thought you would never see them again!

When at last she rose from her bed it was already late morning. She stretched with a groan, her legs and arms feeling sore and stiff. Running her fingers through her hair she felt grit and she could smell smoke in it. She decided then that she would spend extra time washing that morning and instead of dressing, she pulled on a pale green dressing gown over her white sleeping gown. Just then, her mother slipped into her room; she was fully dressed but there was an unguarded look about her face. Mise paused and smiled, the events of the day before had been explained to her last night but she had been so weary and tired that she didn't remember all the details - but she did remember her mother's heroic part. She could hardly imagine her mother galloping out into the forest by herself to ask for help from the Tarven duke!

"Good morning," Loy said as she stepped closer and brushed Promise's hair away from her face.

Mise waited for her to say more but Loy seemed to be at a loss. 'She seems... different,' Mise thought, still strangely sad, but still something had - or was changing.

Then Loy took Mise by the hand and said, "Come with me."

"Oh I was going to wash my hair..." Mise stopped at her mother's strangely excited expression.

"There isn't time for that, they will be waiting for you - come." Loy didn't give her daughter time to ask who was waiting. She hurriedly led her daughter out into the hallway and down a flight of steps. Mise felt a little silly when she caught a glimpse of her refection in a window pane as they passed by it. She still had black smudges on her face from the fire!

At last Loy turned a corner and suddenly they were out on a balcony overlooking the manor courtyard. The whole courtyard was filled with people, from women and children to men, from the Tarvens who lived in the manor to the Garatin villagers, and all had their eyes on Mise! Mise looked about the balcony and just as surprising, the Tarven duke Thrive was there along with her father. Both turned to her and smiled. Thrive held out his hand to Mise which she took with wide eyes. He pulled her until she was in the center and at the edge of the balcony with a clear view of the courtyard below. Thri stood beside her and spoke with a loud and commanding voice.

"People of Fray, you have heard it said that Lord Esteem intended to kill many of you last night. Whatever reasons he had, they were unjust, for he sought to find lawbreakers by killing the innocent." There was a silence over the courtyard, and Mise was thoroughly bewildered.

"This is all true! But he had first sought to find rebels in another way… he demanded that the Lady Promise tell him the namesakes of rebels in Fray. She refused to tell him anything and for that he falsely accused her of witchcraft and tried to burn her at the stake. This Lady of Tarva - sacrificed her own life for you - the people of Fray! It is by her actions and those of her father and mother, that Esteem's unjustness was ended!" Even before he had finished the people began cheering! And throwing their hats in the air. At the end of his rousing speech he raised Mise's arm aloft and the people cheered all the louder.

The wind came up and blew Promise's dark hair away from her face, and her bewildered eyes beheld the people below. Beside her Thrive turned to her.

"I have traveled far, my lady, and have seen much - but you, with one brave and unselfish act have bridged a mighty gulf between Tarvens and Garatins and in so doing have answered the question of how to save this country. My whole mission from the king would have been in vain had I not witnessed what you did here in Fray. My lady, if you had been the general of the king's army sixty years ago when we took this country, I truly believe that there would not have been as much blood shed as there was." He then bowed his head, and Mise could only wonder if this could possibly be the plans that Nity had meant for her.

*   *   *

What happened at Fray was an outrage such as Thrive had never imagined. The thought that a Tarven lord could go so far out of line was more than disturbing, it cast shame on the Tarven name! But when Thri had learned about what Esteem had ordered concerning the village - Thri had been angry enough to kill Estee! If only he could find him, for the last anyone had seen of Estee was when he ran off into the dark the night before. The coward had run and hid under a rock somewhere. 'I'll find him,' Thri thought as he looked about the manor courtyard from the front door steps. Turning about he caught sight of Courage passing by.

"Courage," he called out.

Rage paused then came through the open manor doors to stand before him. "Yes my lord?"

"I wondered if you would ride with me, I'll be going out with another search party looking for Esteem soon." The two of them descended the steps and began walking out into the yard. Rage smiled in ill humor.

"I would gladly ride with you my lord, alas my fool horse was traded last night so that Loyal could bring you back in time."

"I must commend her again for such a valiant act." Looking up both men paused as a ragged and sad looking horse trotted through the manor gates. Screaming he jumped away from a page who tried to grab hold of the rope about his neck. Rage stepped forward with a surprised and outraged expression.

The horse made straight for Rage, thrusting out his head he nudged Rage's shoulder and nickered loudly. "Stream - You dumb beast of burden!" Rage exclaimed. Thri laughed.

"It would seem your horse didn't like his new home - I really think he's smarter than you give him credit."

Rage half smiled, as dumb, useless and stubborn as this horse was, he was touched by the thought that Stream had come back to him. "Fool horse," he murmured with a warm tone, he would have to see about buying Stre back from the peasant.

"Looks as though you're stuck with this 'beast of burden'." Thri was about to say something more when a troop of soldiers rode into the courtyard lead by the head guard, and flung over his saddle in front of him; was a body.

"My lord!" he called out while he dismounted.

Thri stepped closer to examine the body, while Rage watched closely. "What's this?" Thri asked.

"It's Lord Esteem's body, my lord. We found him near the forest edge," the guard said after a moment's hesitation.

Rage noted that he didn't look Thri in the eye. From where Rage stood he could see that Estee had been killed with a sword.

"Confound the man," Thri said. "As mad as he was it seemed as though he had enough honor to give himself justice." The head guard shifted uneasily.

"I wish it were so my lord," he said swallowing hard. "Then I could be at peace knowing I served an honorable man... I killed him, my lord."

Thri was silent as he looked him up and down.

"When he saw your lordship coming, I saw him run, and I feared he would escape so I went after him. He fought to get past me and..." he looked at Thri fearfully. Rage wondered what Thrive would do.

"You should be commended - without you the coward might have escaped," Thri said. "Put that body in the ground where I no longer need look at it."

Turning about Thri began walking towards the manor doors, then he called over his shoulder, "Courage, come, I would speak with you on a matter of importance."

Courage hesitated only a moment before handing over Stream to a stable boy. Rage had been bewildered by Thrive's actions that morning. Whoever heard of a Tarven lord making peace between Tarvens and Garatin rebels!? And now Thri wanted to speak with him privately? Was he after the rebels after all?

Despite his uncertainty Rage took care not to let it show on his dark face as he took up stride beside the Tarven duke. "How is it that the King's emissary should wish to speak to a simple tradesman on matters of import, my lord?"

"You are far from 'simple'," Thrive said with a cunning flash in his eyes.

Rage met his gaze for a moment before looking away again, he felt sure that Thri knew who he had once been. To Courage's surprise Thrive smiled and looked about the grand hallway beyond the manor doors as though he had forgotten what he had just suggested. They continued walking down the hall at a leisurely pace.

"Five months ago the King of Tarva (may his reign go ever on) summoned me to his castle, into his council chambers where he met with me alone. He went on to tell me of how he had sent hundreds of knights, lords, and dukes across the Sea to this country, a country that the king himself has never seen. He said that they have all returned with glowing reports about how the country thrives and blossoms. Of how the people here have welcomed and bowed to the lordship of Tarva." Thri paused and said dryly, "His majesty doubted these reports, and sent me, so that I may tell him of the true state of Garatin." Thri looked at Rage and smiled.

"If the king is pleased with the report I bring, he will make me his Grand Duke! Alas there is not much to be pleased over - the people of Garatin despise the King, Tarven lords cheat and near well plunder Garatins simply because they can. What King would be pleased to hear that?"

The two of them went up a flight of steps. Courage was grateful that he was not in Thrive's boots. He began to relax; it didn't sound as though Thri was probing to find out what Rage knew about the rebels. Suddenly a twinkle came back to Thri's black eyes.

"However I shall take great honour in telling the King about the village of Fray! After all, the tyrant Esteem is gone and the manor has a Tarven lord worthy of the honor, serving under the King once more." He ended with a crooked smile on his thin lips and stepped inside a doorway. It was the council chambers, he moved to the middle of the room and looked at Rage.

Courage couldn't believe his own ears.

"I could search far and wide, but I doubt I would find a man better than you to be lord of this village."

"My lord!?" Rage breathed.

Thri drew forth his sword and held it out as though testing its balance (it was of course perfect) then walked forward to stand before Rage.

"You have proved yourself more than worthy. I would find it an honour to tell the King that you are the Lord of Fray."

Rage let a breath go… This couldn't be real. After all that had happened in the past five years - to be restored to a place of honor and power. Courage's face hardened; the truth had to be known! No more hiding.

"My lord, I have done things in the past that make me a poor choice for the lord of any manor."

Thri looked down. "Whatever it was, I do not wish to learn of it."

He looked back up at him, "if you can swear to uphold the laws of the King, and be lord of the people of Fray in a fair and just way, then you are already a far better lord than Esteem ever was- despite your past, whatever it is." Rage still frowned, he couldn't be the Lord of Fray; he would be duty bound to search out and arrest the Nity followers in Fray!

"And what of the rebels, my lord?" he dared to ask.

"As I alluded to the people this morning, in my opinion the rebels who follow this man Eternity (misled though they might be) pose no threat to Tarven rule, there are many who would disagree with me on that... but- if I am not mistaken; you see things the same as I." He looked at Rage with a cunning glint of his eyes. Rage realized the incredible situation; Thrive knew where his loyalty's lay, but was turning a blind eye to it!

"Naturally if ever there was an uprising in Fray of a violent nature, it would be your duty to put it down. Can you swear to do these things Courage?"

Rage stood absolutely still, Thri was giving him free rein to govern Fray how he wished! To give the followers of Nity freedom... After all he had come through - could this be what Nity had meant for him?

"My lord, I do swear these things. I give my word that I will follow the laws of the King, and rule over the people justly and fairly - no matter if they be Tarven or Garatin!"

"Then kneel." And so it was that Courage the tradesman, the disgraced soldier, and the outlaw, kneeled before Thrive. With solemn grace Thri touched both his shoulders with his sword and said, "By the power given to me by the King of Tarva, I name you lord of the manor and village of Fray and the lands surrounding it. Rise, my Lord Courage."

And so it was that Courage the Tarven began his lordship over Fray.

*   *   *

Loyal stood on a low balcony overlooking the manor's inner gardens. She stood and gazed out over the flowers, but she wasn't really looking at them, rather she was deep in thought and wonder over everything that had happened. It had been a week since Rage had been appointed a lord and still she wondered if it was truly possible that so many things could happen in such short time. Was it possible that all their problems could fade away so quickly?

Loy closed her cinnamon eyes and let a light breeze wash over her, the dark mauve and bright green dress she wore fluttered about her legs, and her hair was unbound and free about her shoulders. A heavy foot step fell behind her, her dark lashes did not fly open as you might think; for she already knew whom it was behind her.

"Hello Loyal," Thrive spoke softly as he came to stand beside her, he looked down at her but she only gazed out at the garden.

"I wondered when you would remember," her voice was low and thoughtful.

His thin lips turned up at one side, "You knew from the first then," he half asked.

Her lips turned up in a tender smile.

"I often wondered what sort of life you had after setting sail from Tarva," he said after a moment.

"It was a long time ago..."

"I always hoped that you would return one day."

"I will not lie, those first few years I very badly wanted to return. I even hoped to see you again." A moment of silence followed.

"Did you ever wonder how our lives would have been different if your father had considered me as one of your suitors?"

"Stop Thrive!" she said closing her eyes to block out the longing she heard in his voice. "Don't do that. Our past and how it could have been different does not matter now," she finished, looking at him.

He smiled, "After all this time you are still true to your namesake... aren't you Loy?"

Her heart ached, "I try to be," she said, her voice dropping to a very serious tone.

They looked at each other for a moment, and both fully understood what had been passed between them without words. If she would have asked, he would have taken her away...

"Farewell Thri."

"Farewell Loyal," he said gently then turned to leave, but stopped and turned back to her and asked a final question.

"Loyal?" she turned to look over her shoulder at him. "Are you happy?" It was simple enough, but he needed an answer, and Loy was glad she could give him the one he hoped for, and her face softened into a smile.

"Yes Thrive, I am."

With a smile of his own, he turned and left, leaving Loy alone. For a moment tears sprung into her eyes as she remembered herself as a sixteen-year-old girl, standing on the deck of a ship sailing away from her home, the city of Tarva. She was leaving behind her family... and Thrive.

After a long time, Loy opened her eyes, and was surprised as what might have been, faded and gave way to the present. She had told Thri that she was happy, and she was, for although there was still distance between her and Rage - she knew that things would get better. Just then there came up behind her someone else; it was Courage. He stood beside her silently for a moment, as if building up his strength.

Loyal's red lips parted in surprise as he broke the stillness and took her hand. He knelt before her and looked up at her with glowing eyes and... there was an openness in his face that she had not seen for such a long time...

"Forgive me, for I have kept you at arm's length for crimes that I should have forgiven!" Loy's breath escaped her and a tear slipped from her eye, for Rage - looked broken before her!

"I let my pride come between us, and rather than giving up that pride I let it drive us apart! I am as much to blame for what happened as you, I should have been there for you to turn to - but I wasn't." Even as he spoke she could see him struggle with his pride, and in the end win. "Now all I can do is seek your forgiveness, for you are my dear wife... my equal. My Loyal."

Loyal turned her head to one side, "And you, my husband, have and always will be the only courage that I have to face another day." She dropped to her knees and held his hands in hers, and her heart ached. For joy can break a heart as surely as pain can. But this Loyal knew, Rage would be there to pick up the pieces.

*   *   *

It was as though a peace settled in Fray such as there hadn't been in a very long time. The villagers had more than accepted Courage as their lord, there was even talk of feasting for days on end to celebrate the good fortune of Fray once the end of harvest came. The villagers lined the streets the morning that Thrive left, and waved him and his guards off. They thought of him as the magical hand of the King stepping in just in time then fading away again. Even Transform and his sons lost much of their hostility and had seemed to tuck their weapons away - at least for a time. The knights and lords of the land seemed relieved to follow Rage and none of them questioned his friendliness to the Eternity rebels.

Promise thought of all this and a smile touched her lips as she did, for it all seemed so... right, like Fray was where at last she and her father and mother belonged. She knew of course that troubles would arise soon but things were too perfect to ruin them with worrying over that. She held in her hand her vial containing the dried flower petals of the Cres'aren she had once grown from a seed. Rubbing her thumb over the glass surface and little cork, she looked down at it and smiled; new life.

That's what this flower meant to her, new life indeed! Mise wouldn't have believed it if someone four weeks ago had told her what her life would look like in the future; but here she was! She couldn't set foot out of the manor without children giving her flowers, and women waving and men bowing to her! As if she were a princess! Even early morning, walking through the manor courtyard leading her horse out for a morning walk, the people in the courtyard going about their days' work would cast her glances and crane their necks to look at her!

She couldn't quite understand it. She wasn't even dressed fancy, she wore a simple brown skirt and a white tunic tucked into a belt, while her dark wavy hair blew about her shoulders freely. Ever since that dark and fiery night Mise hadn't wanted to wear fancy things. The need to impress, was gone, which was strange since now more than ever people were watching her.

She had thought long and hard about herself in the past few days, it was like she could see herself clearly for the first time. She wasn't a fair, noble and graceful maiden of Tarva, but nor did she wish to be - not anymore. What Mag had said was true. Nity had woke her for a reason, he had meant more for her than to just marry a rich man. She had restored Rizon's sight, she had saved the rebels of Fray, and she had helped Mag... who could tell what else Nity had planned for her?

As she left the courtyard she paused and dropped her horse's reins. Gently she placed the vial about her neck, and bowed her head for a moment to lock the clasp. Then she looked up and there coming towards her up the path from the village was Mag! He looked up at her and awkwardly smiled then looked away as though embarrassed. She noticed something different about him, like something had changed...

"I just thought I'd say hello" he said glancing at her.

"Well?" Promise demanded, "Aren't you going to say it?"

Mag looked at her for a moment as though offended that she would be so rude - but couldn't hold back a smile.

"Hello," he said and his blue eyes sparkled.

She noticed that they seemed clear - clear as the blue sky.

"How thoughtful," she said with a slightly coy tone as she picked up her horse's reins again.

"Well really I came to say farewell," he said hurriedly.

Mise frowned playfully, "Make up your mind before you say something you don't mean!" Again they shared a smile.

"Something's... different about you Mag." She turned her head to one side. "Have you had any more trouble with your eyes?"

"No, and I don't think I ever will again" he said quietly.

Mise frowned with an unasked question.

"You were right; it was my anger that was blinding me - I know that now. I blamed Rizon for my father's death, it was better than facing the truth that my father knew what he was doing and did it anyways. Maybe it was my father I was truly angry with... but either way I have carried that anger with me for too long! My hunger for revenge had weighed my heart down and made me blind to the truth."

Mise continued to frown but comprehension was setting in, and Mag took a deep breath.

"I'm ashamed to say this Mise, but I lied to you. When I came to warn Horizon about the ambush, I lied! I didn't want the others to kill Rizon, I wanted to kill him myself! So I followed him out into the woods that night."

"But Rizon got away... didn't he?" Mise asked softly with a faint hint of alarm.

"Yes, he did."

Now she understood, "You forgave him..."

He looked at her with sparkling blue eyes, but his voice was broken with emotion, "Not at first. I let him go, but I was so overcome by my anger that I went blind and stumbled down off the road. When I opened my eyes again it was morning, and I knew I would never be blinded again. I've decided to live with eyes open, and I won't be weighed down by a heart of lead anymore!"

A tiny breath escaped her, and her lips turned up as joy flooded her heart - she could see it in his face - he was free.

"Well that explains why it took you so long to come rescue me!" she said, a child-like playfulness breaking out over her face. He too smiled, and for a moment they just looked at each other. After a silence Mag took on a serious tone.

"I'm leaving to return home to Hawthorn today."

Her smile faded at once, and she looked away. "I suppose you have been gone for too long."

He nodded, and then they turned and began walking down the wide path together. "I said I would return in two weeks-time; it's been that already. Any longer and my dear sister will come out here looking for me!"

Again a silence fell, both knew that Mag had to leave soon - but neither wanted him to go just yet. When they came to Transform's cottage, Mag's horse was waiting for him by the door, fully saddled and loaded down with traveling things.

"You will be careful with him, won't you?"

Mag grinned as he took up the reins. "Don't worry I'll make sure to return him to Lord Favour's stables in good condition."

"I was speaking to the horse," Mise said primly. "Horse thieves are hung you know."

Mag laughed, "Oh yes I know! So I had better restore your good namesake as quick as I can! Wouldn't want you to be hung for stealing him, now would we?"

Mise could only hide her smile as best she could for really she had nothing to say to that - for she had been the one to steal the horse! Soon they neared the village edge and passed by one of the last cottages.

"I can hardly believe everything that's happened!" Mise said as two young girls and a little boy poked their heads out the cottage window and waved at her.

"Look it's Promise!" one whispered loudly with awe. Mise waved back with a shy and even a little embarrassed smile. Mag watched her face and smiled to himself.

"The villagers are treating me like some kind of hero!" she said with wonder after they had passed by the cottage.

"It's true though."

"Not really, Thrive made it sound as though I individually saved each one of them! But really, Mag, I didn't know the namesakes of any rebels - just Transform, and only because you told me you were staying with him, and your namesake of course," she added as an after-thought.

"But you didn't give him my namesake," he said stopping to look at her. Now they stood on the path out in the field that lead up to the forest.

"No - of course not, I wouldn't do that!" she said in surprise.

"But that's just it Mise; a Tarven wouldn't give the namesake of a Garatin to save her own life! That's what the villagers know - and that is why they love you and call you a hero… you've changed things!" he explained it with wonder in his voice.

Mise was touched, but there was something else she needed to know. "And what about you?" she asked softly.

"How do you mean?"

"When we first met, you thought I was an untrustworthy Tarven with a spy for a father. Have you changed your mind?" she asked genuinely interested in his answer. The smile that touched his face was truly something to remember.

"My anger had truly blinded me, for you are, without doubt, trustworthy and beyond compare."

She blinked in surprise, the way he said it made her believe him.

"Oh! Does that mean you will come back to visit me soon?"

Mag's face went blank, "Come all the way out here just to visit a Tarven?!" Mise felt her anger flare up; how dare he!?

Suddenly he smiled widely, "Yes - Promise! I would imagine I will come here again," he said tilting his chin like he thought his choice of words was so clever.

Mise smiled and looked away ruefully. "Alright then! You may leave my presence!" she said waving her hand and tilting her head in a queenly way.

"HA!" Mag laughed at her and she couldn't hold back a giggle.

But the next moment her face was wiped clean by beautiful surprise. For Mag had reached out and gently taken her hand in his own, bending over it, he kissed the back of her hand as though despite her plain clothes, she was a true lady of Tarva.

"Farewell my Lady Promise," he said looking up at her and backing away to mount his horse.

She felt a thrill go through her, "Farewell Imagine."

Chapter 28   Imagine

The sun rose over the grasslands of Hawthorn and spread red light over the village and manor. The wind blew gentle and swayed the grass like waves in the sea. Sparrows and rabbits were about in the early morning but all stopped to turn and look as a young Garatin man rode towards the village, his back was straight and his shoulders thrown back. The young man's face was fair and it shone with hope that had not been seen in that face for many a year. His blue eyes spoke of excitement, one wouldn't have guessed that he had rode on through the whole night - for he had. He had tried to sleep but his heart was too full; an excitement had filled him and he couldn't close his eyes for when they were open - his sight was filled with a dream! A dream so wondrous that one could not sleep! In truth he had pushed himself on through the night for the longer his eyes were open the more he could see this dream. It was an idea for what the world could be like... It was like a Cres'aren seed, so tiny yet within, it held new life! His heart was so full that it should have been heavy! But it was light enough to fly on butterfly wings.

The horse he rode hung his head for how could he have known that the young man who rode him was alive with new life? How could a simple horse have guessed what the young man could see?

A sudden flashback overwhelmed his mind's eye, and again he could see his father's face.

"Son, at some point in your life you must decide for yourself what kind of man you want to be. I can't make that decision for you - only you can. Everyone must decide at some point what they want to fight for. For a long time, I didn't think there was anything in this world worth fighting for. I've decided in my own heart that Nity is, at last, something worth fighting for."

At the time his father had said it, Mag had been hurt and angry, and his father's words had not settled into his heart - but now! Now Mag understood, his father had caught sight of something beautiful, something that Nity himself had started. Yes, now Mag understood, for now he too had decided what he would fight for!

Two weeks ago, he had left as a young man with hatred and revenge; now he returned with something incredible: hope.

Both Perilous and Remember were overjoyed at his return, and both saw the change in him right away. Mag hardly even had to tell them all that had occurred, for they could read it so plainly on his face. His brothers and youngest sister were bewildered by the change in him - rather the whole village was taken aback for Imagine the son of Obedience, was like a new man!

He sent word the next day out to all the Eternity followers and called for a meeting that same night - for what he had to say was too important to wait!

He stood before the men and women in the bakehouse cellar, and they all waited for him to speak, for now they could clearly see that he deserved their respect. For now, on Mag's face they could see something that they needed to understand - his eyes were too clear and his face was too excited to be dismissed. So they waited for him to speak. Ember watched with glowing heart, for she could tell, that all was indeed right with her dear brother. Mag spoke with the voice of his father.

"Imagine a world where Tarven and Garatins live among one another like brothers, without quarrels or faults in one another. A time when men and women of all countries can follow Eternity freely. A world where blinding anger and hatred is left behind in the past, along with our hearts of lead... do not fear if you cannot yet see this new world - but do not doubt it! For I have seen this bright new future - it exists! Let me lead you there."

to be continued...

Heart of Ashes – Namesake Chronicles-Book 3

*   *   *

About the Author

Rachel Lang lives in Orillia, Ontario, Canada. *Heart of Stone* was her first book, and *Heart of Lead* is her second book. Rachel also designs and sews unique animal themed handbags as well as fashion doll clothing. She enjoys painting with both acrylic and watercolor. She appreciates the many beautiful natural parks in Ontario as a camper and hiker. She is pleased to be a respite companion for adults.

Look for the author, Rachel Marie Lang, on the Facebook Page - "Namesake Chronicles".

Her books are available on Amazon, in print or eBook formats.

www.ingramcontent.com/pod-product-compliance
Lightning Source LLC
Chambersburg PA
CBHW022146170626
46807CB00005B/2095